'Quickly asserts itself as something [...] *Treasure Hunt* is a masterclass on what happens when empathy is absent ... This novel marks the arrival of an important new voice.'
GUNTER MAGAZINE

'A fascinating character, as complex and exasperating as a real person. As he mires himself ever further into controversy, it's as gripping as a real treasure hunt. He'll stay with you long after the last clue is solved.' MANDY HAGGITH

Praise and awards for Jane Alexander's short stories:

'A perfectly handled piece of realist science-fiction.' THE SKINNY

'Moving ... relentless honesty.' SOPHIE HANNAH

'A trumpet call of urgency and great promise.' THE SCOTSMAN

WINNER of the Fiction Desk story competition, 2014

WINNER of Sunday Herald's 'A Scottish Wave of Change' competition, 2011

Awarded a Scottish Arts Council new writer's bursary

THE LAST TREASURE HUNT

JANE ALEXANDER

Saraband

Published by Saraband
Suite 202, 98 Woodlands Road
Glasgow, G3 6HB, Scotland
www.saraband.net

Copyright © Jane Alexander 2015

All rights reserved. No part of this publication may be
reproduced, stored in a retrieval system, or transmitted,
in any form or by any means, electronic, mechanical,
photocopying, recording, or otherwise, without first
obtaining the written permission of the copyright owner.

ISBN: 9781908643803
ebook: 9781908643810

Printed in the UK by CPI on sustainably sourced paper.

Publication of this book has been supported by Creative Scotland.

ALBA | CHRUTHACHAIL

Cover illustration © 2015 Scott Smyth
www.ithinkitsnice.com

This is a work of fiction. Names, characters, events
and incidents are either the products of the author's
imagination or used in a fictitious manner.
Any resemblance to actual persons, living or dead,
or actual events is purely coincidental.

2 4 6 8 10 9 7 5 3 1

For Aidan

GLASGOW LIFE GLASGOW LIBRARIES	
C005254727	
Bertrams	15/05/2015
F/ALE	£8.99
HH	GEN

At the edge of the world, in the last of the light, I'm searching for the hangman.

The downpour soaks through my stolen waterproof, floods through stretched seams, finds where the zip won't meet. It drenches my jeans, underpants, skin; flows through my shoes with every frozen step. Rain blurs my eyes, batters down till I can't see the world in front of me – and still I wade on blindly. All I can do: keep walking, away from home and warmth and anyone who might once have cared. Keep hoping I can make good on my promise – the promise I made to the dead. Keep searching, since the search is all that's left. And this time if I fail, there's no way back.

But the cold hurts less, now. Pain becomes numb. Thoughts turn to ice.

Keep searching.

PART ONE

The hunt begins
Where starts the track
From a place the same
Forwards and back

Chapter 1

From the time we used to play together as children, Eve and I were ~~meant~~ *destined to be together. On the face of it, we were two very different kids – she was from a wealthy, bohemian family,* ~~half~~ *equal parts English rose and Italian passion. And I – I was–*

And me, I was–

And me–

From the time we used to play together as children, Eve was a wee dog yapping round my heels.

'Campbell! Campbell, where are you?'

Her proper little voice makes me bite the insides of my cheeks. I hunch into myself. Twigs are poking me all over but I don't want to move in case she looks in our direction and sees the shaking of leaves on a day without wind.

'Campbell!' says Duncs, in a girly voice. 'Darling! Where are you? Ayah!' He rubs his shoulder. 'That hurt!'

'Good. Shut up, or she'll hear.'

There's four of us flat on our bellies inside the hollow hedge: me and my brother, and my cousins Roddy and Jean.

'I think it's a shame for her,' says Jean, in a loud whisper. Jean is nearly as old as Duncs. Roddy says he's as old as me though he's nearly a whole year younger. After the summer he'll only be in Primary Four, and I'll be able to play in the P5–7 football team with Duncs.

'It's not you she's obsessed about,' I say. I can hear Eve moving closer, stamping through the high grass. I know she's going to find

3

us, any minute now. It was her showed me the hedge in the first place. It's my secret place, she said, but you can come here too. We can make up that it's our house, and we live here together.

'Give up, Eve,' I breathe. 'Give up, you can't find us.' But yappy dog Eve never, ever gives up.

We all hear it together. The murmur of grown-up voices. We swap panicked looks, start wriggling backwards. Twigs stab us, catch our clothes. Duncan kicks me in the face and I smother a howl.

'Evie, where are the others, darling?' It's her mum, Jasmine.

'They're *somewhere* about...' says Eve. 'I know I saw them somewhere, just a minute ago.'

Okay, there is one good thing about Eve: she doesn't tell on you.

Jean is first out from the hedge, the other side from where the grown-ups are. 'Oh, *there* you are, Evie,' she says. 'We all thought we'd lost you!'

I burst out backwards, and shake my head upside down in case of telltale twigs in my hair. When I stand up, my eyes go fizzy. I blink and blink till the grown-ups in front of me all stop fizzing, and while I'm busy blinking Eve runs towards me and grabs my hand.

'Now, Cam...' she says, dragging me away from the others. I can hear Duncs sniggering and I know I'll be getting a slagging about holding hands with girls, but in front of all the parents I can't do a thing about it. 'Come and help me with this clue,' Eve is saying.

As far back as always, when we come up to Glenelg, the big thing is a treasure hunt. Last year, the whole week was so wet that the hunt was just in the house. You would think that'd be rubbish, but Eve's house has three whole floors, four if you count the cellar where the treasure turned out to be hidden, so there were rooms we'd never gone into and it took just as long as a hunt outside. (When I asked my mum why two people needed so many rooms,

4

especially when one of them was as little as Eve, she sighed and said, Jasmine always thought she'd have a bigger family. And when I said, So why didn't she, then? Mum just said, You can't always have what you want. When I asked my dad about the house, he said, Well may you ask, Campbell, but even though I was asking he didn't give me an answer.)

This year, we solved the first, second and third clues, but then the fourth clue didn't make any sense.

Good luck you'll need for number four
Both open and closed you'll find the door

Roddy thought maybe we had to go back to the house and look for a door that was halfway open, but we tried that and it didn't get us anywhere. Jean said was there a house nearby that was number four, but Eve said apart from the farm theirs was the only house for a mile, and there were no streets, and anyway round here houses had names instead of numbers, like theirs was Daluaine which meant 'green field' in Gaelic. Then she started showing off by saying words in Gaelic which none of the rest of us understood, and that's when we ran off and hid in the hedge.

Now Eve is dragging me with her to the falling-down sheds, with the others all still watching. When we're far enough away so no-one can overhear, she stands on tiptoe and whispers, 'I know the answer.'

I duck away from her damp breath tickling in my ear. 'Euch, Eve, dinnae! That's disgusting!'

She's still got her hand clamped onto mine. 'I can tell you, if you like. And then we can find it together, so we can both win.'

I stare at her. We'd all decided not to bother with the treasure, once we got stumped. But the idea of winning makes me think again. It's always Duncan that wins, or Jean, them being the oldest – except once it was Eve that found the treasure and the rest of us ganged up and complained it wasn't fair because Eve knew all the places round here and we didn't. (Complaint dismissed: Eve was youngest, which made it totally fair, said the grown-ups.)

'Tell us, then,' I say.

She smiles. 'Good luck,' she says. 'What's something that's lucky?'

'Black cat. Ladders. No, not ladders, I mean, the opposite of ladders ... chimney sweeps,' I say, thinking of Mary Poppins. 'Right-way-up horseshoes.'

'Yes!'

'Horseshoes?'

'Yes! And a door that can be open and closed *at the same time*?'

Once I've guessed, it's obvious. Both of us together make a dash for the old stables, and of course I'm faster. She's only just seven, after all.

'Cam, please slow down!' she gasps.

I check over my shoulder, see the others twig the hunt is back on – they're racing across the meadow to catch us up, and I'm running like it's the hundred metres on Sports Day, and I get there before anyone else and there's the last clue wedged behind the rusty horseshoe that's nailed to the door – I stretch up, get the corner with the tips of my fingers and wheech it out from its hiding place.

Digging into stony ground
Beneath the cairn the treasure's found

I fold the paper, push it back, because the rules are you have to leave the clue where you found it. Biting the inside of my mouth, trying to think, Eve on tiptoes stretching up and Duncs, Jean and Roddy thundering up behind – I'm staring round, trying to look calm–

I see it. Right over by the fence: a heap of stones, piled all loose together. With the others fighting over the clue, I set off – so fast I think I'll overtake my feet and fall on my face. By the time I reach it I can't see straight, but I don't waste a second, I'm shoving the clattering stones apart and inside–

'Hoho, yessss!' I haul out the plastic bag and tip the treasure onto the ground. Like always, there's little parcels for everyone, with all our names on, and then the proper prize, for the winner. 'I am the cham-pion!' I sing. The prize is massive, bigger than my head, wrapped in silver paper. I lift it like a trophy.

'Me and Cam found it together,' says Eve. But everyone else is saying, 'Well done Campbell!' And even Duncs says, 'Aye, nice one, Cam.' I start to tear the paper off, letting it fall to the ground.

It's a frisbee. I've already got a frisbee – but this one's got Power Rangers on and anyway that's not the thing; the thing is, I won it. The thing is, I won.

'Brilliant! Look!' I'm showing it off to everyone, kids and grown-ups too, and then I catch Eve's eye: she is staring, arms folded across her skinny chest, cooried in to her mum with her eyes all big and sad. Trying to spoil my win. I turn away.

'It's brilliant, this!' I say.

In the afternoon we play with it, but frisbee is actually not that much fun, especially when Duncs can throw so much harder than everyone else. After a bit we get bored and decide to build a den instead, a new hidden place that Eve won't be able to find.

When it's time to pack up and go home, I forget all about the frisbee. I only remember when we're halfway home, when it's too late to go back.

Chapter 2

You could sum up my cousin in a single gesture: *shrug.*

'What d'you want to do tonight, Roddy?'

Shrug.

'Roddy, d'you realise it's three days since we last set foot outside?'

Shrug.

'Hey Roddy, aliens have landed in George Square!'

Shrug.

Perhaps it explained how we lived so uneventfully together. For the past seven years we'd been a fine-tuned mechanism, clicking off each other like those silver spheres in perpetual motion toys. The things we did that annoyed the shit out of each other (Roddy's inability to return milk to the fridge; my tendency to leave washing to fester, rather than hanging it out) were outweighed by the advantages of not having to make an effort. Roddy was always there to head to the pub with, or sink a bottle of wine; to sit around with, and say nothing much: my everyday was given another layer – slightly threadbare – because I wasn't alone.

The two of us had our routines. By the time I hauled myself out of bed, he'd be up, installed on the sofa that functioned as his study: semi-reclined, with my Technics headphones, which had somehow become his, squashed over his ears; with his laptop on his knees, and a sea of textbooks drowning the worn, brown couch. Every morning I made tea: my breakfast, his mid-morning cuppa, our days aligned just slightly out of sync. Roddy would make a small concession to my company by demoting the head-phones to the neck area, so an insect orchestra would accompany us as we drank. We tended not to talk: it took me a while to wake up, while he, presumably, was balancing a headful of great and original thoughts, all clamouring to be set down onscreen.

Today, though, when I fitted his tea into a small floorspace amid books and papers, Roddy took the headphones right off and clicked his laptop shut. A little different thing, alerting me to the possibility of a greater difference.

'Cam,' he said, wrapping his mug in both hands, 'I need to talk to you about something.'

'Go on.' I was waiting for the tea to have its effect, like it might steam open my gritty eyes. Last night had been late. We didn't get the hardcore of drinkers out of the pub till gone half one. I could have slept hours longer, except for the noise drifting up from the street. Earplugs. Kept meaning to get some. Where did they go exactly, to block the sound – how far inside? I had a finger experimentally stuck in my ear when Roddy dropped his bombshell.

'Thing is,' he said, 'you're kind of going to be needing another flatmate.'

I pulled my finger out of my ear; frowned, not getting it, yet. 'How would we need another flatmate? Where would they sleep? You planning to rent out the sofa?'

'No, Cam: another flatmate instead of me. Sleeping in my room. Or yours, if you want to swap. You might want to think about that,' he suggested, helpfully, 'mine's that wee bit quieter, being round the back...'

'But ... yes, but...' A great big difference was opening up in front of me, a dark crack gaping in the living room floor. 'Where will you be sleeping? Are you leaving – leaving Glasgow?'

Shrug. 'Aye. See, I've got this thing...' He tailed off, looked about him, like he was waiting for a prompt from off-stage.

'There's clinics for that.' I sat clutching my tea, feeling my palms burn, trying not to panic.

'It's this, ah…' He patted the sofa; freed a sheet that had been half-swallowed by cushions. 'No, wait, that's not it.' He was shuffling pages, delving into piles of papers. 'Wait, it's here somewhere, it just came this morning so I can't have lost it already–'

'Roddy?' I was practically yelling. '*Roddy!*' Finally, he stopped shaking books, started making sense.

'What it is – I applied for this Fellowship. It's like an award, funding for two years, to finish the PhD. And, so I got it. And it's in Atlanta, Georgia.'

'Oh, Atlanta, Georgia? That Atlanta? For a minute there I thought you meant the other Atlanta, you know the lost kingdom of – or, wait no, is that Atlantis? I always get them confused…'

He laughed, which, seeing as my joke wasn't anywhere near funny, had to be kindness. God. I was reduced to a pity laugh.

'A fellowship – isn't that for real geniuses?'

Shrug.

'You sure they didn't get you mixed up with somebody else?'

Another pity laugh.

What do you say? *Fantastic. Well done, Roddy. On you go, cuz. Happy for you.* I said all of those things, I think, getting the words out and meaning them all, and meaning none of them. Then, 'When are you going?'

'Not for a couple of months. So you've got ages to find someone for my room.'

'Yeah, ages. Oh well, that should be fine then.'

'And you should come and visit me. I don't know what there is to see in Atlanta, Georgia – but you should come anyway.'

'Coke. They make Coke, that's the headquarters. Atlanta, Georgia.'

'Right, so we can go on a Coke tour. That's got to be worth flying four thousand miles, eh? Bet you get free samples.'

I grinned, and it felt pretty convincing: my face making the right shape, mouth turned up, all that. Aye, sure, I thought. I'll save my seven quid an hour, be over there in no time at all.

Can't wait.

For once, Roddy had to leave the house: a meeting with his supervisor. I couldn't imagine she'd be gutted to hear the news: she must have been sick of seeing him after four years, or however long it was. Four years, and I still didn't know what he was doing, not really. I'd always thought it was just a way to avoid the real world, which seemed fair enough to me. Who wouldn't want to avoid that?

My arm reached for my guitar, swung it onto my lap. My brain was still re-shaping itself around this new information, that Roddy was ... not that he was clever, Christ, I knew *that* already. My left hand stretched for E minor, right thumb drew the notes, one at a time. It was the realisation that there was some spring of motivation bubbling away, out of earshot, out of sight. That progress and Roddy could go together: that there was such a thing as a plan.

I played the chord: let it hang for a moment, then silenced it. Put the guitar aside. I wandered into Roddy's soon-to-be-vacant room, sizing it up. He was right: it was quieter. Gloomy, though. It got the sun in the early morning: not ideal, given my working hours.

I imagined all of Roddy's books packed into boxes. The single picture gone from the walls. Or maybe I could keep that while he was away: the blown-up photo Jean had given him one Christmas, of our village in the snow; Moulin looking all story-book, with frosted leaves and branches framing the view. You might think it was black and white but the colours were there, subtle and wintry and clearer from a distance than they were up close.

I stood at his window for a bit, gazing down at the jungle of shared green. Didn't they say glass was a liquid? A super-cooled, super-slow liquid, flowing imperceptibly over thousands of years; the top of the pane thinning like a sucked glacier mint, the bottom thickening, molecule by molecule, the whole steadily warping.

Sadness was slow in the room, the whole flat full of absence, and between me and the world was a rippled sheet of glass.

I shrugged, à la Roddy, and felt a stiffness across my shoulders, up into my neck, like I'd been too long in one position; like I'd been tensed without knowing it, poised, for threat or action.

Fuck. I said it out loud, and straightaway the air set around me, like there had never been a sound.

The thing was – who would understand? It wasn't Roddy. I mean, it wasn't just that I'd miss him. I was a grown-up; I could cope with missing a friend. People went places; sometimes they came back again. Sometimes not: what were you going to do, bawl your eyes out each time your world shifted? The pieces settle again, things are different; you're still standing, so get over it.

But now, I was the only one. The only one left, as in: behind. Who would move in here, taking Roddy's place? Someone my age? Or someone ten years younger? Some random student, young enough and green enough not to balk at paying £300 a month for a flat with no heating, where the intercom was fucked, and the stair was a makeshift urinal every Saturday after closing; drunks pissing out the booze I'd been serving them all night, because I was thirty and still behind the bar of the Douglas Arms.

Fuck.

I thought of friends, acquaintances: how one way or another they'd all got it sussed. The folk I started uni with – I didn't know them any more, any of those people, hadn't ever known them for long – but some names had stuck, and now and then I searched the web to see where they were, what they were making of their lives. I found them in New York, in Sydney, in Singapore; found directors and senior executives; found an ex-girlfriend making video art, showing her films in London galleries; found my old friend Amit in Silicon Valley, inventing electronics. From where I stood on the edges, craning towards the centre, their every success was bitter. And the people closer to me, those I'd grown up with. My brother Duncs and his oil money, £70k tax free for working in Kazakhstan six months of the year; his bachelor pad in the Merchant City; his fledgling rental empire – beads of security scattered across the Southside – of which my home was just one tatty part. Cousin Jean, making it as a photographer, travelling the world. Magnus, photogenic and shining gold in fawning broadsheet features about his latest restaurant venture. Eilidh – okay, Eilidh was different. Eilidh was just a teacher. But she had a profession, a life built on solid foundations. And there she was, settled in London – the city that had defeated me, come close to destroying me.

And now Roddy, snatching something that looked very like success from the jaws of mediocrity.

Then, of course, there was the one you didn't need to go searching for. The one whose success was rammed down your throat. The rising star: the face that eyed you seductively from the sides of buses, the face you could see on screen ten times life size. The one, when you told people you knew her, or at least you used to know her, who made their eyes go wide and their mouths drop open.

The yappy dog, turned best in show.

Like an eavesdropper, I opened Roddy's laptop, knowing I'd learn nothing to my benefit. But my fingers on the keyboard had a life of their own; a muscle memory. Without my say-so, they went ahead and typed her name into the search engine.

Eve Sadler.

I hit return.

Search.

Chapter 3

Last time I saw Eve in the flesh, she would have been eleven. Nearly a decade later, her sudden appearance in our living room caused my mum to spill cocoa all over the Turkish rug.

'That's Jasmine! I mean – she's the spit...'

I'd been less than half watching; costume drama not my thing. Now I stared at the screen, at the girl with the huge dark eyes and the tiny speaking part. 'Is it...?' I said, moving closer.

The girl on the TV ducked her head, said, 'Yes, ma'am, immediately,' and together Mum and I yelled, 'Eve!'

The action shifted then to a different scene, and Eve was gone; both of us were standing now, a foot away from the TV, and for the next ten minutes we stayed there, unwilling to sit back down, to glance away, even to blink. Finally, our patience was rewarded. Eve re-appeared in the background of a lengthy scene, standing obligingly still, while we said to each other things like *It is, isn't it? Isn't it? It definitely is...* But I didn't believe it, not really, till the credits rolled and told us in white on black: *Second Maid – Eve Sadler.*

Mum kept shaking her head. It must have shocked her to think, even for a second, that it was Jasmine up there; Jasmine, caught at the age she'd been when she and Mum first met.

'Well, well. Looks like Evie's doing well for herself,' Mum said, as I texted Eilidh and Roddy and everyone who'd known her. *Guess who was just on tv??* 'How nice,' Mum said, 'after what happened, poor soul.'

Over the following year, as Eve's star rose, Mum said the same thing again and again. *She's doing so well, poor soul.* To the rest of us, increasingly, that phrase didn't cover it. Poor soul, with her vast pay cheques; poor soul, with her limitless opportunities. Almost a year after that first appearance, I remember the whole gang of us – me and Duncs, Roddy and Jean, Eilidh and Magnus – crowding round the telly at ours to watch the BBC's flagship Christmas offering. Another costume drama, but this time Eve was the star. To start with, we could barely hear the dialogue for our own shouted comments, our shrieks of laughter; by the end, we were watching in near silence.

After, down at the Moulin Inn, conversation naturally centred around her.

'It's so weird, eh?' said Roddy. 'That someone we know is famous.'

There was general agreement: it was weird, right enough.

Duncs, ever analytical, was the voice of doubt. 'Is she famous, though? She's totally stunning, no argument there. But, properly famous?'

'What's the test?' I asked, sure he would have one.

'If you asked people on the street – if, say, half of them knew who she was, I reckon that would be properly famous.'

'Any street in particular?'

'Who's the most famous person you can think of?' Duncs was ignoring me. 'Sean Connery, someone like that.'

'Madonna, she's more famous,' objected Eilidh. 'David Beckham.'

'Whatever, so ... a really famous person, say nine out of ten people would know them?' Duncs took our silence for assent. 'So with Eve, say three or four people might recognise her, that makes her less than half famous.' He sat back and smiled, satisfied he'd made his point.

'That's maths,' I said. 'Can't argue with maths. Can't argue with an engineer.'

Roddy shrugged. 'She's on her way, though.' With a hand, he mimed a plane taking off, gaining altitude.

'You on your way to the bar, by any chance?' Eilidh waved her empty glass in his direction, and conversation ceased as a fresh round was got.

'The whole thing was beautifully shot; and didn't Eve look lovely?' Jean was smiling, but her voice was sad. 'So much like her mum – Jasmine used to model, didn't she?'

'News to me,' I said, but Duncs was nodding.

'Yeah – when she and Mum were still students,' he said. 'Before she got married.'

'Aye, she scrubs up well, I suppose,' said Eilidh. 'Eve, not Jasmine.' Duncs pulled a face at the understatement.

'And she got to snog Matthew Macfadyen! Bitch.' Jean's smile widened, and Magnus frowned.

'Not my type,' he said, as though that was an end to it.

'Which?' I was pushing it. 'Eve or Matthew?'

'Neither! I'd go for the manservant, personally.'

'It can't be hard, though, can it?' This was Eilidh, oblivious to the double entendre that had Magnus raising his eyebrows. 'Compared to a real job. Compared to a shitty nine-to-five grind-away-in-an-office job. Or till 2am in a kitchen.' She glanced at her brother. 'It's just not very fair, that's all.'

Magnus shrugged, and looked away.

A potentially awkward pause: Jean smoothed it over. 'Did you think they had chemistry? I did. God, it's made me a bit depressed.'

'Depressed? How?' Roddy looked baffled.

'Just. Makes me feel past it.'

As one, we chorused, 'You're twenty-four!'

'I know, I know I know. Maybe I'm on my way up as well.' Jean was still smiling, but it was a crooked kind of an effort. 'Bloody hope so. I can't take another year like this one.'

That was it, really. Nail on head. We were bleakly fascinated by the contrast between Eve's ascent and our struggles. That year had been a tough one. Eilidh had been knocked back from a graduate teaching programme, was stuck in a hated admin job. Roddy had finals coming up fast. Jean was taking whatever she could get as a photographer's assistant, more or less living on air. Duncs was doing well, moving on up: in the New Year he was starting a job in Nigeria, and we all knew the doctor had prescribed beta-blockers for the fear. And Magnus... Magnus was bust, the receivers called in to the restaurant into which he'd put everything: his time, his money, his heart. For all of us, that year, the path of life was pot-holed at best. At worst it seemed a dead end.

Me, I'd already had my dreams crushed flat: blurred, childish dreams of musical success. But that year – thanks to Eilidh, more than anyone – I'd begun to rebuild my life. I had taken the huge step of moving back to a city: to Glasgow. Had got myself a job, behind a bar. Small achievements, from the outside; but inside, after what had happened, it felt like I was moving on. I think I felt hopeful – lucky, even, in comparison with the others. Maybe that's why, back then, I could almost be happy on Eve's behalf. I'd had my troubles, but I'd found my feet again, wobbling only slightly.

I still thought I was on my way somewhere.

Chapter 4

Googling Eve, on Roddy's laptop. It was the kind of behaviour that could end up with me in possession of half a bottle less whisky than I started with.

Keeping up with the trivia of her life – who she was dating since her divorce from Dan Fischer, which movie she was launching, what new haircut she'd turned into a style essential – required zero effort: the information seeped in, via magazine covers, gossip columns, workplace chat. Nevertheless, I did, sometimes, make an effort; I did seek her out. Times when I was down and I wanted to be kicked. It was compulsive, joyless, like calling an ex when you were drunk, like masturbating over someone you hated. These must have been the times I really despised myself.

The first weblinks appeared in a row of pictures: Eve all glossy with red-carpet smiles.

Then came her entry on the Internet Movie Database. This included a handy STARmeter – which told me Eve Sadler was 'Up 29%' in popularity this week – as well as a list of the lads' mags that had ranked her in their hot one hundred babes, and memorable quotations that had flowed from her famous lips. My favourite of these was: *I do truly believe that if you can visualise the life you want, that's a very powerful tool and you can't help but succeed.*

Next up: her Wikipedia entry. Admirably factual.

Her official website, devoid of facts in almost any form.

And then there was Starspotter: a site where people with lives even more unimaginably sad than mine could hunt down their favourite celebrities, and post information about the stars or C-listers they'd spotted. *Woody Allen in Carnegie's, Manhattan*, that kind of thing. Most of the sightings were in New York or LA, but there was a smattering in Toronto, a couple in London.

And today, there was one – just one – much closer to home:

Posted: yesterday: 3.46pm
Morgan Freeman and Eve Sadler. Filming their new movie about a haunted house.
Pollok Country Park.
Glasgow.

Chapter 5

'We won't get anywhere near her,' I said.

Shrug.

'It'll be all cordoned off. Security guards, with tasers...'

Without Roddy, I never would have gone. I'd talked him into it, or maybe it was the other way around – maybe we persuaded each other – but however it happened, with two of us it wasn't stalking. It was an adventure. I spent the whole bus journey conjuring obstacles, and at each fresh objection, Roddy shrugged.

'Aye, maybe. Still. Nice day for it.'

And it was. We were nearing midsummer, with the world for once all promising and bright. As we ambled through the park, past the allotments, the cricket ground, here and there a Highland cow watching us warily from under a floppy fringe, I could almost feel as Roddy did: that the day was already a success, that whatever happened next was irrelevant. All my years in Glasgow, and I could count on one hand the times I'd made the effort to come here.

'Why don't we do this more often?' I said with the sun on my face, and birdsong all about me. We were passing by the woodland garden, nearing Pollok House – a stately home, of the kind you're vaguely pleased to have in your city; that you do mean, one day, to visit.

'Is that a crane? Are they renovating?' As we reached the gate, I could see it wasn't a crane but a cherry-picker.

'Spotlights,' said Roddy.

Spotlights. The film crew was still there; we hadn't missed her. It seemed odd they should need lights on a clear June day. Perhaps the brightest Glasgow sun was still too thin to convince on film.

We stopped by the gateposts. The wrought iron gates were closed, and a sign said in strict capitals:

POLLOK HOUSE CLOSED TO THE PUBLIC.

Roddy shook his head. 'You'd think they'd put SORRY FOR THE INCONVENIENCE. We might have come specially.' He gave a gentle push; the gate swung open. He turned to me. 'Inaccurate, too. They're not closed at all.'

I took a deep breath. 'Are we going to do this?' I was smiling; I already knew we would.

The two of us breezed though the gateway, started walking up the drive, eyes fixed front like we knew our way. Two men and a woman were standing near the entrance to the house, consulting a clipboard. The men seemed very American in caps and over-sized check shirts; both had goatees and, as we watched, one actually raised a hand to his chin, gave his beard a little stroke.

'You know what we need? A piece of paper.'

Roddy shot me the look I deserved.

'No: if you have a bit of paper you can get in anywhere. Wave it about; people assume you're meant to be there.'

'Aye well.' Roddy patted his pockets. 'I'm all out of paper, as it happens. Let's keep walking.'

We were pacing a wide circle round the side of the house, keeping as far as we could from the clipboard monkeys. A half-dozen trailers were parked in a row, elephant-like, nose-to-tail. As we got closer I could read their names. *Facilities*, said one; *Make-up*, said a second. Another looked like a catering truck. Through the open door I glimpsed a man holding a cardboard cup. He looked like my dad.

'Oh, the glamour.'

'Hey, we should get some tea,' said Roddy.

'Tea? Sure. Why not? You wanting a wee scone and a sit-down, too?'

'Make us look like we're meant to be here.' He stared at the truck, jingling coins in his pocket. 'D'you think you have to pay?'

He was right. Tea would be the perfect disguise, far better than paper. 'Doubt it. They wouldn't have cash on them, would they? Actors in costume.' I made for the entrance, acting bolder than I felt. 'We could be runners. Or joiners, or some kind of techies.' With Roddy close behind, I bounced up the three steps and into the truck.

'Alright,' I said to the woman at the counter. I gave her a grin. 'Couple of teas please, darling.'

She poured, silently: nobody's darling. Pushed the cups towards me. I cast around for milk, trying not to look clueless; decided to take it black rather than ask, and risk giving the game away.

There was something so ordinary about tea – the blowing, the sipping – that before long I'd convinced myself we were meant to be there. If someone had asked us to show our passes, I'd have been indignant. Safe behind our steaming drinks, we watched the business of the set. It was pleasant enough, standing there sunning ourselves. But if anything much was happening, it must have been elsewhere. We saw a flash car drive up, a Merc with a soft top; saw the driver get out and walk straight into the house. We saw three dusty-looking guys in wrecked jeans and faded T-shirts saunter up to the truck for some late lunch. We saw a woman with sunglasses on her head talk fast into her mobile, slicing the air with her hand. The back of my neck felt like it was burning. I finished my tea. Opened my mouth to suggest we call it a day.

'There.' Roddy tipped his head: three o'clock.

I followed his gaze. But he'd made a mistake. The girl coming out of the house, the one he was carefully not pointing to, was a child. She wore a long, white dress, like first communion.

'Is it...?' I narrowed my eyes against the sun. The girl was laughing, looking up at a broad-shouldered man in a morning suit. Her laughter carried towards us, deeper and darker than I would have thought possible, and I realised she wasn't a child, wasn't even a teenager. Instinctively I took a step back, sidling behind Roddy. A breeze curled across the forecourt, caught her dress like a flag, so white in the sun it made my eyes water. I blinked, and stared: Eve at work. Here was the glamour I'd hoped for. In the Douglas Arms, sometimes I shared a joke with Angelika, or Kayleigh. This was just the same: more sun, more soft-focus, more lens flare, though I must have imagined that. Less stale-beer stench and stinking toilets. Otherwise, just the same.

Eve stopped laughing. She looked around, raised her hand, and within seconds a young man was at her side. She must have asked him to fetch her a drink: he set off at a jog, straight towards us and the catering truck.

'Now's your chance,' said Roddy, 'if you want to say hello.'

'We're not talking to her! How sad do you think I am?'

He raised his eyebrows. For a minute, neither of us spoke.

'Anyway, what would we say.' I crushed my empty cup in my fist, let it drop. It bounced under the truck, hit a tyre and came to a stop.

Roddy's disapproval was genuine. 'That's a disgrace.'

'It's keeping someone in a job.' Eve's runner climbed down from the truck and passed close by, a triangle of cups balanced in both hands. 'Him, probably. Come on. Let's go before they bust us.'

That was us: we were done. Walking away. But Eve must have turned to see where her coffee had got to, and that's when she must have seen us. Maybe she turned back to her co-star, picked up their conversation, before her subconscious told her we didn't fit: that we were familiar, and wrong. We'd almost reached the gate by the time the past coloured itself in around us, and our names – my name – arrived in her mouth.

'Campbell! Campbell Johnstone!'

I stopped. Turned around; raised my arm in a weird half-wave, a smile on my face. 'Oh, shit,' I said to Roddy. Eve was walking towards us, coffee forgotten. Down the left side of her white dress was a shocking splash of red; her face was powdery-pale. She looked like a haunting, headed straight for me. I straightened my shoulders, stepped out to meet her halfway.

'Campbell, I can't believe it. What are you doing here?'

Eve's words overlapped with the clanging great question in my head. Straightaway, I began to lie.

'Just passing, actually. We had no idea all this was... We're often down here, down this way.' She couldn't possibly believe that. 'Me and Roddy, remember Roddy?' I turned to where Roddy was gawping, halfway along the drive. He lifted a hand, and Eve waved back.

'Of course I remember Roddy. Gosh ... and Jean, and your brother... Wow.' Through her pale make-up, the smile she gave me had red carpet right the way through. 'It's lovely to see you Campbell. So...'

My mother's phrase spilled from my mouth. 'So, you're doing well for yourself.'

She pulled a face that said, *Oh don't*. 'Well, I'm working pretty solidly,' she said, 'which is nice. Tiring, but nice. And you, are you living here, then, in Glasgow?' She pronounced it with a long aah, G*laahs*-gow, and I remembered how her posh voice used to have me digging my fingernails into my palms.

'Aye, me and Roddy share a flat.' I knew she was going to ask what I was up to these days, and to head her off I started blethering. 'Actually, Roddy's about to move to the States. You live over there, don't you? I mean, I don't know but I'm presuming...'

'Oh well, he should look me up,' she said. 'He should come and stay, if he's in LA. You too, Campbell.'

The impossibility of her actually meaning this left me floundering. In my imagination, I saw Roddy turning up at her massive security gates, suitcase in hand. Giving the gates a push... Of course, there was the small matter of an address.

'Nice outfit,' I managed, feebly. 'Looks like you've spilt something, though...'

'Oh. Ha. Yes, I'm all bloody. I could tell you why, but then–'

'You'd have to kill me, fair enough. No, God, don't spoil it for me. What's it called, by the way?'

'So it's called *Never Setting Sun*, though that might change. It'll come out – actually, not sure, over here. Late autumn, I should think.'

'Oh well, I'll look out for it. Is it going to be any good?'

She let a silence stretch between us; held my gaze, her eyes huge, reproachful, shadowed with violet paint. 'Doubt it,' she said, eventually. 'I only do films that I'm confident will be really, really bad.'

I drew breath to apologise, but she cut me off. 'Look, I'm afraid I've got to go, we're so behind.' She tilted her head, looked up at me with a sidelong smile. 'Don't want to keep Morgan waiting.'

'Sure, of course.' While I'd been talking to her, other sounds had faded out: suddenly the volume slammed up again, birdsong piercing my brain. 'Look,' I said, too loud. 'Are you staying in town? I just ... if you wanted to see a bit of the city, you know, I'd be happy to show you round. Though you might have to wear a disguise or something.'

She hesitated. Thinking of a way to fob me off, without being rude. Then: 'Sure,' she said. 'I'm here for a few more days. Why don't you call me. At the Metcalfe: I'll tell them to put you on the list, and they'll put you through.'

'The Metcalfe. Great. Okay, I will, I'll give you a call.' I felt like we should be shaking on it. Instead I shoved my hands into my pockets. 'Take you out and show you the sights!'

'I'll look forward to it.' She gave me that red-carpet smile again; lifted her bloodied skirts and strode off, back to work.

Roddy's face was like good news that couldn't be kept in.

'So, Mr Johnstone: what was it that first attracted you to the world-famous, filthy-rich film star Eve Sadler?'

'Very funny.' I kept my voice casual, kept my hands in my pockets. The ground felt springy underfoot. 'She said you can come and stay at her pad in LA, man. You can hang out with her in the States, hang out with your good friend Eve Sadler.' I nudged my elbow against his arm. 'No; no need to thank me.'

'I don't know if you've ever considered the impressive scale of the United States, and the relative positions of Atlanta and LA on said land-mass...'

She'd remembered my name. She remembered me; was pleased to see me. Roddy's voice was a stream in the background. Of course – Eve was an actress. An Oscar-nominated best supporting actress, no less. If she wanted to look pleased, it would hardly be stretching her capabilities. And the way she'd asked about me, if I was living in Glasgow: I ran it back in my head. Yes, there was just something about it that sounded – what? Like she was the Queen and I was a commoner. Like I was a fan.

'She didn't hang about,' I heard Roddy say. 'Busy being famous, was she?'

'Something like that. Said she didn't want to keep Morgan waiting.'

'Morgan?'

'Freeman, to you and me.'

Roddy's face creased with laughter. 'Morgan!'

And then I was laughing, too. It shouldn't have been funny. She wasn't name-dropping, not really. It's just, he was her colleague; that was her life. Poor soul.

Chapter 6

I didn't call Eve – not that day. But the idea of it lifted me. At work in the Douglas Arms, the hours fizzed past like a party.

'What's with you?' Angelika asked, between pouring pints of heavy. 'Get lucky last night, did you?'

And in fact, that night, I could have got lucky twice over: unheard of, in the Douglas. Eve was wreathed around me, like I'd been drenched in pheromones; my status subtly enhanced. The two attractive girls who'd unaccountably chosen to spend their evening in this shabby boozer could sense something distant, exotic, still clinging. By closing time, the choice was mine for the making. But sometimes it's enough to know you've got options. I gave them a grin as they left, a cheeky wink, and drank in their backward looks.

It wasn't till I was walking home that I began to wonder at how she'd made me feel. It occurred to me that there was an obvious question I was refusing to ask myself: What did I want? What was the prospect that had turned drizzle to diamonds? But it was late. I was too tired to start examining my motives. I walked, and chose not to think: enjoyed the wet street sparkle.

I slept fitfully, woke early, the way you do when you've a morning flight to catch. Then, since I was up, I called Eve's hotel, hoping to reach her before she left for a day on set. As I spoke her name to the receptionist, I could hear myself trying to inhabit it, take ownership of it. To make it sound natural, from my lips; a name I said all the time.

After a pause, the receptionist was back on the line. 'Miss Sadler is not available at present,' said the sing-song voice. 'May I pass on a message?'

I'd already missed her. Filming started early, no doubt, making the most of the light. I left my number, and a request for her to call me back; hung up with a feeling of frustration.

'So, what's the story then?' Roddy, still in his boxers, had wandered into the lounge. He scratched his head with both hands, setting his hair on end. 'You and Eve, are you seriously, like...?'

'Naw. God, no!' I shook my head. 'I mean, come on: Eve?'

His shrug spread from arms and shoulders to his expressive face; mouth turned down, eyebrows raised. 'Aye, but. She's all grown up, Cam. She remembers you. Maybe she still has a wee thing for you; childhood sweethearts and all that.'

'In her dreams.'

'I know you were! Maybe still are, what d'you reckon?'

'Roddy!'

I knew he didn't believe me. Fair enough; I only half-believed myself. Eve was more or less universally lusted over, was, if memory served, number 17 in *FHM*'s Hot Hundred. How could I not have intentions that were less than honourable? She's all grown up, Roddy had said: straightaway, I was thinking of that infamous sex scene, the one from *Concrete Moon* – and from his suggestive intonation, I guessed that's what he'd thought of too. We had seen that film together, after all, and when the credits rolled we were out of there as soon as we could. Bloody hell, we'd said to each other: to think she was ... and we didn't discuss it any further than that. I've never seen the appeal of watching a porno with your mates and, as arty as the shagging was, that's basically what we'd been doing. And I don't know about Roddy, but for me there was something else disturbing about it – something shameful. That scene would easily earn a place in your library of fantasies, but to feel myself respond to it – and show me a man who claims not to have found it a turn-on, and I'll show you a gay man or a liar – was

28

like getting an erection over a ten-year-old girl. Or, given Eve's resemblance to her mother, like lusting after a dead woman – neither of which could be good.

Maybe that's why I was still dodging last night's question. Or maybe you could question yourself too much; all thought, and no action.

That night, late, on the back steps of the pub, I called the hotel for the fourth time. Because I'd played it cool, hadn't phoned yesterday, now I was forced not to play it at all: tomorrow was my night off, and if we didn't meet then, she'd be gone before I was next free. Standing by the overflowing bins, inhaling the perfume of stale food in high summer, I could sense the luxurious cleanliness of the hotel; could just about hear the soft music, the heels click-clicking on marble floors. As I held, I imagined Eve relaxing in her suite, a glass of something expensive in her hand, gazing down at the city lights where the rest of us scurried about our tiny business.

When the voice on the phone repeated the brush-off – 'Miss Sadler is unavailable at present' – I felt something bright and covetable slipping from my grasp.

I was home by one; sat up for an hour or so, slumped on the sofa amid Roddy's paper landslides, drinking whisky from a chipped glass that kept catching at my lip. I could have put on some music, turned down low so as not to wake Roddy – but tonight, whatever I might choose to listen to would wrap itself tightly round my chest, and tighten till it crushed me. There was no song to lift my dark mood, or to glorify its ugliness.

It was the worst thing, maybe, about failure: what it spoiled. How it curdled what you once loved.

Instead, I reached for a memory: one I kept carefully, accessed rarely, so as not to use it up. The festival, ten years ago. On stage, me and Amit: his laptop, my guitar. Finger-picking simple melodies into his beats and glitches; an improvisation, looping and shifting, because we didn't believe in songs, because everything flowed into everything else, because what we were doing was stopping time, for as long as we kept playing: two nobodies down at the bottom of the bill, but a circle of friends around us – new friends from uni, and old friends too, Eilidh there at the front of the crowd – and a wider circle of strangers beyond them, and the sun high and blinding so the memory was flared with warmth, with light.

The glass pulled at my lip again: I tasted blood in the whisky, iron through the smoke. That younger man, with the sun in his eyes: he was nothing to do with me. His stage, his audience – all that was lost, too distant. He and I were strangers.

I could set the alarm, try once more, reach Eve before she left for work in the morning. I tongued blood from my mouth. Stared up at the ceiling: the paper moon shade, the tidemark from last year's leak. My brother was a shit landlord. Next time he was in the country, I would get assertive, demand a fresh coat of paint at the very least before trying to hook a new flatmate with acceptable domestic habits.

Fuck it: the ball was in Eve's court now. The court of Eve: I thought of some olden days queen, dressed in jewels and ruffles, surrounded by toadying courtiers and maid-servants to cater to her every whim.

How easy it would have been, yesterday, for her to say she couldn't meet me. How simple to say she was leaving that night, flying back to LA. How very many ways there were for a movie star to let you down gently. All those teenage boys with posters of her on their walls, with their *Concrete Moon* DVDs on permanent pause: how little she needed another fan to chase her. I thought of Eve aged eight, her hand grabbing mine, her prim little voice saying, *Cam-pbell, Cam-pbell...* And I wondered at how long a woman might bear a grudge.

I drained my whisky. Went to bed, alarm un-set.

'How's the chase?' asked Roddy next morning. He was throwing some stuff in a rucksack, heading up the road to break the news to Auntie Linda and Uncle Donnie that their son was off to the States for the next two years.

'There is no chase,' I said. 'She's got my number. If she wants me to show her around, she can give me a call.'

He didn't push it. Went on packing: a bundle of T-shirts, socks and pants still damp from the wash.

'Are you taking your laptop?'

'You wanting to use it?'

'Only if you were going to leave it.'

'Sure, no bother. I can use my mum's.' He disappeared into his room, called back through: 'Remember and clear the history if you're looking at specialist sites...'

Specialist sites. The address leapt up as I typed the first letters: Starspotter...

I browsed through the most recent entries, till I found the one I was looking for: Morgan Freeman and Eve Sadler. Filming their new movie about a haunted house.

Underneath was a tab marked Update. I clicked.

Spotted? Tell the world!

A window popped up with a dialogue box, a flashing, beckoning cursor: inviting me to share what I knew.

I typed, Eve Sadler, staying at the Metcalfe hotel in Glasgow.

Clicked Post.

Then I cleared the site from the browser's history, made myself a cup of tea. Switched on the TV with the volume down; picked up my guitar, and let my fingers play. I drank without tasting, watched without listening, strummed without engaging my brain. This was normal. This was life.

Twenty minutes later, the phone rang, and everything changed again.

Chapter 7

'You know who's staying here?'

The man looked perfectly ordinary: youngish, smart-casual in jeans and striped shirt, clutching a plastic bag. He'd been watching me kill time, as I paced the quiet street outside the hotel. Now he spoke like he'd recognised a fellow hunter.

I gave him a nod. 'Aye.'

He took a few steps towards me, eager to share. 'I've been here since three,' he said, and I wasn't sure if it was meant as a boast, or just fact. 'Haven't seen anything yet. There was some others; there was quite a few of us – and there was a guy, looked like from the papers, he seems to have disappeared, anyway...'

He saw me glance at the bag he was carrying. 'Going to ask her to sign them,' he said. He delved inside, pulled out a *Concrete Moon* DVD. A magic marker fell to the ground, rolled towards me. I picked it up, handed it back.

'Thanks,' he said. 'Not got anything for her to sign?'

'Nah.'

I pulled out my phone, checked the time. Give it another couple of minutes: I didn't want to be early.

Striped-shirt guy was busy with his phone, too: scanning the internet for the latest clues. 'Nothing,' he said. 'Thought there might be an update, like if someone's spotted her somewhere else, but...' He slid the phone back into his pocket. Stared up at the Georgian facade; the lighted windows. 'I'll give it another hour,' he said. 'Another couple of hours.'

I toyed with telling him. *Don't bother; tonight, she's drinking with me.* Instead, as I scudded up the stone steps to the front door, I settled for some gentle advice. 'Maybe don't wait too long. Not sure you're going to be lucky!'

Inside, the Metcalfe was just the way I'd heard it on the phone. Tinkling, calm; washed with warm light. I walked up to the front desk, expecting to see the receptionist with the sing-song voice, the one who'd spent the last two days brushing me off – hoping she'd know me when I spoke. But the desk was staffed by a man: grey suit, pink tie, and a face that wouldn't smile till he knew what I was after.

'Hello. Hi. Campbell Johnstone, here to see Eve Sadler.'

'Just a moment, sir.'

The man picked up the phone. His nails were manicured, the white lines at their tips precisely two millimetres wide. I looked away from his hand, up to his carefully impassive face. He was acting like she was just another guest, but I could see it, the glow under his skin. A vein pulsed at his temple; his hand on the receiver seemed to clutch a touch too tightly. Eve was taking her time in answering. Perhaps she'd invited me here just to stand me up. No: I stopped that train of thought. I'd misjudged her once already; had spent an age scrabbling round the Starspotter website in search of a delete function. Perhaps her phone was at the other end of a suite the size of a football pitch. I tugged my left shirt-sleeve to even it up, so the same length of cuff showed at each wrist. My outfit was the result of some fine calculations: smart enough so I wouldn't be barred from her glitzy hotel; not so smart that I looked gauche. In the end I'd gone for a charcoal suit (borrowed from Duncan's flat; the only suit I owned was shiny enough to see your face in) with white shirt left open at the neck. If I was overdressed, I reckoned I could ditch the jacket.

Still I felt like I'd trailed dirty footprints across the pristine floor.

'Sir.'

I looked up. Praise be, he was smiling, just barely.

'Miss Sadler asks if you wouldn't mind waiting in the residents' bar; she'll join you there.'

Eve's approval was my backstage pass: the receptionist summoned a minion to show me the way, a young woman uniformed in sharp black and white, and I followed her in the opposite direction to the public bar, to a place I would never have found on my own. Which I suppose was the point of a residents' bar. Everything here was designed not to be noticed. Most of the seating was in private booths. The lighting was low. Strings played at a perfect unobtrusive volume. I sat at the bar, the only spot Eve would easily see me, and ordered a beer – bottled, in deference to my surroundings.

'And do you have any crisps, peanuts or something?' I didn't know whether Eve would want to eat, and the last thing I wanted was to get accidentally steaming and make an idiot of myself.

The barman placed my bottled beer on a little padded napkin. 'We have *edamame*, or soy-boiled peanuts.'

I had never heard of the first option. I ordered the nuts, which came in the world's smallest bowl and turned out to have been boiled in their shells till they were weirdly soft and looked like tiny cat turds.

'Your room number?'

'Sorry?'

'Can I have your room number, sir?'

Panic: they were going to throw me out because I wasn't a resident. 'I'm meeting a friend,' I said. 'She's staying here, I'm not sure what number–'

'Certainly, would you like to settle now or shall I put it on a tab for you?'

'Oh. Now, I'll pay now, thanks.'

I could have cried as I swapped him a tenner for a pound coin in a saucer. I couldn't even claim my change, which would have done me for the train home; that saucer told me clearly that this was his tip. Sitting there alone, I wondered how long Eve would be, and how long I could nurse my lager without blowing my cover as hoi polloi. I wondered what the etiquette was for poor barmen when it came to sticking your drinks on the tab of a rich and famous woman.

When she walked in, I almost laughed. She was wearing a black dress and dark bug-eye glasses: it was such a cliché, so unimaginative. She looked like the cover of a gossip rag. She came closer, and again I was shocked at how slight she was: standing in her heels, she was shorter than me as I sat on the bar stool, and when I rose to greet her I towered over her. The only jewellery she wore was a cuff round her bicep, plain silver a couple of inches wide – chosen, no doubt, to emphasise the slenderness of her arms. I couldn't help thinking an ordinary woman – Eilidh, for instance – could have worn it as a bracelet.

Eve stretched to kiss my cheek, and I stooped to meet her halfway. She smelt of perfume, not the usual flowers or fruit, but something dry and adult that caught in my nostrils: the fragrant equivalent of an acquired taste, of olives, coffee, whisky.

'Nice to see you,' I said. 'What are you drinking?'

'Vodka tonic, thanks,' she said, and straightaway the barman started pouring. He kept his eyes down, as though Eve was too bright for him to look at.

'And the same again for me,' I added.

'Let's get a booth.' She stalked off without waiting for her drink.

'We'll be just over there,' I told the barman, and the nod he gave was newly deferential.

Eve had sunk into the farthest booth, the most hidden corner, shades still shielding half her face. I slid onto the opposite bench.

'How do I know it's really you?'

'Sorry.' She took them off, ducking her head as she did so. 'It's just, someone's tipped off the fucking paparazzi that I'm here.'

Was I really sitting drinking with someone who had just said that? At the same time as trying not to smile, I made sure I was meeting her eyes, not looking guilty. 'I guess that happens all the time, does it?' I suggested.

'Well anyway, we should be fine in here. Cameras are banned, so even if some arsehole did get past the desk...' Her drink arrived; I noticed the slight tremor of the barman's hand, as he placed her glass squint on its napkin, then re-set it, perfectly centred. Eve seemed oblivious to the effect she was having. She wrapped her fingers round the glass. I was briefly fascinated by her fingernails: like perfect pink shells. Then she raised her drink and smiled, and it was like standing under a shower as it turns from cold to hot.

'Cheers, Cam,' she said. Our eyes stayed locked as we sipped.

'So, gosh,' I said, 'it must be fifteen years since I saw you last.' I didn't know why I'd said *gosh*. I never say *gosh*, and she'd already said *fucking* and *arsehole*; it must have been the sheer poshness of my surroundings, like soap and water, washing my mouth out. Eve was smirking.

'Yes. Gosh,' she said. 'Well then. Tell me all about it.'

I'd planned for this. Of course she was going to ask me what I'd been doing. How my life had turned out. And there's ways and ways of saying things. 'Well ... I was in London for a bit,' I said. 'I studied down there; did a bit of DJing, messed about making music, just generally having fun ... then I wasn't too well, unfortunately, that put a damper on things, had to go back to Moulin for a bit.'

She made a concerned face, and I raced on before she could ask. People don't, usually; if you don't offer, they don't like to dig – but I remembered how tenacious Eve had always been. If she wanted to know more, social niceties wouldn't stop her.

'But I've been in Glasgow a few years now. I'm managing this bar.' I took a risk: given that a pack of rabid photographers was apparently stalking her, we'd probably not be leaving the safety of this booth. 'It's a great wee bar,' I said, mentally glossing the old guys with their pints of heavy, the curling lino floor that might once have borne a recognisable pattern, the panelling thick with forty years of gluey varnish. 'Kind of stylish, but edgy; it's a real party place, you know. So: that's me.'

'Wow, that's great to hear you're doing so well,' she said, eyes wide. 'And Duncan, and Jean and Roddy, what are they up to these days?'

She kept me talking, pitching fresh questions whenever I thought I'd finished, and my beer was done by the time I realised she'd said nothing about herself. All the time I'd talked, I'd been seeing myself through her eyes, forgetting to look at her. So now I swung it round.

'And you, Eve: seems like no time ago, you were monkeying around on your wee pink bike, hiding out inside hedges' – she pulled a face – 'and now look at you. How did it all happen for you?'

'Last time you saw me was after my mum died.' She held my eyes, saying straight out what I'd been avoiding. As she stared I felt my face grow hot: I hadn't behaved well on that last visit, when she came to stay with us in Moulin. I had a sudden fear she was going to call me to account. *I was only thirteen*, I nearly squeaked. But instead she smiled a sad kind of a smile, and – oh, that's why the camera loves you, I thought. It was just the face for emotional goodbye scenes, when there's no choice left but to leave. I was the camera zooming in, her face filling my screen; no-one could resist the gravitational pull of her dark liquid eyes.

'I went to my dad's for a bit,' she said.

'Yeah, that was in London, wasn't it?'

She nodded. 'I didn't really know him, back then. It was pretty ... weird. So then, my cousin was going back to school, to boarding school, and I begged to go with her, and I think he was glad not to have me around all the time. And that all worked out a bit better. It was fun, mostly. It was sort of like a home. And loads of other girls there with fucked-up families so I felt... normal, for once! You lot always made me feel like some kind of an alien; I know I was different but–'

37

I was ready to apologise, since that seemed to be what she was angling for, but she waved it away.

'I suppose different is what makes you – I don't want to say special – it destines you, maybe, for something out of the ordinary... So anyway: when I was sixteen this production company came to hold an open audition for some kids' drama, I don't even remember what it was and they didn't pick me, and I didn't think any more about it but then some *other* director asked me to audition for *Catriona* – see, they thought my accent was Scottish even if you didn't!'

'Eve, you're as Scottish as Rod Stewart. You sound like Princess Di.'

She smiled and shook her head. 'Just as long as I don't *sound* like Rod Stewart. You were always teasing me, Campbell.'

'Affectionately, though.' Strike me down for telling such a blatant lie: there was nothing affectionate in my 'teasing' of Eve. 'It was probably the making of you. You should thank me, in fact. All of this: down to me, really.'

'On the shoulders of giants.'

'Aye, something like that. Can I ask, when you're shooting a scene with Morgan Freeman, do they make you stand on a box?'

She did a kind of outraged pout. 'I'm not that short. I'm taller than Kylie, I'll have you know.' She leaned forward as if to confide a secret. 'She's got bigger feet, though. It was so funny, I was at some awards thing – what was it? In London, anyway – and Kylie ended up borrowing my shoes. She'd flown in from somewhere, New York I think, and all her luggage had gone missing which, I know, you wouldn't think that could happen to someone like Kylie, but it did, and...'

I watched her full lips moving, knowing I should be fascinated by this behind-the-scenes gossip; by the reality of people I didn't quite believe were real. Kylie surely didn't exist, not in the same way that I did. She was a Christmas tree fairy, she didn't shove her sweaty feet into borrowed shoes a half-size too small.

But what I was thinking as Eve talked on was: you're still trying to impress me. Just the way you used to with your Gaelic words, your secret hiding places. Is this all you've got, stories of people more famous than you? And then I thought of how I'd turned the Douglas Arms into some city-centre style bar, and how desperate that was. We were the same, then: we were almost the same. I listened to her scattering starry names, her world so shining and limitless and small and scrutinised; looked at her bug-eye glasses folded on the table. Where Eve was trapped in this gilded cage, I could walk out of here, walk down the street, into an ordinary pub. If I wanted to.

But I stayed where I was.

After a while, I realised my silence was encouraging her.

'So, do you hang out with any of the real A-listers?' I asked, and saw her smile vanish. 'People like Keira Knightley? I mean I know she's more mainstream Hollywood; you're a bit more arthouse, aren't you?'

'Not really. I wouldn't say so.' She reeled off a list of recent films: an action movie, a thriller, a romantic comedy.

'I suppose I'm just thinking of stuff like that one ... *Concrete Moon*, was it?'

I was trying to make her blush, but she stared me down – eyes hard now, obsidian – and it was me that turned red.

'You saw that one, did you?'

'Well, aye.' I coughed. 'Me and Roddy went.'

'Yeah, I'm proud of that.' She leaned back in her seat, crossed her legs and draped her arm along the back of the bench. The silver cuff glinted tight round her tricep. The straw in her drink pointed directly to her mouth. 'It really stretched me.'

Too right it stretched her. Was she doing this on purpose? I couldn't help responding: a thick warmth, both welcome and unwanted. I glanced around to check we weren't being watched, then back at Eve, trying to read her intention.

She turned away, displaying a perfect profile. Bored with this game. 'I need a cigarette.' She put her shades on. 'There's a court-yard. D'you want to come?'

There was nothing for it. 'Lead on,' I said, and stayed where I was till she'd left her seat. When I got to my feet, my hands went straight to my pockets, subtly rearranging things down there as I followed her outside.

It was still light, the sky a deep summer-night blue, but the path was already decorated with hundreds of pin-prick spotlights. Light washed up from raised beds of flowers, and palm trees glowed luminous green. We sat on metal chairs beneath a tree – again, she'd chosen the most private place to settle. She had her arms wrapped round her, though it wasn't cold; huddled like a wee girl, all skin and bone and eyes. Fifteen years ago I'd have run off, left her shivering.

'Here.' I took off my jacket, handed it to her.

'Are you sure? That's so kind. But then you'll be cold.'

'I'll survive.'

It draped almost to her knees; she had to push up the sleeves before she could light her cigarette. For a while, we sat quietly. Nearby, illuminated water trickled through a stepped pool, find-ing its level.

Eve finished smoking. Warmer now, inside my – Duncan's – jacket, she showed no sign of wanting to move.

'Campbell,' she said, eventually. 'Why did you want us to go for a drink?'

I pulled a face. 'So I could tell all my pals about it. Maybe sell my story to the tabloids, who knows.'

'Never get a straight word from you, will I?'

'You think I'm joking?'

She leaned back, gazed up at the palm leaves. 'This is nice. Most nights I get back and I'm just … shower, dressing gown, climb into bed and watch TV. That's it.'

'The loneliness of fame?'

'No, I know you're laughing, but it can be. Imagine, you're away from home, months at a time. A week in one place, a few weeks in the next. It's so hard to sleep, when you're always somewhere new. And relationships – forget it. Seriously. That's what happened with Dan, you know – well, part of it.'

There was a certain amount of presumption there, that I'd been following her life from down in my gutter, that I would know who Dan was. Irritatingly, of course, she was right. I could tell you they met on the set of *Astonishing Beauty*, were married in Italy, split up not long after.

'I always saw that described as "amicable".'

That made her sit up. '*He* may have been amicable about it. Let's just say, when a person can't cope with a few weeks of chastity, and when that person can't see he's done anything wrong, it doesn't leave me feeling friendly.'

I felt myself staring. She looked indignant, her cheeks flushed pink. For the first time tonight, her expression was real. I couldn't begin to count how often I'd seen her face reproduced. But no matter how good the light and how sharp the focus, no matter how long the camera lingered, showing every angle, I could never see her clearly enough to recognise her. I could never understand what she looked like, even with her face ten-foot tall in front of me, couldn't understand that it was her. Now, as I stared, her expression changed: a flash of something still real, something like surprise; and then she blinked, and as her lids descended they veiled her eyes with self-awareness, and a new face appeared, one she'd practised. A professional expression: anticipation. She was expecting me to do something.

I was so, so tired of doing nothing.

I did what she expected me to.

What was it like to kiss a movie star? I imagined myself answering the question, years from now. The answer: like kissing any other woman. Taste of make-up and cigarettes. Smell of perfume. Her lips damp and soft. She half kissed me back; pulled away. I pulled back just as fast.

She was glancing all round, like checking for snipers. Then, 'What was that?'

'Sorry, I thought – forget it.'

'No, it's just – I don't know. Not out here, for sure. D'you want to be on the cover of *Closer*? Eve's Mystery Man?'

'Not especially. Like I said, forget it.'

'Fine.' She folded her arms, hands retreating into the tunnels of her sleeves. My sleeves. Duncan's sleeves. Then she narrowed her eyes at me, and said, like a code word, 'Don't tell.'

'Obviously.' Now I was really hacked off. Did she honestly think I'd be off to the tabloids to sell my tale of a brief half-kiss?

She shook her head. 'No: remember? The hunt.' Her look was like a shared secret. 'It was raining...?'

I had no idea what she was talking about. But I didn't want to offend her, so I just smiled like I'd put two and two together, and I was on her wavelength.

'Always interrupted,' she said; and then, softly, 'Fuck. It's never simple, is it?'

I shrugged. 'Isn't it?' Because it was pretty simple for me: life, love, everything; you could write it all on a postcard. I really had no idea how it might be for her. But she was about to tell me. She sat there beautiful and vulnerable, cooried into my jacket; sat with what was probably a thousand-pound handbag tucked beneath her chair; sat with her legs crossed, dangling thousand-pound sandals from her bony feet: she sat there with everything, gazed at me and told me how hard she'd had it. I didn't want to hear.

Ten minutes later, I didn't want to have heard. Some of it was nasty. Dan, mostly. You'd think if you were married to a bona fide film star, a woman more famous than you and far more beautiful – you'd think you'd keep it in your pants. If you did fancy something on the side, you wouldn't need to pay for it. And if hookers were part of some dark sexual quirk you just couldn't suppress, you'd be suitably ashamed. You'd do all you could to keep it hidden from your other half. What you wouldn't do is engineer an expensive threesome, and emotionally blackmail your wife into making it four. That was Eve's story, at any rate. I believed it. She was pink-eyed by the time she finished, arms folded tight.

I didn't know why she was telling me. What she wanted me to say.

'What an idiot.' The words fell limp and inadequate from my lips.

She glanced up at me, then looked away. 'After that,' – her voice was low and gritty – 'all I wanted was to be with someone nice. Someone ordinary, someone who's not… spoiled.' Her mouth tugged down on that last word.

For a moment we sat without speaking. Then Eve leant forward, fished her bag from under her seat and stood, wobbling a little in her heels. 'Scuse me.'

I waited, minutes ticking by. I wasn't sure she was coming back. Wasn't sure what I should do now. *Someone nice, someone ordinary.* Perhaps she'd meant me to follow her – to make my way up to her room. No: I dismissed the idea. She hadn't mentioned her room number; her back view, hurrying off, had not been an invitation. It was dark now, as dark as it would get on this summer night. I half-closed my eyes, and a thousand lights stretched and blurred. I could pick out one single light, just the one, because it was on the blink: flashing on and off; mostly off. With my eyes open, I lost it again.

When Eve reappeared, runny-nosed, hanky in hand, it was obvious what she'd been doing. It was obvious from the way she perched on her chair clutching the edge of the seat, from the way her right heel played a tat-a-tat-tat on the paving, from the way her breath came quick and shallow. I could feel my own pulse start to race, like it had been me cutting lines in a toilet cubicle. I could feel panic barging in.

'Sorry about that,' she said. Her voice was still croaky. She cleared her throat. 'Didn't mean to splurge.'

'No no, that's fine.' I smiled, breathing slowly, trying not to see her white knuckles, her jittering legs. I was riffling through possible exit lines, because I couldn't be around this, because I had to leave; but how could I, when she'd just cracked open her heart? I started to speak, to lay the ground for my escape – something about an early start for me and for her – but as I did, she exploded into a monster coughing fit. My dry-mouthed words were lost.

'Oops,' I said instead. 'Something go down the wrong way?'

She held up a hand; caught her breath; started to cough all over again. I was half-laughing, embarrassed for her.

'You alright there?'

A pause: another fit.

'Wait and I'll get some water.' I went to fetch it from the bar, arriving at the same time as a gent who so clearly took precedence in every possible way – age, class, wealth – that I might as well have been invisible. I stood, and waited, and waited. Mr Precedence wanted his drink just so. I'm needing some water for Eve Sadler, I wanted to say – you know, the film star? She's coked up and coughing her guts up out there in your fancy courtyard. But I held my tongue.

'A glass of tap water,' I said, when eventually it was my turn. 'Just water, it's fine–' But just water wasn't done, apparently. The barman went on messing about with ice, lemon, straw. Another quilted napkin under the glass.

When I finally made it back to Eve, she was still coughing; a rough, barking noise that ripped through the courtyard, and fighting for breath between barks.

'Here.' I crouched beside her, held out the water. The ice shook against the glass, water slopping over the rim as she took it, took a gulp and seemed to struggle to swallow. She shoved the glass back at me, almost dropping it, and made a grab for my arm.

'Allergic.'

'Allergic?' Sure, I thought: sure it's an allergy. 'What is it, asthma? What do you need, have you got an inhaler? What is it you need?'

44

She was wheezing now, and still barking. She sounded like a dying dog. 'Adren – adrenaline…' she managed. '…pen – my bag–'

Her bag. Under her chair. I went to grab it. 'Eve, it's not here. Where's your bag?'

She bent over, drooping, head on her knees.

'Eve! Where did you leave it?'

Eve caught her breath, seemed about to answer, and then–

'Oh, Christ!'

She'd spewed, pure vodka tonic, all over her feet in their strappy sandals, and over my trousers. Till now I'd thought, *panic attack* – but I'd never seen anyone throw up from anxiety. Jesus, what if she was having a heart attack? 'Your bag, did you leave it in the toilets? Eve? In the ladies?'

She might have nodded, or it might have been a spasm of coughing.

'I'm going to fetch it. Okay? I'll be back in a minute.' But I didn't want to leave her like this. Folded into herself, pooled with vomit, gasping for breath. 'Oh shit,' I muttered. 'What do I do?' I crouched there, swithering. And then she retched again, and I saw her lips all ghostly, tinged with blue, and I jumped to my feet and ran through the courtyard, into the bright inside, staring wildly, searching for the ladies. I couldn't see it. I couldn't see it. Eve was outside, alone, fuck knows what wrong with her, and I couldn't see the… An age passed before I spotted the symbol – so small, so discreet – and I barrelled straight in there not caring who I might surprise, and there was her bag on the side of the basin. I snatched it up and I ran back outside, and as I ran I was shouting, 'Help, I need some help out here…'

Eve was still slumped forward. She'd stopped coughing. Was that good or bad? 'Okay, Eve, I've got it, I've got it.' I tipped the bag out onto the ground. So much stuff: fags, phone, make-up. 'Eve, what am I looking for, what does it look like?' A syringe, to inject the adrenaline? I looked for a syringe. 'Like this?' A long black box: I held it up. 'Eve! This?' She made a kind of gurgling sound. I

45

tugged it open. Inside, a tube like a glue-stick. No needle in sight. The stick thing had writing on. Shaking hands. It danced in front of my eyes. I couldn't read – there wasn't time–

'What do I do? Eve!'

I grabbed her hair, tilted her head back and almost passed out. The whites of her eyes were blood red.

'Oh Jesus, Jesus. Oh, help!'

Finally, they came running. Someone snatched the stick from my hand. Yanked off a lid, stabbed the pen straight into Eve's leg, and held it there. 'Okay,' she was saying, 'It's alright, hen, we've got you.' Another woman was on the phone: I could hear her calling the ambulance, giving the address, and at the same time a man was saying, 'Eve Sadler – it is – it's Eve Sadler.'

'An allergy,' said the woman, 'I think it's an allergy, a reaction. Is she breathing? Check, someone check, is she breathing?'

Eve was on the ground now, still wrapped in my jacket; it had slipped off one shoulder, and above and below the silver cuff the flesh of her arm was swollen, purpled. I crouched at her side. Her eyes were closed, her hair stuck to her face in dark streaks. Ice-white circles on her cheeks. Her lips were parted, were blue, and when I leaned close I could hear just a whisper of breath.

'She's breathing,' I said. 'She's still breathing.' Her mouth was damp and soft against my ear. 'Tell them she's breathing. Tell them she's still okay.'

I don't remember a camera. All I remember is Eve lying on the ground, and me bending over her, hoping against hope that she was still breathing. How could it be? How could this happen to her? Minutes ago we had shared a kiss; she had opened her heart to me; she had told me she wanted to be with me, that it was all that mattered. As I rode with her in the ambulance I held tight onto her hand and spoke to her. Knowing she couldn't hear, I begged her not to die.

Though I don't remember it, of course that camera must have been there. The evidence is still all over the internet: that as Eve lay dying, in her last minutes, someone was standing by – not helping, not even frozen in horror, but instead taking picture after picture. Pictures that are familiar now to hundreds of thousands of people.

By the time one of them appeared on the Daily News website, with the story that Eve was in a critical condition, she was already gone. And by the time the evening papers caught up with the sites that had broken the news to the entire world, my life had changed forever.

PART TWO

On dry land
Bound south-east

PART TWO

Chapter 8

'Duncs! Go and time us!' I'm on my bike, ready to race with Eilidh and Roddy. Down to the burn and back again.

'Get *lost*.' Duncs has his back to us, talking to Ross and Graeme and two girls from their year at school. They've been there for ages, leaning against the wall. Doing nothing. I don't see why he can't time us. I'd do it in under three minutes, I'm sure.

I ride past the five of them, turn in a circle and pass them again, so close that Duncs reaches out and tries to shove me over. I'm too fast for him.

'Fuck off, Heinz!'

I pretend I haven't heard, but my hair feels suddenly heavy and hot round my face. I've been growing it since the start of the holidays and Duncs thinks I'm copying him. His hair is down past his chin now and he thinks it makes him look like the singer out of the Stone Roses. I shake my head, and straightaway my stupid hair slips back into my eyes. Maybe he's right. Maybe I do look like a German boy. I'm going to ask Mum to get it cut. But it'll have to wait for a week, cos tomorrow we're going to Glenelg.

This year, it will be different. This year it's just Roddy and me. The others have grown out of it, Mum says – and yeah, last year they did spend the whole week sulking and moaning and really annoying the rest of us. It's *dull*, says Jean, and Duncs says nothing but you can tell he's too old for treasure hunts just looking at him.

'I've grown out of it too,' I said to Mum when I heard Duncs was staying behind. I don't know if it's true. I'd still want to go, if everyone else wanted to. I'd still want to do the treasure hunt. And I don't understand why they've gone off it, when they used to think it was the best fun ever. Every year when we came back home, we'd try and make a treasure hunt of our own, so Eilidh could join in and sometimes Magnus too. Every year I'd say, It's better at Glenelg because ... till Eilidh went in a huff and left us to it. But it's true. Up there, it was always the best.

'I can't stand that Eve,' I told Mum. 'She's always chasing after me. She *annoys* me.'

'Like you annoy your brother?'

'That's different.' Which is what Mum says all the time, so I was being clever, using it against her. But she'd made up her mind. So we're getting packed off, no matter how much I complain.

Now, Roddy and Eilidh are practising wheelies.

'Cool! Who can balance longest? I'll be judge,' I say. 'One, two, three, *go!*' And they yank their handlebars and rise up onto their back wheels, sitting in mid-air and dancing the handlebars side to side. Even Duncs and his pals turn to watch. In the distance thunder rumbles like an empty stomach. A few fat raindrops darken the pavement.

'Boys!' Mum's halfway down the path, arms folded. 'I need you to come inside.'

Roddy's front wheel bounces back down to earth. Me and Duncs look at each other, like, *What's going on? It's way too early for tea.* But her voice sounds sharp and rough like it would shred any arguments. She's on her way back inside, not waiting for us to follow. Then she stops.

'Roddy, you'd better go home too.'

Roddy has his mouth open to ask why, but Mum's hurrying into the house, looking kind of hunched. Eilidh is still dancing in mid-air. The open door is waiting for us.

I've never seen Mum like this before: white face, red eyes. Never heard her speak like she's half-swallowed her voice and it's stuck all thick in her throat. Dad has his arm around her. Duncs gives her an embarrassed hug. I stay where I am, staring at the carpet. Your mum shouldn't need comforting; it's her job to do the comforting of you.

'At least I won't have to do that stupid treasure hunt.' I don't know why I say this, but I mean it. I mean for them all to look away from me, for Mum to leave the room, for Dad to slowly shake his head. And then I feel bad, bad to the pit of my stomach for saying such a thing, and I can't ever take it back.

I follow Duncs up to his room, hover in the doorway.

'I don't feel anything,' I say, 'like sad or anything. Do you?'

Duncs shrugs like he doesn't care, but he looks a bit sick. He kicks at his door, and it swings shut in my face.

I'm left standing alone on the landing. Around me the house is silent and listening, full of hiding people. I grit my teeth; run downstairs, stomping hard on every step so the sound of me thumps through the house, and I burst outside and slam the front door behind me.

It's raining, big lonely drops spattering the street. Eilidh's still messing around on her bike, pushing hard uphill, sailing down again. 'What's up?' she calls as she passes me.

'We're not going to Glenelg.'

'How not?'

I look at the pavement, scuffing my foot against the kerb. 'Eve's mother's died.'

Eilidh scrunches to a stop, wheels backwards till she's alongside me. 'She *died*?'

'Aye. She had a...' I can't remember the word. 'Something in her head, like, bleeding or something.' Kick, kick at the kerb. All I feel is angry: at Mum, for her white and red face; at Duncs for shutting his door. It's not my fault if I don't feel sad.

Eilidh is silent, leaning on her handlebars. When I glance at her face she doesn't look horrified or sick. She doesn't look anything, really. She's just watching me with her orangey eyes. She didn't know Jasmine, not really, same as she hardly knows Eve.

'Want to race?' she says. 'Top of the hill, past the church, over the burn and back again?'

'Aye, alright.' I fetch my bike from where I dropped it, wrap my hands around its solid handlebars. I line up alongside her, ready to go. 'Cool.'

Eilidh nods her head, just the once. 'Cool.'

It's because Mum feels responsible for her that Eve comes to stay two months later, bringing her sadness into our October holiday. I wish she wasn't here. I can tell Mum's upset, probably because Eve makes her think of Jasmine. And I don't know what I'm meant to say to Eve, and she doesn't have much to say for herself. Her big eyes follow me everywhere, but she doesn't try to play or sit close beside me like she always has before. Which is good – but even though she's keeping her distance, and keeping her mouth shut, she still makes me feel bad. Like she's dangerous, like if she wanted she could get me into the worst trouble ever.

Plus, because of Eve, everyone has to be miserable.

The first night she's here we're not allowed to go out after tea. We have to all play *Monopoly*, which is Mum's suggestion even though she hates board games. Eve gets to choose her counter first and she takes the dog. Normally, I'm the dog.

At first it's like she doesn't even know how to play, but then you can see her forgetting stuff, forgetting about being here without her Mum and feeling weird and all of that, and you can see she wants to win. And you can see everyone making exceptions for her, Duncs as well as Mum and Dad, letting her off with fines and stuff. I'm biting my tongue, telling myself, *Her mother's dead, her mother's dead.* And we all let her win, and she looks happy and then after a minute her mouth droops again, and it's like, why did we bother letting her win if she wasn't even going to enjoy it?

Next day, Duncs is up and out first thing, into Perth to meet some friends. I'm on my way to chap for Eilidh and Roddy, but

Mum grabs my arm before I can get out the door, grabs me really hard.

'Ow! What?'

'Where are you going?'

I tell her, already sulking cos I know what she's going to say.

'You're to take Eve with you.'

'Mu-um!' I kind of whisper it, so Eve won't hear.

Mum gives me a look, then she drags me out into the front garden. I can see Eve through the kitchen window, staring at nothing.

'I am so disappointed in you, Campbell. The girl has lost her mother!'

'Yeah, I know, but it's not fair, Duncs doesn't have to–'

'Stop!' She holds her hand up like a traffic sign. 'Don't give me *not fair*. I'm sick of hearing it. Now you will *take* Eve with you and you will be *nice* to her, and I *mean* it.' She folds her arms, glances back at the kitchen window. In a lower voice, she says, 'Have a little compassion, for God's sake.' And I think she means for Jasmine, and maybe for her, as well as for Eve, and I also think 'compassion' is a drippy word and kind of embarrassing, like an RE lesson or a Christmas service.

I stomp back into the house and say to Eve, casually, 'Want to hang about with Roddy and that?'

She slips down from the stool she's perched on, and nods.

'Come on then. It's cold, you'll need your coat.' There. Compassion.

Together, not speaking, we walk round to Roddy's house, then the three of us go in for Eilidh. We don't stop there for long. Her house is too small, plus last week Magnus told them he was joining the army and since then it's been almost as bad as it was last year when he gave up on school.

It's better having three of us with Eve. Roddy's younger, and Eilidh's a girl, so they can both look after her better than I can – and even though Eilidh hardly knows her, already she's telling all about

Magnus, about how he made a bonfire from his school books and his tie and came home stinking of lighter fluid, how her dad locked him in his bedroom so he climbed out the window onto the shed roof and disappeared for two days. About how he was too clever for school, and how he's too good for the army as well. At the time, me and Roddy were pretty impressed but we've heard it a million times. I'd never sook up to Duncs the way Eilidh goes on about Magnus, I'd be embarrassed, but then Duncs is nowhere near as cool. Anyway, Eve is looking all wide-eyed, and Eilidh's happy with her new audience, so me and Roddy hang back till they're out of sight and then it's just like normal, like Eve isn't here.

We take our time catching them up. When we reach the flat rock by the burn, which is our usual place, Eilidh's sitting there cross-legged, looking fed up. She's on her own.

'Where have you been?'

'Where's Eve?'

Eilidh shrugged. 'She said she'd catch up. She was waiting on you.'

'Where was she waiting?' I stand on the rock, hands on hips, looking around for any sign of Eve's red anorak. 'Bloody hell, Mum's going to kill me. Where did you leave her?'

'I didn't leave her, she left me.'

'Yeah, okay, where did you see her last?'

'Just when we got to the river, she said she was going to wait.'

I look down at the water. It's rained a lot this week and the river's high and fast, with plenty of white foam. I have a bad feeling. If something's happened to her, I'm going to be in trouble for the rest of my life.

'We can't have walked past her,' says Roddy.

'She's gone off somewhere. Crap.' I jump down from the rock, back onto the path. 'Come on, help me find her.'

We walk back the way we came, and when the path goes away from the river we stick by the water, pushing through bushes and trudging through mud.

'Eve! Eve, where are you?'

It's Roddy that sees her first. 'There!' He points: a flash of red, at the edge of the water. Still as anything.

I have to slide down a muddy slope to reach her. She's crouched down, and at first I think she's fishing something out of the river.

'What have you lost?' I say.

She turns her face to me. Her hand's still stuck in the water, which is freezing. I grab her arms and yank her upright.

'What are you *doing*?' Her hand is clammy and red with cold, her coat sleeve soaked. 'Idiot!'

I rub her fingers, trying to warm them up, cos if she gets frostbite or something it'll be my fault. Her lips press together like she's about to cry, like her hand's so cold it's sore. So instead I push it up against her face.

'Breathe,' I say. She puffs like she's putting out a candle. 'Bloody hell, not like that.' I breathe for her, holding her hand near my mouth, breathe hot and deep. 'That better?'

She nods. Her wee face looks just as frozen as her hand.

'Right. Come on, we're going home.'

I'm scared to let her go in case she runs off again, but I need both hands to grab onto branches and pull myself up the muddy bank. As soon as I get to the top I turn round and make sure she's following.

'It's like looking after a baby,' I say, watching her scramble. I say it to myself, quietly. I don't think she can hear.

When she gets near the top, I reach out to pull her up the last slippy bit. Her hand is still dead cold.

'There,' I say. 'You're okay, eh.'

Chapter 9

They didn't want to let me go. They questioned me: their voices gentle, matter-of-fact. Were you aware of any allergies Eve might have had? Did she eat or drink anything unusual? Had she complained of feeling unwell? Are you the next of kin? That one, I could answer with confidence. I didn't know who was her next of kin, I didn't know how to find out. Before I was allowed to leave, a policeman took my details. 'Is this all because she's famous?' I asked. He shook his head: standard procedure with sudden deaths.

From the bad dream of the hospital into early morning dark: dazed, I walked into an ambush. 'That's him,' someone said – and the world exploded.

'Can you tell us how she is?'

'Is there any news?'

'Tell us what's happening!'

My hands leapt up to shield my face; a hopeless, belated gesture. I had nothing to hide behind; my jacket lay back in the hospital. Head down, half-blind in the strobing light, I hurried for the waiting taxi. The flashes kept coming as I slammed the car door, as we pulled away.

'Do I want to know what that's about?' said the driver. 'Naw, don't tell me. Where to?'

We swung onto Dumbarton Road; the empty streets, the lights smearing past.

'Where to?' he said again, as gently as a gruff Glaswegian can.

I still couldn't tell him. My face was wet, and knives packed my throat.

I'd forgotten Roddy was away. I stood in the empty flat, and it waited to see what I would do next. My legs were shaking, and my hand when I held it in front of me. The shaking meant that what had happened was appalling. Of course it was appalling, there was no question about that; but it reassured me that my body knew it too.

In the kitchen I poured some whisky, thinking it might help. Sweet tea: that's what I should have been drinking. No-one had offered me tea at the hospital. They should have done – for the shock. I began to feel angry that I hadn't been given tea. I gulped the whisky, and it didn't help at all, just made me feel sick. When I closed my eyes, I saw Eve's eyes scarlet with blood, and I blink-blink-blinked that sight away; pressed the heels of my hands hard into my sockets, till all I saw was spirals of coloured light, and their dancing made me come loose in the world and I had to run for the toilet.

I made it, just. Stayed there, bent over the bowl, slack and emptied. Being sick felt good, like the right thing to do. I concentrated on the scoured, stinging feeling in my nose and throat, and when the pain passed I stood up, rinsed my acid mouth, and did the only thing I could think of, which was to go to bed.

My sleep was shallow, easily broken by the phone. The ringing stopped as I registered it; started again just as I went to check the number. The voice was male, unfamiliar, asking for me.

'Speaking.'

'Campbell, sorry to disturb you but I believe you were with Eve Sadler last night?'

Was it someone from the hospital? The police? 'Sorry, who did you say this is?'

'My name's Tom Bell – would you be able to confirm that for me, Campbell? That you were with Eve when she was taken ill?'

'Yes, I was. But what, who – who told you?'

'And you were in the ambulance with her, is that right?'

'Where are you calling from?'

'I'm from the *Mercury* and – listen, Campbell – we want to tell your story. We'll make it worth your while to talk to us, only to us. You'll get to put your side of the story before everyone else starts telling it for you...'

I didn't say anything for a minute. He kept on talking. Making offers. I thought of all the things I could say, wanted to say. I didn't open my mouth; didn't want him even to hear my breath.

I hung up.

Seconds later, the phone rang again. I let it ring, and at the last moment I answered. I didn't say anything.

'Campbell? Don't hang up now–' It was the same guy. Straightaway I ended the call: again the phone rang. This time I let it go to voicemail, then unplugged it.

That firing squad of photographers outside the hospital; the scavenger I'd just spoken to – I went to the front door, locked the deadbolt and put on the chain. Peering through the spyhole into the stair, I don't know what I thought I might see.

4am: too early to call anyone, to tell them about Eve; but I called Eilidh anyway. Voicemail, of course. I left her a message: something had happened, I said, and please call back. Then I crawled into bed once more.

This time I plummeted into a dead sleep, and when I next woke it was in a sudden hot panic, fear throbbing through me. I was in trouble – such bad trouble. *Don't tell*, said Eve. *Remember?* I sat up gasping.

I remembered. I remembered she was dead. I kicked the covers aside. Moved like a zombie through to the kitchen to make some coffee. It was light outside. I carried my mug into the living room, eyed the phone. Plugged it in, and heard the broken tone that meant I had voicemail.

It wasn't just the *Mercury* that had somehow tracked me down. I listened to brief, urgent messages from the *News*, the *Record*, the *Star*; from *Now* and *Heat* and *Closer*, deleting each as soon as I heard who it was from, and when the phone was clean I yanked the jack out of the wall again, grabbed my mobile. Called Eilidh.

There were other people I could have called. Other friends, or family: Roddy, my mum, Duncs long-distance. But it was Eilidh I needed. It always was Eilidh, those rare times I wanted to talk. I could rely on her not to ask stupid questions, to accept what I told her – to understand, or at least not to say that she didn't. And since right now I didn't understand myself, I needed the rock of someone who could.

'Cam. What's up?' She sounded sleepy, and worried.

I should have planned what to say; now I found myself lost. Where could I start?

'What is it? Cam? Are you there?'

'Yeah, I'm here. Something's happened – a bad thing, and I wanted to talk to you. Is that okay?'

'Of course it is. Take your time, I'm listening...'

Her voice was calm now. I could hear the sounds of her getting up. The water running into the kettle. She's not a rock, perhaps, more like hard-packed sand. Solid, giving. Her voice made the ground firmer beneath me.

'Eve, Eve Sadler – she died last night.'

'Oh. God.'

'No but, I was with her. I was with her when she died.'

'Oh my God, are you okay?'

'We went for a drink. She was here, she was filming in Glasgow, and we went for a drink. And she had this attack. I thought it was – it was like an allergy. And she just ... her eyes, Eilidh, her eyes went bright red. She couldn't breathe.'

'What's happening now? Where are you, who's with you now?'

'At home, and the press have been on the phone and I don't know what to do.'

'Roddy's there, yes?'

'He's in Moulin.'

'You're on your own?'

'Shit, Eilidh, what do I do?'

'Is there anyone you can call, to come over?'

'Yes but – what for, how will that help?'

'You shouldn't be on your own.' There was a pause. 'I'll get on a train, I'll come up.'

'No, no, it's fine, I just–'

'I've got prep and planning this afternoon; I can take that with me. Someone can cover my morning classes. I'll be on a train in an hour. Be in Glasgow by one.'

She was coming to rescue me. That must have been what I wanted when I called; what I expected. It was what Eilidh did.

All I needed to do now was hang on till she got here.

I turned on the radio, waiting for the news. Eve had made the headlines: *The actor Eve Sadler has died after apparently suffering an extreme allergic reaction. The star was rushed to hospital after collapsing at the Metcalfe Hotel in Glasgow, where she had been filming, but doctors were unable to save her and she was pronounced dead in the early hours of this morning.*

Seven-thirty: I imagined my mum listening to the same bulletin. She'd freeze, in the middle of making breakfast; her hand would go to her mouth. She would think of the little girl we used to know; and she'd think of Jasmine, who at least made it into her thirties. She would rub her eyes; sit down, maybe, at the kitchen table, where the tea was starting to stew; stare at the radio. *Poor soul*, she would say.

There was no mention of my name. Of course not – why would there be? This whole thing with the phone, it was crazy. As long as I ignored their calls, they'd go away. Give them nothing, and they'd have to leave me alone.

Over the next few hours, the radio told me the news again and again and again. As time went on, they added a few new sentences: *The actor is best known for appearing in* Absolute Beauty, *for which she was nominated for an Oscar. It is believed that she may have previously suffered minor allergic reactions. Her family has issued a statement asking that their privacy be respected at this time.*

I had never thought before of what lay behind a statement like that, but now I guessed at unplugged phones, and her family – her father? her cousin? – sitting behind closed curtains, ignoring the doorbell's chime.

As a test, I re-connected my phone line. It was silent for all of thirteen minutes before they started calling once more. I didn't pick up, of course; sat listening to the ringing, saying out loud to the empty room, in my politest voice, 'Fuck you ... fuck you ... fuck you, too.'

Early afternoon: when the buzzer went, it jarred right through me. Normally, I'd just press the button to open the main door. Now, cautiously, I lifted the handset.

'It's me. It's Eilidh.'

I felt like running down to meet her, but by the time I'd released the chain, unlocked the deadbolt and turned the snib she was almost at the landing. She slipped inside, shoved the door shut behind her. When she gave me a hug I smelled newsprint, felt the rolled-up paper she was clutching damp and cold against my neck.

'How are you doing?' She fixed me with her rusty eyes, looking worried; as though I were fractionally different from myself, and she didn't quite recognise me.

'Oh, not so bad now,' I said. 'I think maybe I was panicking.'

She pursed her lips. Handed me the paper. 'It's not in the tabloids yet. But it's all over the *Evening Times*. Your name and everything.'

Eve's face was huge on the front page. **STAR DIES IN CITY HOTEL** ran the headline. Inside were stills from her movies, shots of her on set outside Pollok House. I perched on the kitchen counter, reading, while Eilidh made tea.

'I don't get it, how did they find this out? Look! *Sadler is reported to have spent the evening at the Metcalfe Hotel with city barman Campbell Johnstone.* How do they know that?'

Eilidh took the paper off me. 'It's their job, isn't it? Thing is,'

– she handed me a brimming mug – 'when I was coming in, there were people outside who were just hanging around. And I reckon they're journalists. I bet they're staking you out. Or door-stepping you, whatever you call it.'

I stared at her. 'You're kidding.'

'Are they still calling you?'

On cue, the phone rang. I smiled, feeling it come out twisted. Jumped down from the counter and went to the living room window. I stood back from the glass, like the outside world was a war zone. Peered round the edge of the frame.

'There.' Eilidh was at my side. She pointed to a couple of guys and a woman on the opposite side of the road. 'They're still there.'

'Did I tell you, there were photographers at the hospital?'

'What, inside?'

'When I came out. They were waiting for me.'

'Wonder where they were from,' she said. 'Not the *Evening Times*, judging by your absence from today's edition. Well, Cam, I hope you've got plenty of food in, and plenty of drink. You're not going anywhere for a while.'

Chapter 10

I know how wrong it sounds, how repulsive, with Eve's body lying cold in the hospital morgue. But for the next two days, Eilidh and I had fun. We pulled the quilts through to the living room and made a sofa nest in front of the TV. We worked our way through a stack of DVDs. We made random meals with whatever ingredients we had: egg and chips with pesto; bacon sarnies with tattie scones instead of bread; rice seasoned with soy sauce and vinegar. We ran out of tea and drank hot water and whisky instead. When it started to rain, heavy drops battering the windows, we laughed at the thought of the journalists getting soaked outside. Every so often, Eilidh checked the phone for messages: *delete, delete, delete.*

'Cam, this one's from your mum.'

I called her back on my mobile; I didn't want to touch the landline. She'd read it in the *Herald* – so my name had reached the broadsheets. I was described as 'family friend Campbell Johnstone'. It seemed that someone had been persuaded to talk. I wondered who it could be; whether I'd ever find out.

'I didn't know you were friends with her,' said Mum. 'I didn't know you knew her still, or I would have phoned before. They've written here that you were with her when it happened.'

'Yeah, I was.'

'Oh, Campbell. That must have been awful. How are you feeling?'

'Eilidh's here,' I said.

'Oh well, fine. Fine. She'll look after you then.'

When Mum rang off, we poured the last of the whisky, and put on *Terminator*.

Halfway through, my mobile went. 'Pause, please,' I said. 'Roddy...'

'I've been calling the flat. Where are you?'

'We're here. We're hiding.'

'We?'

'Me and Eilidh.'

'Have you seen the papers?'

'It's in the *Herald*, I know. Mum called–'

'The *Herald*, aye, and every other paper. Cam, there's pictures of you in all the tabloids. The *News* has got *pages* of it – you kissing her, for fuck's sake! I mean it's fuzzy but that's what it looks like. Is that for real?'

I felt sick, whisky churning in my stomach. 'I did – It just – Oh God... how?'

'And this picture of her lying there: fuck. With you beside her. It's a picture of her dying; it's unbelievable. I can't believe they'd print this. And then loads of them have got you outside the hospital and you look like a wreck, I've got to say.'

'Jesus. Has my mum seen them?'

'Dunno. Don't think so. Look, Cam, it's not just the photos. Listen, here's the header. *Eve snapped in passionate kiss with mystery man – moments later, she is dead.* Then it goes, *The star was rushed to hospital after ...* da da da ... okay, hang on ... here: *Her companion has been identified as family friend Campbell Johnstone. The Glaswegian barman was–*'

'Glaswegian?'

'*...was at Eve's side in the ambulance during the emergency dash to the Western Infirmary, where the actress was pronounced dead in the early hours of Friday morning.* And then it says, *Johnstone, 32–*'

'What? Thirty-two? Where did they get that?'

'*...is said to have been consoling Eve following her high-profile divorce last year from Dan Fischer. Sources close to the star have revealed that Eve had recently spoken of a new man in her life. The couple, who spent the evening in the bar of the exclusive Metcalfe*

Hotel, were spotted sharing this intimate moment just minutes before Eve collapsed.'

'They already said that bit.'

'Campbell Johnstone was seen leaving the Western Infirmary in a disorientated state and has since been unavailable for comment.'

'Well, that's one thing they've got right.'

'Which? The *disorientated state* or the *no comment*?'

'Okay, two things.' I blew out a sigh. It came out all wobbly. 'Um. Thanks for the heads up.'

'What are you going to do?'

'Ahhhh ... nothing. Nothing, I think. I mean, what can I do?'

'But all this stuff about you consoling her...'

'It's what they do, isn't it? They make up stories. Basically, I'm staying here till it dies down. It'll all go away if I just keep a low profile. When they realise there's no story, they'll forget it. It's just a case of waiting them out: and they're outside in the cold and rain and I'm in here watching *Terminator*, so who's winning so far? Only, we have run out of whisky. You haven't got a hidden stash anywhere?'

It was Roddy's turn to sigh. 'Aye, under my bed. Emergency supplies. I guess this counts.'

In my room, I lay awake, head swimming with booze and lies.

I felt like I needed to see the papers: I needed their ink on my fingers, or it would never seem real. Out there, outside the window, were millions of people who now knew my face, my name. Over breakfast tomorrow, people I would never meet would talk about me as they turned the pages of their dailies. There was a time – wasn't there? – when that was what I'd wanted. But no: not this. Never like this.

A thought struck me: that from now on, forever, if I were to search the web for Eve, my name would appear alongside hers.

But it wasn't so bad, what they were saying about me. Apart from the Glaswegian thing. What they were saying, between the lines, was that I was the lover of a Hollywood star. A dead Hollywood star. I wondered what it would be like to say that to people, instead of, *I'm a thirty-year-old barman and general underachiever.*

I'm the tragic lover of the late Eve Sadler.

In the black, with my eyes closed, I tried to understand what it meant that she was dead. I had seen her dying. Not dead. Not final. Carefully, thoroughly, from head to toe, I tried to imagine her body. But I could only conjure it piecemeal. Her face. Her arm, her hand. Her feet. As each part came into focus, the rest of her vanished – in the same way that her appearance had eluded me, even as I stared at her on a widescreen.

Something else was eluding me. Eve's eyes, holding mine. *It was raining...*

I turned over and over again. My legs were twitchy. I'd hardly moved all day, and though my brain was like a wrung-out dishrag, my body wasn't tired.

I wondered if they were still calling. I wondered how long their interest would last, for how long I'd be part of the story. We'd unplugged the phone before we dragged the quilts back through to the bedrooms. Eilidh would be crashed out, always a good sleeper and she'd put away her share of Roddy's whisky. It was just me awake.

I sat up, swung my feet to the floor; padded through to the living room and scooped up Roddy's laptop. Back in my room I fired it up, and searched for the website of the *News*.

Eve's death was still the top story. The text blurred in front of my eyes. I recognised phrases that Roddy had read out: *passionate kiss with mystery man; old family friend...* The pictures loaded, and I clicked for enlargements. The hotel courtyard unfurled down my screen: palm trees, lights, tables. Me, crouching. Eve stretched on the ground: you couldn't see her face, you couldn't tell, if you didn't know. My jacket; I'd forgotten she'd been wearing my jacket. Duncan's jacket. There were other people in the photo. A woman in hotel uniform; she must have been the one to call the ambulance. The woman who wasn't afraid to use the EpiPen. But right in the centre, me: open-mouthed, stretching an arm towards her, like I was pulling her to me and fending her off, both at once.

Who had been there, unseen? A professional? Someone I'd summoned, with my message on the Starspotter website? Or an opportunist – a guest, or a member of staff – reaching for their phone?

I closed the laptop, got up and moved over to the window. At first, I couldn't see a soul. Then I noticed a figure in a car parked just around the corner, on the side road that ran uphill from my street. I watched: for a long time, I watched. Well past midnight, a strange man parked in an empty street: looking for me. Me, concealed, looking out at him.

We both slept late the next morning. As I was making coffee, Eilidh emerged, wrapped in Roddy's quilt.

'Ow. Ow. Ow.' Her eyes were puffy, her hair a state.

I poured the coffee, passed her a mug. 'No milk. Sorry.'

'I need painkillers.'

'Again – sorry.'

'Right. One of us needs to go to the shops, and I don't suppose it's going to be you.' She carried her mug over to the window. 'Wow, they're breeding. Five of them this morning. Two with cameras. Do you think they do it in shifts? I don't recognise any of these from yesterday.'

She finished her coffee, shuffled back to the bedroom and re-appeared fully dressed; pulled the hood of her top down low over her face. 'Just in case. Don't suppose you've got any shades?'

'You already know the answer to that. Listen, can you get me some of the papers?'

Even with her eyes concealed, I could tell she was frowning. 'You sure about that?'

'I just need to see what they're saying.' I felt around in my pockets, came up with a fiver. She waved it away.

'Keep your pennies. I'll take your keys, though.'

Ten minutes, and she was back. 'Christ, they're fast. They clocked me on the way out and they were waiting by the door when I came back. They literally door-stepped me. I suppose it's pretty obvious, with all these.' She opened her arms and let a wodge of newspapers hit the floor. 'I haven't read them,' she said. 'They were asking, are you a neighbour of Campbell's? Are you living with him? Are you his girlfriend? Is Campbell in there, will he speak to us?' She pushed at an imaginary door: '*Slam*. I got some guy in the face, I think. Milk. Bread. Bacon. Loo roll. Drugs; I'll have those back, thanks. I'm going for a shower.'

I took the paper mountain through to the sofa, started to work my way through the pile.

The story was dying. On the front page of the first paper, there was no headline, no photos. Only a flash:

Eve: her last moments – Inside

Nice. I could tell them about her last moments. I could tell them about the sickening choking sounds she made, about her hands clawing at her throat. I could tell them how her eyes had saturated with blood. But they wouldn't want to print it. Or, they probably would. I felt my own throat thickening. Shook my head; turned the pages. There she was, a double-page spread devoted to her. A childhood snap of her with Jasmine, along with red carpet pics, movie stills, a shot of her accepting some award.

Most of the papers had similar spreads: the same pictures, the same half-facts and outright lies.

Eve: her charmed life and her tragic death.

Tributes pour in. Send us your comments.

The SHOCKING truth about allergies.

Skimming the text, here and there my name tripped me. It was all a re-hash of what Roddy had reported last night.

'Fascinating reading, is it?'

I tore myself away, flipped shut the paper I'd been looking through. 'It's nothing. Just the same stuff. The same crap.'

Eilidh bent down, shampoo and freshness replacing cheap paper and ink, lifted the rags into one big armful and dumped them out of sight round the side of the sofa; making room to sit.

'Sounds like they're losing interest,' I said. 'At least in the mystery man angle.'

'Good. So what now? I've got three hours till my train. We could watch *The Wicker Man*?'

While Eilidh made bacon rolls, and coffee with milk, I sorted out the film, and ten minutes later we climbed back into our sofa ship. Watching the opening shots – the northwest coast, the village street, the unexpected palms coddled by the Gulf Stream – it could have been Glenelg. The bleached, yellowed quality of '70s film stock was the tint of childhood memories, the sort that should make your eyes go soft and your mouth curl into a smile. Instead, just for a moment, I was stuck in that same slug-slime of guilt I'd woken with two days ago. I blinked, breathed in coffee steam, resisting everything but here and now.

Eilidh's hand on my shoulder. 'Alright there?'

'Alright.'

Eilidh had to go.

'When's Roddy back?'

'I think tomorrow, or soon, anyway.'

'I can stay. If you need. I can tell them it's a family emergency.'

The truth was, Roddy would be away for at least a week, and it would have been a comfort to have Eilidh stay. On a purely practical level, she could help with the shopping. But I owed her so much already that I'd never been able to pay back. What had happened, years ago: it still skewed things, sometimes. The equilibrium we had was delicate. She hated to take time off work, to let people down: the fact that she'd offered meant a lot, but it threatened to tip us out of balance. Just as much, I hated to always be the one in need.

I smiled, shook my head. 'Go on, Miss MacDonald; back to your kids. It's already blowing over. They'll get bored, and I'll be fine. I'll call if I need to. And if it gets really bad – I can always go home.'

She gave me a measuring look. 'Maybe stay off the booze tonight?'

If anyone else said that, I'd want to know who put them in charge of my choices. But I knew what Eilidh was getting at, what she was concerned about. I shrugged. 'None left, anyway.'

She called a cab, asked the driver to wait for her several doors down, and when it arrived she gave me a hug. Her leather jacket creaked as I squeezed her shoulders, and the smell of it stayed once she'd left. I watched from the window: I saw the reporters and the photographers flow across the road, moving like a single animal, then lost sight of them as they came in close to my building; I saw the cab, a flash of black in the wet grey street, and then the press reassembling across the way. Ever watchful; ready to jump.

With Eilidh gone, I didn't know what to do with myself. I put on another movie, but on my own I couldn't concentrate. The story seemed irrelevant, disjointed; I was distracted by jump cuts on a screen inside my head. And the largest part of my mind was itching towards the pile of papers on the floor. I kept myself away, resisting, for as long as I could. And when I gave in and reached around the side of the sofa for the rough slide of newsprint, there was nothing but carpet under my fingers. Eilidh had moved them; she knew I'd be drawn back. And she knew, presumably, that I shouldn't let those stories into my head.

I sat and watched another few minutes of the movie. I was beginning to think Eilidh was right: I shouldn't stay here alone. If I could scrape together a tenner, I could do what she had done

– call a cab, make a dash for it with a hood pulled over my face. I could pack my bags, head for Queen Street. Jump on the first train home.

A last glance out the window: the photographers, the journalists were still massed on the other side of the street. I decided to make my escape.

But the cupboard in the hall, where I thought my rucksack might be, turned out to be where Eilidh had stashed the papers.

I carried them back to the living room. Taking my time now that I was alone, I turned the pages. Allowed myself to read every word. Looking at all the pictures of Eve, spreading them out on the floor around me, now finally I began to see her clear, complete: pinned down, once and for all. Like she was finished. I read, and looked, and read, turning page after page, turning from paper to paper till an image – unexpected – hooked me, pulled tight in my gut. A picture of my house. Not my flat, not where I was hiding now, but home: Mum and Dad's. The caption beneath was:

Campbell Johnstone's family home in the Scottish Highlands, where Eve often stayed as a child.

I raced my eyes across the text, and they caught on the sentence:

At his family home near Pitlochry in the Scottish Highlands, relatives refused to comment.

So it wasn't just me they were after. That *refused to comment* – it almost made me smile. It certainly didn't sound like Mum. I bet she gave them a bollocking: you should be ashamed of yourselves, call this a job... But I didn't smile, because actually it wasn't the least bit amusing. It was as if I'd brought the baddies to their door, to the ultimate safe-house. Who else had they gone after? My Auntie Linda and Uncle Donnie? Roddy, or even Magnus?

I rang home, but the phone went to voicemail: I had a vision of

Mum and Dad sitting strained, refusing to answer for fear of yet another reporter chasing the scraps of a story.

The press had been busy in Glasgow, too: running down connections; speaking to people who could tell them precisely nothing, then drawing out that nothing into a hint of something. Somehow, they'd tracked me to the pub.

Staff at the Douglas Arms said Campbell had not turned up for work since last Wednesday. Barmaid Angelika Czarnecki said: 'Campbell never mentioned her. If they were having a relationship, maybe they wanted to keep it a secret from the newspapers.'

The heading read:

Eve's secret love

In a way, you had to admire it. While the rest of the press was letting me slip quietly out of the picture, this one paper – the *Sunday News*, it was – had decided I was part of the story. The total lack of information about me mattered not at all. My family, my friends, my job; all were material, to be woven into a news-worthy version of events.

On the floor in front of me, my home sat defenceless among half-truths and lies, looking like some kind of evidence.

I took a deep breath, but the air was thick and stale. The room was shrinking round me; I had to get out. I snatched up my house keys, and in the hall I stretched for the door ledge, scrabbling through dust for the key to the shared green. I let the front door slam behind me, jogged four flights to the ground floor, and out the back way.

Out here, the wet had sent things wild. Nettles and foxgloves were shoulder-high, escaping over the far wall; I studied the stone for footholds. But the wall backed onto another row of tenements.

Even if I hacked my way through stinging nettles, climbed up and over, all I'd achieve was being trapped in someone else's garden. And say I found a back door unlocked, made my way out onto the street – where would I go, to be safe? Everywhere was invaded.

They had me surrounded. They'd made sure I had nowhere to go. But it didn't mean I was powerless.

I had a choice. I could stay here, under siege: wait things out. Or I could get tactical. I could change the terms of engagement. There must be a way to draw off the pack. Give them what they wanted, and they'd forget about my family, my home. Give them what they wanted and they'd write the story they would have written anyway – just with me at the centre.

I had a choice.

Back in the stair, I stood, split. Walking out there would be like kissing Eve: like doing something so I wasn't doing nothing – whether or not I wanted it, whether or not it was wise. I ran my hands through my damp hair, stretched my sweatshirt and shook it so beads of rain leapt up into the air. Was I really going to march out and face them? Was I going to offer myself? Anger could maybe have carried me: the image of our house; *relatives refused to comment*. But still I didn't move: not till I heard keys turn in the main door, saw a stripe of light as it opened, and the guy from upstairs – same guy who'd leaked on our ceiling – appeared. He glanced over his shoulder: a moment's hesitation, as he tried to figure it out – should he hold the door open, or slam it in their faces, or...? Before he could make up his mind, one of the pack was beside him. 'I'm here to see Campbell Johnstone,' I heard the reporter say. 'Flat six, but I think his buzzer must be–' And then he clocked me. 'Campbell!' he called, and somehow he was inside, straight past the upstairs guy, setting him aside with a move that was half-dodge, half-shove, and smiling all the while. There was no camera slung round his neck, but his hand was already in his pocket – reaching, I guessed, for a phone. In the dark of the stair, I reckoned he'd get nothing but shadows, but I wasn't giving him any chances. I strode towards him, got right up into his face – and when he opened his smiling mouth to speak, I cut him off.

'What paper are you from?'

The smile didn't shift. 'Chris Carter, *Daily News*.' He took a step back, stuck out his hand. I put both of mine in my pockets, and stared him down. He was round-faced, receding. About my age. Casually smart in jeans and waxed jacket. I kept on staring till he got the message, and dropped his hand.

'Okay, Chris Carter.' I gestured to the stairs. He was going first; I wanted him where I could see him. 'I gather you know what number it is. On you go.'

He went. As he began to climb, I glanced back at the door, where upstairs guy was hovering like a spare prick. 'Hey,' I said, 'do us a favour? Since it was you let this scum in.'

He started. 'Eh, aye,' he said, 'what's that, then?'

'Outside: the rest of these bastards. Go and give them a message, would you? Tell them: get tae fuck.'

EXCLUSIVE: CAMPBELL'S GRIEF OVER TRAGIC EVE

Campbell Johnstone talks **exclusively** to the *Daily News*

When Campbell Johnstone shared a passionate clinch with Eve Sadler last Thursday night, he couldn't have guessed that this would be their last ever kiss.

News of the *Astonishing Beauty* star's sudden death has caused shockwaves around the world, but no-one is more shocked than Campbell.

The 30-year-old barman had been a close friend of Sadler's since they played together as children in the remote Highland village where the actress grew up.

Though the two had lost touch in recent years, they rekindled their friendship following her divorce from actor Dan Fischer.

In her last weeks, Sadler was filming *Never Setting Sun* in Glasgow, where Campbell lives in a shared flat in the city's Southside.

Sudden

When he talks of what happened on Thursday night, Campbell's voice is low and he fixes his eyes on the ground.

'It was incredibly sudden. We'd been talking, laughing. Having a couple of drinks. We were sitting in the courtyard of the hotel. There was no warning, really, she just started coughing, and wheezing.

'It sounded like an asthma attack, but then she said she needed her adrenaline, she needed an injection.

'I emptied her bag, but I didn't know what I was looking for. By this time she couldn't speak, she could hardly breathe. I did find the adrenaline, the EpiPen, but I didn't know how to use it, to give her the injection she needed.

'By this time I was shouting for help. It seemed like forever before someone came but it can only have been a minute. A woman helped give her the injection and she was still breathing, but she was unconscious, and her breathing was so shallow. I remember saying, "She's okay, she's going to be okay," something like that.'

Campbell takes a deep breath before continuing his story.

'I was saying it in the ambulance, telling her she was okay even though I knew she couldn't hear. By that stage I don't know if she was still breathing by herself, they had an oxygen tube on her. I was trying not to get in the way, but I kept telling her, "You're okay, you're okay."'

Shock

Anaphylactic shock triggered by an allergic reaction has emerged as the most likely cause of death. Sadler had previously reacted severely to certain foods, thought to include nuts and shellfish.

But Campbell says she didn't eat during their night together.

'She drank a couple of vodkas with soda, with slices of lime, and that was all. I was with her all the time and she didn't eat anything at all.'

Campbell had no idea that Eve suffered from serious allergies, or that she carried an EpiPen in case of problems.

An EpiPen is an auto injector that is used to deliver an emergency adrenaline injection.

'I suppose because she wasn't planning to eat, she didn't think to tell me about her allergies. If I'd known what I was doing, I could have reacted quicker and maybe if we'd been able to get the adrenaline into her sooner she would have had a chance.'

Kiss

When questioned about the embrace that was caught on camera shortly before Eve's death, Campbell is reluctant to talk in detail about the relationship.

'It is what it is,' he said. 'Yes, we kissed. The camera doesn't lie and that was obviously an intimate moment.

'But I don't feel it's respectful of Eve to talk about that.'

Chapter 11

Mum hadn't met me at the station in years. But when the train pulled in, there she was waiting in the old blue Skoda. I threw my bag on the back seat, climbed in the front.

'Thanks for the lift.'

She was starting the engine before I even had the door shut. As she pulled out and turned up the main road, her eyes jumped constantly from side to rear mirrors. I followed her shifting gaze; I couldn't see anything out of place. No sign of the ladies and gentlemen of the press.

'What's been going on, up here?'

'Let's just get home, then we can...' She swerved for a pheasant, jerking me against the door. 'Shit. Sorry.' But she didn't slow down.

I sat quiet till we reached the house. Mum had her keys in her hand even before we got out of the car; she marched up the drive, head down, eyes fixed on her destination.

'Dad not in?' I asked, as she unlocked the door.

'He's upstairs.' She closed it behind us, turned the key again. Locking us in. 'Just to be safe.'

In the kitchen she filled the kettle, then forgot to switch it on. I dropped my bag on the floor and went to give her a hug. She felt small, even fragile.

She sighed. 'All this...'

'Has it been bad?'

She shook her head. 'Nothing we can't cope with. But what are they after? I don't know what they want from us.'

'Have you seen any of them today?'

'No – thank goodness, they seem to be giving up.'

It was the same in Glasgow. By the time I left the flat today everyone was gone, apart from a single photographer. I'd copied Eilidh, pulled my hood down low so all he could snap was a hunched, anonymous figure; then I'd jumped into a cab and made my escape. He didn't try to follow me: I was *News* property now. My story was sold, and there was nothing there for the rest of the scrum. Nothing for them to do but break up and drift away; back on the sniff for their next story.

The stairs creaked: my dad appeared in the doorway.

'Hello there. You made it, then.'

'Mum was just saying, they seem to be losing interest.'

He shook his head. 'What a job. How do they look themselves in the eye, I'd like to know.'

'Oh well, if they're giving up...'

'But – are you managing? I mean it must have been... Being there with her, when it happened.'

My mum looked stricken. 'Yes, goodness, are you alright? Sit down, what can I get you?' She glanced at the silent kettle, clicked in irritation and switched it on, set about making tea.

The strange thing was, having told the story to the guy from the *News*, the last thing I wanted was to go through it again. And I felt bad about that. But maybe it was better, not to burden them with it. I could imagine how Mum would fret, quietly, over what I'd seen, over how I must be feeling. That's what they want, isn't it, parents? More than anything – they want, they need, to protect the children, to keep them safe.

I hadn't told him everything. The guy from the *News*. He'd been easy to talk to; he'd seemed pleased with my story. Impressed, even. But I hadn't told him everything. There was stuff I didn't want him to use. For instance, I hadn't told him about her eyes.

'Is that my room?' Roddy stared at the photo of me on the front page.

As soon as I'd convinced Auntie Linda that yes, I was coping, Roddy and I had retreated upstairs to his bedroom. There, door safely closed, I handed him the paper I'd bought in the station. The cover bore a smiling Eve, inset with a much smaller picture of me.

'Sorry,' I said. 'It was tidier than mine.' I hadn't wanted to let them into my own room – not Chris Carter, and definitely not the photographer he'd summoned.

I waited for Roddy to shrug, to tell me *fair enough*. But his shoulders were steady as he opened the paper, spread it across the bed. There was a large shot of me on page three: I looked worn and shadowed from lack of sleep and too much booze, but it easily could have been grief. It fitted with the story, how Chris Carter had told it.

'It's an alright picture, don't you think?' I said. 'Considering.'

'You let them into the flat.'

I settled on the floor, uncomfortably cross-legged. 'It was the only way to get rid of them. They were up here, they were after Mum and Dad...'

'Aye, I know. They were knocking on our door as well.'

'See? And now they're away. Because there's no story anymore. It's all in here.'

Roddy blew out a breath, folded the paper and threw it back at me. 'You think that's it, then? They'll leave you alone now?'

'Well. Yeah. I mean – yeah.'

'Hope you're right; it's a bit drastic. This is out there, you know? All of this. Anyone can read it.'

Anyone, like the woman at the counter in WHSmith: she'd recognised me, I was sure of it. Hard not to when I was paying for a paper that had my own face all over it. She had looked me in the eye, taken her time giving my change in spite of the queue behind me. I'd been suddenly conscious of my ancient jacket with its fraying sleeves, the fact I hadn't shaved. At the same time, I'd stood taller under her gaze. I wasn't just another person passing by her counter. I had been acknowledged.

'So forget all that,' Roddy was saying, nodding towards the *News*. 'What was it – I mean, like, was it … are you … how…?'

This was painful. 'I'm getting old here. Are you trying to ask if I'm okay?'

'Aye, I s'pose. And I just – can't really get my head round it. That you're part of all this.' His face creased into a comedy frown, eyes half-closed and mouth half-open: as though he wanted me to explain it in words of one syllable, or to understand it for him.

'I know,' I said, and I felt like my face was probably a mirror of his. 'I mean, actually, I don't. I don't know.' I picked up the paper, rolled it into a cylinder.

'We never knew anything about it, did we?' Roddy said. 'About allergies or anything? I've been trying to think, I'm sure I remember her eating just normal food. Maybe not shellfish – but she must have had nuts, peanut butter and stuff like that.'

'We definitely would have known, if she'd had it then.'

'So it must be something you grow into.'

'I guess. In her case, it must've been.' I thought of what Eve had grown into: a body that gave her the beauty to lay the world open, then turned on her and took the lot; thought of what had been waiting for all of us – and what must be crouching further down the line, patient and unknowable.

'What about your mum and dad?' Roddy said. 'Have they seen the story?'

I glanced down at the newspaper tube, realised I'd been wringing it with both hands, twisting it tight. Now I let it unroll, smoothed it out. 'Doubt it,' I said. 'If they have, nothing's been mentioned.' One of the benefits of selling the story to the *News* was its status as paper-most-hated in my family circle. It was the safest bet for going unread among everyone I knew. 'Don't you say anything,' I warned. 'If I don't show them, there's no reason they should know... What?'

Roddy was shaking his head. 'No chance, Cam. You think the neighbours won't be round waving their copies? There is no way

82

your folks won't see this.'

He was right. By the time I got back home, it had happened. A well-thumbed copy of the *News* sat in the middle of the kitchen table, brought kindly to my parents' attention by Mrs Wishart from over the road. There was something about the way it had been pushed just out of reach that made me imagine my mum and dad leafing through it with tongs, so their hands wouldn't be fouled by its pages.

'I take it you've seen this?' I said.

'You spoke to them.' Mum was slicing onions; she didn't lift her gaze from the chopping board.

'Yeah, but only so they'd stop stalking you guys. That's why they're all away – because I did speak to them. That's why there's no-one outside the door right this minute, that's why there's no-one harassing you every time you go outside.' She didn't seem to get it. 'That's why it's safe here,' I pressed on. 'You don't need to lock yourselves in now.'

'Well.' Chop. Chop. 'You certainly didn't need to do this to protect us.'

'No, okay, but – I had to do something.'

My dad had heard me coming in. He stood by the fridge, rear-ranging the magnets that held receipts, bills, shopping lists. 'Did they pay you for this?'

It sounded like a polite enquiry, but I wasn't fooled. As far as Dad was concerned, there were no shades of grey. His moral code came direct from my grandad – a Greenock docker and shop steward, who'd spent his life fighting for the right thing. In my dad's eyes, you did what was right, and if not, it was simple: you were in the wrong. The trouble was, in this case I couldn't be sure which answer he wanted to hear. If they didn't pay, I was being exploited: I was a mug, boosting their sales, swelling their capitalist coffers. If they did, I was cashing in.

Trying for the safest middle ground, I said, 'Not for talking to them, exactly. It was more so I wouldn't talk to anyone else.'

He nodded, sliding the unused magnets into a neat line along the edge of the door. His face was unreadable.

Mum spoke more gently, still without making eye contact. 'It does imply there was something going on between you and Eve.'

So typical of my mum: not to question me directly, but instead create the space for me to tell. She was always good at that, when I was younger and bursting to talk, to share a joy or a misery – and usually a misery – but hating to show my need. She had a talent for making me feel I was doing her a favour by letting her in on the secrets of my life.

'You know what they're like,' is all I said.

When Dad laid the table for dinner, he lifted the paper and very deliberately inserted it into the bin. Then he tipped the dregs from the teapot on top of it, and a heap of vegetable peelings on top of that.

I knew I should prepare them for what was to come; the stories that were slated to run over the next few days. Like Roddy said, I was kidding myself to think they wouldn't see any of it. It would be out there for the world to read – a world that included my parents. But I didn't say anything.

We ate in a tense atmosphere. My mum, trying to talk of other things: Roddy's fellowship in the States; how Linda and Donnie would be going out there to visit him; Duncan's next trip home from Kazakhstan. As I did my best to chat along with her, Dad just chewed and grunted. I knew I had given the wrong answer.

CAM'S LIFE-LONG LOVE FOR EVE
'She's still with me'
Exclusive interview – inside

CHILDHOOD SWEETHEARTS
A love that endured from childhood – an innocent love between an ordinary little boy and a girl who would grow up to be famous – was cruelly cut short when... (CONTINUED ON PAGE 5)

THE TRUTH ABOUT EVE'S LOVE FOR BARMAN CAM
Was star planning to wed again? Sources say marriage was on her mind >> *read on inside*

Chapter 12

Sometimes, if you put something off for long enough, the gods will find a way to excuse you from doing it at all.

I still didn't quite believe it, the amount of cash in my current account. The bank had called to express concern that I was losing money by not putting my earnings in some other kind of account where it could be making money. I had never needed to think about such things before.

It wasn't until I finally forced myself to sit down and write the flatshare ad that I realised: rather than renting this fleapit off my brother, I could conceivably buy a place of my own. At the very least, I could rent somewhere by myself. Somewhere that boasted a working lock on the main door. Somewhere with a ceiling free of stains.

That said, I was pretty much on my own here anyway. Last week Roddy had come back from Moulin (bringing tales of parental dismay at my frequent appearances in the *News*); after a couple of days he'd vanished again, this time to spend a few days with Jean in Berlin. He'd been happy to report, at length, my dad's opinions on the newspapers, but Roddy had little to say for himself. His main feeling seemed to be one of grudging relief that I hadn't let any photographers loose in his room again.

'I don't know, Cam,' he'd said, when I pressed him. 'You said they were going to leave you alone, and then there's stories in the paper every day about you. And where are they getting this from? About you and Eve getting married, I mean that's just crazy talk...'

'It's like I said, they write what they want to write. Obviously it's not what I've been saying. What they do, they get a source to say something – and the source is probably like a make-up girl or a runner – they *pay* them to say something like, Eve wanted to get married again, at *some point*, to *someone* – and that's all they need. The journalist just chops it about till it fits in with their story.'

A classic Roddy shrug: 'It just seems like you wouldn't want to have anything to do with it.'

Eilidh, on the phone, had been even less forthcoming. 'There's no point even talking about it. It's what you decided to do, and you did it for a reason. It's not up to me to have an opinion on whether it's right or wrong.'

So here I was, on my own on a Wednesday night: and whether it was right or wrong, for the first time in the whole of my life, I wasn't poor. I had a cash card that could take me anywhere, and after so many years of scratching by, I had absolutely no idea what to spend my money on. My ambitions, my aspirations had shrunk to the point of invisibility. I closed my eyes, and tried to envisage what a wealthy person might do if they found themselves free for an evening in Glasgow.

I could spend the night in an exclusive hotel, ordering room service and drinking the mini-bar dry.

I could take a cab to the city's most expensive concert, and drink champagne in the interval.

I could afford to eat at Magnus's.

I walked in like it was my natural environment: the dark glossy wood, the dimmed light washing walls painted deep aubergine. I had eaten here twice before: once with Eilidh, before it opened to the public, on a friends and family freebie, and the other time when Magnus closed the whole place for his pre-wedding dinner. His parents were meeting Paolo's for the first time: it could have been strained, but in fact it was a glorious mess of a night, chaotic and boozy, with everyone willing things to go well. In my memory this place was filled with boisterous chatter, Italian and English colliding mid-air, with people laughing and shouting and even some tears from Paolo's *mama*, Magnus's mother-in-law to be.

Tonight, though, the atmosphere was soft and rich. At the front desk, a black-clad waitress gave me a smile that faded only slightly when she realised I hadn't booked. She studied her list of reservations.

'Is Magnus around tonight?' I said, and this blatant piece of name-dropping seemed to do the trick.

'He'll be in the kitchen,' she said. 'Actually...' – she tapped her pen against the clipboard – 'we can just squeeze you in.'

I followed her to a vacant table, handed her my coat.

'Would you be able to let Magnus know I'm here? Campbell Johnstone.' Did I imagine the flicker of recognition as I told her my name? Probably I did: the great and the good must dine here all the time, and a few appearances in the *News* hardly put me up there on the A-list.

I settled myself at the table, gazed around the restaurant. It felt odd to be here on my own. Everyone else was part of a pair, or a group. Your skin is thinner when you're on your own, your ears and eyes keener. Things that wouldn't have registered if I'd been with someone else were clear-edged: the music; the sharp, delicate sound of steel on china; the interplay of voices and the underneath rhythm propelling it all, the distant thumping of the kitchen. People leaned forward into their meals, towards their dining partners, feet hooked round ankles (the women) or square on the floor (the men). Little wavering pools of light spilled from candles. The waitress approached my table, soft-shoed and swift.

'Magnus says to let you know he'll be out in a minute.' She handed me the menus, touched her lighter to the candle on my table. The flame caught, dwindled to nothing then leapt up tall and smoking. A candlelit dinner for one. I leaned back in my seat, satisfied: began to study the menu – lingering over the descriptions, ignoring the prices. There were some French phrases that meant nothing to me: the hare, apparently, came *à la Royale*, and I imagined a sauce flecked with gold; thought I might order it just to find out. Just because I could.

'Mr Eve Sadler, as I live and breathe.' Magnus, shining in kitchen whites, filled the seat opposite. With a wave he summoned my waitress. 'Bring us ... bring us the Valpolicella Ripasso, would you?'

'One glass, or two?'

'Just bring a bottle. Thanks, darling.' He turned his gaze on me, the same rusty eyes as Eilidh's, the eyes that on Magnus, with his mane of gold, were positively leonine. Mum always said what a shame it was that Magnus got all that blonde hair while Eilidh was plain sandy.

'Alright?' he asked, warily solicitous: accepting that I might not be, and if so, if I absolutely must, I could talk about it – but please, not at length. But since I was alright, I told him so, and his face lifted. 'So: what brings you here, all on your own-io?'

'Money burning a hole in my pocket. Thought I'd treat myself.' As I spoke, the waitress returned with the wine.

'Just leave it there, thanks Sarah,' said Magnus. 'You ready to order?' he asked me. 'Want me to choose for you?'

'Sure.'

'The terrine, and ... the hare. You said you had money, right?' He tipped wine into my glass, poured himself a smaller measure.

'Don't you worry, I'm good for it. For once. Cheers.' We clinked, and drank.

'And let me guess why that is,' said Magnus, setting his glass down. 'I've been reading all about you. I guess your stories don't come for free.'

I opened my mouth, and he raised a hand to cut me off. 'No, and why should they?' I stared at him. It was another shared resemblance between Magnus and Eilidh: a reluctance to judge – even the times you couldn't help but judge yourself.

Like he was reading my mind, he said, 'I hear Eilidh was up

to see you.'

'Just for a weekend, when it was all happening.'

'I won't be offended she didn't make time to see her brother...'

'It was a bit last minute, you know.'

He nodded understanding. 'And how's she doing?'

'Yeah, fine. She doesn't think much of all this press stuff. I mean, she hasn't said anything, but...'

'No, she wouldn't.' He looked at me closely, head on one side. 'She doesn't. So: she's fine. You're fine. Everyone's fine. Fine! Just, Campbell: be careful.'

'Of?'

'You feel like you're in control. Yes?'

'Well...' I shrugged.

'They've got their agenda. Remember: it's never the same as yours. I know whereof I speak. That's all. Class dismissed.' He knocked back what was left of his wine, rose to his feet. 'Enjoy your meal,' he said, his hand landing briefly on my shoulder, and as he left my starter arrived, looking for all the world like a tiny perfect piece of art.

He did know a bit about it: as I ate my amazingly rich terrine (foie gras and venison, with a compote of seasonal fruit) I considered his words. You could say Magnus was a local celebrity, a regular in the weekend features pages of the *Herald* and, despite being a Glasgow adoptee, the *Scotsman*. But he hadn't always made friends of the press. When his first restaurant went under, there had been sniping diary pieces; column inches giving voice to disgruntled former employees, cheap insinuations about his sex life. All this was 'BP' – Before Paolo – so I'm not saying what they wrote wasn't true, but it was none of anyone's business. Still, Magnus rode it out: now, the worst you'll read about him is that he's 'a survivor'.

So you could say his success undermined his warning. You could see it like that.

Whatever. It didn't matter now: I was done. The *News* had its stories, my family had their privacy back and I had a bank account in the black. From where I sat, everyone was a winner. I re-filled my glass; sat back, and toasted the arrival of the hare.

When I got back to the flat, half-drunk and completely full, the phone was ringing.

'Campbell? It's Chris here from the *News*.'

I didn't make any effort to sound welcoming. Chris from the *News* didn't seem to notice.

'Have you spoken to any other papers?' he said.

'No, when do you mean? You're the only ones I spoke to.'

'I mean today.'

'Nope.' I was sleepy and happy and I wanted him to get on with it. Phone in hand, I crashed onto the sofa, swung my legs up over the arm and lay on my back to ease the fullness in my stomach.

'They've released the results from the post-mortem. Sudden fatal cardiac arrest, caused by severe allergic reaction.'

I yawned. 'Which is what they said two weeks ago.'

'Traces of nut protein on her lips, but not in her stomach.'

'She didn't eat any nuts, she didn't eat anything. I've told you that already.'

'We know that, Campbell. And we also know it was peanuts she was allergic to. Shellfish, and peanuts. So the question is, how did she have a reaction to something she hadn't eaten?'

'Ask the doctors. Look, I've kind of had enough of this.'

'We've done better than ask the doctors. I spoke to the barman who served you that night. He backs you up, Eve drank two vodkas with soda and lime, nothing to eat. You drank three bottled beers. Good memory he's got, this guy, but I suppose it's the sort of thing you might well remember given what happened next, eh?'

'So, it's like I told you: she didn't eat!'

'No, but you did.'

'And?'

'And what did you eat?'

'Some weird kind of monkey nuts boiled in their shells...'

'Monkey nuts, that's the same as peanuts, yeah?'

This guy set a new record for stupid. I was on the verge of hanging up. 'Yeah, but Eve didn't have any. I ate them before she turned up.'

'So you're saying you definitely did eat peanuts, what, an hour, two hours, before you kissed her?'

I stared at the ceiling-stain. I could hear him breathing. Waiting for my reaction.

'What *you're* saying – it's not even possible – surely…?'

'Come on, Campbell, it's what you've just told me. You ate the peanuts; you kissed Eve. Yeah?'

'Yeah–'

'And minutes later, Eve, who is extremely bloody allergic to nuts, is on the floor, she can't breathe. *Traces of nut protein on her lips.*' He let a silence stretch. Then, 'We're going to run this, Campbell. But if you keep talking to us, only to us, we'll look after you. We can set the tone.'

The stain was bigger; darker than before. I was pretty sure it was growing. Foie gras and hare and truffle sauce sat sickly in my stomach, and ashes filled my mouth.

'So. Campbell. Do you want to give me a comment?'

They called it the kiss of death.

Of course, the *News* got their exclusive. The fuzzy close-up of the kiss filled their front page. My comments were reported in the three-page spread inside – the comments I'd wrenched from nowhere the night before, slumped on the sofa at midnight with my hands over my face.

By the next day, variations of the headline were in every tabloid. *Killed by a kiss. Poison kiss. The kiss that sealed her fate.* The broadsheets ran with soberer splashes, on pages two and three. And in all of them, that picture. Pixellated, gritty, obscuring as much as it revealed.

Before, it had been an indiscretion that was caught on camera. But context is everything. Now it was so much more: it was Christmas come early. The picture's new meaning was spelled out in a caption run by the boldest, most brazen rag – a single, careful question mark keeping them free from the threat of libel.

Eve and Campbell: the kiss. Murder scene?

Chapter 13

On the day of the funeral, it rained. The weather seemed to mirror my feelings of desolation.

Though I wanted to say my final goodbyes to Eve, right up until the day before I had been undecided about whether to attend.

All of the papers were reporting 'the kiss of death'. Even though the inquest had recorded a verdict of death from cardiac arrest caused by a severe allergic reaction, with no certainty as to the cause, the idea that she'd been killed by a kiss was a story too good not to believe.

If I turned up at Eve's funeral as I wanted to, would I be seen as an assassin? Would her family be hurt, offended by my presence?

What persuaded me to go was an unexpected call from Eve's cousin, Mariella. She let me know that I would be welcome, and that Eve would have wanted me to be there. In the midst of the family's grief, she thought about mine, and opened a door to me. And as I listened to her kind words I knew that she was right: Eve would have wanted me to be there – just as much as I wanted to be there myself.

What persuaded me to go was Chris from the *News*.

Go to the funeral, he'd urged. If I gave them the story, they would keep their photographers out of the way, run a sympathetic piece. Hadn't he promised he'd look after me?

But it's true that without that call from Mariella, I still might not have brought myself to turn up at the church. Mariella: the cousin who took Eve under her wing, after Jasmine died. When she called and introduced herself, I didn't know what to say. Should I tell her how sorry I was? Or should I be receiving, not offering, that sentiment?

I settled for: 'Eve told me a lot about you.'

'Likewise.'

'Really?'

'When she was younger. She was obsessed with you, completely obsessed.'

I laughed, not knowing what to say.

'I hadn't realised you were still so close. I haven't been reading the papers, of course, but – you can't really miss it.' She sounded like she'd bitten into something bitter.

'It's just a story for them,' I said. 'They don't care...'

'No. Well. The reason I called – Eve would have wanted you to be at the funeral.'

'Yes.' As she said it, I found myself nodding. 'I suppose she would. Is it–'

'It's at eleven, tomorrow. At the West London Crematorium, do you know where that is?'

I already knew the when and where: because Chris knew. Because Chris knew everything. What I was going to ask was, is it okay, for me to be there? Whether she read the papers or not, it couldn't have escaped her, what everyone was saying: like a murderous Georgie Porgie, I'd kissed her cousin and made her die.

'It's going to be a private funeral, no hangers-on, no gawkers. No press.'

It was a command, her voice hard, precise. And the only way I could promise *no press* was to go along just as Chris had told me to, and then give him what he needed to patch into a story.

That's why I went to the funeral; that, and the fact that Eve would have wanted me to. It's something people say – *she'd have wanted it this way* – to comfort themselves or justify their actions. But I knew it must be true, knew just how and when she'd wanted it. Ten years old, lying in her dorm in her horsey school, imagining she was dead; imagining herself beautiful and tragic, laid out like her mother; imagining me at her funeral. Me, weeping over her death. My realising, too late, just how much I'd loved her.

So I booked my flight, texted Eilidh to ask if I could stay. Luckily, there was a dark suit hanging in Roddy's wardrobe, and with the trousers turned up once, it just about fitted. Duncan's was a better suit, and a better fit, but – even if the jacket had ever emerged from A&E – admittedly inappropriate.

From the moment I woke at first light, the day was like a dream. I moved from cab to departure lounge, from plane to cab, without effort or thought. As my taxi neared the cemetery gates, I watched the photographers with detached fascination: they were clustered at every vantage point, balanced on ladders with their foot-long lenses. I pressed into my seat as the car swung past, so they'd get nothing but a rain-pocked window.

'Who is it then, what's all this in aid of?' asked the cabbie, and when I told him he whistled through his teeth. 'Sad, that was. Right sad business.' He lapsed into silence as we passed along the tree-lined drive and on to the crematorium, pulling up alongside a dozen other cars. As I handed him the fare, shoulders hunched against the rain, he did some belated arithmetic: two and two made four, and recognition flashed across his face. 'You're brave, then,' he said, as the window rose between us and the streaked glass stopped me from asking what he meant.

All around, dark cars were delivering mourners. Most had sunglasses paired with umbrellas – double protection. I was defenceless, in comparison. I merged into the stream of black, towards the crematorium. A notice tacked to the door announced: *Photo ID Required For Entry: No Cameras*. I offered my passport to a black-suited man – the uniform of security, rather than mourning – was checked off a list, and allowed inside.

An entrance heaped with flowers: we passed through, into the chapel. It felt foreign, the way things do in dreams: flooded with light despite the weather, warm in shades of cream and gold. Nothing like the cold stone of northern churches. I slid into the back row. Kept my head down. A few people turned, snatched a quick glance, but nobody stared. Eve's family and close friends seemed to number a hundred at least; among them there would be far bigger names, more famous faces than mine. It occurred to me that Morgan Freeman might be here; I dared to raise my head and cast around the crowd. He should have been an easy spot, but I couldn't see him anywhere.

The first notes of the organ stirred up something in me – a weird excitement, like I was looking forward to what came next. But as the coffin was carried past, laden with flowers, I bowed my head and began to think more appropriate thoughts. The funerals I'd been to before were for old people. My nan. Gran and Grandad. Great Uncle Will. One of my teachers from secondary, but he'd been in his late fifties; when I was seventeen, that had seemed old enough.

Eve wasn't old enough.

The vicar spoke of celebration. He talked in hymns about how bright and beautiful she was, the pleasure she'd brought to so many. He spoke of how she would live on: eternal life he was talking about, of course. Heaven, about which I was doubtful, verging on disbelieving. I didn't know what Eve had believed (other than if you can visualise your life as you would like it to be, that's a very powerful tool). But it was a fact that she would live on in one sense, at least. If I went under a bus tomorrow, all I'd leave of me would be the usual family snapshots, and the digital ephemera of a life: pictures on hard drives, emails in inboxes, items almost entirely lacking physical substance. But Eve would always be here, on film: on reels, in canisters, in archives.

We rose to sing 'Nearer My God to Thee' – Eve's favourite hymn, it seemed, though how many people of our age could really have favourite hymns? From the usual sludge of bad and timid singing, two beautiful voices rose – one male, one female. They soared up to the high white arches, leading the rest of us, and I thought I recognised the man's voice: though I craned my neck, lifted on to my toes, the congregation was so dense I couldn't pick out its owner.

We sat. Those of us who knew Eve, said the vicar, and I thought, as though I were defending myself: yes, I did know her. I was thinking, I suppose, the sort of thoughts she would have wanted me to have. About how things could have been different. How we could have been friends. How we could have been more than friends. *Always interrupted*, she had said. *Remember...?*

I pinched the back of my wrist, feeling hardly awake. Shifted on the pew, knees nudging the row in front. A cassock hung ready, in case I should want to pray for forgiveness. Which people, lots of people, must have thought I should do. Intention, though; doesn't that get taken into account? The kiss was what she'd wanted me to do – her eyes closing; opening – was what I had thought she wanted me to do. How would that play with St Peter, if it came to it? Standing outside the pearly gates – there would be a queue, probably, for borderline sinners, borderline killers like me, and a side entrance where we'd wait for a chance to plead our cases. Meanwhile the good and the bright and the beautiful, the Eves of this life, would waltz straight in through the main door, applause falling round them like summer rain.

Another hymn, unfamiliar to me; I mouthed the words, let the soaring voices do the work. Then it was over.

As the family walked towards the exit, a song started up – Bob Dylan, 'Forever Young' – and after all those hymns it felt like that moment in the hotel courtyard when, briefly, I'd glimpsed the real Eve. I watched them approach, a small group: an elderly man who must have been her father; a couple of young women, either of whom could have been the cousin. Their eyes were fixed on the floor as they walked, arms around each other. Concentrating, I suppose, on getting out without stumbling.

Behind the family, mourners began to filter from the chapel.

Now, in a dreamlike way, I saw faces I knew: several actors, a well-known fashion designer. Had they been asked to flash their passports at the door? I joined the tail of the slow-moving crowd; having paid my respects, and done my duty by the *News*, I hoped I might be able to slip away. Into a cinema, perhaps: somewhere dark where I could close my eyes. I could almost feel myself sinking into the seat, its plush embrace – and then a fair woman standing by the exit took hold of my arm.

'Campbell?' I could see her likeness to Eve, though her features were cruder: the looks of a supporting actor, as compared to a star.

'Mariella?'

She nodded. 'Thanks for coming. It would have meant a lot to her, I'm sure.'

Now she was more than a voice, it felt natural to say it. 'I'm so sorry.'

She inclined her head just slightly. 'Thank you. Do you have a car?'

'No, I got a cab.'

'Good. There's room in the second car. Come back with us.'

The city slid past; sitting on the broad back seat, I was almost as comfy and out-of-time as I would have been in the cinema – except for Mariella beside me.

'I'm glad you could come,' she said. 'There are some things of Eve's we thought you might like to have.'

'What kind – what a kind thought.'

'They're just silly things, bits and pieces from when she was younger, you know. But you do crop up rather a lot, so we thought... It seemed right that you should have them.'

'But are you sure you want to give them to me? I mean...'

She turned to me. 'Listen. If you're worrying about the press, all those stories: don't. We know how beastly they can be. We know the lies they tell. And there's nothing you can do, of course. Of all people, we know. So: don't worry about that, at all.'

The car was gliding along wide streets, past the most enormous houses, like stately homes. I couldn't tell where I was, other than somewhere north and west. The strain of saying the right thing was giving me a real thirst and I hoped there would be something to drink where we were going. It was past midday now, after all.

We swooped into a gravelled drive, drove up to where a number of other cars were already parked.

'Is this – ah, where are we?'

'Uncle Alessandro's house. Eve's father. This is where Eve lived, after Jasmine passed away. You've never been? No, I don't suppose you would have.'

She opened the door and swung her legs out, one graceful movement taking her onto the drive. They probably learned that at the boarding school, she and Eve both: how to exit a car like a lady. It was good to know Eve's schooling had equipped her well for her red-carpet career; the knack of leaving your limo without flashing your knickers was probably just as important as being able to learn your lines. Somewhat less gracefully, I clambered free of my comfortable seat, and followed Mariella up to the house.

The door stood open. We walked through a slate-tiled entrance into a double-height hall that was roughly the size of my flat. Straight ahead rose a wide staircase; above, a chandelier sparkled with frozen tears.

The room Mariella led me into boasted double doors, and was twice as large again: even the charcoal-painted walls couldn't make it feel anything less than vast. Straightaway, Mariella was absorbed into a group gathered near the door. She placed a hand on someone's arm, and I recognised him from the church. Eve's father: Uncle Alessandro. White-haired, dark-skinned, he stood very straight and still, and I was suddenly terrified he might see me, know me, question my presence in his house. I turned, hiding my face.

A waiter passed with a tray of drinks. I helped myself – thin-tasting sherry – deposited my empty glass on a side table, and moved to the other side of the room with a plan to inter-cept a different waiter. Spotting a familiar face, I started to smile, searching for a name, a context – and then it came to me; I knew her from TV, some drama I'd seen. I slid my eyes away from her, directed my smile across the room. Let it fall away.

Another waiter: I claimed my second glass. Stood hugging the wall, hoping to become invisible. The mourners moved like shad-ows against the black, heads and hands seeming to float. Layers of conversation rose gradually, shrank suddenly, swelled again – a roomful of people used to being heard, all trying to mute their voices. I fixed on the familiar pattern of a Scottish accent; glanced up to find its owner. It took a few seconds to place him. Forrester Scott, talking to a thin beautiful brunette. Where would he rate on Duncan's scale of fame? No more than a five, perhaps – halfway between heartthrob and character actor – but still, I felt myself starstruck. As if he sensed my stare, he looked over, and nodded. I dropped my gaze, edged closer to the wall, but when I glanced back he was making his way through the crowd, coming towards me.

'You're Campbell Johnstone, aren't you?' He offered a hand.

We shook: should I respond with a similar *You're Forrester Scott, aren't you?* Was it cooler not to recognise him?

He pre-empted me. 'Forrester. Nice to meet you.' His voice was comforting in this dark sea of yah-yah. 'How are you coping?' he said.

With losing Eve? With the press? With this hellish gathering? 'Och, you know. Managing. Were you close, to Eve?'

'We worked together years back. Her first film, I think it was. Up in Ross-shire. She was from round there, of course, though you'd never have guessed, would you, she lost the accent pretty convincingly.'

'Actually, she always spoke like that even when she was living there, when she was little.'

'Course, you knew her when she was wee...' He shook his head. 'Terrible. You can't believe it.'

Could it be that I really was sleeping? That I'd manifested Forrester Scott as some kind of psychic comforter? But Mariella, reappearing, could clearly see him.

'Forrester,' she said, and embraced him briefly. 'Thank you so much for coming. I must just show Campbell something; are you here for a while longer? We'll speak before you leave.'

She steered me towards another double doorway – this room was long enough to need two entrances. I found myself at the foot of the curved staircase, struggling to keep my bearings.

'It's a bit of a trek, I'm afraid.' She set quite a pace, sure-footed in her heels; I was flagging from my 5am start, quickly out of breath. Up two floors we climbed, then she led me into a corridor lined with a Persian runner that stretched for miles. We passed several rooms before she stopped. With her hand on the door-knob, she paused, looked at me, and in that moment – that moment only – I saw she was undone. Her face was naked, as though she couldn't believe what had been lost; as if I could help, or anyone could help; and then she turned away, opened the door and stepped into Eve's old bedroom.

Considering the size of the house, Eve's room was small. It was pretty much filled by a single bed with bright-coloured bedding, and a dressing table flounced with frilly skirts and a garland of lights shaped like flowers. A wall of posters showed beautiful girls and girlish young men, none of whom I could name; a corkboard was filled with snaps of teenagers grinning for the camera.

Mariella slid back the door to the built-in wardrobe. It looked half-full, clothes still hanging from the rail. She crouched, lifted a box from the wardrobe floor and held it up to me.

I took it with both hands. Held it like a relic. I didn't want to open it.

'Like I said, just a few bits and pieces.'

'Thanks.' More: she needed more from me than that. 'This means a lot,' I lied. 'To have something of hers.'

She smiled like we'd shared something. 'Let's get out of here.'

We re-joined the dark room of guests through the doorway near the staircase, and as soon as Mariella was caught up into another conversation, I detached myself, walked the length of the room and slipped out through the second set of doors. I moved through the hall with the frozen tears, still clutching the box; out onto the drive, and into a smirr that seemed to hang rather than fall. Past the fleet of parked cars, I crunched over wet gravel. It took at least a minute to reach the road. I had to get back into town; to Liverpool Street, where I'd left my bag. All I knew was that I should be travelling east. I checked the sky, trying to get my bearings: with cloud solid overhead, there were no clues. The road stretched wide and quiet in both directions. I chose one at random, and started to walk.

I caught a cab eventually and, as I'd promised, called Chris at the *News*. The moment I heard his voice, Mariella's words were in my head: *We know how beastly they can be. We know the lies they tell.* We did a phone interview as the taxi carried me across town; I gave him a string of clichés, words as bare and as empty as I could get away with.

For the rest of the afternoon, until it was time to meet Eilidh, I wandered. I wandered from Liverpool Street across Bishopsgate, and east to Brick Lane; I navigated the bleak brick and tangled concrete of the Old Street junction, along with the memories of a decade ago – passing alley-mouths, locked doors, shuttered windows that might still have been hiding those old haunts; those bars and clubs filled with temporary friends, with late nights and early mornings; those darkened rooms where I listened, and danced, and once or twice I played: me and Amit, in that bar where our stage was four square feet beside the gents; in the club where we shared the platform with a dozen clubbers who knew they were part of the music, and the music was part of them. Good times, that seemed to merge into a single fractured night – one I couldn't recognise as belonging to my past without owning, too, the black morning after: and so I walked faster, south to St Paul's, where the sky cleared and let through enough sun for me to buy a pair of sunglasses, put them on with a silent apology to Eve for dismissing her shaded eyes as a Hollywood cliché. I crossed the silver sword of the Millennium Bridge, skirted Tate Modern and curved through the back streets of Southwark until finally, with aching feet and my bag strap carving a dent in my shoulder, I reached the New Kent Road and the gates to Eilidh's school.

As uniformed girls streamed past, chatting and calling like a sky full of starlings, I began to worry that my sunglasses made me look like some kind of predator. I took them off, dropped them into my pocket. A knot of pupils, maybe sixteen years old, eyed me in silence as they strolled by; as soon as they had passed me, they exploded into excited laughter. One of them shouted over her shoulder, 'Give us a kiss!'

When at last Eilidh appeared, in clothes disarmingly smart, I was so relieved I practically ran to meet her.

Her hug was perfunctory. 'If my kids see,' she said, glancing around, 'they'll decide you're my boyfriend.' She stood back, stared at me. 'Nice suit, shame it's too big for you. Roddy's?'

For her benefit, briefly I stuck the shades back on. '*Reservoir Dogs*?'

'Aye, right. Come on then, Mr Pink. Let's get ourselves on a train.'

'I'll pay for a taxi.'

'It'll be twenty quid at least!'

'Doesn't matter.' I could have managed the rush-hour train, probably; deep slow breaths, and it would have been fine. But at the thought of it, my heart was already dancing in my throat, a quick one-two, one-two.

We flagged down a cab on the Old Kent Road. My whole body sighed with relief to be sitting down. 'Isn't this the way to travel?'

Eilidh's stare told me straightaway that – taxi or not – she, at least, was not going to give me an easy ride. 'What the hell is going on?'

I rolled my eyes in the driver's direction. 'Can we wait...?'

'No, we can't wait. I don't know where to start with you.' She pulled a clip from her hair and raked her hands through, tugging hard. 'Okay: is it true?'

'Is...?'

'The stuff about – the kissing thing.'

'Ahhh... It's true I kissed her, yeah, that's true. The other – I don't know, I honestly – I don't even know if it's really *possible*. I mean they're all saying it is, the papers are, but they'll say anything for a story. I even, I called NHS 24 to ask–'

'And?'

'And, they were shit. They said, we advise anyone who has suffered an allergy to avoid the allergen and get it checked out and blah blah. And I said no, that wasn't what I was asking, and they just repeated it again, like they were reading a script. Probably they're in a call centre in Bangalore, probably they don't even know what anaphylactic shock means.'

'You're avoiding the question. And plus, that's racist.'

'Eilidh, I truly don't know. Maybe. Yes.' My hand shook as I reached out and opened the window a crack, feeling the need for air. 'I don't see how else it could have happened.'

'Christ.' She thought for a minute. 'And can you be charged or anything?'

'Charged?'

'For – because – if it *was* because of what you ate...'

'Oh. God. No. No, nothing like that. I mean, the inquest, the verdict didn't even mention what had caused it. So they're not even sure, you know. It's only the tabloids that seem to know exactly what caused it. Funnily enough.'

'Right. That's something, anyway.' She gave me her stern look again, forehead one deep straight line of frown, and I thought she was as worried as I'd ever seen her. Which worried me in turn, of course, but also made me feel safe: she was looking out for me. 'What are you doing all over the tabloids?' she said. 'Are you seriously still talking to those scumbags?'

'Just the one, just the *News*.'

Teeth clenched, she hissed in a sharp breath. Closed her eyes.

'Only because, I knew they'd write it anyway, they'd make up whatever they wanted to. So, I give them exclusives to keep the rest of them away. Or like today, I gave them the story from the funeral so they'd keep their photographers away.'

'The *story* of Eve's funeral?'

It sounded bad, right enough, and once again I heard Mariella's words: *We know the lies they tell. There's nothing you can do.* 'Like I said, it was so they'd stay away, it was for Eve's family.'

'And did they? Stay away?'

I gazed out the window. We were turning into Eilidh's road: I could see the block where she lived, low-rise ex-council. Sometimes it seemed I needed someone looking from the outside to point out the holes in my thinking. Gaps big enough to drive a truck through, and on my own I simply didn't see them.

'I just want for you to be sure about what you're doing. All of this stuff, it's going to stay with you forever. It's not like yesterday's news is today's fish and chip wrappers, not any more.'

She spoke quietly, and she didn't tell me anything I hadn't known, but the word *forever* hung about in my head, and I felt slightly sick as I paid the cabbie and we went inside.

As far as anywhere could in this city, Eilidh's flat felt like sanctuary. Its tiny spaces were filled with her solid presence. If there was a hint of unease, it was only the knowledge that her lodger could arrive home at any moment. But Astrid worked evenings and weekends, was hardly ever here, and if I had to be anywhere in London, Eilidh's minuscule kitchen was the place I'd choose. I pulled out a bottle of wine I'd bought earlier, cracked the screw cap.

Eilidh pulled a face, her no-but-yes face. 'Small glass, please, I can't cope with classroom hangovers.'

We sat at opposite sides of the breakfast bar; lifted our glasses. The first swallow tasted like the bottle wouldn't last long. The second gave me a coughing fit, and the third soothed my throat again. Big swallows: I found I needed to top up my glass already.

I lifted my bag onto my knees, and pulled out the box Mariella had given me.

'Eve's cousin gave me some of her things.'

Eilidh's face registered surprise.

'I know, it's a bit weird.'

'What's in it?'

I shrugged. 'Let's see.'

It had probably been a child's shoebox: Eve had covered it neatly with pink and blue striped wrapping paper. The glue had lost its stick over the years, and the paper was peeling from the corners. Carefully, I lifted the lid.

Inside were bright little squares of our past. On the top was a photo of all us kids, up at Glenelg: me and Duncs, Roddy and Jean, and Eve aged eight or nine, sitting next to me, leaning in. I passed it over to Eilidh. Another showed me on my own, standing astride a bike – a blurry snap, and from the look on my face as I eyed the lens, it was Eve behind the camera. Though I didn't remember her taking this picture, I was pretty sure the very next moment I'd have been pedalling away, as Eve called after me: *Wait for me Cam, slow down!*

Eilidh was staring at the group photo. 'Oh,' she said, and her voice was sad. 'Look how much she liked you.'

Under the photos was a bundle of tickets, to family movies. *Babe. Free Willy. The Flintstones. 101 Dalmations.*

'Why would she keep these?'

Eilidh was still studying the photographs. 'I used to collect sweet wrappers, remember?' she said. 'Kids are just weird, that's all.'

Next was a bundle of cards. Happy birthday! Eve is nine; she is eight; she is seven. There were cards from school-friends, from her father, from Jasmine. I opened one with a hot pink '9' on the front and saw my mum's writing: *To Eve, Happy Birthday from*

Margaret, Bill, Duncan and Campbell. Did Eve keep this simply because of the looping ink that formed my name, in my mother's hand? I handed them across for Eilidh to see.

A notebook, fat and square. *Diary*, it said in silver script on the front. It was the kind a little girl would choose, pink with a strap and a flower-shaped popper to keep it closed. Eilidh looked at it, and up at me.

'I guess it's okay for us to read it,' she said. 'Eve's cousin did, and then she gave it to you...'

But I didn't want to read it. Not with Eilidh there.

I put it back in the box. There wasn't much left, now. A badge saying, *I've got friends in London.* An egg like you'd get from a vending machine, with a cheap ring inside. A star from a Christmas tree, white plastic showing through the glitter. A brown-and-white speckled feather. An old French franc. A piece of amethyst, and some round white pebbles. Some folds of paper, crinkled and stiff like they'd been dampened and dried out. There were a couple of these pages: gently, I spread them out.

The writing was in an adult hand. The first sheet started with scribbles and crossed-out words, and then four lines were written neatly:

> *The hunt begins*
> *Where starts the track*
> *From a place the same*
> *Forwards and back*

Underneath, more crossings out led to another finished verse:

> *A traveller's rest*
> *Where land meets shore*
> *Look for the tallest*
> *Tree of doors*

I passed it to Eilidh. 'From one of our treasure hunts. Must be Jasmine's writing. I never thought how much time must have gone into them, coming up with clues that rhymed.'

'Hah. These are good; better than the ones you used to make up for us. *Look at someone's bicycle / A clue is hidden in the wheel.* Genius, that was.'

'It rhymed though! Well, kind of...'

'So who won this one?'

I took the page again, skimmed through a few of the clues. 'I don't remember. Actually, I don't remember any of these. *The hunt begins / Where starts the track / From a place the same / Forwards and back.* Where would that have been?'

Then I realised. None of us had ever seen these clues. We didn't solve them, didn't find the treasure. The workings were here because Jasmine hadn't made the fair copies, bold capitals on coloured slips of paper. She had planned the hunt and then, days before it was meant to happen, she had died. That's why Eve had kept these scribbled sheets. But why had she stashed them here, in this box of childish love-tokens? They were nothing to do with the crush she'd nursed on me.

'Ah ... *a place the same forwards and back.*' I looked at Eilidh, pleased with myself, to see if she could guess. She shook her head. 'Glenelg. It's Glenelg. The hunt was meant to start ... *where starts the track* – from Glenelg, *from* Glenelg – to where? Well, anyway. Doesn't matter. Doesn't matter.'

I packed Eve's keepsakes back into the box. Rubbed at a speck of gold on my hand, till it disappeared. When I made to top up Eilidh's glass, she covered it with her hand.

'Sure?' I filled my own, took a drink and studied her more closely. 'You look knackered.'

'You say the sweetest things.'

'I like to compliment a lady. Working too hard?'

'Always.' She smiled, dodging the question. There were blue circles under her eyes. Eilidh cared too much, that was her trouble.

Good for the people around her, me included; not so good, maybe, for her. 'Food,' she said. 'I'm not sure what I've got in...'

'Takeaway? On me. You know you want to.'

We ordered curry. I drank the rest of the wine, we watched TV, and it felt as if everything was normal, except that I'd paid for the takeaway. By eleven, both shattered, we called it a night.

But I couldn't sleep yet. I waited while Eilidh brushed her teeth, washed her face, padded back through to her bedroom. Clicked her door shut. Then, safely on my own, I reached for the box of memories.

I unpopped the flower that fastened the diary, let the book fall open somewhere in the middle. The pencilled writing was round and neat on the lined pages:

Tomorrow me and Claire are going to go horse riding, I am really really looking forward to it.

I turned the pages; sank backwards through time.

I decided I am not talking to Claire because of what she said about me and Fiona. When I have my party I will not invite her. She is the only girl in my class I won't invite so she will be left out. I went to see the film A Little Princess, it was brill.

She was a diligent diarist: the book allowed a page a day, and every page had been used; sometimes filled right to the last line, sometimes just with a sentence or two. I read my way back till I reached the start. Then I flipped to the middle once more, and started reading forwards. I was looking for something, and I wasn't sure what. Something ... something about rain, on the glass above our heads. About dust, on the attic floor. On our clothes – on her skirt...

Went round to Fiona's for a video, we watched Mrs Doubtfire, it was quite funny. They're allowed to have Coke! And we had crisps too. 24 days till Campbell comes.

I paused: a twinge of pity, at the mention of my name.

Today, baked with Mum. We baked a strawberry cake, we used the strawberries from the garden. 21 days till Campbell comes.

I turned the pages: more of the same. 17 days. 15 days, 11 days. 4 days. And then the entries stopped, and the next part of the diary was empty pages.

I never did come, of course.

I burst from sleep, stretched on the sofa, twisting and sticky with guilt, the knowledge of something awful, irrevocable, gripping my chest so I could scarcely breathe. Like Eve, desperate, gasping for breath – but for me the air came, my lungs hauling it in like there could never be enough, then slower, and gradually calmer. She had been in my dreams. She had stared, scarlet-eyed, and whispered, *Don't tell.*

I sat, sweat-damp face in hands that felt filthy, like they were smeared with newsprint ink. And that was me, awake for the day.

In the airport I kept my sunglasses on, kept my distance from the newsagents; ignored the discarded tabloids scattered across the waiting areas. My hands still felt dirty, no matter how much soap I used in the bathroom, how hot the water ran. By the time I was in the air, on my way back to Glasgow, I'd decided to call it a day. Game over: Chris, the *News* and all the rest of them would have to find a new story. They could write what they wanted, but none of it would come from me.

I'd go back to work, if I still had a job. I'd find myself a better place to live, a flat to myself. I'd get a new phone number. I was leaving this behind me: Eve, and all of this.

So when we touched down, and I checked my voicemail, Chris's unwelcome tones had me poised to delete his message. It was morbid curiosity that made me listen: what fresh angle had he dreamed out of nothing? But this was something else, something unexpected.

'Campbell. I've had a message from some people who want to be in touch with you. Anaphylaxis Alert, they're called.' He stumbled slightly over the words. 'They're a charity for, what, raising awareness, and stuff. Anyway, I said I'd pass it on, if you want to speak to them...' He left a name and number. 'So: we're running a follow-up to the funeral story and I'd like to get a fresh quote from you for that – it won't run till the day after tomorrow so, plenty of time – I'll keep trying till I get you.'

I played the message again; then I saved it.

A charity. Perhaps they were after a donation. That seemed fair enough, if a little quick off the mark. The *News* had promised to pay for the funeral story, and something about that felt like profiteering. Of course, my dad would have said that's what I'd been doing all along. But it seemed to me there was a line, albeit ever so fine, and up until now I'd stayed on just the right side. Now, though, I was ankle-deep in murky moral swamps. I thought how I would feel if I gave the money away. How clean. How light.

Maybe I didn't have to give the whole amount.

Maybe half would be enough, to feel good about.

Chapter 14

I was drinking sludgy coffee on Sauchiehall Street, waiting for Hilary Steel. I had on a whole outfit of new clothes. Nothing flashy: new jeans, new trainers to replace the pair with holes in the soles. A new summer jacket, sleeves un-frayed. And I still felt shabby.

In a weird way, I was looking forward to digging deep in my pockets. Deep-ish, at least.

On the phone, Hilary Steel had sounded gentle, with something West Country in her accent: a touch of warm, slow vowels. She was director of something-or-other at Anaphylaxis Alert, and she was travelling from London just to meet me. She had to be after a serious donation, but she hadn't mentioned money. *So sorry for your loss*, she had said instead, and I'd realised it was the first time anyone had said that to me. To my surprise, I'd found myself welling up, self-pity congealing in a hard ball at the top of my chest. I'd had to remind myself that my loss was more or less fictional. Someone whose job involves making people feel sympathy for others must naturally be able to make them feel sympathy for themselves. Without trying, probably; without knowing she was doing it. Either that, or it was part of a strategy to make me more inclined to stump up on a grand scale.

Arranging where to meet, I'd started to tell her how she could recognise me. Then I'd stopped.

'Well. I suppose you know what I look like.'

She'd agreed, and I could hear a smile in her voice. 'We've seen a lot of you lately.'

She arrived ten minutes late, pink-faced and apologetic: her train had been delayed. She paused to unwind a scarf from her neck and shoulders, draped it over the back of her chair before she sat. Middle-aged; broad, and comfortable-looking. I tried not to be obvious as I studied her and made my judgements.

'Thank you so much for meeting me.' She sat with her hands clasped on the table between us. 'I told you a little bit about our work, didn't I, on the phone?'

I agreed that she had. Briefly, we were interrupted by the waiter: with a pot of tea safely ordered, she resumed her soft sales pitch. By the time her tea arrived, my coffee was finished, and she'd reached the crux of the matter.

'I'm sure you appreciate the importance of what we're aiming towards, with the terrible time you're going through. Campbell, we very much hope that you might be willing to help us in our work.'

My chequebook was folded and ready in the pocket of my coat. I had to get in first with what I could offer. 'Absolutely,' I said. 'I'm more than happy to, to do what I can, you know. To give what I can afford.'

She set down the teapot, lifted her cup and held it steaming at her chin. 'Of course donations are always welcome. But what I'm getting at, really, is another way you could help. The media have gone to town on this, there has been just so much coverage, over the past two or three weeks. You could use that; the media interest. We want to raise awareness as widely as possible, of the risks of anaphylaxis, and we want people to know about us – to know where they can come for information and support. And with all the interest there is in you – in you and Eve' – she paused, just slightly, before she said Eve's name, almost as though she were asking permission to use it – 'we hoped you might consider acting as an ambassador for AnAlert.'

'So – what's that then, what would I do, if I was an ambassador?' I was wondering if she'd ever actually drink her tea, or if it was just a prop.

'What we would ask you to do is spread the word about AnAlert; talk about us, in the media. Make sure that we're mentioned at the end of a story. Perhaps you might take part in some of our campaigning, the fundraising events we run. I don't know how you would feel about speaking about your experience, to different sorts of groups...' She must have seen my reluctance. 'But it's very much up to you, the kind of involvement you'd be interested in.'

It sounded simple. Just mention them when I did an interview. Except that I wasn't going to do any more interviews. Except that the story was over. *We know how beastly they can be. The lies they tell.*

'I don't know how much help I can really be,' I said, 'that's the thing. There's nothing more for them to write about.'

She nodded as if she agreed, but when she spoke it was to say just the opposite. 'My sense is that, handled right, there's plenty of mileage in this – in you. Your story is so unusual, and so touching. People want to know more about you. They want to hear all about this love that was there right from childhood. And for us – I'm sorry to say this, but for us it's a tremendously powerful story because it shows what people stand to lose. If you'd known about the allergy, if Eve had explained to you – given you the information – what happened, needn't have happened.'

Again, that tiny pause – as though Eve's name was a precious possession of mine that she hoped to borrow. She took a sip of tea, set the cup back in its saucer. She was waiting for my reaction.

What she'd said was quite true: Eve ought to have told me. Even if she'd talked about it in an interview, chances are I would have known; I would have stumbled across it on the internet. Eve herself could have acted as an ambassador, and raised awareness of her own condition. But she'd chosen to keep it private. You could say privacy had killed her. It was all about information: information I hadn't been given.

I had come here in search of a simple transaction. A wodge of cash, for a clearer conscience. But my chequebook stayed curled in my pocket. Hilary Steel with her friendly vowels, her good cause woven through the tone of her voice, offered another kind of exchange. These stories I'd been selling, they weren't just voyeurism. People were touched. They cared. And by sharing what had happened, I could do some good.

I sat back as the waiter took my dirty cup, wiped a coffee-ring from the table. When he was gone I lifted my water-glass, took a long clean swallow.

'I'd have to think about this,' I said, and she nodded.

'Naturally.' Then, 'You don't have anyone – an agent? A PR advisor?'

'No, what for?'

'No, of course... It's just that you've done so much press. I thought you might have someone handling it for you.'

Did people have agents – people like me? The idea of someone to handle Chris and his ilk – to keep them at a distance, and keep the story going whilst I did my bit for a good cause – struck me as inspired.

'I could ask around. Get you some names,' she said. 'If you thought it would be useful.'

'Perhaps I should.' I looked at her, wanting her approval. Saw her smile, ever so slightly. 'I think, perhaps, I should.'

TRAGIC CAM IN CHARITY PUSH

The picture could be of any group of children. But the little girl sitting close beside a young Campbell Johnstone was destined to grow up to be a star, before her life was tragically cut short...

When Eve Sadler's family gave Campbell a box of keepsakes the star had collected as a child, he didn't know what he would find inside.

'It was emotional, to see these photos,' he says. 'Even though we were close as children, I didn't know she had kept these pictures of us together. Obviously they meant a lot to her.'

Also in the box was Eve's diary. Campbell won't reveal its contents, but he does tell us he was deeply moved by the youthful memories it brought back.

Since it was revealed that the most likely cause of death was the peanut snack Campbell had eaten shortly before he and Eve kissed in the courtyard of Glasgow's luxurious Metcalfe Hotel, Campbell has been struggling to accept what happened.

'It's ironic, we had everything ahead of us, and the very moment that everything seemed to fall into place for us was when it all fell apart.

'I'll never know whether it really was the kiss that killed her,' he says. 'That uncertainty is something I'll have to live with for the rest of my life. But what I do know is that if I had been aware of Eve's allergy – how severe it could be, and how to deal with an attack – she might still be here today. That's why the work they're doing at Anaphylaxis Alert is so vital.'

Now Campbell hopes to raise awareness of anaphylaxis through working with the charity. 'Eve's death shouldn't be in vain,' he explains, 'and if I can help spread the word about Anaphylaxis Alert, then it won't be.'

Anaphylaxis Alert offers information and support for people with severe allergies, and campaigns for a safer environment for sufferers. For more information on allergies and anaphylaxis, visit www.analert.org.uk

Chapter 15

It was striking how little of my old life I wanted to keep.

The stuff I was taking with me made a very small pile on the bed. My new clothes, including a suit of my own (whisper: Armani, charcoal wool with a silk lining... More beautiful than my brother's, than Roddy's by far). New laptop, new iPhone. Eve's box of memories. My newspaper clippings.

I hadn't seen the flat, but I'd been assured it would be fully furnished. Amanda, my newly acquired advisor, had helped me find it. She was keen for me to be on the spot, to make the most of opportunities and maximise her twenty per cent. After three trips to London in the last week alone, I wasn't arguing. I had to be at the centre of things.

From the doorway, Roddy was watching.

'That all you're taking?'

'Don't need anything else.'

'What about your guitar?' He nodded towards the corner where it was leaning, filmed with dust. I hadn't picked it up in weeks.

'I can always get a new one, if I want it.'

'Uh-huh.' He stood, arms folded, eyes following me.

The thing is with Roddy, his face is like glass. He can't hide his thoughts. 'Come here a sec,' I said.

'What, where?'

I grasped his shoulder, steered him into my room and stood him in front of the wardrobe mirror.

'What am I looking at, dust?' he asked. He ran a finger across the surface, leaving a clean streak.

'Your face. I can see what you're thinking.'

He stared. Shrugged. 'I'm not thinking anything.'

'That's maybe generally true. But right now it's bollocks.' I turned my back on him, added a bundle of socks to the pile on the bed.

'If I am,' he said, 'it's just...'

He didn't finish. In silence, I carried on assembling my belongings.

'Have you told Duncan you're going?' he said, eventually.

'Have *you*? Told him *you're* going?'

'I thought you were getting a new flatmate. He didn't particularly need to know.'

I lifted my suitcase onto the bed. Started to pack.

'I'll tell him when he's back next week,' said Roddy. 'So ... I mean, are you alright about this?'

'What do you mean, alright?'

'Like, about London. Going back.'

I looked him in the eye, held his gaze till he glanced away, down at my case. 'It'll be different,' I said. 'It'll be fine.'

Again, his face spoke for him. *Aye aye*, it said. *You really think?*

'If I don't take this opportunity...' I said.

'How do you mean, opportunity? For what?'

'God! Just ... to be in the centre of things. To do something! To achieve something.'

He looked at me, uncomprehending.

'And it's for AnAlert; raising awareness–' I broke off, irritated: with myself as much as Roddy. Why should I justify the choice I'd made? 'I'm going, alright? Whatever anyone thinks. I'm not letting this get away from me.'

'Do you not think you'll look back and wish – like, in the longer term...?'

That was precisely what I couldn't afford to do: to think in the longer term, the too much and the not enough of it. He must have seen my face snap shut; held out his hands. Truce.

'Listen,' he said. 'I'm not trying to be an arsehole. I'm just – it doesn't seem like you.'

And there it was. The nub of it. Why would I want to seem like me? Where had that ever got me?

'How are you so concerned,' I said, 'all of a sudden? You disappear for weeks, then as soon as you're back you're telling me what I shouldn't be doing? What's that about, eh?'

He shut up then. He left the room, and across the hall I heard his door close.

I placed my laptop in the case, cushioned in layers of clothes. Making himself scarce: it was what Roddy did, when things got sticky. It had to be easy, for him. He couldn't cope with the hard stuff, the fucked-up stuff, hadn't ever been able to. Not back when I needed all the friends I could get; not now that things were changing.

I was done here. My case sat waiting at the foot of my bed. I turned out the light, went into the living room and picked up the book I'd been reading. But I was all churned up. I couldn't leave it. On my own, disconnected – from Roddy next door, from my folks back home – it was a bad sense of falling backwards through my own life, just when I was fighting with fists and feet and teeth to go forwards.

I threw my book aside, strode to Roddy's room and banged the door open.

He was lying on the bed with his eyes closed, face set in a frown. He was using my headphones; he pulled them down as I entered.

I wanted to tell him why it was his fault we were fighting. I wanted to tell him he was wrong. But there was too much needing to come out all at once, and my throat was a bottleneck. I stood, mouth open. From the corner of my eye I could see a packing box half-filled with books, at the start of their journey up to his mum and dad's.

'So it's alright for you to go,' I said. 'It's just me that has to stay here.'

'Eh? That's not what I said.'

'You've got no idea.'

'Fine.' He sat up. 'I've got no idea. It's obviously nothing to do with me, so forget I said anything.'

'You're right, it's nothing to do with you. It's nothing to do with anyone.'

He hovered the cushion of the headphones over his ear, asking, *Are we done here?* 'Can I?'

'Those are mine by the way.'

'Oh right, you going to take them to London, are you? Here you go.' He yanked them off, pulled the jack from his iPod and flung them at me. 'Catch.'

They hit my chest, and I caught them there. There was no room left in my case, but I'd have to squeeze them in now, somehow.

Roddy lay back down again, arms folded. He closed his eyes. Listening to nothing.

'I can't stay,' I said.

His eyes remained closed. 'So go. Nothing to do with me, remember? Go on. Go!'

I went.

PART THREE

*Here the right choice
Could prove wrong*

Chapter 16

Any second now, it's going to be too late. Duncs is muttering to himself with his eyes shut, Jean's got her hands to her mouth like she could pull an answer out, Eve's face is dark with thinking – and I'm glaring at Roddy, shouting *GO ON,* but shouting it silently, shooting it straight from my brain into his. And Roddy – he's staring down at the toes of his shoes, staring up at the tops of the trees, staring anywhere that's not at me.

'*This year's story's nearly told / What we discard can turn to gold ... to gold, to gold...*' It's like, if he says the clue often enough, Duncs reckons the treasure will just appear by magic in front of him, all bright and glittering.

I try to act like I'm guessing too, so no-one gets suspicious. '*No need to dig. Beneath the grass,*' I say, '*The treasure waits for you at last.* Oh ... I can't think. Roddy, come on. You're not even trying.'

He shrugs, like he has no ideas in his head. His mouth is all pressed shut, and I want to hit him right in his stupid, frowning face. If he didn't want to win, he should have said so at the start.

The whole entire point was that Roddy had never won. Duncs has won loads of times, of course, and Jean won last year, and me and Eve have won as well, once each. And Roddy always said he wasn't bothered – but back at the start of the holiday, when I said this year we should put our heads together and be joint winners, he didn't say no.

'All we need to do,' I told him, 'is find the clues before Jasmine hides them.'

'You mean – we should cheat?'

'No! It's not cheating, cos we wouldn't look at all of the clues. We'd only read the last one, just so we had a head-start.'

'But that's still cheating, is it not?'

I shook my head. 'We'd still have to solve the clue, wouldn't we? It would be cheating if we were looking for the answers. But not if we have to guess same as we always do.'

I could see he wasn't sure.

'We're just making it more fair,' I said. 'Duncs and Jean have got an advantage because they're older, and Eve's got an advantage too because it's her house. This would be our advantage.'

It made sense, Roddy could see that. Everyone should have an advantage. It was only fair. 'So if we did – did look for the clues ... where d'you think she would hide them?'

I'd been thinking about this. We were allowed pretty much anywhere in the house. 'Well, where's the one room in this whole house where we wouldn't ever go?'

Roddy's eyes went wide. 'Jasmine's bedroom?'

If someone guesses right now, it'll only take two minutes – two minutes running fast to where the treasure is. Jean's looking around for inspiration: for a moment she stops, gazing up at the house, and I think she's got it. I think she knows. I can feel my fists clenching, and if Roddy's not going to guess I'm going to do it myself, and I'm staring at him, staring...

Jean's gaze moves on. '*What we discard*,' she says. 'So: rubbish. But not the dustbin.' We've already looked in the dustbin, which was empty, lucky for us. We've biked over to the farm and the house beyond that and checked their rubbish too. 'And it's buried, but you don't need a spade...' She makes a baffled noise.

I need to give Roddy a prompt, to make it easier for him to pretend-guess – but it's risky, because anything I say could give it away to one of the others instead.

'Like ... rubbish that isn't thrown away,' I say. Roddy looks up, meets my eyes – and then he looks away. I can't believe it. He's chickened out. He's not going to guess at all.

Neither of us had ever been in Jasmine's room before. It felt emptier than a normal empty room, and it had a smell, sort of powdery and cold. I'd thought it would be clean and tidy like Mum and Dad's room, but there were clothes all piled over chairs instead of put away in the wardrobe. Along one wall was a shelf with some cupboards and a dusty mirror, and the shelf was covered in *stuff*. Loads of paper, all heaped in with bottles and pots, and piles of necklaces and earrings and that, and empty smeary glasses and a dirty, dried-out mug that must have been there for ages. I poked at some of the paper piles, letters and envelopes, but they were mostly typed not written. Plus, the clues were always on bright coloured paper, and all these pages were plain.

Roddy was hovering by the door, hands in his pockets like he was scared to touch anything.

'Look in the drawers,' I told him.

He shook his head. 'I don't think we should.'

'Jessie! Just – keep watch, then.'

The table on one side of the bed had a pile of books on top and three glasses of water that had been there for days – you could tell because they were all bubbly, the way my stomach felt. It looked like that was the table she used most, so I crossed the carpet and pulled the handle of the drawer – opening it just a little way so I could see inside. Tablets. A book. A tube of cream or something. A pair of glasses. I didn't even know she wore specs; that seemed like a kind of secret. But no coloured bits of paper. I shut the drawer, sneaked round to the other side of the bed, to the bedside table that was empty apart from dust.

'Quick!' Roddy whispered.

He was right, we had to hurry. Eve was bound to be searching for us, even if nobody else was. I wiped my hands on my jeans, opened the second drawer.

There! There they were: black marker on coloured paper – red, yellow, blue, green. All numbered, all in order. I made myself skip straight to the back, and clue number six – read it once, twice, three times, making sure I'd remember it, so I could tell it to Roddy. Then I shoved the clues back in the drawer, pushed it shut and together we raced from the room – getting out just in the nick of time, because there was Eve climbing the stairs towards us.

'I hope you're not hiding from me,' she said. And the secret of where we'd been and what we'd been doing fizzed up inside me and exploded into laughing, both of us laughing, me and Roddy, killing ourselves, and when one of us stopped the other one's face was enough to start us all over again.

I can see Duncs getting it. First, he stops muttering. He blinks, three times. Then he stares up at the house.

I shout it before he can. 'The compost heap!'

But he's already running. I set off after him, and behind I can hear Eve shrieking, 'Cam, run!' Up the slope, towards the house, as fast as I can but he's faster. Jink around the side of the house, down the path, Jean at my heels, but by the time we reach the back garden Duncs is almost there, almost at the compost heap. I slow down, let Jean overtake: sick from running, and from knowing I'm beaten.

The treasure's where I knew it would be: under a pile of fresh cut grass, at the side of the compost. Duncs swooshes grass into the air, and reveals a fat package.

'That was soooo close,' says Jean, all breathless. 'Wasn't it? You both guessed at the exact same time! Just – Duncs is a faster runner. You should almost be joint winners.'

'Yeah, almost,' says Duncs, tearing off the wrapper. 'Bad luck, Cam!' Inside is a pogo ball. It's too young for him, really, but he starts to play with it anyway, balancing with his arms spread out, tipping off and laughing, and balancing again. It looks like brilliant fun.

Behind me, Roddy is watching, not saying anything. If I hadn't waited for him, given him a chance – if he hadn't chickened out – I definitely would have won.

'Doesn't matter,' I say. 'I've already won once anyway. But it's a shame for Roddy, though, not to win – *again*.' I stare at him. 'Doesn't seem fair that you've never won at all.' I keep staring, to make him look away.

But he looks straight at me, and then he shrugs. 'Maybe next year,' he says. 'But Duncs won this time, eh. Fair and square.'

He says the words slow, and it's me that looks away – to where Duncs is wobbling and laughing on his new pogo ball, and Eve and Jean are shouting for a go. 'Aye – but it was close though,' I say.

And it was: it was totally close.

Chapter 17

An allergy sufferer, a specialist and me: of the three of us, I was pretty sure I was the main attraction. You might think I'd have been offered a cup of tea; that someone would have run through the questions I'd be asked; at the very least, that I'd have been introduced to the presenter before we went on air. Instead, we spent a half-hour being ignored in the waiting area – like the doctor's, but with comfier seats, better magazines and added nerves – before, with less than a minute to go, a girl with a face like a tension headache rushed us into the studio. Jeremy's notes had gone missing, she said by way of apology. Not to worry: he'd wing it.

This level of organisation, I was learning, was par for the course. Made you wonder how they ever got the programmes out.

We squeezed ourselves around the desk. The allergy sufferer took the furthest seat from me. The chair dropped a little under his solid frame; he had a rugby player's build, and a knocked-about face to match. I wondered if he was afraid of me. Afraid I might breathe on him, or spit in his eye.

The producer counted us in: *five – four – three* she said out loud, then *two* and *one* with silent beats of her hands.

We were on.

'Hello, and welcome to *Good Health*, where this afternoon we're going to be looking at allergies...'

Outside the studio, it was neglectful chaos; inside, you were special. Headphones cushioned my ears; Jeremy's voice was like warm bath-water. I couldn't help but sink in, and relax. It came to me that I was starting to like radio. Once I'd managed to forget the thousands, even millions, of listeners – and it was easy to forget, in this dim, intimate space – being here was strangely restful. The producer, the presenter, had a tight hold of the seconds and minutes. I was free to let go of time.

Of course, I wasn't meant to relax. This was work. I'd been coached by Amanda. I had the list she'd given me of everything she thought I should say. It was folded in my pocket; it was there if I needed it. But it told in my voice when I read instead of just talking naturally; plus, I didn't want the mic to pick up the flutter of paper, the way it had in my first interview. I'd thought my nerves would kill me: it had seemed impossible to squeeze in all I had to say, as well as remembering to listen through the racing of my heart – and to answer in proper sentences – and to try and not sound like a dick. I still wasn't sure my brain was quick enough to get it right, but it was easier each time. It was becoming automatic: to refer to the childhood I'd shared with Eve, to hint at untold stories. To mention the AnAlert campaign, before the presenter wound me up or cut me off.

Across from me, Jeremy raised his arm in my direction; making a loop with forefinger and thumb, drawing me in. 'Campbell Johnstone knows perhaps better than anyone how serious an allergy can be...'

I took a couple of slow breaths. The most useful tip Amanda had given me: forget it's radio, and pretend you're there with just one person, someone you're totally comfortable with. I conjured Eilidh: she rolled her imaginary eyes at me, then started pulling faces in a wildly inappropriate attempt to make me laugh.

Jeremy's voice was rich with sympathy. 'Campbell. Tell us what happened, if you could, that night.'

I leaned forward, ready to unreel my story.

Afterwards, I followed my voice out of the studio, into thick London sun. My performance ran back through my head, a kind of reverse rehearsal: what I'd said, how I'd sounded. My heart was a little fast, my breath a little shallow, but slowing now, deepening now. Coming down. There would be a time – and I knew it would be sooner than I could imagine – when this would become routine, mundane. For now, balanced midway between excitement and anxiety, I made myself savour it.

It had been just right, I thought – the tone, the content. I imagined my just-right words vibrating through the sky: pulsing through the traffic fumes that hung in the heat, that hazed the light, softened the streets and set buildings afloat; imagined them pulsing through the airwaves, to be picked up by receivers in analogue radios, in cars and kitchens and workplaces. Imagined packets of digital data delivering my words to mobiles and laptops all over the world. A massed choir of my voice was all around me. Invisible pieces of me: duplicating, dividing. Shooting off into the air, in electromagnetic particles–

Stop.

I brought my thoughts back to here, now, concrete. Back to my feet on the pavement.

I could have caught a cab, but I had hours till my next appointment, and so I walked, under the sun that had shone almost every day since I'd got here. It was a different sun down south. Heavier. More opaque. All sorts of things felt different – the way I moved: purposeful, keeping a fast beat. The faces of people I passed. The mild thrill of recognition; the subtle stare. Eyes drawn to mine, searching my shades, seeking confirmation. Then the sudden change of focus, the pretence that I was no-one, just another anonymous pedestrian – even as they stored me up as an anecdote: *Guess who I just saw in the street? Yes: on the Strand, just walking.* And I let my gaze pass through them, in turn; kept a neutral expression, so as not to let on what a buzz it was for me, to be known.

That buzz was reason enough to walk. But there was something else, too. Before – when I was a student here – I'd hardly walked at all. My London was patches, small and separate. I zipped between them on tubes, trains, buses, without any sense of how they were joined. And maybe that had been part of the problem. When things pulled apart, there was nothing that could hold.

What I was doing now, walking like this, was making sure it all held together. Across the bridge, along the Thames: my marching steps were stitching up the seams, strong and tight.

Chapter 18

AnAlert occupied one floor of a bland '80s office-block, south of the river. I'd been there once before to meet with Hilary and Simon, the campaign manager. Then, late in the day, the office had been deserted: the carpet, worn to a dingy neutral, the walls painted Elastoplast-pink, the empty desks divided by walls made of something like sacking; all this had left me feeling drab.

Today was the opposite.

'We've had to take on some more staff,' said Hilary. 'It's just gone wild – in a good way, of course. It does mean we're a little cramped at the moment.'

Every desk accommodated at least two people: they hunched into phones, hands pressed against ears, or leaned into screens, fingers darting over keyboards. Landlines and mobiles rang unanswered. Most of the women were barelegged, the men in short sleeves; even Hilary was unscarved in the heat. I felt sweat blooming under my arms. Windows had been thrust open to admit some notional fresh air, and the drone of traffic rose from Waterloo Road.

'So, this is our team...' Hilary gestured, left and right. We were edging between desks; some of the workers glanced up as we passed and, in amongst the tapping of keys and mice, I could almost hear little clicks of recognition. Out on the streets, strangers' stares might be bright and acquisitive or politely, professionally blank; here each glance was accompanied by a friendly nod, an acknowledging smile. I smile-and-nodded back. I might not know these people – for all that they recognised me, they didn't know me either – but that didn't matter. We were a team, working together, for the same thing. For a good, a worthwhile thing.

And we weren't the only ones. All around, on every desk, were screenfuls of kisses. Girls kissing boyfriends, husbands kissing wives; women kissing women and men kissing men. Parents kissing kids, from newborns to toddlers to teens, and grown kids kissing ageing parents. Brothers, sisters, best friends – even cat-people and dog-lovers smooching up to their pets. Each picture, each bright fragment, was one small part of what we were doing: one hundredth of a thousandth of *Give With A Kiss*.

Send us your kisses and make a donation, in memory of Eve. I'd been unconvinced, worried at first that the idea was in poor taste: weren't we asking people to celebrate the cause of her death? The very act that had – probably – killed her? Hilary had listened, open-faced, then turned my concern on its head: the kiss was a symbol of love, and the story of me and Eve was a love story, after all. I'd been persuaded; and Hilary had been right.

In the middle of the office we stopped, by the lone desk that hosted a single occupant.

'Simon,' said Hilary, 'I know you're busy. Are you able to join us, for a quick update?'

'Sure...' he said, frowning at the vast, multi-coloured spreadsheet that filled his screen. Till recently, I'd have said Simon was younger and more successful than me. I'd still say he was younger. He was also more American, and with much less hair; looking down, I had an aerial view of his scalp gleaming sunburn-pink. He swung round in his chair. 'Sure,' he said again, standing up. 'Campbell, great to see you back. Pretty buzzy in here, huh?'

We settled in the meeting room, a long space sliced off one end of the office. Through windows that ran from waist-height all the way to the ceiling, I had a clear view of almost the entire staff.

'They're all working on the campaign?' I said.

'And some people who're working from home, too,' said Hilary. 'We had thought we were well enough resourced, but it really has taken us by surprise.'

Simon was nodding. 'It totally helped that we had some famous faces picking it up nice and early, Eve's friends in the business, her co-workers. By the way,' he said to Hilary, 'did you see we've had kisses now from a couple of politicians?'

Hilary pulled a face: delicate disapproval. 'Oof. If that doesn't kill it...'

'No, no, we got one from that MP who just came out – what's his name again...?'

'Oh. Oh, really? Well, then, that's brilliant!'

Simon turned back to me. 'We've got them working in shifts now. 7am till 11pm, there's always someone on it.'

I looked out at the crowd of twenty-somethings. All their scrolling and sorting and sharing, their selecting and responding – it was like tending a fire. Feeding it, building it, keeping it alive; coaxing the flames to leap higher and higher. At the desk nearest our window a young woman with a ponytail wiped a sheen of sweat from her forehead, then clasped a hand to the back of her neck, and squeezed. Pinned to her hessian desk-divider was a sheet of A4 that said:

- OPENNESS
- OPTIMISM
- EMOTIONAL CONNECTION

That was my voice. My public voice; the voice of *Give With A Kiss*. Simon and Hilary had brainstormed these values, passed them to me for approval. Which I'd given, of course: I wasn't a sociopath. These keywords kept the tone consistent – in every utterance, across all social media – allowing the campaign staff to become professional versions of me. Not that they were impersonating me – at least, most of them weren't. Though there was a Campbell Johnstone username for each platform, the majority of the work was happening under the campaign banner, *Give With A Kiss*. But as Hilary had explained, it was all about branding. It was about my brand.

And it was a strange feeling. My name was central to the campaign, as was my so-called voice – but me, I was nowhere. Which was why I'd suggested dropping by for an update I could have had over the phone.

I listened as Simon described, with extravagant hand gestures, the campaign trajectory; how they'd achieved maximum virality; how far ahead they were on their targets for raising awareness, and raising cash. 'The guys in fundraising pull off an update once a day – over there, that's yesterday's total.' He was pointing through the windows, to a whiteboard where someone had written £1,301,000!! and decorated it with red and blue stars.

'It's a tremendous achievement,' said Hilary. 'And without your help, it wouldn't be happening.'

I wasn't here for a pat on the back – but it did feel good to be appreciated. 'God, it's my pleasure.' For the first time I noticed how knackered Hilary looked; at the same time, there was a glow about her. She reminded me of the photo of Mum, propped on hospital pillows, one of us – a miniature me or Duncs – cuddled close to her chest, tilted towards the camera. This campaign was Hilary's baby, and something about her weary pride helped me formulate what I wanted to say.

'Look, I know it's my name, my story, that's the best way I can help. And that's great – but then – I keep reading in the *Metro*, or wherever: what celebs are sharing their pictures, how there's people posting from the States, Australia, Japan, all over... And I'm thinking, I've got a bit of time at the moment, and ... I'd like to be a wee bit more involved.' I had to admit the campaign so far hadn't suffered from my lack of engagement; still, I thought they might be glad to use me. At the least, I'd be another pair of hands.

Hilary looked at Simon. 'I think – we'd be thrilled by that, wouldn't we?'

'Sure!' he said. 'That would be great.'

They both smiled at me: their enthusiasm was convincing.

It seemed obvious I should begin by contributing as myself, under the Campbell Johnstone usernames. 'You want to get started?' said Simon. 'Let's go take a look how these guys are working, then you can have a shot. Sound good?'

It did. Outside the meeting room, Hilary thanked me once again – it was tremendous work I was doing, she said; my support was much appreciated – then left us to get on with it.

With a clap of his hands, Simon scanned the room. His gaze fell on an empty chair. 'Karin... Are you on your own here?'

It was the same girl I'd watched rubbing her neck. She glanced at the vacant seat, as though it had just appeared. 'Uh, yes. Tom's gone for a coffee.'

'Mind if we perch?' He gestured for me to sit, spun his own chair across to join us. 'Campbell, this is Karin; Karin, meet Campbell. He's going to be helping us out, getting his hands nice and dirty.'

Karin smiled, turned back to her screen with a flick of blonde ponytail. 'Nice to meet you, Campbell.' She had a faint accent – Scandinavian? – and when she frowned in concentration, her lips pressed into a kind of pout.

'Just Cam is fine,' I told her.

'Okay,' Simon was saying, 'so actually, Karin's already logged in as you. That's great. Now this here's your dashboard, it's what you'll see when you log in – all your various platforms across here – don't worry about that stuff over there, we'll set you up so you don't even see it...' He rattled along, switching back and forth between explaining the basics of social media and of what Karin was doing. 'See now, she's favouriting loads of stuff; like, everything that's coming in? That's because someone's posted a negative comment. When that happens, we can't delete it – but we can bury it with positive content.'

'You can't report it?'

'Only if it's libellous, or threatening or whatever.'

Karin laughed. 'Yeah, or when they post sex pics,' she said, still busily burying the negative post. 'Sometimes, it's not the kind of kisses we want.'

Every couple of seconds the streams refreshed, new content appearing: pictures, comments, conversations, moving so fast I found myself trying not to blink. All that love; all that self-love. I wondered what made them do it. The desire to be seen? To show they cared? The need to join in, to be part of something bigger than themselves? In a few of the photos, I thought I saw genuine intimacy: love bubbling up, warm and alive, tickling kisses into smiles. In most, I saw performers: all stagey pouts and eyeing the lens.

'Does it not get overwhelming?'

'At first, it is a bit,' Karin said. 'But I'm not the only Campbell Johnstone – there are two of us logged in right now – so then between us it's easier.'

I watched as she typed a thank-you message to someone who'd just donated. 'The people who're posting pictures, have they all given money?'

'Not all,' said Simon. 'But a good proportion. And even the people who don't donate, they're still contributing. They're helping us build the buzz.'

So it wasn't as simple as altruists and narcissists. The lines were blurred. Somehow, I found that comforting.

'What we'll do,' said Simon, 'is we'll get our guys to flag stuff for you to respond to, so whenever you log in you won't have to wade through everything. What d'you think, are you ready to take a turn?'

Karin moved aside, and I settled myself in her place; I could feel her body-heat stored in the chair, the mouse. Tentatively, I copied what she'd been doing, highlighting all the positive posts.

'Perfect. Okay, now wait – see this one?' Simon pointed at the screen: a picture of a woman kissing a curly blonde toddler. The comment read, *My angel Tyler aged 3, seriously allergic to many foods, but he's a tough little fella! Proud to #GiveWithAKiss, keep up the good work.* 'Let's reply to that.'

I thought for a second, then typed out my message. *Thanks for sharing your kiss, what a beautiful boy! We appreciate your support!*

'Okay?'

Karin reached over, tapped on the keyboard; I caught the tang of her sweat, mingled with some clean, floral fragrance. 'Maybe just…' The exclamation marks vanished, were replaced by full stops. 'It's more sincere,' she said.

I'd been thinking *optimism*, but she was right: her version was better. She had the *emotional connection* spot on. I posted the comment, watched it appear in the streams.

'Great!' said Simon. 'You got it!'

He and Karin watched as I replied to a few more posts, variations on a theme. *Many thanks. Thanks so much. Beautiful picture, thanks for sharing.*

'Hey – I just had an idea!' Simon's chair squealed as he pitched himself forward. 'What about if we get a pic of you guys, Cam kissing Karin? We can post it with, *Campbell says thanks to our hard-working team*, something like that… Just a peck on the cheek – what d'you think, Karin?'

Karin shrugged. 'Fine with me – if we can do it right now? Because I finish at five.'

'Of course – and we should do in front of the whiteboard, right? Then we'll have the total there in the picture.' As an afterthought, almost, he turned to me. 'That okay?'

For a moment, I hesitated. My reluctance was the same as I'd felt over *Give With A Kiss* in the first place: was this asking for trouble, given the last time I'd been snapped kissing a pretty girl? But I wanted to be involved; I wanted to help. And if Karin didn't mind getting closer, it was no hardship for me.

I glanced at the **£1,301,000!!** on the whiteboard.

It was only another picture.

'Sure,' I said.

In under a minute, the pic was posted. Straightaway people began to share it, tag it, like it. Instant approval: every response a thumbs-up, a burst of applause. I supposed I could see the appeal. Karin, gathering up her belongings, kept glancing back at the screen, checking progress. 'Hey, yeah!' she said. 'Look, I'm getting pretty famous!'

As she hitched her bag over her shoulder, I decided I was ready to leave too. 'Are you heading out?' I asked her. 'I'll come with you.'

But away from the screen, waiting for the lift, I wasn't sure what to talk about. I should thank her for showing me the ropes; I was opening my mouth when she spoke first.

'Does it help?' she said, eyes narrowed.

'Does it...?'

'I mean – out of something so awful – that you can make something that's good, like this.'

'It does,' I said, unthinking – a public response, one I'd give to an interviewer. But it wasn't quite true. *Does it help?* she'd asked – but I didn't need to be helped; not the way she meant. What I needed were reasons: for what had happened, for my altered life. What I needed was a story that accounted for it all. Trying to put it into simple words, I pointed back towards the whiteboard, the £1.3 million. 'It's like, that kid in the picture, the wee blonde boy. For him, everything's a risk – it's going to be tough, growing up. But this – okay, it's not curing cancer – but it really can help. You know? This is what it's about.'

With a ping, the lift arrived: I heard the doors tug open, but neither of us moved. Without fanfare, a middle-aged man was approaching the whiteboard. He checked the piece of paper he was carrying. Picked up an eraser, and wiped off yesterday's total. The babble of office noise dropped a notch, people nudging each other, turning to watch, as the man glanced down once more. He lifted a marker: changed his mind, chose another colour. Finally, in blue, he wrote, **£1,512,000!!** Then he stepped back. Studied the board. With a squeak of his pen, he added another exclamation mark.

Somebody whooped: someone else began to clap, triggering a wave of applause. The office throbbed with approval, louder than ever. As Karin summoned the lift once more, there was a general movement: people logging off, standing up, collecting jackets. This was the moment they'd waited for, before finishing up for the day. And it was on the tip of my tongue to suggest a celebration drink. Karin and me, a few of her colleagues: I had a feeling she would have said yes. Only, Jean was due on my doorstep, and I had to get back home.

With reluctance I put the thought aside: a pint with the team, at the end of a day of good and honest work.

Another time, perhaps.

Chapter 19

'Hey stranger!' I swung the door wide open. 'Come along in.'

'Hello, hello! Don't you look smart!' Jean paused on the threshold to wrap me in a hug. Her handbag slipped from her shoulder and swung between us like a pendulum. I'd expected her to be weighed down with cases and cameras.

'Where's your stuff, are you not staying here? Not trying out my sofa?'

'Och no, thanks, I would, but I'm booked in at this B&B in Victoria; I've left all my gear there. It's so seedy, it's fantastic, I love it. It's like stepping into the '50s. I always think I'm going to need a shilling for the meter.'

'Oh well, try my sofa anyway, it's dead comfy. Sit.' I waved towards the couch, but she stayed standing, gazing round. 'Or – shall I give you the tour? Got five seconds to spare?'

It wasn't much of an exaggeration. The flat was an executive apartment, and executives, apparently, were built on the small side. I whizzed her round the bedroom, we popped our heads into the bathroom, and before you could say *bijou* we were back in the lounge that was also the kitchen. The place was beginning to fill up, with CDs, DVDs, clothes – all newly bought. It's not like I was going crazy with the spending, but to choose a bundle of new album releases and hand over my card without a thought was such an unaccustomed pleasure. It was a kind of freedom for me.

'I suppose you don't know how long you'll be here,' Jean was saying, and I could tell all she saw was two small, thin-walled rooms: a white-and-beige box with cheap laminate floors and a building site outside the bedroom window, smack in the centre of unlovely Vauxhall.

'Look,' I said, and tilted my head back. Jean did likewise. We stared up at the ceiling. 'No stain.' I took three steps over to the window and made a show of caressing the radiator. 'Central heating, not that I've needed it but still... And...' – I took a few more steps, into the kitchenette – '*nobody leaves the butter out of the fridge*.'

She was laughing now. 'It's great, Cam. I mean, what more do you need? The last thing you want is to be rattling around somewhere.' She dropped her bag by the sofa. 'Oh, hey, though,' she said, 'this looks pretty special...'

Leaned up against the couch was my new guitar.

'Can I stroke it?'

'Go ahead.' It was my most extravagant purchase ever; even someone like Jean, who didn't play, could tell it was a beautiful instrument. I'd walked into a shop in Denmark Street and asked for the best acoustic they had in stock. Ridiculous: all I played on it was simple stuff, listening over and over to my favourite songs till I'd figured out the chords. But the spruce and rosewood gave it a bright, warm tone; my hand around its neck felt smooth, and my strumming sounded a hundred times more accomplished.

'Gorgeous,' said Jean. 'You'll have to give us a tune later. Here, I must just use your loo...'

'Sure. Don't get lost.' I switched on the iPod dock, pressed play – thin walls: you could hear a spider land in the bath, let alone your cousin having a pee – and busied myself with corkscrew and glasses, opening the good white wine I'd bought not as a three-for-two but in a case of *two dozen*. This was me joining the adult world.

Jean re-emerged, running her hands through her hair. She was sporting a very Berlin cut, short and stark. It didn't suit her, but even the brutal fringe couldn't harden the pink-and-white softness of her face, the wide-open smile that crinkled her eyes. 'That's better,' she said. 'Talking of butter–' (Had we been? I jumped backwards through our conversation; ah yes, butter...) 'Have you spoken to my brother lately?'

'Uh, not for a while.' Roddy hadn't been in touch since I left Glasgow. From the overly casual way she'd asked, I was pretty sure Jean knew that already. 'He's busy, I'm busy, you know how it is. Wine?'

'Actually, I'm really thirsty, could I maybe get a glass of water?'

'Strange choice, but sure.' Another step took me to the sink. 'Delicious London tapwater coming your way.'

She sipped, pulled a face. 'Mmm. Isn't it. Thanks. So: bit of a change... It's all been happening since I saw you last, eh? I couldn't believe it when Mum told me.'

For a moment, I wasn't sure what she meant; what, exactly, she couldn't believe. But she meant Eve, of course, what had happened to Eve. I could tell by the way her face had drooped, gone all sorrowful.

'What a tangle. For you to be there, when it happened. Getting caught up in all this. It's just...' She shook her head. 'Anyway though – how're you managing?'

Jean would have made a great interviewer. She had the knack of drawing out what you'd rather keep inside, of gently disembowelling you with careful, concerned questions. I could sense her lining those questions up, could guess how she'd work away at my practiced answers until she cracked them open. She was a whole new audience, and I didn't know what kind of truth to tell her. So I closed her down before she could start. 'I'm managing,' I said. 'So listen, it's great to see you: how's everything, how's Dieter?'

She blinked at the sudden change of subject: went along with it. 'Yeah, Dieter's good, he's great. Everything's going fine.'

'And the job? Tell me again, what's it about?'

'Okay, have you heard of Urban Arboretum? They campaign for trees in cities.'

'Right, right. Good.' Jean had slowly and surely built her reputation as a nature photographer: close-ups of flowers so sharp you could count the grains of pollen on their stamens, ferns unrolling their lizardy heads, that sort of thing. 'You'd think that would be an easy sell – who doesn't like trees?'

'I guess. So anyway, they're doing these posters – huge posters, to go on tube platforms. It'll be great – don't you think? Imagine, down in the hot, dark, stinky tunnels, and you're staring at an enormous tree. Sun in its leaves. Beautiful.'

You could tell she was seeing it. Leaves dancing behind her eyes. Her words brought something else to mind.

'Hey. You might know this. What would be a *tree of doors*?'

Her forehead creased beneath her unforgiving fringe. 'A tree of doors? Where's that from, then?'

I hesitated, then, 'Hang on, I'll show you.'

The box was under my bed; I fetched it out, carried it through. 'This was Eve's. It's all stuff from when she was a wee girl; her cousin gave it to me.' Jean's face filled with more questions I didn't want to answer. 'I know,' I said, 'I'm not sure why. But anyway.' I took out the folded sheets of paper with the treasure-hunt workings, gave them to Jean. 'You can guess what these are.'

She read them through, one by one, handling them like they could crumble into dust. 'Oh my God,' she said softly. 'Jasmine?' She looked as if she might cry: her cheeks and the tip of her nose were bright pink.

'But we never did this hunt,' I said. 'At least, I don't think so. I don't remember any of the clues.'

Jean shook her head. 'No. Me neither. But then – didn't you and Roddy go up that last summer, without me and Duncs?'

'We were going to. It was like, two days before we were meant to go that Jasmine died. So I think, she made up all these clues, and then – we never played it.'

'*Tree of doors.*' Jean was holding the second clue. 'My guess would be an oak. You know different trees mean different things,

146

like rowans are lucky and all that? So, oaks are meant to be a doorway between worlds. In Celtic mythology, it's like a portal, into the spirit world. Or the underworld. Actually, the Celtic word for oak was *duar*, or *duir*, or something like that – and that's meant to be where our word "door" comes from.' Carefully, she handed me back the clues. 'Bit hard though, that one, if you're not into trees and stuff. I don't know how she'd have expected you to guess.'

'Wow. Thanks. You certainly know your trees.'

'A gateway to the underworld,' Jean said. 'And Jasmine and Eve both gone through...'

The front door buzzer startled us both.

'That'll be Eilidh.'

I stood well back from the whirl of enthusiasm as the girls greeted each other.

'Look at you!' squeaked Jean. 'New hair!'

'At last, someone's noticed! Thank you.' Eilidh gave me a pitying look, as she accepted the wine I'd poured for her.

'What, is it shorter?' I shrugged. 'Whatever. It's nice. It's always nice.'

Eilidh ignored this. 'And you look incredibly stylish as always. That's Jean, not you,' she clarified.

'What, I'm not stylish?' I took a step back so she could see the whole impression. 'Genuinely: tell me.'

She took her time, running her gaze from my face to my shoes, back up again. 'You're smart enough,' she said. 'Aye, you'll do. It's nice of you to make an effort for us.'

'Well, I was going to say... What do you want to do tonight?'

'I thought just get some food, have a few drinks?'

Jean nodded agreement.

'Cos if you wanted ... there's this function I've got an invite to – one of Amanda's other clients is opening some new club, over in Shoreditch. I've got a plus one, but I'm sure I could bring two.'

Eilidh and Jean swapped lukewarm looks.

'We could eat first,' I said. 'It's not till late. But I can ditch it, if you don't fancy it, I mean it's not like I have to be there.'

'Late, how late?' said Eilidh. 'Some of us have to work, remember.'

Jean glanced down at herself. 'I'm not sure I'm dressed for a private function. Or up for a big night, to be honest.'

'And I'm definitely not dressed for anything that involves being photographed and possibly appearing in next week's gossip mags – which is what I suspect might happen...?'

I held up my hands. 'Okay, no worries. We'll skip it. Food and a few drinks. That's it.'

'Speaking of drinks, and early nights...' Eilidh was staring at Jean.

'What?' I said. I glanced from one to the other. 'What am I missing here?'

Eilidh's stare didn't waver, but she was smiling too. 'Jean? Nothing you want to share with the group?'

Jean was beaming like she'd just won a prize and was trying to be modest about it. 'Erm. Me and Dieter are kind of ... having a baby.'

'Ah!' I said, realisation arriving somewhat after the fact. 'The water!'

'The water,' Jean agreed.

'Wow, that's brilliant! Congratulations!' I sneaked a look at her belly, which seemed perfectly normal to me. 'So ... when's it, when are you...?'

'February: my due date's actually Valentine's Day!'

'So romantic,' said Eilidh, straight-faced. I couldn't tell if she was being serious.

'You knew?' I asked her.

'Yup.'

I turned back to Jean. 'And who else knows? Just so I don't say something I shouldn't.'

'Just Mum and Dad, and Roddy.'

'God: Roddy's going to be an uncle. Ha! You're going to be a mum!'

'That is how it works.'

'And what will I be? Second cousin, something like that?'

'Um, no, I think you'll be once removed?' She put an arm around Eilidh. 'And you'll be an honorary auntie.'

'Of course,' said Eilidh. 'So – how are you feeling?'

'Oh, tired. Sick. But no, it's not too bad. It was worse earlier on. I just can't really manage a late one. But your thing, Cam,' – Jean put a hand on my arm – 'your opening: don't let us stop you. You could go along later. I'm sure Eilidh will be wanting an early-ish night, too.'

I looked at Eilidh. She shrugged. 'Sure.'

'I'll just – I'll maybe take the invite with me,' I said. 'Just in case. Won't be a sec; talk amongst yourselves...'

I darted through to the bedroom, guessing I'd left it somewhere in the pile of papers that was accumulating on the chest of drawers. From next door, the girls' voices rose and fell, fast and low, with just the odd phrase breaking through the music.

'But is he alright?' said Jean, and I stopped mid-search, a bundle of papers in my hand.

'Yeah, I think he...'

Their voices sank to murmurs, then rose again.

'But from what Roddy said, that's not how it was...'

'I know, I know.'

'So then why...'

More murmurs; and a silence. Then, clearly, I heard Jean say, 'Is he *really* alright, do you think?'

I pulled a face; abandoned my paper pile. 'Can't find it,' I called as I rejoined the girls. They turned to me, their faces bright, and I made sure to mirror their smiles. 'Never mind. Doesn't matter.'

A last look round before we left: I saw the contents of Eve's box were still spread across the floor. 'Just let me put all this away,' I said, 'then I'm ready.' I kneeled to gather her bits and pieces, and Eilidh crouched beside me.

'Is that Jasmine's clues? Have you two been treasure-hunting?'

'I was just asking Jean about something.'

'*Tree of doors*,' Jean offered. 'We think it must be an oak.'

'What about the others?' Eilidh asked me. 'Have you figured out anything else?'

'I've not really looked at them.'

'But you've got the starting place, at Glenelg. And now you've got an oak tree. Don't you want to guess what comes next?'

I shrugged. 'Not really. Not especially.' I scanned the first of Jasmine's pages. 'The next clue would be ... okay, this one: *A pirate sleeps / Beneath the yew.*'

'A pirate... Something to do with the sea, boats...'

'Except the yew,' said Jean. 'That must be significant.'

'How's that?' I asked.

'Well, they won't grow by the shore, I don't think. And also, yew is a tree of death.'

'Oh. Good. Nice and upbeat. We were what, twelve? Thirteen?'

'But also transformation, rebirth. Because they're poisonous, but they live forever: thousands of years. You know there's one near us at home that's meant to be five thousand years old – the oldest living thing in the whole of Europe?'

'I did not know that.' I mimed tapping on Jean's forehead. 'Enquire within upon everything.' But I felt, suddenly, that I didn't want to pick through the clues for the guessable bits. I wanted to keep them to myself: an echo of how we'd hunted for real, co-operating only so far. At the start – and again if we all got stuck – we'd share our suggestions, but the moment you picked up the scent you'd be racing off on your own. I put the lid back on the box. Stood up. 'Right then, ladies: are we ready to go?'

Eilidh knocked back her wine; Jean grabbed her bag. It was just as we were heading out the door that I caught sight of my invitation, peeking out from a heap of mail. It fitted neatly inside my Armani suit jacket. Like it was made to measure. Smart enough; I would do.

Chapter 20

When I made it to Amanda's, late next morning, she was on the phone. She gestured for me to come in anyway, and I dropped into the empty chair; rubbed the back of my neck to ease the ache of too much drink.

The Gately Agency was a one-woman show: a phone, a laptop, two chairs and a desk in a Clerkenwell warehouse that had been partitioned to house scores of small businesses. There was some chain of links between Amanda Gately and Hilary from AnAlert, which I hadn't quite followed – but it meant that when I'd first dialled her number, without the faintest idea of what I was meant to say, Amanda was expecting my call, and just about all I needed to do was tell her my name.

I signed up with Amanda because it was simple. That she was just about bearable was an added bonus. And so far she'd proved more efficient than I'd ever have guessed from her office. Her desk was a junkyard of newspapers, magazines and Starbucks cups. If I craned my neck, I could read an upside-down headline about some celebrity divorce. SPLIT! it said. As she talked on, I gazed round at the now-familiar wall display: a gallery of past and present clients, in photos and framed cuttings. From what she said, Amanda had worked in every sector you could test her on, and the variety of has-beens and also-rans arrayed on her wall seemed to bear her out. The first time I'd sat in this chair, I'd remarked on an old NME cover featuring a band called Cask. Three lads from Cambridge, they'd been briefly successful around the time I was a student. I had seen them once, in a sweatbox in Camden, support-ing the band I'd really come to see. Amanda seemed delighted by this point of contact: now she mentioned them practically every time I saw her, reminiscing or passing on snippets of current news as though we were all mutual friends with a shared past.

If she'd only known it, there was different cutting on her wall that established a real link between us. A double-page feature from a long-defunct music mag: an interview with a folktronica artist I'd met once – at the Oxfordshire festival where Amit and I had grabbed onto the tail-end of the bill. I hadn't heard her men-tioned in years, this artist; would have been mildly, genuinely, interested to know what she'd done with her life since her moment in that dim spotlight. But that would have meant coming clean to Amanda. Confessing that yes, I was in a band, and no you wouldn't have heard of us. No, we didn't make it, didn't come close. Played a handful of gigs to a handful of people who didn't know who we were, and cared less, and then – gave up. *I* gave up. Coming clean would have meant admitting to the existence of a third cutting: one I'd destroyed long ago, but which nevertheless existed forever on the internet, and forever, word for awful word, in every cell of me; the only known review of *Jodrell Bank*, the eponymous EP we'd recorded in Amit's bedroom, then burned onto discs, care-fully packaged with hand-drawn artwork, and posted out to the music press; the review that warned readers we sounded *like the bastard sons of Orbital and Joni Mitchell, and if that sounds like a compliment it's really, really not*, that told them our EP *would be excellent evidence for the prosecution of formless digital twattery,* except that *the guitar/vocals are, if anything, even more hateful*; the review that had a single redeeming feature, in that the author was so busy burying us he omitted to spell my name right.

No. What I wanted Amanda to see was potential – not failure. So I kept my mouth shut, and when she told me another anecdote about the pouting boy singer from Cask, I nodded and smiled along.

'Speak later... Campbell, how's things?' Amanda was talking to me before the receiver hit the cradle. She studied me through pale eyes fringed with blackened lashes, framed in turn by angular plastic specs. I found it hard to say how old she was: she could have been my age, or into her forties. I thought she probably did have a soul, somewhere, hidden away under the paint and the efficiency. 'I gather you did eventually make it to the opening last night?'

I leaned forward. 'What, am I in the paper?'

'No, darling: your eyes look like someone's punched you, and you reek of booze.' She smiled blandly. 'That was a nice slot the other day, the *Good Health* one. We're pleased with that.'

'We are? Good, that's good.' At first, her habit of using the word *we* instead of *I* had confused me. I'd thought, after all, there must be more than one of her. Then I'd wondered if it was a self-important thing, a royal we. Now, I thought I had it figured out: the *we* was *us* – me and her. She'd review an appearance or an interview and let me know when I should be pleased, as well as when I shouldn't.

'Erm. Did I get paid for it?' I asked.

'No fee. But it's raising your profile. Good audience for you: housewives, thirties to sixties.'

'Sure... And – anything coming up where there *is* a fee?' Getting paid: it wasn't a worry, as such, not with tens of thousands stashed in the bank, but it did seem that money was ages coming in, and every week I was paying out a painful sum for my flat.

Amanda consulted her laptop. 'To be honest, Campbell – the paid gigs are tailing off, a bit. But I'm working on getting some bits and pieces off the back of the *Kiss* campaign.' She looked up. 'Now that really has paid off, in terms of growing your fan base – your social media stats are rocketing. A genuinely smart move.'

She'd got it the wrong way round – as if the purpose of the campaign was to build my stats, when it was the purpose of my stats to build the campaign – but before I could gather my thoughts to object, she'd pressed right on.

'But if we're talking cash... Let's see. There should be payment coming in for the *Living* spread, any day now.'

'They still haven't stumped up? That was weeks ago.'

'They're notoriously slow – but trust me, as soon as I get it, you get it.'

'And that's what, three grand?'

'Yup. So you'll see ... just over two.'

'Oh, so that's – with your twenty per cent. But hang on, that should still be–'

'And the ten to AnAlert.'

'Right. Course.'

'And remember, that hasn't been taxed; so you'll keep at least a third of it aside. But your accountant will sort that out for you.'

My theoretical accountant would doubtless have understood the figures – but who knows how many thousands they'd have charged me for the pleasure? I nodded, changed the subject. 'So. Anything else on the horizon?'

She looked like she was mulling something over. She sucked in her cheeks, shadowing the faint orange smears that showed where her cheekbones should be. 'I want you to know,' she said, 'that this isn't coming from me. It's not my idea. But: there is a particular publication who've said they could use a picture of you at Eve's memorial.' She blinked, and blinked again like she was fending off my stare. 'As I say: not my idea. But I agreed to run it past you.'

'Oh come on, that's a bit grim.' The thing was, I could see why they wanted it. I could almost see the photo they had in mind: me wearing the expression you see on the covers of women's weeklies, next to unbearable captions like, *My husband was killed the day my daughter was born* – an expression that's meant to be tragic, but manages against all the odds to seem merely constipated. The shot would be taken from a low angle, would show me under a heavy sky, standing in front of – of what?

'We don't even know where her memorial is.'

It was Amanda's turn to stare, and mine to blink. 'West London Crem,' she said, as if to an infant. 'Kensal Green.'

Well, of course Amanda would know; she'd made it her business to find out.

'I mean, we don't want people to know where. Anyone to know. I can't believe anyone would suggest that.' I felt I'd been caught out. 'How would that be for her family? Imagine, if it became some kind of shrine for weirdos...'

'Fine, fine. It's a definite no. I thought it would be. But...' She sighed. 'Campaign stuff aside, that does leave things fairly empty. We need to think about how we're going to move the story forward...'

I was half-listening, if that. Did Eve have a headstone? A little cubby in the crematorium wall with a plaque alongside, like my grandparents? I couldn't ask Amanda, though she'd probably have the answer; I ought to have known. And I should have been to visit. It hadn't even occurred to me, and I was surprised how guilty I felt. Like forgetting someone's birthday; someone who mattered.

'At some point,' Amanda was saying, 'we'll probably want to pair you up.'

'Sorry – pair me up?'

'With someone else who needs a push. Get you into the gossip mags. You know: you're spotted out together, we get them to take some pics ... then you'll split up, get back together again, etcetera. But Eve is still what people want to know about, and we don't want to screw that.' A thought stopped her. 'You aren't seeing anyone, by the way?'

'No–'

'Good. Don't.'

'Listen, I don't think I want to go out with someone just for the magazines.'

'It's not real, Campbell. Well, I mean, it could be. Doesn't have to be. But anyway, that's down the line. Right now, what we should be talking about is ... *Green Man*.'

Green Man: the last film Eve completed before she died. A climate change action movie, with Eve in a small supporting role: it was premiering next week in Leicester Square.

'Fine,' I said. 'Good. Talk away.'

Under the make-up, Amanda's face shone with satisfaction. 'We're on the list.'

'For...?'

'Hire yourself a tux, Campbell.' She actually winked. 'The red carpet beckons.'

Chapter 21

All the next week I woke early. 5am would find me lying motion-less, trying to kid my body I might still return to sleep, while my brain danced over the surface of upcoming appointments: the when and where I needed to be so people could take the same photos, ask the same questions over and over again. Deeper, somewhere in my chest, lurked the premiere, occasionally sur-facing – a fin slicing into conscious thought – and making me fizz with nerves.

There was a trick that helped a bit: it couldn't lull me back to unconsciousness, but it calmed me, stilled the fizzing and the dancing. I imagined myself back in Glenelg, and instead of counting sheep I solved treasure-hunt clues. Or, I tried to solve them, from a distance of more than fifteen years and six hundred miles. I'd worked out the first clue, and I had a good idea what the second clue meant, thanks to Jean, but my sense of where things were in relation to each other – the pub, the beach, a patch of grass and trees – was muddled and vague.

I remembered in snapshots, and in feelings, more than any-thing. So the pub was tables in the sun, was Coke and crisps; was a dark inside, where we were allowed only to use the toilets, where we'd sneak round to the heart of the place. Was a high bar, and men with enormous drinks and deep, loud voices, and laughter that shook the floor. Forgetting the clues, I'd get lost in imagining – and after an hour of this kind of wakefulness I'd give in, get up, start my day.

I established a routine: a walk down the river, as far as the South Bank; a takeaway coffee and something to eat, on a bench where I could watch the flow of traffic into the city centre. Trains came every minute or so, pulling over Blackfriars Bridge. Up on Waterloo Bridge, a steady stream of buses ferried workers across the water, and railings cut across the pedestrians striding towards their offices – towards days laid out, ready-filled. I'd told Jean I was busy, my excuse for not speaking to Roddy, but it wasn't true, not really. As Amanda had observed, I had acres of idle time; and what work I had – if you called it work – couldn't be easier: be punctual, and don't be difficult.

For days, I'd been just about to phone my cousin. Now I sat on my bench, and watched the river, and occasionally I reached into my pocket, toyed with my mobile. I let my eyes lose focus, feeling the weight of my week of insomnia. But it was cool this morning, refreshingly so; the sky hazed with cloud, the river grey as the Clyde. This was something I had never done in Glasgow: sat by the water – though there were places you could, now, land newly developed, attractions and riverside walks. But for me, the Clyde was just something you passed over, or under, on your way into town. Above me, the traffic flowed south to north; the Thames tugged from west to east, and in my imagination the Clyde was tugging differently, east to west. And somewhere the bright thread of the Moulin burn danced and fell and tumbled as well, a clear, peaty brown.

I swallowed my last cold mouthful of coffee, stopped making excuses, and pulled out my phone.

I felt weirdly nervous. I almost hoped Roddy wouldn't pick up, that I could leave an upbeat message as if everything was fine between us, and leave the ball in his court. But on the fourth ring, he answered.

'Hi,' I said, 'how's things? You busy?'

He took his time replying. 'Aye, pretty busy; plenty to do, you know.'

'Preparing to head off, packing and stuff?'

'Yeah, all of that. You?'

'Yeah, the same, just – busy.' *Listen: you doubted me, but I was right – right to come down here, to take the chance, to use it for something worthwhile.* But I didn't say that. Instead: 'You'll maybe have seen it, all the fundraising stuff?' I thought he might say, *Well done*, however grudgingly.

'Uh-huh,' he said – and I didn't press it.

'Although, not today. I've taken a day off.'

'Aye?'

'I'm down by the river, having breakfast,' – my half-muffin sat in its bag on my lap, empty cup on the bench at my side – 'sun's out...' Almost: give it half an hour for the haze to burn off, and it would be another beautiful day.

'Sounds good.'

In person, I'd have known where we stood. Those comedy expressions he couldn't control, wasn't even aware of, would show just what he was thinking. But on the phone, I couldn't tell. He might be distracted, or disapproving; still scunnered with me, or just busy, like he'd said. His voice sounded far away, for all its familiarity, and I wondered if what I wanted was for the phone to erase time as well as distance.

'So anyway,' I said, 'I saw Jean the other night.'

'Oh aye?'

'Yeah: congratulations!'

'Oh, right ... you know it's not me having a baby?'

'Yeah, but – you're going to be an uncle, that's pretty exciting.'

'Course, aye, it's exciting.' I could almost hear him shrug. 'Good news.'

'Yeah, brilliant news.' There was a moment of emptiness. A gull coasted low, on the scrounge; I tossed the remains of my muffin onto the ground, and it swooped to snatch it up. 'I do think you've gone over the top though.'

'What, how d'you mean?'

'Well, I know you'll be wanting to get out of your babysitting duties, but moving four thousand miles away is just ... excessive.'

Roddy gave a yelp of laughter; I could hear his surprise. 'If it gets me out of changing nappies: well worth it.'

I felt easier now I'd made him laugh. 'Well – guess I'd better let you get back to your packing.'

'Sure. Enjoy your day off.' Then, just as I was cutting us off, he said, 'Thanks for phoning.'

'Yeah. Yeah, no worries.'

Thanks for phoning. It sounded to me like a line you'd receive along with bad news, but perhaps it was a normal, friendly thing to say. Perhaps he was practising to be an American – have a nice day, a great day, a fabulous day. I dropped my phone back into my pocket, gathered up my rubbish. The sun was out now, just like I'd told him. It was going to be hot again.

I was nearly back at the flat when my pocket buzzed an alert. A text, from Roddy. *Forgot to say, having drinks for my leaving. Moulin Inn, next Sat. See you there?*

As I climbed the stairs I thought of a trip home: of everyone being there. Duncs would be back. Maybe Magnus and Paolo. Eilidh, for sure.

Sounds good, I typed. *See you there.* Thought for a moment then, smiling, added, *No flatmate = no need for headphones. Free to good home.*

Chapter 22

Kensal Green. The day of the premiere seemed like the right time to visit Eve.

A funeral was ending as I arrived. Some of the party were smiling, even laughing, as they headed for their cars; jackets slung over their arms, shades guarding against sun instead of cameras. I guessed the deceased had been the right age for dying. Good innings, and all that; and a far better day for it than we'd had. I slipped my own sunglasses on, consulted the scrap of paper that was my map to Eve's memorial. I'd called ahead for directions. I hadn't seen much of the cemetery at Eve's funeral, but I'd had the sense of it stretching in all directions: a green and silent city of the dead, where I'd be well and truly lost if I didn't know where to look. The man on the phone had given me what sounded like a postal address, complete with street name and plot number: to me it seemed as cryptic as Jasmine's treasure hunt clues. He hadn't hesitated, hadn't asked me to wait while he fetched the information, and I'd wondered how many times he'd answered this same question. Perhaps I wouldn't need the address he gave me; the memorial might be signposted by a mass of grieving fans.

Keeping my distance from the mourners, I set off in what I thought was the right direction. I walked through fields of pale stone that shone in the sun, past mossed, weathered crosses that sank into green, subsiding softly into leaves and rough grass. The path I was following turned, split, crossed with other paths, forcing me to wander. I struggled to keep myself pointed east. Somewhere beyond the cemetery walls a gasometer rose, criss-crossing the sky: like a trellis, giving the illusion of support to a tangle of trees.

I passed through an opening cut into a hedge, found myself in a garden filled with cherry trees. A man in work clothes was piling pruned branches into a wheelbarrow. He nodded when he saw me, straightened up as though to signal his readiness to be interrupted. Then he pointed a gloved hand at something.

'Look. Moorhen.'

It took me a while to spot it: dowdy brown, camouflaged against the dirt it was pecking at. 'Oh yeah,' I said. 'I see it.'

'She's always here, that one, always about. Lovely bird.'

Above our heads, I realised, the trees were squealing with birds, their branches bouncing and swaying.

'What kind are they?' I asked, gazing up.

'Parakeets, those ones.'

'They live here – wild?'

'Yeah. Lots of places that have got them, round here, from when people had 'em as pets.' He glanced at me. 'And they escaped, like, or people just…' He opened his hand, and an imaginary bird flew free.

'Amazing.' For a minute I stood and admired the riotous parakeets, their lemon-and-lime flashing undersides. Then I held out my map. 'Do you know, am I going in the right direction?'

He peered at the scribbled address. 'Yeah, more or less. Straight across, out there,' – he pointed towards an opening that echoed the one I'd come through – 'and take a left, and you'll get there. Look, she's showing you the way!'

Sure enough, the moorhen was picking its way along the path, out through the hedge. I followed the bird, turned left as directed and was suddenly in a newer part of the cemetery. Here the headstones were packed together – more urns, and fewer coffins. Softened stone gave way to sharp-edged granite, black glossy hearts heaped with plastic flowers. The names seemed to come from everywhere. Some looked Eastern European, or African or Arabic; some were spelled in unfamiliar alphabets. Plenty of the headstones had pictures printed on them, brass-framed photos of the deceased. A few of the photos were so bad it was almost funny. Funny, and sad – that these were the best snaps the families could come up with.

A woman trundled past with a pushchair, and I nodded a greeting. I should be near, now, if I'd read the map right. I began to search for markers nestled in the grass, for numbers that corresponded with those I'd been given. Slightly off the main path, the man had said: I walked back a row, and back again, scrambling over tussocky ground and stamping down nettles. I was looking for a bench – and there, I spotted one, and made my way towards it. But the wood was old and weathered; the shrub it faced was thick-stemmed, as tall as me, and weighted with fat roses. This had to be wrong. I was turning away when the plaque on the bench flashed me to a stop: sun on brass, shining and new.

JASMINE SADLER
DEARLY LOVED

EVE SADLER
LOVED BY MANY

A butterfly danced past at eye level. I could hear bees at work nearby. I hesitated, then sat down on the little bench.

Eve felt crowded in here, bumped up against so many other headstones and memorials. But it was peaceful; and at least it wasn't lonely. The sun dripped through the leaves, and pooled at my feet. I cast about for the sadness I must surely be feeling, and found in myself a still, gentle sorrow that was almost pleasurable. I prodded deeper, searching for something more raw. I knew I could give myself the horrors thinking of her damp lips and her scarlet eyes, could freak myself out on demand, that way. But that wasn't what I was after. I was hoping for something profound – something that fitted the story of Eve and me.

It was all at one remove: like when Eilidh's dad died and I was sorry for her and for Magnus, and hardly at all for myself.

At the foot of the rosebush, people had left tokens of

remembrance. Bouquets of flowers. Coloured jars with burned-out candles. A cut-tin lantern. They looked junky. Abandoned. I bent down, straightened one of the jars, pushing its base deeper into the green glass chippings. Cleared away the deadest of the flowers.

'Sorry I didn't bring you any. You probably would expect I'd forget.' My voice sounded self-conscious, and not like my own. 'I'll come back,' I said, not sure whether I would.

Loved by many, I thought as I walked away. I liked that, liked the understatement. It made me think of Mariella: her brisk kindness, her extended hand. Her undone face. Guilt stirred in my stomach. By now she'd have a dartboard covered with my press cuttings. I regained the path, my foot just missing a family of mushrooms sprouting along the edge. I was so focused on the ground that I nearly collided with a runner, shooting past in shorts and vest. I thought maybe he gasped an apology, but he was moving too fast for me to be sure. Strange place to choose for a run: disrespectful, almost. These paths were meant for a slow pace, a stroll that acknowledged the weight of vanished lives. Not for hammering feet, disturbing the ashes and bones; for rude breath and all of that hot life rising in waves. I turned to stare, as though he might sense my disapproval fired at his back, and as he dwindled into the distance I saw someone else move through the trees, in my direction. Fair, longish hair, a dark denim jacket. A man: carrying flowers, making his way across the grass, past rows and rows of headstones towards Eve's memorial.

He had been here before, that was clear. I watched as he reached the bench: saw him crouch, lay the flowers down by the rose; stay crouched. A fan: imagining himself connected to her, though they had never met. Imagining his pilgrimage made a difference.

He raised his head and turned to me, just as though he could hear. For a moment he stared – like he was a mirror, striking my thoughts right back at me. I raised a hand, and I might have been going to greet him, I'm not sure; but instead I ended by hiding my face, as I turned and walked away.

Chapter 23

Eilidh had agreed to meet me straight after school, for a shot of Dutch courage. Since I'd been in London, I hadn't been drinking all that much: vanity, partly, because I'd reached the age where a few pints the night before meant a puffed, sagging face next day, and that's not how I wanted to be seen by the world. And partly self-preservation: as with the walking, staying clear helped keep things together. But today it was medicinal.

'Looking sharp,' said Eilidh.

'Aye well, big night, got to make the effort.' I nodded, trying to look like it was nothing: fooling neither of us.

It was a perfect afternoon for outdoor drinking, and we were holed up instead in some rough old boozer on the Old Kent Road – preferring not to be seen together by pupils or paparazzi. The pickle-faced punters were far more interested in their pints than in the two of us tucked away in the corner. Their glances rolled across us, and back to the business of the bar. In a few hours, I'd be swapping the company of these dedicated drinkers for faces familiar from screens and magazines, everything smooth, bright, beautiful. I focused on the sandiness of Eilidh's hair, the promise she was of normality.

'D'you know who's going to be there?' she asked. 'Are we talking A-list?'

I reeled off some names, and she whistled through the gap in her front teeth – a trick I used to be wildly jealous of when we were kids. 'A-plus,' she said.

I swallowed a cool, flat gulp of heavy, then another, trying to quench my nerves.

'So did you go on to your function, the other night – your launch or whatever it was?'

'I did.'

'And was it fun?'

'It was standing around drinking loads of free booze, small-talking with a bunch of strangers. So, yeah. It was fun, I guess.'

'Mmm. Sorry I missed it.'

'You and Jean just head home, aye?'

Eilidh nodded. 'She was definitely needing her bed. So was I, mind you.'

I had wondered – briefly – if I should be offended that Eilidh had heard Jean's news before me, but concluded it wasn't favouritism: just a girl thing. 'When did she tell you?' I asked now.

'Couple of weeks ago. She'd have told you, if you ever bothered to phone.'

'Come on, I'm a guy. I don't need to be on the phone all the time to my pals, or my family.'

'Apparently not.'

I held her eye, challenging her. 'What's that meant to mean?'

'It means, when are you going to phone Roddy?'

I paused before answering, stretching out in a bath of smugness, and enjoying the unaccustomed warmth. 'I'll have you know I spoke to him only days ago.'

'Did you?' I couldn't blame her for being surprised. 'Sorry, then.'

'But thanks for the reminder. You'd make a good PA; I should pay you, really.'

'And?' she prodded.

I shrugged. 'And ... he's okay.'

'And *you* and him? Are you okay?'

'Aye. I think so, pretty much. He said about Saturday, drinks for his leaving. I presume you're going?'

166

'Yup. Why, want a lift?'

'Seriously. I should pay you.'

'Well...' Her face flashed into a smile. 'Feel free to buy the petrol.'

'Deal.'

We clinked half-empty glasses, and I took a drink; sneaked a look at my phone to check the time. Eilidh noticed, of course. 'I'm not keeping you?'

'Loads of time.' I wished it were true: that I had hours ahead of slow drinks and easy chat. Breathed, and chose not to think about the red of the waiting carpet.

'I wonder who'll be next to have a kid,' Eilidh was saying.

'My money's on Magnus and Paolo,' I said. 'It's funny, when she told us – told me – I thought: she's a bit young for that. But she's not, is she? Not at all.'

'So the rest of us should be getting on with it?'

'Jean's always wanted kids though; she's always been more grown up. It's an eldest thing. You and me and Roddy, we're the wild ones, the youngests.'

Eilidh laughed. 'If that's true, God help us. In fact, it couldn't be less true. I mean: out of me and Magnus...?'

I saw her point. 'Yeah, okay. I take it back. Well then, what about you, if you're so grown up? Do you want kids?'

'Dunno. Probably.' She pulled a face. 'Though the way I'm going, it'd have to be conceived through a mad, passionate affair with the internet.'

A mouthful of beer went down the wrong way, stinging my nose; she waited till I'd finished coughing and laughing, then, 'What about you?'

I shook my head. 'I don't think the internet can get me pregnant. Alright, alright, don't sigh at me! Yeah. I mean, I've not ever thought much about it, but – aye, I'd like to have kids one day. Eventually. Need someone to have them with first, of course.' The suggestion was obvious. 'Tell you what. In ten years' time – or five, maybe – if we're both still single and childless–'

'*Barren*,' she said, doomily.

'That's not – doesn't barren mean you *can't*? Oh, never mind: what I'm saying is, if we're both still *barren*, you can have my sperm.'

Eilidh's glass stopped halfway to her mouth. She looked like she might topple either way: laughter, or horror.

'What?' I said. 'It's a genuine offer. I'm good for it.'

'Euch. Campbell.'

My full name: I was in trouble. 'Plan B. We'll be each other's back-up.'

'Thanks,' she said. 'But fuck off.'

We were still joking, kind of. 'Come on,' I said. 'Everybody wins, what's the problem?'

Her eyes narrowed; I could see the teacher in her. 'I'll have you know, I'm nobody's back-up.' Her glass finally made it to her lips. She turned away slightly as she drank.

I picked up her mock-offence, and ran with it. 'Right, well. Be like that. But you'll be sorry. There's plenty women would jump at a generous offer like that. If you'd any sense, you'd be pinning me down, making me sign something.'

She said nothing: just looked at me, one eyebrow raised.

'So, don't be changing your mind. That was a one-time offer.'

There was a hint of a smile on her face, but it spoke more of endurance than amusement.

'I'm changing the subject now, yeah?' she said. 'So ... tell me: what's new in *Heat*world?'

*Heat*world was Eilidh's catch-all term for everything I'd been doing these last few weeks: every TV show, every magazine; even *Give With A Kiss* wasn't exempt. Sarcasm was her default setting, but I thought I heard an extra jagginess in her tone, a rougher edge than usual. Perhaps that's why I decided against telling her about that morning's trip to the cemetery. 'Same old, same old,' I said instead. 'What about you?'

'Me? What about me?' The edge was still there, and I wondered if somehow I had actually offended her. I kept a smile on my face, pretending not to notice.

'Come on, talk. How's work? How're the little angels?'

'Two days till the weekend. Seven working days till the holidays, if I make it that far.'

'Oh ... that bad?' 'Yesterday I was threatened with a pair of scissors and told to watch my back when I'm walking home on my own.'

'Fuck, I hope the kid's been expelled for that.'

'Yeah, only it wasn't a kid, it was her mother...'

As she talked, I was trying to pay attention. But it was all so negative: what she was saying, the way she was saying it. I didn't want to listen, to let it seep inside me.

Instead, I started to imagine what it would be like to step out of the car, to stand on that red carpet. There would be shouting, an artillery of flashes; I'd be prepared though, and it wouldn't faze me. I wondered, should I smile for the cameras, or look serious? I tried a combination, kind of solemn but warm, to see how it felt.

'What's funny about that?' Eilidh sounded indignant.

'No, sorry, nothing.'

'I'm serious. If all those celebs can do it...'

'Sure, sure.' I had no idea what she was talking about.

'And it's not like I'm not qualified; I'm more qualified than they are.'

I nodded.

'So, what do you think?'

It was too late to admit I hadn't been listening. 'It's not about what anyone else thinks, is it?'

That seemed to do the job. 'No, you're right. It's up to me.' She finished her drink. 'Got time for another, or...?'

I was itching and squirming in my seat, trying to kid myself that the beginnings of panic were really excitement. My palms were damp: I rubbed them dry on the threadbare fabric of the bench. 'Actually ... I'd better get home, start getting ready.'

On the pavement outside, she stood with her hands in her pockets. 'Good luck then. Knock 'em dead.' She scrunched up her face. 'I mean...'

I was smiling, shaking my head. 'S'alright. Thanks for the drink.'

I watched her stride away, heading for the bus stop: bag slung across her body, bouncing at her hip. Then I started to walk in the opposite direction, eyes peeled for a cab.

When you know you're going to be photographed alongside bona fide film stars, it's amazing how obsessed you can get with the details of your hair. By the time the car arrived I'd spent the best part of an hour in the bathroom: waxing, spiking, ruffling it back to square one and starting all over again.

Black suit, rental limo. I'd been here before. This time, though, it wasn't a funeral. When we picked up Amanda from the office, she was slinky in purple, surprising me with a va-voom figure.

'Nice,' she said, as she slid across the back seat. A spiced, heavy scent wafted with her. 'Smart.' She reached out with both hands, tweaked at my hair. 'Better.'

'Whatever.' I made as if to muss it up again, but secretly I left it just as she'd arranged it. 'You look different...?'

'Lenses.'

Of course. The plastic specs were gone. She looked older – loose skin pillowed under her eyes. Older, but less fearsome.

She'd talked me through it already, at length, and now she started again. I didn't mind. It was better than sitting in silence, than having to actually think. I was deep-deep-breathing: even so, my brain had gone clear and gelid. All I could do was pretend to listen, and watch the streets move far too fast. In between issuing instructions, Amanda was on her phone. Just setting things up, she said. I nodded, with no real idea of what she was talking about, and soon – too soon – we were there.

The driver turned into a side-street and stopped. Engine running, we sat behind a black Merc that matched our own. What were we waiting for? Then the car in front pulled away, and a guy in a fluoro jacket appeared at our driver's window. The men exchanged a few words; the security guy made a mark on his clipboard. Stepped back. We were through.

Up ahead of our crawling limo, the action was underway. A man's voice, deep and distorted, somehow familiar: 'She's one of our fastest-rising stars, a genuine home-grown talent, let's turn the volume up and give her a warm welcome...' Like the caller at the carnies that used to pitch up in the big field back home. Strapped-in, waiting, I had that same nausea as when I was about to be lifted in a fairground ride, swung upside down, round and round, every which way.

We were reaching the head of the queue.

'Ready?' Amanda's voice was distant.

I unclicked my seatbelt.

We emerged to a dazzle of floodlit daylight. I felt myself melt in the glare, I had to sit down or, God, I felt my guts loosening– Hold it. Hold it together. Amanda: I had to keep her close. Amanda knew what to do, where to go. Which way to face. Now her hand clamped my arm, steered me towards the barrier. To the bodies pressed against it, the mass of fans; shoving, reaching, shrieking, with eyes and mouths stretched wide.

'Walk slow.' My arm was freed. 'Give them a good look.' We were in a stream now, following the flow, of black-suited men, of tight shiny women, of hair and skin like honey. All walking slow, being seen, on a carpet that was not red but green: why? Why was it green? Ahead of me a man I recognised was clutching the wrist of a woman I didn't, raising a hand to the fans who were calling his name.

'I love you!'

'You're gorgeous!'

'Over here!'

He paused near the barriers, and the crowd erupted, a Mexican wave of phones.

No-one was calling for me.

My hands tried to hide in my pockets, but I was scared of looking scared. Tried one hand pocketed. Better. Bolder. And suddenly Mr Gorgeous was gone, beckoned by his handler towards someone with a microphone, and it was me leading the field, winging it on a pitch where there were no rules of play, or everyone knew them but me, and at the same time the voice of God came down from the sky saying, 'Here's Campbell Johnstone, close friend of Eve Sadler, and of course this is Sadler's final appearance on film so a sad day for Campbell, no doubt.'

My name, picked up by the crowd. Scattered voices, calling, *Campbell! Campbell!* And one, louder: 'Campbell, sign this for me!' A woman stretched over the barrier, paper waving. A flyer for *Green Man*. I took it, and the pen she offered; with nothing to lean on, scrawled an approximation of my name. Speak. Say something. 'You'll be wanting some more famous names than mine,' I managed. She blushed, squeaked a thank-you.

'Move on,' Amanda murmured, behind me still; and I moved on, paced along the barrier, found myself face to face with a crying girl, red-cheeked, black-streaked. 'Campbell!' she sobbed. Crying at me. *Move on.* Someone was chanting: it was – oh God…

Give us a kiss! Cam, give us a kiss!

A chorus, a gang of women. I pulled back, panicked. 'Amanda…'

'It's fine,' she said. 'We're moving on…' And I followed her, faster now, towards a man with a mic at the junction of the carpet, and on to where fans were replaced by cameras and satellite dishes, by interviewers and banks of photographers.

A Japanese woman caught my eye. 'Campbell!' she called, and held out a furry microphone. TV ASAHI, said a sheet taped to the barrier. I stepped towards her. Amanda caught my arm.

'Not them; waste of time.'

She steered me away, brought me to a halt in front of a girl with a mic and a man with a camera. PRESS ASSOCIATION. Amanda spoke briefly to the girl, then, 'Okay, go,' she said.

'Campbell,' said the girl, 'what's it like to see Eve's last film?' She pushed the mic towards me.

What a dense fucking question; ask me when it's over and I'll tell you then. I took a breath. 'It's bittersweet,' I said. 'You know, she was such a talent.' As soon as I'd spoken I saw my words in quote marks on a printed page. They'd do. Amanda would say, *We're pleased with that.*

'What does it feel like to be here?'

'It's just – a real privilege to be here with so many talented people…' Damn. Repeating myself already. 'Everyone who worked with Eve, you know. She was so excited about this film, the, ah, environmental message. And I'm just…' I was running out. 'Just, it'll be emotional but – I'm really looking forward to seeing her up there on the screen.'

Amanda led me from one mic to another, so I could say it again and again. I swapped *talented* for *amazing*; ended up repeating that word instead. All the time, all around me, cameras flashed, and press called out like market traders, hawking their tabloids, stations, gossip rags to stars and D-listers alike, all hungry, endlessly hungry for promotion. And sated, too, and sickened – unless that fairground nausea was just in me.

We were close to the end now, nearly at the entrance to the Odeon. The facade was hung with *Green Man* banners, the stars twenty feet tall. No Eve; her role too small for banner status. How sad, that no-one was calling her name. That she wasn't here to strike that shop-window pose all the woman did, or to sign her name for the pressing crowd.

'Campbell, smile for us!'

Loved by many. Forgotten by more. I did as I was told: I smiled and smiled, all the way into the Odeon.

Inside, I let the grin fall from my face. Amanda turned to me.

Her cheeks were flushed; she looked ten years younger. In the cinema foyer, with its promo posters and its sweet, stale popcorn smell, her slinky purple looked like fancy dress.

'Well done,' she said. 'Great; really great.' She spoke each word with equal, heavy emphasis, to show she was genuinely pleased with my performance.

We followed the flow of people into the auditorium, passing under plastic coils of greenery. The foyer was faked up to look like a forest; belatedly, I understood the colour of the carpet.

In the stalls, we found our seats set out with freebies: publicity bumf, chocolates, bottles of water. I kept the water, gave the bumf and the chocolate (Peanut Butter Cups: nice touch, I thought) to Amanda, who slipped the lot into her Tardis bag. Onscreen they were showing a live feed from the square. I watched the parade of guests; watched, minutes later, as the same people walked into the auditorium, as though they'd stepped straight from the screen. Amanda kept up a running commentary, pointing out everyone she recognised, with no distinction between those in the square outside and flesh-and-blood arrivals. There were several big names, I noticed, who appeared on the carpet but never seemed to make it into the auditorium. When I asked Amanda, she was clearly amused. 'Out the back way,' she said, as though it were obvious. 'Once they've been seen, there's no reason for them to stay.'

It seemed like a cheat to me. But it didn't seem to bother the ordinary people who'd somehow secured their golden tickets – through prize draws, giveaways, well-connected friends. The air was filled with babble, and now and then a flash as some ordinary person held up a phone to capture a shade of fame – an image, blurred and distant, that would prove they'd been here; had breathed the same oxygen as people who weren't real but idols and gods. Who you might imagine touching, kissing, without any real sense of their physical solidity: the fact that her mouth would taste of cigarettes. That he'd be patched with sweat. That she would be bones in your arms.

'Ah. Eve's family.'

My head jerked up. On the live feed, or here, actually here?

'Look.' Amanda pointed at the screen. I saw a blonde head move through the background: Mariella. 'No. She's gone.'

I curled into myself; willed the lights to go down, though I knew that couldn't happen till the stars had arrived, the director spoken. From the corner of my eye, I could see Amanda too was watching the entrance.

When Mariella walked in, she was on the arm of a youngish man. Her partner, I presumed. I'd expected her uncle, Eve's father, to be with her. She paused to look round the auditorium, and I could feel the floodlights from outside stabbing down at me. Her gaze travelled slowly: towards me; past me. Her face registered nothing. The two of them made their way along the aisle, passing out of my field of vision. I might have been unspotted. I might have been seen and snubbed. It was impossible to know.

Amanda had turned to watch them find their seats. 'We might try and talk to them, after.'

I sank further down into mine. She might do anything she liked, strike up a nice wee chat with Eve's cousin if that's what she fancied doing. I had no intention of tagging along.

It was a loud, bad movie when it finally started. Eve was playing a reporter. Since she died I'd seen her, oh, a hundred times – in papers and magazines, but never onscreen. I'd seen her static, and here she was moving, talking: gazing with her huge dark eyes straight into mine. And because there was something cold about the screen, something absent, it wasn't a contradiction for her to be talking and moving and dead. She kept saying, in a standard American accent, *I need to find the truth about what happened here.* But she never did, because halfway through they killed her off with a car bomb. I was relieved she'd been exploded, and I didn't have to see her as a beautiful corpse.

Shortly after she'd gone I was so desperate for a slash that I pushed my way along the row and ran to the bathroom, and once I'd been, the last thing I wanted was to sneak back in for the ending. Instead, I went to find myself a drink.

The Circle Bar was crowded, and scattered with faces I knew but didn't know. I ordered a double whisky – Glenfiddich: London default, only decent one they had – and claimed a seat at the bar.

It didn't take long for someone to be curious enough to want to talk.

'You're Campbell Johnstone.'

She was blonde, solidly tanned, in a nightie-style dress; pretty, and so generic as to be sexless – except for her eyes, which were wide, icy blue.

'I am. And you are ... someone I should recognise. Sorry.' I took a drink, medicine burning my mouth in that bad-good way.

'Cody.'

It told me nothing. I smiled anyway. 'Want to sit?' I gestured to the seat beside me.

She hitched herself neatly onto the stool and waved at the barman.

'Let me.'

'Nah, we've got a tab ... mojito, please.' Something else to learn: there was always a tab. That explained the barman's surprise when I'd offered him cash. Cody's voice was London stage-school. I had no idea who the *we* might be, till she gestured to a glossy group of women and men: all in their early twenties, some vaguely familiar. All pleasing to the eye. 'You should join us,' she said.

'Aye,' I said, 'maybe.' For now, though, I stayed where I was. 'So, you werenae enjoying the film?' I was doing that thing I hated, that I'd found myself doing more and more often since I'd been back in London: exaggerating my accent to cover my lack of ease, and in some rough way to seem more appealing. Playing to a stereotype, basically.

'Not my cup of tea, I'm more *Mamma Mia*.' She turned her wide eyes on me. 'No offence.'

'None taken. It's not going to win any Oscars.'

Her eyes grew wider, if such a thing were possible. 'It must be hard for you to watch, I'm not surprised you had to leave.'

'Och well.' I took another drink. Still playing: man of few words, drowning his sorrows in whisky and, maybe, women. The silky blue of her dress flashed, like sea, like salt and sun in my eyes. It made me blink.

Her hand was on my arm. 'You miss her, don't you? It's obvious.'

People see what they expect, don't they? I saw a dumb blonde with only her iced eyes hinting at intelligent life. I saw someone who knew the game.

Whatever Cody saw, she seemed to like it.

'Coming to the after-party?' she said, stirring her drink with a straw. Ice shivered against glass.

I drained the last of my whisky, a trail of fire from my lips to my heart. Called on my most charming smile.

'You asking?'

Free drink. Beautiful people. Girls packaged like sweeties, bright and shiny. It was too loud for conversation, but that didn't stop anyone trying. I stood in the centre of the bar, shouted and grinned and nodded, at people I recognised and others I didn't – always aware of a blue dress, flashing now here, now there, at the edge of my vision. And the blue was what made me think of it: of an opposite party – where there were friends instead of beautiful strangers, and sun instead of midnight glamour. Where something had happened – something had almost happened. Three years ago, at Magnus and Paolo's wedding. That's when people are meant to make inappropriate pairings: swept away by romance; tipsy, filled with love, and nowhere to pour it.

It was at our local, the Moulin Inn. Reception in full swing, and three of us outside, smoking – years since I'd smoked, I'd fallen off the wagon for the occasion – three of us, me and Eilidh, and Paolo's best man. I remember Eduardo was flirting, eyeing up my kilt. 'I like your skirt,' he'd said, in heavily accented English. 'Very stylish.'

I took mock offence. 'Hey, that's fighting talk. You know we keep knives in our stockings?'

'Yes, really?'

I spun around, gave him a flash of the dirk stuffed in my sock. 'Really.'

'Oh my. And what do you keep in here?' He reached for my sporran.

'Gerroff!' I leapt backwards. 'In our culture, Eduardo, that's a very intimate act.'

Eilidh looked on, amused. She'd been forced out of her jeans and T-shirt; she was encased in a shiny column of a bridesmaid's dress, kingfisher coloured with no sleeves or straps. I felt a little sorry for her. She was showing a perfectly nice figure, a good figure even, but somehow she looked chunky and awkward. It was the shoes, as much as anything else – sandal things with high heels, and above them her strong legs. When a woman chooses shoes like those, contrast is probably not what she's aiming for.

'I can't help feeling I'm missing out here,' she said.

Eduardo turned to her. 'And what are you missing?'

'Well, you know: it's meant to be the bridesmaid and the best man getting together. Traditionally speaking. But I see I've got no chance...'

'Oh, I'm sorry. Just, I looked around at everyone here, and I thought Campbell could be a best man, for the best man.'

'Why thank you.' I was flattered, and embarrassed.

'Sure he is,' said Eilidh. 'I'm just not sure he's the best man for you.'

'Ah-ha ... well then.' He winked. 'I should leave you to it.' He stubbed out his cigarette, and drifted back inside.

Eilidh leaned up against the sun-soaked stone of the pub wall, fag in hand, gazing straight ahead. I thought of an athlete dolled up for a photoshoot. You could say *gilding the lily*, if you were striving to be kind. What did look kind of amazing though was the way she'd painted turquoise round her eyes, so the weird orange of her irises was glowing as she faced into the sun.

'Best man, eh?' I said.

She turned, looked at me with a half-smile. 'Best man. Bridesmaid. The weight of tradition on our shoulders.' She ground her cigarette against the wall with unpainted fingers. 'So…'

So. It shimmered in the air. *Why not?* I remember thinking; drunk enough to disregard the many very excellent reasons why not. I think I staggered slightly as I moved towards her, alerting us both to the fact that I was well in my cups. And that might have gone either way, for or against, if Duncs hadn't burst out of the pub at just that very moment.

'Speeches!' he said. He looked from Eilidh to me, oblivious. 'C'mon, quick. You too, hot lips.'

I remember Eilidh's frowning face as we followed him inside. Annoyed at the hot lips, I think.

In all the years we've been friends: one drunken moment. That's all.

Cody turned out to be a soap actor. And once we'd been snapped arm in arm leaving the afterparty, she was *Cody Comforts Tragic Cam.*

Warmth, softness under my hand; silk slipping over skin: you could say there was comfort there. I don't remember looking at her with the hunger the photos caught. But it's on the web: all you have to do is key in my name and hers. A second for the file to load, and it's there, will always be there.

Her bleached, slippery hair fanned on the pillow, tangled round my fingers. Her tan was like a disguise. Like she was trying to hide anything that made her alive; her veins, her blood. When I touched her skin, it was doll-smooth and weirdly dry; her breasts were the first fakes I had felt, too round, too resilient, a subtle scar concealed in each crease.

But she smelled real. She felt real, inside.

Cody Comforts Tragic Cam. As you'd imagine, we were not pleased with that.

Chapter 24

The morning after the night before. My phones rang and rang – mobile and landline. I silenced the one and ignored the other: guessing who it must be, and guessing she'd give up eventually. But an hour later, the entry-phone started splitting my head in two.

Swearing, I went to the living room window and peered through the blind. In the courtyard the only sign of life was a man, youngish and fair: he was standing with his hands in his pockets, very still, and he seemed to be looking up at me, with a kind of endless patience – though all he could see from there would be the slats of the blinds slightly parted. I knew him from somewhere; I'd seen him before. Press, maybe – chasing a quote or a photo. But as I watched him, the entry-phone shrilled again: Amanda, after all. I snapped the slats back into place and, to save my aching head, I let her in.

Her greeting was abrupt. 'What the hell were you thinking?'

I was unslept, hungover, not in the mood. Not in the mood for any of this. I left the front door open, went to the kitchenette to make some tea. Amanda followed me in, placed herself right in front of the cupboards.

'Scuse me.'

She moved a couple of inches, just enough for me to get at the teabags. Now she was blocking the fridge.

'Amanda…'

She moved again, a single step. I had never seen her so eager to displease.

'What's your problem?'

She slapped the papers onto the counter: three red-tops, each one folded open at a picture of me with Cody. I stared. I don't suppose I was surprised; instead, I had a strange sense of completion. Part of the pleasure of a one-night stand – part of the point – had always come after the event, with the telling of the tale. Not in any sordid depth – just, other people knowing was what made it real. And this morning I had slipped away from Cody's place, caught a cab home, and found myself with no-one to tell. Though Roddy and I were speaking, we weren't yet back to normal. Duncs was home from Kazakhstan, but he'd never been the kind of brother I shared my conquests with. I could have called Eilidh, regaled her with the story, but I somehow didn't think she'd be impressed with me. And when I realised that, I stopped feeling impressed with myself. That morning-after feeling, edgy but smug, shrank and sharpened. Just edgy.

Now the story had told itself, to anyone who was interested.

'You should be happy,' I told Amanda. 'At least I made it in.' I dumped her mug right over my newsprint one, took my own tea over to the sofa. 'Anyway,' I called, 'I thought pairing me up was part of your plan.'

'Please, Campbell. Try not to be a fucking idiot.' She stood, mug in one hand, newspaper in the other, looking pinched; tired as well as furious. 'At Eve's premiere? Your timing is atrocious.'

I shrugged.

'I hope you got something out of it; I know she did. Page two. Page four. Page four. Pretty good, I'd say, for a cookie-cutter soap actress.'

'Yeah well, she got more than publicity, I can assure you.'

She pulled a face. 'Christ, spare me the details. Look. I'm trying to explain to you that this is serious. No-one's running a picture of you on the red carpet. No-one is quoting anything you said about Eve. The interviews you did: pointless. *This* is what people are seeing.' She shook the paper at me, threw it to the floor. 'This is what they'll remember. And the tone of these pieces...' She set down her mug. 'You've had an easy ride so far–'

'Easy? Reporters harassing my family? Staking out my flat? Calling me every five minutes, all through the night?'

Amanda laughed. 'Oh ... you have no idea what it can be like. No idea. And if the tide turns, you'll find out and I can promise you... The sympathy, the goodwill – it's all for Eve. You've been coasting on public sentiment. And last night, to the public, it's like you're cheating on her.'

She wasn't telling me anything I didn't know. More and more, it seemed that what Eve had, she'd left to me. I walked down the street with shades glued to my face, and people knew me; I saw my fame, such as it was, reflected in their eyes. That recognition came straight from Eve. I worried about getting paid, but I was richer than I'd ever thought possible; that too was down to Eve, as surely as if she'd left me the cash in her will. If I'd inherited the compassion that was meant for her, well, that made perfect sense. Sometimes it seemed she'd given me her trouble sleeping; though it wasn't every night I woke with the weight on my chest, struggling to breathe. Only occasionally. Once a week, or twice. Three times at most.

The question was: did I want what she'd bequeathed? Not this part of it, or that part – did I want the whole package?

I knew what I didn't want: to listen to Amanda for a second longer. I put down my tea, picked up my guitar and started to strum. I was playing for comfort, softly, to soothe myself through the edginess, but it was good to have a barrier between us.

'Do you understand what I'm saying?' she said, acting the headmistress. I nodded. Carried on playing.

'You won't do it again? Anything like this?'

I played on, just a little louder. Just enough to force her to raise her voice.

'I'm working on your behalf; that means you take my advice. Or we call it a day.'

If it meant her closing her mouth and getting out of my flat, that sounded fine to me. I reached the chorus of the song; started to hum.

'Jesus,' she said. 'Can you stop that.' And then she fell silent.

I played louder, faster, watching my fingers jump from chord to chord. Feeling her watching me. I flicked my eyes up: in her face I saw the start of something: an idea, glittering.

My fingers missed their places, and I struck a bad note. Grabbed the strings to silence the discord.

When Amanda spoke next, her voice was quite changed. 'You didn't tell me you were a musician.'

I gave a snort. 'That's cos I'm not.'

'Well. Let's not split hairs: you're not awful. Why didn't you say you could play? Do you play with a band?'

'Nope. I did, once. About a hundred years ago.' I wasn't bothered now whether she knew or not, about my being a failure. Not now I'd stopped trying to impress her.

'And – were you any good, would I have heard of you?'

'No, God. We were nothing. We were called Jodrell Bank. Me and a friend with a laptop and a pirate copy of Cubase he picked up in Bangkok. This was before GarageBand: a hundred years ago, like I said. The high point of our existence was playing at the Shed festival in two-thousand-and-something, can't remember. We were millionth on the bill, give or take.'

'What sort of stuff?'

'Like ... digital-acoustic, samples-and-guitar kind of thing.'

An eyebrow twitched. She looked unimpressed, as well she might. But she ploughed on: dog with a bone. 'So you have some songs of your own?'

I shrugged. 'We didn't really do songs. Or, actually – just the one.'

She sat herself down in the armchair opposite me; hands folded, head on one side.

'Play.'

Chapter 25

It was true: the song I played for Amanda was the only one I had –
unless you counted my very first compositions. In my early teens
I was briefly allowed to play in a band with Duncs, two of his
friends, and Roddy on maracas. We were called, hilariously, Sonic
Transmission Device – or STD. We played an unholy mix of metal
and white-boy rap, very, very badly. At least, I played badly, guitar
and backing screeches, and Roddy played worse – for a mathe-
matician, he had an impressive lack of ability to count four beats
in a bar. Duncs and his mates were better. Duncs, in fact, played
lead guitar and played it well – technically. You could tell his heart
wasn't in it though. He was too straight to be a rock monster.

Anyway, they sacked me and Roddy before we'd played a single
gig. They went on to achieve giddying success on the local pub
circuit. (We had one local; they played it twice.) They played the
school gym, too. Duncs would come home after a gig and try to
make me jealous.

'One word, Cam: *groupies*.'

Okay, so he succeeded. And he spurred me on, to practise and
practise, trying to be as good as him. I wanted them to beg me
to come back. I planned how I'd turn them down, form my own
band (Penicillin) and storm the pub circuit, with STD as my support act. Then Duncs left home, the band fell apart and I stopped
playing every spare hour I had, just took my guitar to parties
instead where I learned that girls really, really liked a boy with
an instrument. My teen Casanova years were down to Duncs, I
suppose. Though I never could play like he did.

For a while when I got to uni, my guitar gathered dust. Back then it was all about decks and your vinyl collection. I'd play now and then, at idle moments; or when I felt stressed I'd use it to block things out, concentrate on learning a new song, practising a new chord till its shape became part of my hand. But my fingers had grown soft, and the strings blistered my skin. It wasn't till Amit and I became friends – started sharing the music we liked, then making our own, messing about with his laptop and my steel-string – that I built up the calloused tips once more.

Nineteen years old: London opened up to me, was the life I'd always wanted. Amit and I came up with a name, called ourselves Jodrell Bank. We were in demand at parties. Got a regular gig at the student union, the last Thursday of every month; occasional slots in Shoreditch bars. Started to think we could go somewhere: after all, why not? Amit passed his exams, and I failed mine; sat summer resits, scraped into second year. Drank a lot, smoked a lot, took enough happy pills to make an elephant grin and gurn. Pretended not to worry about my fluttering chest. Smoked my way through crushing comedowns. Clung to dub records through mornings after. So far, so standard: the best years of my life.

Then a friend of Amit's got us a gig in a Brixton bar: a prime slot in a venue packed with cool club kids. For a week before-hand I let it slip into every conversation. We were so thrilled, we couldn't see how wrong it was. It was the timing that did for us. Our stuff was gentle: no big beats, no songs, just tracks that merged one into another, with improvised words over soft washes of sound; perfect for the end of a night, for a Sunday afternoon or a weekend in a field. Not so perfect for Saturday night, 11pm, and a crowd that wanted it loud, fast and up. Within minutes they'd turned their backs. The delicate ebb and flow of our digital acous-tica was lost in the chatting, the flirting, the hype of the night to come. The worst thing: there was this girl I'd asked along, mean-ing to impress her. Ten minutes into our set I found her in the crowd, doing her best to listen, with sympathy in her eyes. Next time I glanced up she was gabbing away to her pals like all the rest of them – as if we were nothing but background, the beer-sticky floorboards beneath their feet. We played on – we needed the money – and when at last we left the stage, not a soul reacted. At midnight we slipped out of there, just Amit and me. Headed down the road to the Fridge, where the music was so loud we wouldn't have to speak, and the beats would vibrate through our flesh and our bones, shaking the shame away; where we could pool our resources, knock back whatever pills we had on us, and escape our humiliation.

It was late the next afternoon that it all fell apart.

I hadn't slept, dodging the comedown that was chasing my heels. The winter sun had come out blaring like a siren, and it was obvious I could never leave the house again. The world outside was enormous, was pushing to get inside my head. And then my flatmate shouted for me: Eilidh was at the door.

I'd forgotten. We'd arranged to go and see an artwork: a sound installation in a lighthouse near the Docklands.

Eilidh chattered away as we rattled on the train, talking about her Saturday night. It was tame enough: she never did any of that serious party stuff. A good drinker, sure, she'd always been that. A bit of spliff now and then. But she was too solid, too steady for anything else. She was at South Bank Uni, lived the other side of the river; she had her own friends. We hadn't seen much of each other that year.

The trek to the lighthouse from Canning Town felt like miles through a freezing wasteland. You could see too much of the fading sky. We trudged in silence, Eilidh stopping now and then to check the A-Z. After an age, we reached the wharf, a ruined playground of metal. Shipping containers sat next to skips, pylons next to rusted machinery that must once have shifted heavy car-goes. Ragged steel spiked the sky: spiked, like my brain felt. But everything I'd taken had been on purpose. What was that pur-pose? Not to think, maybe. To go deeper or wilder, into my life.

Alone with Eilidh beside me, I scuttled across the wharf, and the too-huge sky stared down.

The lighthouse appeared like a gift, glowing through the dusk: a Chinese lantern. Uplights warmed its walls; two porthole windows caught the last daylight and burned like gold suns. The panes that would once have flashed with warnings and reassurances were illuminated with blue, and the whole structure was topped by a cherry-pink beacon.

While Eilidh stopped to take photos, I went on ahead, shivering and eager for shelter. I was battling troughs of blackness, which I knew were only payback for the nights before. I breathed my way through them, humming quietly like someone lost and trying to keep their spirits up.

Inside, the wooden space was like a ship, or a sloping attic. Screens glowed; an apparatus with wheels and wires and bells was placed at one end of the room, and a bronze bowl at the other. A concrete staircase clung to the curve of the tower, climbing to a metal platform that formed the floor of the lantern room. Up here, it was almost as cold as it had been outside. The astragals on the storm panes sliced the sky into diamonds: I could see the Millennium Dome crouched low in the ebbing light.

The noise crept up on me, so gradual I didn't recognise it as music. It could have been the echo of my boots on the steel floor. It could have been the infinitely slow collapse of all the rusting metal we'd passed on the wharf, stretched so a second become a minute, a minute an hour. The platform vibrated under my feet.

Eilidh's steps sounded on the floor below. 'Did you read? It lasts for a thousand years,' she called up to me. 'Till the end of the millennium.'

A bright note spun on its axis, swung in circles too big for my brain to contain. A lower note swelled and contracted underneath: dread pressed against my ribs, throbbed in my throat. A thin sound scraped inside my skull, and caught; fishing twine pulled taut. Somewhere was a scuttering, soft and scarcely there.

A whistle of tightening airways. A thousand years. A thousand years singing inside me. The floor shook. I shook. Outside was a blue halfway between day and night; at the moment I noticed it, the sky darkened; the blue was lost, was gone. It was nothing. One day gone from a thousand years.

In fairytales, when you're young, forever is signified by a hundred years: forever being far too long to comprehend.

Eilidh appeared at the top of the stairs; gazed around, then sat in one of the listening chairs. Her eyes closed. She sat relaxed, feet apart on the metal floor, hands loose in her lap. She was twenty years old. Both of us were twenty years old. In her jeans, hoodie, leather jacket she seemed always to have been the same. I felt myself fly apart in contrast. She was solid as I was dissipating, dissolving into molecules. My centre could not hold. She kept her eyes closed. I kept mine open, staring through the window at the lost blue.

I don't remember getting home.

I remember being in bed. I had a book, I thought I was reading this book, but I didn't ever turn a page, just clutched it like a sleeping toy. I slept a lot, and when I couldn't sleep I stayed still, still, still, and pretended to sleep. I remember hugging the pillow, finding it damp. I remember hanging on white-knuckled to the edge of the bed.

My flatmates knocked, stood at the bedside, creased their foreheads. They brought me tea, took the cups away cold.

I remember, sometime later, Eilidh in the doorway. Her familiar voice.

'Get dressed, now,' she said. Laid out clothes for me, pulled the quilt aside, wrinkling her nose. Turned her back. Arms folded; waiting. Not taking no for an answer. 'Come on, Cam, put them on.'

I remember the terrifying back seat of her ancient Citroën: how thin the metal skin seemed, how close the speeding road, and the hugeness of the traffic. The smell of the engine, and the noise it made, endless, always the same. I remember Eilidh's voice, steady from the front seat: the words all but swallowed, the tone a rope to cling to. I remember her singing with the radio, her voice a blunt instrument – dulled, dented pewter, not silver or gold. Plain, and always flat by a fraction of a note: each phrase only the length of her breath.

I remember opening my eyes. Trying to focus on the details. Eilidh's hair, shining like wet sand. A spot of grease on the head-rest in front of me.

And then I was at home, in my own room, in bed; Mum and Dad and Eilidh voices down below. And I stayed in my room for a long time.

People came to see me. Christmas holidays: Roddy was back. He sat with me and we watched TV till I told him to turn it off, then we sat in silence till he couldn't take it, made his excuses and ran. Jean dropped in, and Magnus. Jean hugged me, and cried; Magnus told me about his own breakdown – his 'mad time', he called it – which had far more entertainment value than mine. Duncs came home for ten days, and swung between taking the piss and acting like nothing was wrong. Christmas Day came and went. I hadn't got presents for anyone. Mine arrived in a pile on the end of my bed: I was scared to open them, scared of I don't know what, and Mum had to open them for me. I made it down-stairs for Christmas lunch, a painful hour where we all tried to pretend things were normal. That I was normal.

Somewhere between Christmas and Hogmanay, Eilidh fetched my guitar. She'd brought it from the London flat where all my stuff was, where I was still paying rent, thanks to the Bank Of Mum And Dad, though I already knew I wasn't going back. I held the guitar on my lap, not touching the strings, not wanting it to make a sound. I hadn't been able to listen to music. I was ter-rified of what might happen inside my head. I tried it sometimes, imagining the sounds of the gentlest music I knew. All of it was tainted. What ought to have soothed me was drenched with fear:

with a hundred comedowns, with the unbearable proportions of a thousand years.

By now, I could read. Mum brought books from the library; I read one, sometimes two each day, in the quiet of my room, sitting on my bed with my back against the wall.

Hogmanay. Everyone was going to Roddy and Jean's, to Linda and Donnie. Mum had frowned at me when I said I'd be fine, and I'd managed a smile. I would see the old year out alone, with a cup of tea and an Ian Rankin. It really was fine. But an hour before midnight, Eilidh turned up, toting a bottle of tequila. We sat in my room, and some of the time we were quiet and some of the time we talked: about people we knew, times when we were growing up. The bells from the kirk were almost unexpected when they came, and the cheers floating up from the street. Eilidh raised her glass, straight tequila, and I raised a water-glass in return. Hug. Kiss.

'Play us a song?' she said. '*Should auld acquaintance be forgot...*'

And I picked up my guitar and fumbled through the chords, F, C7, F, B flat, and Eilidh sang in her blunted-pewter voice, and my head didn't explode so that was alright. That was alright, then.

After that, my guitar was a security blanket, constantly in my arms. I strummed and picked phrases rather than entire songs, some of them melodies that had worn themselves into the pathways of my brain, and some that composed themselves under my fingers. And slowly some of these phrases began to slot together, and build into a song. I hummed it as I moved about the house. I could do that now: leave my room, wander up and down the stairs, even out into the garden, frosted grass crunching under my feet, breath puffing out deep and slow, keeping calm, keeping it together. It was just the three of us in the house now: me, my mum and dad – Duncs away at uni, everyone else back to their lives. Everyone moving forwards. Eilidh came back to visit once or twice a month, called a couple of times a week. Just checking in, she'd say – rather than checking up, which was what we both knew she was doing.

The words, when they came, when they fitted themselves into the song, were about nothing in particular. Standing outside as the sun slipped behind the garden wall, I thought: on the coldest day, you can see a slant of sun. And there was the first line.

Well, maybe it was about something.

Anyway, when the words and the tunes were all in place I gave it to Eilidh. I mean, the next time she came to see me, I played it to her; I didn't say, I wrote this for you, or anything embarrassing like that. I just played it, sang her the words, and she said she liked it. And I told her I felt a lot better now, and it was a long time since I'd seen the inside of a pub, and together we left the house and walked right down the road to the Moulin Inn. Inside we had to stand, but that was okay. I managed to stay for a drink. I sent Eilidh to the bar, and when she came back with our pints I told her thanks for looking after me. I know she knew what I meant.

The only song I ever wrote. It bobbed up from the depths, from the darkest, sharky depths. The place I don't ever want to go again.

And now, Amanda wanted a chorus.

Chapter 26

Eilidh's car these days is a more solid affair than the battered old Citroën that rescued me ten years ago. The door made a good heavy clunk as I closed it.

Me, I'm more solid too than I was back then.

I chucked my bag on the backseat alongside Eilidh's, on top of her purple waterproof. 'Looks like you won't be needing that. Brilliant weather, eh?' We pulled out into early morning traffic. It was the first day of the school holidays, and we were heading home for Roddy's leaving night. 'Hey – six weeks of freedom starts here!'

Eilidh kept her eyes on the road. 'Yep.'

'Got any plans?'

'I haven't had the energy even to think.'

'You should go away. Somewhere hot; you need it, that's obvious.'

She didn't reply. I was ready to list some possible destinations when she whacked the horn and cut me off – the car in front had been slow away from the lights. I glanced at her: her face had a shuttered look as she scowled at the traffic. She should have been demob happy, but it was a stress thing, maybe: like those people who work all hours with never a sick day, and fall ill as soon as the holidays start. The frustration of the term just gone, working its way out.

For a while I tried to lift her mood, chatting about nothing much, but she gave me flat replies and one-word answers all the way. Round Birmingham I lost patience, shut my mouth and turned on the radio. At least she hadn't brought up the Cody thing. I'd expected to be skewered for that.

So I sat there in the hot car, sweat slick on my forehead and prickling under my arms, thinking I'd be there already if only I'd flown. And at the same time, I was nursing Amanda's idea, hugging it close to my chest. If she'd been in a better frame of mind, I would have shared it with Eilidh. But her foul mood did away with that temptation, which was doubtless for the best. At this stage it was only a notion. Amanda was speaking to some people, putting out some feelers. The whole thing could easily prove to be a non-starter.

In any case, there was nothing doing without a chorus. *Give it a hook*, Amanda had said. *Make it about Eve.*

Four lines. A few chords. How hard could it be? But I'd plucked and I'd strummed till I couldn't hear straight, and as yet I had nothing to show for it. The longer I tried, the more it felt like staring at a wall. Now, in the car, tranced by the roadscape, I let my mind go slack till the engine became a pipe-like drone and I played off it, in my head, setting notes against its background, fumbling for a melody. But anything that came sounded like a dirge. My mood began to match Eilidh's.

When we stopped at the services near Carlisle, I bought us ice-cream bars. Finally, Eilidh cracked a smile. I unwrapped hers, and she ate one-handed once we were back on the motorway.

'Chocolate,' I said, when she'd finished.

'What?'

'On your chin. See you. Can't take you anywhere.'

She rubbed.

'Still there.' I pointed, and she pulled away. '*What?*' I said, irritated. 'What's up with you?'

She didn't answer. Licked her finger and rubbed again. 'Now?'

'Aye, you're fine.' From behind my sunglasses I stared at the road, straight line to the horizon: feeling the weight of another two hundred silent miles.

By the time we reached home, I was sweaty and cramped and gagging on a drink. Eilidh dropped me outside the house.

'You coming in?' I said.

'No, I'll see you in the pub. Say hi from me.'

I didn't try to persuade her. And I didn't linger at home, staying just long enough for hugs and hellos. That cold, clear pint was brimming in my mind's eye.

'There's some food for you,' said Mum.

'Thanks, I'll maybe have that later. Is Duncs about?'

'In his room.'

I jogged upstairs, dropped my bag on my bed then chapped on Duncan's door. 'You ready?'

'Aye, be there in a sec.'

Back downstairs, I popped my head round the living room door. Mum and Dad had gone back to the reading my arrival had interrupted: a novel for her, the paper for him.

'That's us off now,' I told them.

'Oh well, have a good time,' said Mum. 'How are you getting on, anyway?' Her voice was light, pitched to indicate interest rather than concern.

'Fine,' I said. 'I mean, I guess you'll have seen a lot of the stories and stuff.' It was only as I spoke that I realised: they were bound to have heard about Cody. They would have no idea who she was, but someone would have mentioned it, Mrs Wishart if no-one else: *I see your Campbell's in the papers again, him and some blonde-haired lassie that's no better than she should be...* I could feel I was blushing.

My dad turned the page of his broadsheet. 'We haven't really been following it.'

'Ninety per cent of it is total rubbish, of course,' said Mum. 'We know that.' She looked like she needed me to agree.

'Absolutely,' I said.

Duncs was behind me, shrugging into his jacket. 'Beer o'clock, is it? Let's go if we're going...'

The sun was melting towards the hills as we strolled down to the pub.

'So: how're the Kazakhs?' I had very little idea of his life over there: living on a compound, in a country I'd thought was a joke till he announced he was moving.

'Wouldn't know, it's all Russians and French. So!' He clapped his hands. 'No need to ask what you've been up to.'

'Aye, well.' I slapped at my neck, thinking I felt a midge after its tea. 'Did Mum and Dad say anything? They're pretending they don't know about it.'

'Not to me – but I heard Mum having a go at Mrs Wishart: totally polite, like, but real teacher mode. We're not in the least bit interested in the – what was it? – the *gossip and fictions* that seem to pass for news these days. That's what she says. Pretty impressive.'

'Oh, God.'

'It was true, I take it?'

I didn't answer. Just looked at him and shook my head, meaning, *Yes, and let's not talk about it.* But Duncs didn't take the hint.

'You've been busy,' he said, 'since I saw you last.'

'God, yeah, that's right. I haven't seen you since – everything.'

'I'd imagine it's been a rollercoaster of emotion?'

'As they say. From laughter to tears and back again.'

He glanced at me; looked away again. 'That Cody girl, though. A bit tacky.'

I bit back a defensive response, knowing silence was my best answer. Kept my mouth shut till he backtracked.

'Alright, I know, none of my business. But do you not think it kind of cheapens her, a bit?'

'Cheapens who? Cody?' The word in my mouth felt old-fashioned; a strange word for Duncs to choose. It made him sound like a Victorian patriarch, protecting the reputation of a precious only daughter.

'Not Cody: Eve,' he said, like it should have been obvious.

I was genuinely bewildered – by the idea itself, as well as the fact that Duncs should care. 'D'you want to get down off that white charger?' I said. 'You'll be getting blisters on your arse.'

He didn't reply.

'It's not like – not like Eve was sleeping with Cody.'

He smirked. 'Now *that* would sell some magazines.'

'If it makes anyone look cheap, it's me, surely? D'you think I'm cheap, Duncs, is that what you're saying? You think I'm damaged goods now, no classy girl will look at me?'

'Never.' He placed a hand on my shoulder. 'Don't let anyone make you feel dirty for what you've done.' I shrugged him off, laughing. We'd arrived at the pub, and I was glad to let the conversation go.

Roddy, Eilidh, Magnus and Paolo were all sat outside; Donnie and Linda too. Only Jean, understandably, hadn't made it over. I was pleased to see Auntie Linda. There was something I wanted to ask her.

'Here,' said Donnie, making space, 'we're just heading off, we'll let you young ones in.'

I turned to Linda. 'Can you not persuade him to fork out for another drink?'

She laughed. 'Ach, one glass of wine is all I can cope with these days! Nice to see you, Cam – taking care of yourself, I hope.' She reached up, touched my arm. 'You're doing awful well with the fundraising, I keep hearing – how much is it now, that you're up to?'

It was what I'd hoped my parents would say – the *well done* I'd been waiting for. 'Nearly two million now – but it's not down to me, not really. There's a whole team...'

'Two million!' She shook her head. 'That's amazing. That's a good thing you've done there.'

I gave her shoulder a squeeze. 'Thanks, Linda. Oh – listen, before you go, I was meaning to ask...' I dropped my voice a bit. 'Do you have any old photos, holiday photos, of us lot at Glenelg?'

Linda tilted her head to one side. 'I'm sure I must do,' she

196

said. 'I'm never very good with pictures, but. You'll've asked your mum already?'

I made a vague sound, because I hadn't asked Mum. She'd have been instantly suspicious, worried I wanted to sell them to the press.

'Just she's better with photos, usually. I always mean to put them in albums, all properly, but ... I never seem to get round to it. Is it anything in particular you're after?'

I didn't quite know what I wanted the photos for. It was something to do with the treasure hunt, and Jasmine's clues; it was to do with how I found myself wondering about oaks and yews, about pirates and graveyards – and how jumbled, how incomplete, my memories were of Glenelg. I thought if I could hold them up against photos – compare them with something real – somehow the memories might take on more clarity, more body.

'No,' I said, 'nothing special. Just whatever you've got would be great.'

'There's shoeboxes full of them, from when you were all little. You'd be welcome to have a rummage, see what you can find, but they're in no sort of order at all.'

'Brilliant, thanks. Maybe tomorrow?'

'Of course. We'll not expect you too early though...' She gave a wave to the table. 'Have fun, folks!'

I got in a round for the six that were staying. When I settled on the bench with my pint in front of me, a sigh I hadn't known was there pushed its way out of me. It seemed an age since I'd been here: not in this pub, but anywhere with friends.

'Cheers,' said Duncs, 'to Roddy.' We lifted our glasses. That first gulp tasted every bit as good as I'd imagined.

'Thanks, everyone. Thanks for coming.' Roddy sounded pleased and awkward. He caught my eye as he spoke, and I nodded. I was hoping whatever had happened between us was over, done and dusted. I couldn't remember, quite, why it was we'd fallen out, or whose fault it was. But perhaps it didn't matter; perhaps now we could kick it under the table and get on with things.

Whatever: it was Roddy's night. I was well aware of that. Of course, people would want to know what I'd been up to, how my life had changed – but I had to be careful not to steal his thunder. No more than half an hour of telling stories, and after that I'd be sure to shut up.

We drank, and we talked: about what Atlanta would be like, about the flat Magnus and Paolo were hoping to buy; about Jean's news, Duncan's brand new motorbike and Eilidh's students. Eilidh was keeping pace with us, pint for pint. She seemed to have shrugged off whatever had been eating her, and in Roddy's honour she'd put on some make-up, even a skirt. She got a round; Paolo another. The sinking sun slid into my eyes; I fished my shades out of my pocket, braced for the inevitable slagging. But no-one said anything. They talked on: the sky turned a dark glowing blue. The warmth went out of the night. I hunched into myself.

'Shall we go inside?' someone said, at last.

The conversation dipped as we moved, reassembling ourselves in the booth furthest from the bar. Now, finally, someone would ask. Surely. Roddy or Magnus or someone: ask, *how's things with you?*

'So d'you think you'll be back for Christmas?' said Eilidh to Roddy.

'Aye, maybe. See how things go, but I'd like to come back for Hogmanay, anyway.'

'Although – it might be fun, New Year in the States...?'

It came to me that they were doing it on purpose. I didn't think they'd schemed it. But every one of them was taking a cue from the others. Giving me a message: that I'd got above myself.

In an instant, my mood turned black. That's how they wanted me, right enough. Never changing, always in the same place, where they could rely on me to be. It didn't matter what I'd achieved, didn't matter I'd raised two million quid. They still thought I should be squashed flat up against the edge of my own life. And I remembered exactly why Roddy and I had fallen out: like I was still stood in his bedroom. Like I'd never stepped away.

I could feel a bitter wave cresting, ready to crash and sweep me down into the depths of resentment. But I made my face into a smile. I didn't have to sulk like a child. If I wanted to talk, it was up to me. I readied myself for a gap.

And then, in a sly way, the conversation spun round to me anyway.

'I couldn't believe it when she said the baby wasn't his.'

'God, I know, didn't see that coming. And then, when she says, *I'm calling it after its dad–*'

It took me a while to get what they were doing. I'd never watched the soap that Cody starred in. Until a week ago, I doubt any of them had either.

I kept on smiling. 'Yeah, very good.'

'Have you been watching recently?' Eilidh said. 'It's totally brilliant, specially that Patsy...'

Patsy, of course, was Cody's character. 'Look, just leave it, eh?'

'Oh come on, don't get coy. I mean, the world and his wife know all about it, so there's no point being secretive with us.'

'If it's true, that is,' said Roddy. 'It might not be, you can't always believe what you read. Eh, Cam?'

'It's fun though, you've got to admit ... who knows what we'll read about next?'

Duncs jumped in. 'Aye, what is coming next?'

I couldn't resist. I just wanted to see their faces. 'What's next,' I announced, 'is I'm recording a single.'

The silence, the stares were worth waiting for. Roddy's mouth actually fell open.

'Yeah, so my ... Amanda, when she discovered I can play guitar a bit, she had the idea we should try to release a song.'

Magnus's eyebrows were almost touching his hairline. 'What's the song?'

'It's one I wrote. Ages ago.'

Across the table, Eilidh narrowed her eyes, and I smiled because she'd guessed.

'Yeah,' I said, 'it's that one.' I turned to the rest of them. 'I wrote it years ago, like. It's called "The Coldest Day".'

'Wow.' Duncs looked genuinely impressed. 'Wow.'

Paolo, leaning forward, said, 'But I didn't know; you're a musician?'

'No, not really, I'm not at all. It's just, well, she – my advisor – she's asked me to re-write it a bit and make it more so it can fit with the ... the Eve thing. And then she reckons it might do well, you know, cos people are still interested in ... in that.' Why was I backpedalling? Something to do with the slits of Eilidh's eyes. 'But I mean, it might not happen, she's talking to some people about it and I don't know...'

For the first time that night, Eilidh asked me a serious question. 'What do you mean re-write it? How does it fit with "the Eve thing"?'

'Oh, just add a chorus, mainly.' *Just add a chorus*: glossing over the dark suspicion that this was beyond me. 'And then it's about how we promote it.'

I had never seen that expression on Eilidh's face before. Or I had: it was the way she'd looked as she flipped through the tabloids, back in my old flat when this whole thing was just starting. A sort of detached disgust. I felt myself grow hot with shame – like I was one of her pupils caught copying my homework – and I didn't know why.

Magnus glanced from Eilidh to me. 'Well, whoever knew you were such a songbird,' he said, smoothly. 'Duncs. Do you still play?'

And Duncs was off, talking about the covers band they'd started in Kazakhstan, how they played on the compound at the social club and the secretaries loved them. I sat there, wondering what had just happened. Eilidh had half-turned away, making a show of listening to Duncs, laughing like she'd never heard anything so funny. I caught Magnus's eye, and frowned a question. He gave the ghost of a shrug.

Later, when Eilidh went to the toilets, I got up too, and hovered by the door. When she came out I stepped in front of her, blocking her way back to the booth.

'Are you going to tell me what's wrong?'

She stared at me, disbelieving.

'Look, look. I've obviously done something to upset you, so – what is it? Just tell me, what have I done?'

'Jesus. If you don't even know–'

I threw my hands up. 'Aw, here we go! *If you don't know then I can't tell you*, is that it? Don't be such a woman about it!'

I thought she might say something then, but instead she pushed past me, back to the booth. When I caught up, she was grabbing her bag.

'Sorry folks, I'm out of here.' She bent, wrapped her arms round a startled Roddy and kissed him on the cheek. 'Look after yourself over there. And email, okay?' She gave a general kind of wave to the table as a whole, slung her bag over her shoulder. 'See ya.'

I stepped aside: she walked by without so much as a glance.

It was Magnus who broke the silence, with a tilt of his head in my direction. 'Nice one, lover boy.'

I'd have ditched the place myself, then – because, whatever was going on, I wasn't obliged to stay and be the object of everyone's disapproval. Only, the last thing I wanted was to chase after Eilidh. So instead I dropped back into my seat, lifted my pint – and for the rest of the night, I spoke barely a word.

I woke wishing myself four hundred miles away, snug in my Vauxhall box. It was late already; Linda would be expecting me, to look through those boxes of photos. I already knew I wasn't going. Chatting to Linda would have been manageable, and Donnie as well: it was Roddy I couldn't be bothered with. Roddy, and all the rest of them. Instead, I went for a run.

It was raining half-heartedly, rotten weather for it, but I forced myself out anyway. I'd started to run after seeing myself on the telly. In quick succession I'd appeared on a breakfast show and an early evening programme. For the breakfast one, a woman had sprayed me with make-up till I looked like a waxwork just back from its holidays. For the evening show I'd refused the airbrush, and I looked like I hadn't slept for a week. Realising my options came down to a dishonest healthy glow or looking honestly fucked, I'd decided I had to get fit.

So far my terrain had been city streets; muddy hills were a shock to the system. My trainers slipped and sank on damp turf as I struggled up the hill, gasping for breath. The hangover wasn't helping. But today, I needed it to be hard: it was either run after Eilidh, try to chip away at that stony face she was wearing – and she'd already had Duncs run after her last night, to see she was okay – or run it out of my system.

That look of disgust. Every time I thought of it, I felt shame, swiftly followed by indignation. I hadn't ever asked for her approval. And if I turned up on her doorstep and she met me with that look, an apology – for whatever it was I'd done – would be the last thing she'd get. And Duncs – when had he become so chivalrous?

With my heart trying to escape my heaving chest and my legs on fire, I pushed myself on: slow-motion upward-stagger, slope shoving back at me, like I was hauling a body twice my weight. I could collapse, easily; slogged on instead, foot by foot closer to the crest. Reaching the top was like breaking through cloud to a mountain summit. I bent in half, hands on thighs: for a wheezing minute my mud-clarted shoes swam in and out of focus. My breath began to steady. I wasn't going to die. I straightened, still gasping, and turned my swimmy gaze to our houses crouched small at the foot of the hill. Beyond them, on the other side of the village, green woods smothered the lower slopes of hill upon hill. It was beautiful, of course, but I was too destroyed to appreciate the view. I flicked a salty mix of rain and sweat from my forehead. Shook out my arms, my hands. And then: let go.

My feet were brakes but still I fell faster and faster – racing towards gravity – my freewheeling reward. I felt like a boy, running for the joy of it: pelting over rough ground, leaving everyone far behind. Thinking of nothing but treasure.

And where the drum of my feet *prestissimo* met the shining idea of treasure, something started to happen.

> *The hunt begins*
> *Where starts the track*
> *From a place the same*
> *Forwards and back*

A place the same. A place the same. It hammered in my head.

A magical place
A place that's the same
Forwards and back...

I ran, letting it build, letting it come.

> *Forwards and back...*
> *I first heard your name*

> *Forwards and back*
> *All the way through*

Through thinning cloud the sun flared, D to C sharp major.

> *Forwards and back*
> *All the way through...*

The whole of my life
I give it to you

The whole of my life
I gave it to you

I was so fast, so amazed, I forgot to look at where my feet were landing. Suddenly, ground wasn't there: I stumbled and slid, my ankle turning as I went. The earth slammed hard into my back: my lungs went on strike, for long seconds. *The whole of my life, the whole of my life...* Relief, as cool damp air flooded back into my body, and I lay there sick and elated – from running too hard, from the pain in my ankle, from the words and the tune that were soppy as hell but just what Amanda had asked for and I knew now. I knew this was going to work.

Sweat stung my watering eyes; I rubbed, rubbed, till the white, clouded sky sparked into stars. In spite of everyone. Because of everyone. I was going to make this work.

Chapter 27

In this business – whatever the business was that I found myself in – the things that should happen fast (say, getting paid) moved like glaciers. And those you thought would take forever were on you before you knew it.

The day after I flew back from Moulin, I played my new chorus to Amanda, who pronounced it Just The Job. That same day, I recorded a quick and dirty version on my laptop, and Amanda emailed it round some of the people she'd been sounding out. By the following morning, she'd arranged for me to meet someone at PGR, a little label with big digital ambitions. By the end of that week the paperwork had been drawn up and I was sitting in the PGR offices, poised to sign.

I tried to keep my face straight as I formed my name on the bottom sheet of the contract: twice over, one copy for the label, one for me. Despite myself, I felt my cheeks pulling up into a grin. Inside, I was dancing, fist in the air, shouting, *Fucking yes!* Sure, it wasn't quite how my sixteen-year-old self used to imagine it: for a start, in my dreams I was part of a band – not alone with The Man from the label, in a bare anteroom off an ordinary office. Also, I'd never envisaged the *Daily News* being involved – but this was the deal: the song would be free to *News* readers as an exclusive download, which would get some word of mouth going online, and we'd go for a general digital release on the back of that. Then there was the advance, which couldn't be further from the hundreds of thousands I'd dreamed of. But if it sold, the royalties would be good – and besides, when does anything ever happen the way you imagined it? If my teenaged self was unconvinced, the me of six months back was watching open-mouthed from the margins, speechless at what I'd achieved.

I re-capped the pen. Sat back in my seat. 'No champagne?' I joked.

The Man, a perfectly nice public school chap whose name was Rob, looked concerned. 'Lager? We've got lager. Should be cold, I think...'

'It's fine, just kidding.'

'No, come on.' Rob jumped to his feet. 'Our newest client – we should have a drink.' He called through to some kid in the main office, who appeared a minute later clutching a couple of vaguely chilled bottles of Becks and then had to make a second trip to fetch a bottle-opener.

We clinked – *Cheers!* – and I took a big swallow, and thought, yes, I deserved this. Because this was the first thing that had anything to do with me. All the rest of it was Eve, was me trailing on her coat tails. But this song was mine: I'd written it, and it felt like the first thing that wasn't smoke and mirrors.

When we'd downed our beers, I left the PGR office and made straight for the nearest pub. There, I sat with a pint and considered my options. There was no shortage of new acquaintances whose numbers were in my phone, but no-one who wouldn't find it weird and slightly sad if I called them out of the blue, inviting them to celebrate my signing. I scrolled through names. Forwards. Back. When it came down to it, there were two people I could try. Eilidh wasn't speaking to me; Cody was a one-night stand whose surname I knew only from the tabloids.

Fuck it. I made my choice.

She didn't sound horrified to hear from me – quite the opposite – even when I told her I'd come to hers, because this time Amanda would cut my balls off if we were seen.

It was coincidence Duncs descended the night before the recording session: a day in London on his way back out to Almaty. When he asked to tag along, I let him think I was doing him a favour even though it felt like the other way around. There was more than butterflies in my stomach. It felt like a full wash cycle going on in there. I'd have been happy even to have Amanda to hold my hand, make sure everything happened like it was meant to, but I wasn't her only client and she was otherwise engaged. I told myself anxiety was the brother of excitement; it was all in how you framed it, and this should be fun. With Duncs there, perhaps that's what it would be.

'Maybe,' I told him as we walked along the river to London Bridge, 'when we get there the guitarist will have cancelled, been taken ill or something, and you'll have to step in.'

'My big break. Could be.' He flexed his fingers. 'Don't worry, bro, I won't let you down.'

We crossed the street, ducked out of the sun and into the dank, shadowed echo of the railway arches. It took us a while to spot the place: a plain blue door with an entry panel, and the smallest of signs that said, *Commotion Studios*. When I spoke my name into the intercom, the lock unlatched; we passed through a dingy lobby, pushed against a heavy door, and arrived in a room crammed with people. There were a dozen, at least – and then I saw that one whole wall was a mural, and half the crowd was paint.

The underground light made everyone flat, painted or not. I had to stare and blink before I could disentangle the real band from the pretend. The checked-shirt guy with the beard, holding the semi-acoustic: real. And the woman with fried-looking hair – somehow I hadn't expected a woman. A black guy held a saxophone and stood motionless. Paint. Good: I didn't want some filthy '80s sax smeared all over my song.

A face I recognised had to be real: I'd met the producer back at the meeting where we thrashed out the details.

'Campbell!' He came over and clapped my shoulder. 'You found us, well done.' He turned to Duncs. 'Hi. Hi there. I'm Nick.'

Nick smiled as Duncs introduced himself, and somehow his face suggested I should have let him know I'd be accompanied. 'Bit of moral support, is it? That's fine, we can just about squeeze you in. Let me introduce you to the guys...'

The room we were in was half-lounge, half-studio: one end furnished with sofa, armchair and coffee table; the other filled with instruments and dominated by a grand piano, black lacquer begging to be stroked. The musicians – the real ones – had migrated into the studio on our arrival, freeing up the lounge. I parked my guitar by the side of the sofa as Nick led us over to meet the band; I hadn't been sure whether to bring it, and I didn't want to come over like I thought I could cut it with the professionals. Guitarist, bass player, drummer: we shook hands with them all, and with (alarm bells) the keyboard player. Alarm, because in all my imaginings of how this song would sound, keyboards had not figured – and sue me for anti-'80s prejudice but I couldn't see how they could possibly be a good thing. I smiled politely.

Nick led us through into a smaller space, where a chubby guy sat by a mixing desk. 'Control room,' said Nick. 'This is Kev, he's the engineer, knows what all this shit does and makes the magic happen.'

Kev swivelled to greet us. For some inexplicable reason he was wearing a trilby, but his grin was the friendliest I'd seen so far today and I thought, despite the hat, he might not be a total arsehole. Everything here was smaller than I'd expected, and more office-like: computer screens and executive chairs. Instead of the banks of *Star Trek*-style controls I'd visualised, the mixing desk was tucked inside a wooden casing, like those kid-on traditional cabinets where people used to hide their TV sets. Speakers and amps were propped at ear-level and shoved under the mixing desk. A pair of guitars waited on stands. A wave of cool air passed my face as a fan turned, ruffling a pile of papers weighted with a dirty mug, and making me realise how warm it was in here. Like the rest of the studio, the control room smelled of bodies with a top note of air-freshener.

'Vocal booth in there,' Nick was saying, pointing to what I'd thought was a fire-door, 'so that's where you'll do, obviously, your vocals, once we get to that. And then, back down the corridor – kitchenette and toilet.'

We turned down tea or coffee, as keen to get started as everyone else must be. Nick took us back into the studio. And then they played my demo.

We listened all the way through. My face grew hotter than ever as each fumbled chord change, each slip of my voice rang out clear for everyone to hear. More than anything, I was conscious of Duncs beside me. I knew he'd have played it better. And that chorus I'd been so thrilled with embarrassed me now, its sentimentality inviting ridicule. Duncs would rip the piss out of me later.

When it ended, there was a brief silence, then Nick skipped straight back to the start and played it through again. This time, I didn't listen to the words. Unexpectedly, like it belonged to someone else, I'd fallen in love with a thing my voice did: a line where it thinned and scraped a little and sounded like I meant it. I found myself glancing round to see whether anyone else admired it; thought I saw a flicker on the keyboard player's face. Yes! She got it: and suddenly I loved her, too.

But there was something else: a musical phrase that sounded wrong, now; had always been wrong, and I hadn't thought it mattered, but now the wrongness was overwhelming. Nick was asking for a first run-through from the guitarist: this was my last chance to make a change before the song would be fixed, always and forever. I was going to have to speak.

'Scuse me–' They'd half-forgotten I was there; turned to me in surprise. 'Can I just…? There's a bit that's not quite how I want it.' Silence: they were waiting. 'Um. I suppose – I'll just show you?' I bent to open my guitar case. As I lifted the guitar, I could feel I'd gone red. I knew they'd recognise a serious instrument; knew as well that as soon as I started to play they'd peg me as a dabbler with more money than talent. Truth hurts, but – there was nothing for it.

'So it's starting at, um, it's a G, just after the first verse, and on the demo it goes...' I played the phrase that was bugging me. 'And it should be, I think it should be like...' Now I played it the way I wanted it, but nerves got the better of me and it was full of bum notes. 'Sorry, should I do it again?' I played it once more, and this time I got it right, more or less. Looked up at the band to see whether it made sense. They could have been paint for all they moved; faces expressionless. Then the guitarist nodded, and Nick said, 'Okay, that's great, thanks Campbell. I think we've got that, have we Loz?'

I hugged my guitar on my lap as they ran it through again and again. Loz played it first on his own, getting the new part of the melody perfectly; then gradually the drummer came in with a chugging rhythm, and the bassist underpinned it. Only the keyboard player sat silent, foot crossed over her knee, eyes closed. As the song came together they communicated with brief words and looks – *faster, louder, softer, up, more* – and the music stretched and tightened and brightened, and with every version it sounded more like a real song and less like mine. I watched how Loz moved his fingers, and I copied him, nearly silent, forming the chords and the notes, with my right hand just barely brushing the strings: a ghost accompaniment. Until they finished a run-through, and Loz turned to me. 'Sorry mate, can you not...?'

I laid my beautiful guitar back in its case.

Could you be fascinated and bored, both at the same time? Beside me on the sofa Duncs kept shifting his legs about. I could tell he was plain bored. On the wall behind us, the painted figures were silent and still, and I was one of them.

I'd had the idea of how I wanted this to sound. I just didn't know exactly how to get there. I wanted it lean, stripped, my voice right up front, with all its imperfections; and behind, some guitar, acoustic, intricate finger-picking like I knew I couldn't do. But that idea was blurred now – still there, somewhere, but smoothed away under all these brighter, better versions which, for all the skill, all the perfection, sounded somehow lacking. Perhaps it was just the stillness: the musicians moved, of course, they hit and pressed and strummed, but so economically it felt almost like an insult – even as they paid me the compliment of playing so professionally. Of course, they weren't hired to be passionate.

Now they were playing in chunks, to the stitched-tight rhythm of a metronome: tap-tap-tapping like someone trying to get my attention. The intro: once, twice, three times. First verse, again and again. Chorus. To me, each section sounded flawless first time, but their ears were more attuned, I guess. Open it up, the producer said, making circles with his arms, and they all seemed to know what he meant. Then everyone fell silent apart from the drummer. Sitting at his kit, which sat in turn on a circular rug like a mat curved round a toilet, he knocked out the rhythm: a textured beat, walking pace with some hopping and shuffling in between steps.

Eventually, from the control room Nick announced, 'Okay, let's break. Back here in half an hour.'

The band unhooked themselves from their instruments, trooped towards the exit while Nick wandered through to find us.

'Coming along, isn't it? What d'you think?'

I shook myself awake. 'Yeah, God, it's amazing how they can just … how they seem to know exactly how you want it.'

'Oh, they're good guys, this lot. No pissing about. If only all musicians were this easy, I tell you!'

'Listen…' I checked to make sure the studio had emptied before I finished my sentence. 'Nick, I'm not sure about those keyboards.' The painted musicians watched and listened, and noted my treachery. In fact, I'd hardly noticed the keyboards come in:

the arrangement was sympathetic enough. But I wanted to make myself difficult, to assert my ownership; just so Nick knew I had an opinion. Maybe, as well, I wanted Duncs to see I was more than an observer. To show myself I was more.

'Uh huh, well – don't worry,' said Nick. 'We don't have to keep them in, we're not tied to anything. It's all about options, at this stage.'

'Oh right, good.'

'So listen, we won't be doing the vocals until this afternoon now, so – don't feel you have to hang around all that time.'

'Sure, okay.'

'So long as you're back by … say, one.' He gave us a code for the door, retreated once again into the control room.

Outside, Duncs and I went looking for something to eat. For both of us, it seemed an effort to leave the shady dream-state of being a spectator; but stepping from the arches into mid-morning sun was like waking up. We glanced at each other.

'Sounding alright, eh?' said Duncs. 'It's not a bad song. Although, I probably don't ever need to hear it again.'

'Yeah, snap. Which could be a problem.'

'When d'you write it?'

'Ages back. Remember that time I was at home.'

'Oh aye.' He nodded, respecting the rule: we don't talk of such things.

We stopped outside a cafe advertising TEA COFFEE ALL-DAY BREAKFAST.

'Here okay?'

'Aye, fine. And which is the new bit – the chorus?'

'Yep. Can you tell, does it sound different?'

He considered, as I ordered tea and bacon rolls. 'Not in a bad way,' he decided. 'It's Glenelg, is it? The same forwards and back.'

'Spot on.' Duncs always had been quick with the clues.

'It's funny,' he said, hesitantly. 'I don't remember all that stuff. I mean, I remember Glenelg, obviously. What was it, six, seven years we were going up there? And I mind she had a wee thing for you, did Eve. But as I recall you were always running away from her. I don't remember it like childhood sweethearts or anything like that.'

He looked at me. I'd been waiting for someone to say it, I realised now. 'No,' I said, 'but you weren't there all the time. And you know when you're young, you might not always act the way you feel.'

'When you're older, too.'

I gave him a questioning look, and he shook his head just slightly.

'No, nothing.'

The waitress was on her way over with mugs of tea; I waited while she placed them in front of us. Then, 'The attic,' I said. I watched his face. 'That time – it was raining. I think it was you … interrupted.'

It took a moment: I saw the memory rise to the surface. 'That?' He gave a short laugh. 'I thought that was dodgy, right enough. There was no way that clue was up in the attic.' He picked up his mug. Blew on it. Put it down again. 'Memory's a funny thing, eh? I suppose, who's to say what way it really happened? You've got it one way, and I've got it another.' He mimed a scale with his hands: perfectly balanced. Fifty fifty. 'And then Roddy maybe remembers it another way again. And Eve, we'll never know.'

Our order arrived, and we were quiet for a bit, eating and drinking. I thought of Eve's diary, and reckoned I did know how it had been for her.

'You sorted things out with Eilidh?' Duncs said, through a mouthful of bacon roll.

'What? I don't even know what we're meant to be sorting.'

He shrugged.

'Why, has she said anything? Have you seen her?'

'I got a lift down with her.'

'I thought you flew.'

'Nah. She was driving anyway so … it made sense.'

I wiped ketchup from my fingers, scrunched my napkin and dropped it on the plate. 'Well? What was she saying?'

'I don't know, just… It's nothing to do with me, like.'

'Aye, but: what did she say?'

'Well, she's no your biggest fan at the moment.'

'Whatever. She'll need to tell me what's up if I'm expected to do something about it. Was that all?'

'We didn't spend ages talking about you.'

'Right then. Fine.' I was getting annoyed with this conversation. He was fishing, thinking I must know what it was all about. And maybe I did; I thought I did. I wasn't about to tell him, though. Didn't want to think of it myself, because of how it was in the way of everything I was looking forward to, everything I was excited about. In the way of what I was doing right now.

Duncs gave up, or perhaps he was never that interested in the first place. Pulled out his phone to check the time. 'What are you doing then, heading back, or…?'

'I know he said I didn't need to, but I kind of think I should be there.'

'Okay. Well, look, I was thinking I might shoot off.'

It was what I'd hoped he'd say. I had found my feet now, would be fine on my own; better, without him sitting bored beside me. And best, I could sing without him listening.

I was walking back to the studio when I heard him call my name. 'Cam! By the way. You're right about those keyboards.'

By the time they wanted my voice, I was itching to contribute. At the same time, I felt hollow with a mix of nerves and hunger; I'd skipped lunch to keep my throat clear, and that bacon roll seemed a long time ago. The booth was tiny, white-walled, with padded boards jutting at various heights and angles. It was a long way from Amit's bedroom, the primitive recording capabilities of his laptop. Nick took me by the shoulders, positioned me side-on, a pace away from the mic.

First, they got me to sing a verse and chorus with just my vocal coming back through the headphones. I closed my eyes, shielding myself from the embarrassment of everyone listening hard to my uncertain voice. Halfway through the chorus my vocal transformed into something stronger, richer, and my eyes popped open.

'How's that sound? Okay?'

'Sounds great.' What trickery had Kev done? I wanted to ask, but it didn't seem the right time for *Recording Engineering for Dummies*.

'Okay, let's try it all the way through. Follow the keyboard, that's your guide track.'

Music poured in: drums and bass low in the mix, keyboards nice and clear. Even so, with the headphones on I had no idea if I was in tune. I kept glancing through the window as I sang, watching Nick and Kev for signs of approval.

Once I'd made it to the end, they got me to tuck one side of the headphones behind my ear, and we ran it through again. Better: I could hear myself hitting notes, and missing a few too.

'Campbell,' said Nick, his voice feeding straight into my left ear, 'don't worry when you're off pitch. We can always tweak it, you know? There's all sorts of stuff Kev here can do. It's sounding great, really. I just wonder, can you get some more feeling into it? You wrote the words: what do they mean? What did you feel when you wrote them, yeah?'

They were simple questions: it was no-one's fault but my own that the answers were confused. Take your pick ... the for-real feeling from years ago, when I wrote the verses – and that was relief more than anything, to be still there, still me, in more or less one piece. The package of loss and enduring love I was meant to feel for Eve. The top-of-the-hill, freewheeling feel of that triumphant chorus. Did it even matter, as long as there was some kind of emotion to animate the lyrics? I closed my eyes, tried to fumble my way inside the words.

What I reached, in the end, was a colour: an orange glow, sun flaring off a lens in a place unreachably far. Orange, and the magic of ten years old in eternal summer. I could feel myself loosen: cheeks, throat, chest, belly, shoulders. I could actually feel the sun on my face. I sang, hearing warmth and light in my voice; thinking of memory sealed in the vocals. How it would be built into the code with which the song was digitised, and how that coded memory would reach a million listeners, and their worlds would turn orange too.

I didn't need Nick's thumbs up, his wide smile, to know I'd done it. The sun shone inside me; the song was mine once more.

Chapter 28

The rough cut sparkled. Rays shot off the disc as I spun it round my finger, and even the dirty old Thames was glittering as I marched alongside it. Nick had promised to email the final track as soon as it was ready. For the meantime, this zinging circle was a silvery promise, waiting to be cashed in.

I swung into the courtyard of my building, and slowed. Outside the front door next to mine was a half-familiar figure – the fair-haired guy I thought I'd seen staring up at my window, the day after Eve's premiere. I stopped outside my own door, reached in my pocket for my keys; my hand closed around them, but I paused a little longer than necessary. For a minute or so, the guy stayed where he was, as if he was waiting for someone to let him in – but I noticed he didn't push the buzzer. Then he turned and walked away. I watched him go, still trying to catch where I knew him from, and why he felt like – not a threat, exactly – more like being nagged over something I should have done, but hadn't – or shouldn't have done, but had.

When I reached the flat my heart was beating a little too fast. A long day, and then I'd taken the stairs two at a time. I unlocked the door, and it caught halfway; I crouched and stretched my arm around to retrieve a thick letter. Pitlochry postmark, handwritten address, but not in my mum's writing, nor the lesser-seen hand of my dad. Inside I propped my guitar in the corner and opened the envelope, tipped it out on the kitchen counter: a bright slither of photos. Of course: Linda. It was kind of her to remember, to go to the trouble of sorting through. She'd enclosed a brief note. *Hope these are what you wanted. Look after them please! L x*

I flipped through the snaps, a dozen or so of them: a jumble of years, faces, weathers and places. At some point I'd look at them – really look. Now, though, I kicked off my shoes, and slid my precious disc into the DVD player. Alone, I could listen properly, and honestly.

I still liked my voice, for the most part: rich, but rough round the edges. If you listened hard you could hear my accent on certain words, and to me that made it sound more genuine.

When the song stopped, I played it again. I wondered if it was the sort of thing I would choose to listen to. Maybe not; but I wouldn't turn it off, either.

If I'd spoken up more, perhaps it would sound more like I'd thought it could. It's true no-one had asked me how I wanted it to sound – but I could have told them anyway. There must have been moments when I could have stopped the whole thing and said, *Listen, this is what I want. Like this.* If I did it again... If there was another song... That was the thing about first times. By the time you'd figured things out, got the measure of a new place, a new situation, it was over.

But it was good. I'd done good. I slipped the disc back in its wallet, swapped it for a DVD from a stack of new movies I'd bought. Let myself sink into the sofa, cold beer close at hand, and as the film intro started I got ready to switch off my thoughts.

The screen was half-hidden by sun-stripes aiming straight through the blinds: I hauled myself back to my feet, moved over to the window. And stopped with my hand raised to close the slats. There he was: the fair man, the still watcher. He must surely be a photographer – but there was no sign of a camera, no heavy bag or case. He was standing, hands in pockets, staring up – not directly at my window, but as though he was searching for something. He couldn't see me through the blinds, but I had a long clear view of him.

I knew, now, where I'd seen him.

Behind me the film unrolled. There was music. They started to talk.

Light hair, dark jacket: walking towards me, towards Eve's memorial.

His gaze moved up, along, till he was looking straight at me. He can't see, I told myself. He can't see, he can't see. But even so, I twisted the handle to close the blinds. Twisted it the wrong way. Just for a second I stood revealed, right in front of him, before I managed to close the slats, slice myself thin and thinner into invisibility.

What did he want? My heart kicked in a quick drum-beat: not again – not again.

He had to be after something. And this time – what did I have to offer?

What was there left to trade?

Chapter 29

It took them two days to finish the song; days I spent away from the flat. Slitting the blinds to survey the courtyard before I left in the morning; in the evening, glancing over my shoulder before I unlocked the door. On the third day, an email popped up in my inbox with a link and a login to a secure server. *Have a listen,* said the message from Nick – *hope you like!*

I clicked through, accessed the server and started to stream the file.

I listened. I listened all the way through. And then I started a reply to Nick's email. *Nick,* I typed: *this–*

Delete.

I don't–

Delete.

I sat, cursor flashing in an empty window. Then I abandoned the message, and called Amanda.

'Have you heard it?'

'Haven't had a chance yet; I was just about to. Is there a problem?'

'Yeah, there's a problem. Listen to it. Call me back.'

I sat there, waiting, for half an hour, growing more and more agitated. Just recently, Amanda had taken on two new clients, on the back of what she'd done for my profile – the ex-partner of a Premiere League footballer, and the widow of a soldier who was campaigning to bring our boys back home. Amanda was stretching herself thin, I felt. I was used to being treated like her number one priority, and it riled me to feel I might be slipping down the list.

'I've heard it,' she said when she finally called. 'It sounds fine. It sounds good. What's wrong?'

'Amanda. It sounds like – It doesn't even sound like me.'

There was silence on the other end of the phone. I'd expected her to hear the problem straight away. But she didn't want to, I guessed. I was going to have to fight to even get her on my side. I marshalled my arguments. Tried to stay calm.

'Right. Here's what's wrong. One, they've done something to my voice so you can't even recognise it's me. Two, they've got some girl singing awful, breathy backing vocals. Three, they've put strings all over it and they're not even real strings, they're fucking horrible *synth* strings–'

'Okay. Okay, calm down.'

'I'm calm, but seriously – it's like the third cousin twice removed from itself. It sounds like they've drowned it in honey. I feel sick just listening. You've got to do something.'

A sigh. 'Let me talk to them.'

It was another hour before she called back again: an hour of pacing, of shuddering at the fake strings sawing away in my head. It got so bad I turned the radio on and up to drown it out. If Nick had purposely set out to make the song unbearable, he couldn't have done a better job. It was hard to say why the sheer polish of it upset me so much – other than: it mattered. The song mattered; it had to, because of the trade I'd made. And it was slipping away from itself, from where it had started, from what it was meant to be. With its imperfections, its idiosyncrasies lost, it sounded like a sugared betrayal.

'No go,' said Amanda when I answered the phone.

'What do you mean, no go?'

'That's it; that's the version they want to go with. I talked to Nick; and to be fair I can see where he's coming from. You've got to think of your audience. The *News*; the kind of people this is going to appeal to–'

'No, no no!'

'I'm sorry, but they're not budging on this.'

'Well, then tell them they can't have it!'

'But you've signed a contract, Campbell. Now, you can renege on that, but if you do you're leaving yourself open to legal action. You would pay back your advance, obviously; you would definitely have to meet the costs incurred so far: studio time, musicians' fees, production costs. I don't know how much we're talking – thousands.' She paused. 'And no-one else will touch you. Word spreads.'

It was my turn to be silent.

'Look, I'm going to be straight with you. The way you want it; it's not going to work. That's what they're saying. You can't carry it.'

'But, I know it wouldn't be perfect, but that doesn't matter. That's the point, almost. That rough-around-the-edges thing.'

She sighed again. 'I'm sure Nick wouldn't want me to repeat this, but – the way he put it, what he said was: bet you sound great singing in the shower. Yes? Not the same thing.' She let that sink in. 'But what they've said is, let's see how this sells, and if it goes well, if they release it on disc, they're willing to release the rough cut you like as an additional track.'

'So that's it?' I could hear the bleakness in my voice, and it angered me that she should hear it too. That she knew how much it mattered, this failure.

It was like she was trying to console me when she said, 'If this does well, next time you'll have more clout, more say. The contract you signed is for this one single. Chin up, Campbell. With luck, and a following wind, we'll be able to re-negotiate from a position of strength.'

That was the carrot, then. That position of strength: if she hadn't dangled that in front of me, I think I would have balked. Would have backed out, carried the cost, taken the risk that they'd sue me for breach of contract. But *word travels*; I hadn't known how much I'd wanted this, and now it was close, so very close ... I could throw this away, this one soiled chance – but to throw away all my future chances?

Maybe, after all, it wasn't as bad as I thought. Just, different from what I'd imagined, and good in its own way. I should listen once more, pretending it was a new thing, nothing to do with the song I'd written. But the thought was appalling. It was only a sound, a set of sounds. Yes, to me they dripped with inauthenticity, with overblown sentiment and manufactured emotion–

I couldn't do it. Couldn't listen again. The laptop, the keyboard repelled me.

I glanced at the empty courtyard. Slung on a jacket, and left the flat.

Was it only when something had been wrecked that you realised its value? That song now seemed a fragile, delicate thing, with its own integrity. The chorus dropped away, leaving verses that had never tried to be more than they were: small and simple, something that had grown, emerged, rather than being constructed. The song fluttered inside me, a hurt bird in my chest.

Stupid. Over-reacting. There was no reason for this, for the lumpishness in my throat when I swallowed and swallowed.

I was walking east along the river, roiled grey and green under an overcast sky. Walking nowhere, just walking: but when a 159 pulled to a stop beside me, I had a destination. I jumped on, heading south. It was the first bus I'd been on since I got here: I breathed deep, feeling like I deserved to suffer. On the top deck I sat by the stairs, in case I needed to get off in a hurry. But it was the middle of the day, and quiet enough, and I kept myself calm by watching the slow streets pass outside the window.

She might not be at home, of course. She might not even be in London. But the 159 was an omen, and what else was I meant to do today?

Eilidh opened the door, a few inches at first, and stopped dead when she saw me. Then she took a step back and said, 'Come in, then.'

In the kitchen she filled the kettle without asking if I wanted anything. I perched on a stool; she stayed standing on the other side of the breakfast bar, arms folded.

Now we were face to face, I didn't know where to start. 'I wasn't sure if you'd be here.'

She shrugged, as if to say: well, here I am. There was silence, apart from the rising sound of boiling water.

'I know why you're pissed off,' I said, eventually.

'Yeah? Why?'

'About the song.'

The kettle clicked off. She made us both tea, waiting for me to go on.

'Because I kind of ... wrote it for you.'

She pushed a mug towards me. 'And?'

'And I should have said something. Told you about it.'

She stood, one arm wrapped across her waist, other hand clutching her mug. Steam blurred her face. 'Well. Yes, you should have.'

'So. I'm sorry.'

She seemed to consider this. 'You're sorry you didn't tell me what you were planning to do.' She spoke slowly, as though she were working something out.

'Uh, yeah.'

'And so – now what are you planning to do?'

'What d'you mean?'

'Well, you're sorry, blah blah, all of that – but are you going to do it anyway? Are you still going to do the song?'

'It's done.' I took a sip of tea. 'We've recorded it, they've mixed it, it's done. I should warn you – it's quite different.' As I spoke, I thought maybe this was really what I was apologising for: the way it had turned out, all trimmed and sugared.

'You've done it already.' She was staring at me.

'Aye. Last week.'

'So hang on, I don't quite get this. What is it you're apologising for?'

I wondered if she'd been out late the night before. She certainly seemed to be struggling with this. And she did look rough, come to think of it, kind of baggy round the eyes. 'I just told you. Because I should have let you know what I was doing.'

'You just … you think you should have kept me informed.'

'I should have done, yeah.'

She frowned. 'If I asked you not to release this song, what would you do?'

'Well – you wouldn't ask me that, so... I don't see what that's got to do with anything. It's a hypothetical question.'

'Is it? Or, okay: what if I asked you at least to be honest about how you wrote it? Or at the very, *very* least, not to lie about it, not to go wanking on about you and Eve and your fictional childhood romance.'

'Wow, look, Eilidh.' Her cheeks were patched with pink. 'I think you're over-reacting a bit. It's just promotion! And besides, some of it *is* about Eve now. The chorus, that's about me and Eve. And to say it's *fictional* is a bit...' She didn't say anything, so I carried on. 'But that's kind of what I'm trying to explain: see the recorded version, it's like it's not the same song, even. You know, I feel funny about it too, I feel like it's been – taken away from me. But it's nothing really to do with me, d'you know? It's like, the song I wrote back then, that's still the same as what it was.' Her face was blank. I was convincing myself more than her, I could tell. 'And this single is something different, nothing to do with either of us, really. Oh … when you hear it, you'll see what I mean.'

'I hope I never do hear it.'

'Steady, it's not that bad! And you will hear it, it'll be on the radio, it'll be – hey!' She had taken my mug from where it sat in front of me. I watched as she carried it to the sink, tipped the tea away. 'What are you doing?'

'You've no clue, do you?' she said. 'I don't know why you're even here.' She walked around the breakfast bar, and held the door open.

'Eilidh–'

'Yeah, I know. I'm over-reacting. Would you mind leaving now.'

'You – you're not throwing me out?'

She didn't budge. Just stood waiting: waiting for me to get lost.

'You're not,' I said again. But she was. I got up, and realised there was nowhere for me to go but out the door. I passed her, close enough so I could see the pink gone from her cheeks, could see her face fixed, indifferent. I looked away. My own face felt hot: my chest was hurting, like I was struggling to keep something in, something fierce.

'I hope it works out for you,' she said, and her words dug into my back. 'But don't bother letting me know.'

I should have been running to get out of range; but fear dragged at my heels: fear that when I left her house, when I stepped onto the street, this – me and her – would be irreparable. So every step was slow, small – and I didn't understand what was going on, I had come here, I had apologised, and how had it all gone wrong? – slow and small steps, but there were only so many seconds I could string it out for. And when I stood on her doorstep and turned to say, *This is crazy...* it was already too late.

The cold sound of the door clicking shut was the sound of the end.

Chapter 30

Once, we spent a weekend in Glencoe. It was somebody's birthday – Roddy's, maybe. Book-ended for me, now, in an easier time: post-breakdown, pre-break-up. Everybody was there: Roddy and Jean, Eilidh, Magnus and Paolo, Duncs and some girl he was seeing. Friday night, we celebrated in the Clachaig Inn, with drink, food, more drink. When Paolo asked about the sign that said, *No Hawkers or Campbells*, we realised he didn't know the story, and battled each other to tell it.

'You seriously don't know? Okay, so this used to be all ruled by the MacDonald clan. We're talking hundreds of years ago–'

'–1600s, maybe.'

'And they were, like, majorly powerful. They were the Lords of the Isles, which meant they were in charge of pretty much the whole of the west coast, from Skye in the north all the way down to Kintyre, which is as far south as you can go. So by sixteen-when-ever, their power was on the wane, and King ... William?'

'William. William the third.'

'King William, demanded that they swear allegiance to the crown. And they kind of hummed and hawed about it, putting it off, and then ... what happened next...?'

'Then, cos they knew they really had no choice, the clan chief set off to Fort William to sign this oath of loyalty. But it was mid-winter, it was all ice and waist-deep snow, and he got delayed and he missed the deadline. He missed it by one day.

'So the government, or whoever, decided to make an example

of them. They paid this other clan, the Campbells' – Paolo pointed at me; I smiled an acknowledgment – 'to take out the MacDonalds. So the Campbells came here, to Glencoe, and basically infiltrated the MacDonald settlement. Cos it was a Highland thing that you had to offer hospitality to any guest.'

'Kind of like being Italian...'

'So the Campbells stayed for two weeks, eating MacDonald food, sleeping in MacDonald beds. And then the order came, and in the middle of the night they rose up and slaughtered their hosts. Men, women, children.'

Paolo's face was a picture. '*Quegli stronzi!*'

'Hence, Glencoe Massacre.' Magnus concluded the story. 'You're meant to be able to sense it. The ghosts. The tragedy. Soil soaked with blood. Etcetera.'

Next day, as we toiled up the slopes of Beinn Fhada, cursing our rotten hangovers, Eilidh said, 'This is where you kill me!'

Through the heaving of my breath and the pounding of my heart, not to mention the wind pummelling my ears, I thought I'd misheard.

'This is where you *kill me!*' she called again.

'Kill you?'

'Your lot. Killed my lot. Betrayed our hospitality. Betrayed our trust.'

'Oh, right. That.'

'Although ... I don't suppose it was your lot really, given that you're not actually a Campbell, Campbell.' She grinned. 'No stories about the Johnstones, are there? Not that I know of, anyway. Dull bunch, you must have been.'

'Just cos you don't know them doesn't mean there are none, and anyway I was named for my mum's dad's mum. She was a Campbell. Apparently.'

'Ah!' She paused for breath, and I stopped too, relieved. 'So it *was* you, then. I never knew that about you.' She shouted at

Magnus. 'Did you know that? Cam's a genuine Campbell?' But he was too far in front to hear: showing his army training as he struck out for the summit. The wind tugged her words back around us, buffeted them to pieces.

'So, yeah,' I said. 'Sorry about that.'

Years on, I imagine her words resounding, trapped like the Glencoe ghosts in the scoop of the valley. Lighter than flesh, denser than air. *Betrayed our trust. This is where you kill me.*

Had we been lucky? Five people in the world I'd always depended on. Six of us looking out for each other. We were the net, tight-woven to catch – catch, as in save, catch as in trap. Somehow, we'd unravelled. Somehow I'd unravelled us.

The MacDonalds' revenge, after all these hundreds of years. *Don't bother letting me know.* Eilidh: it's you that's killed me.

Chapter 31

An hour-long run. Heading west, steady and fast: back and forth across the river, keeping it close at my side. As I ran, a hundred years un-happened, time turning back from box-fresh riverside apartments to quiet Georgian grandeur, to the pleasure gardens of the Chelsea Embankment. My ankle, aching still from my fall on the hillside, jarred with each heel-strike till endorphins flooded, rinsing pain away. With my shades on, strolling people who seemed barely to be moving had no chance to put a name to my face, no time to act on any recognition before I left them for dust.

My turning point: Battersea Park. I looped, and the morning sun bounced off my shades.

It came together, sometimes, like today: a perfect run. Rhythm right, feet just glancing; body coping, in control. Crossing the fairytale Albert Bridge, Disney sugar and icing. Shoulders set, hands loose-fisted. Light and deep. Light and deep.

Too easy. I pushed it, into a sprint. Started, at once, to struggle. Light turned heavy. Deep turned shallow. To distract myself I started to practise: question and answer. What would they ask when the single launched? What was the tale I'd tell, on the radio slots, the daytime TV I was booked in to do? I practiced what Amanda had said: turning the song to a story. *What does it mean – a place the same forwards and back? What's the song about? Have you always wanted to be a singer?*

Home stretch, back to the bleak, box-like present: breath frayed to ragged gasps, gravity glued to my feet. MI6 HQ, squat as a tank

– toytown Meccano, Vauxhall Bridge: I roped the landmarks in my mind, used them to haul myself on till I reached the point where I could slacken off, call it a cool-down, and instead, I pelted on – *treasure in sight* – heaving chest, salt-sweat eyes – blood-red–

Stop.

From nowhere, he was in front of me. I jinked, staggered towards the wall. Caught at rough, wet brick. The wet was from me – sweat, pouring off me.

'Sorry to interrupt,' he said.

I couldn't speak. Could hardly breathe: bent, chest heaving. My shades slid from my sweat-slicked face, and I caught them, just. Sun bounced white off concrete that blurred in front of me. His shoes, black leather, were knife-like, stabbing into my field of vision.

'I was hoping to have a word.'

I lifted my eyes from his black feet. He was wearing the same dark denim I remembered from the cemetery. I straightened to my full height; even then, he had a good half-foot on me. Gradually, my breathing slowed, though my heart was still sprinting.

'I'm a friend of Eve's,' he said. 'Was a friend of Eve's.'

'Aye?' I took a couple of steps so I was out of the sun's glare, standing square on to him. 'There's a coincidence... Me too.'

'Obviously. I know that, everyone knows that.' His tone was deadpan. 'But, I'm guessing you don't know about me.'

Full marks so far. All I knew was he'd visited her, more than once; had visited me as well.

'I've seen you,' I said. 'Hanging round here.' It wasn't a question, but I still thought he might offer some explanation.

Instead he said, 'There's something I need to ask you.'

If I'd had more breath to spare, I would have laughed. He could have approached me weeks ago, in the cemetery – or when we passed in the courtyard, just the other day. My feet swelled and burned inside my trainers; my sweat-soaked shirt clung to my skin.

'You think this is the best time? To ask me your questions?' But as I spoke, I realised. It could be the best time – if he needed me weakened. And if this was his moment, the moment he'd chosen, it had to mean that whatever he wanted, I wouldn't want to give. Well, he'd chosen wrong. I wasn't weakened, I was ready. My muscles were hot and strong, filled with blood and oxygen. I flexed my legs, rotated my shoulders: tiny secret motions.

'Eve never mentioned me?' he said.

I shook my head. 'Pass.'

'No. Well. She wanted to keep it quiet.'

He was watching for my reaction. I made sure to give him nothing. 'You and her...?' I said it casually.

A little colour had risen up into his pale face. 'She didn't want the press to get hold of it, that was the thing. She'd had all that with Dan, and she just wanted … said she wanted to keep them away from us. She wanted us to be ordinary.'

When were you together? I wanted to know, but didn't want to ask. 'She never said.' She hadn't. When she gave me that midnight look in the watery courtyard, she hadn't said a thing. Unless – *someone ordinary, someone who's not spoiled...*

'Which makes sense, right. At the start, to keep things quiet – it does make sense.' He sounded as though he were thinking this through step by careful step – though each one of those steps must have been slippy-smooth by now. 'Perhaps she said something similar to you?'

Again, his gaze fixed me. I didn't reply.

'It would never have occurred to me, if you hadn't been all over the papers, I never would have thought it. But maybe she had another reason for keeping us quiet. Like you. Like you were the reason.' He was staring now, and his voice was suddenly louder. 'I don't believe it. I really can't believe it. Me and her was real. We both knew it. We both felt the same.'

He shut his eyes, briefly, as if he could close out this swarm of treacherous thoughts. I stretched my neck, side to side to side.

His moves were laying themselves out in front of me. But I had to wait, be sure. Stay back. Stay ready.

'I do have some understanding of how it works: the publicity thing, the game.' His eyes were wide now, and serious, and underneath the words he spoke he was saying something else. I had to tilt my head slightly to meet his gaze. Even so he put me in mind of a trapped animal, crouched and staring upwards. I was the one keeping him trapped: I was his hope of escape.

'You and Eve, from what I've read, you were ... close, from way back. We weren't together long, me and her – not quite four months – but long enough for me to see how crazy it is, that world, how fucked up. How people will do anything for a ... an angle. To get noticed.' His mouth twitched upwards in what might have been a smile. *I know how it is*, he was saying to me. Scrabbling for common ground – common ground other than Eve. 'So, like I say. I would understand that,' he said, and I felt, unexpectedly, some kind of truth swelling inside me.

You're right, I thought; felt the words rising in my throat. She was yours, and she's still yours. You and Eve. That's what was real. I could almost see the sun rise across his face. If I spoke those easy words – if I gave her back to him – he could taste his grief pure. Untainted. I could tell him exactly what had happened, and I'd be light. I'd be clean. And all the things I'd lost... It danced in front of me, the promise of confession. If I was his hope of escape, he was mine. We were mutual. We were each other's mirror.

I was ready to tell the truth.

And then Eve's face was before me: her eyes close-and-opening, telling me to *go on, then* – telling me to act. Eve's voice: *It's never simple*. Eve saying, *Don't tell*.

What would her truth have been?

She was yours, and she's still yours.

Neither he nor I could have them back, the lost things. Eve stayed dead, no matter what I said. My home stayed invaded. My parents stayed ... disappointed. My net of friends stayed sliced

233

apart. Eilidh stayed indifferent as a stone, and her words – *I don't know why you're here* – stayed trapped inside me.

He was still talking, trying to make it easy for me. 'I can see how it would happen – you were such old friends…'

You and Eve, that was real.

I could say it, and tomorrow I'd read it back in the newspapers. Amanda would be on the phone to tell me I'd breached some obscure clause of my contract with the record company; that the song was history, and I should get ready to have my arse sued all the way back to Glasgow, to Moulin, to my invaded home, to the cell of my bedroom, my disappointed parents, the ghosts of my vanished friends. All that was lost still lost; and all I'd traded it for gone too.

'It's not a game,' I said.

He flinched. His eyes were such a pale, pale blue they should have been able to laser fiction clean away from truth. But they weren't scalpels of light, they were water, or broken glass; and the light was streaming the other way, in through his cracked irises.

I folded my arms across my chest, rubbed hard at my biceps. I'd never landed a punch in my life, drunken scuffles aside, but now my arms and shoulders ached and I felt like I'd jabbed him with a left-right-left. I'd been too long in the shade; the sweat had chilled on my skin.

We stood for an ice age, neither of us able to look away, and at last his stare slackened.

'I wasn't on the *guest* list,' he said.

I shook my head, just fractionally. I didn't know what he meant.

'For the funeral. I couldn't even go to her funeral.'

I was starting to shiver: the cold that comes after the heat of exertion, that fingers its way into your bones before you know it's on you. 'I'm sorry,' I said. 'Really, I'm sorry about that. But there's nothing I can do.'

As I walked past, he seemed to shrink. I didn't look back.

My ankle twinged as I climbed the stairs to my flat; when

I shoved my key into the lock, my hand was shaking. Inside, I pushed the door closed, and tugged it, testing to make sure it was secure. Left my clammy clothes where they dropped: stepped straight into the shower. Let it rain hard on me.

And now here was another annoyance: I was going to have to call the lettings agency, because the boiler was playing up. No matter how hot I turned the water, it wouldn't get me warm.

EXCLUSIVE FOR DAILY NEWS READERS!
Campbell Johnstone single
Download FREE from iTunes – offer ends today
Interview inside >>

Tell us about your first single, 'The Coldest Day'...
It's a song I wrote for Eve, to tell her how I felt about her. At
the time I wrote it, we were just getting to know each other
again and all these old feelings were coming back – I knew I
had to tell her how I really felt, but I had no idea if she still felt
the same way as she had done back when we were kids. Every
time I tried to find the words to put into an email or a letter it
was like I just froze, and I couldn't imagine telling her face to
face or over the phone. It wasn't until I picked up my guitar
that the words came easily. So that's where 'The Coldest Day'
comes from.

Sounds like it's very close to your heart?
It is, because I never had the chance to play it for her. So when
I recorded it, that was like I was singing for her, putting it out
there into the world, all the hopes and dreams I had for what
could happen with us.

*The song is attracting a lot of attention. Why do you think it's
so popular?*
I think people respond to the sense of hope. I mean, there's a
sadness in the vocals, of course, but the words are filled with
hope. Already I've had messages from readers who say the song
means something to them because it's helping them through
their own hard times. And I feel proud to be able to do that, to
help a wee bit when life gets difficult.

*Until recently, you worked in a bar in Glasgow. Have you
always had musical ambitions?*
I remember Eve said to me once, I think you know if you're

destined for something out of the ordinary, you know from when you're a kid if you're going to be – I don't want to say special – but if you're going to achieve something, live a different kind of a life from most people. And I always felt like there was more out there. It just took me a while to find my passion.

You've been working with the charity Anaphylaxis Alert to raise awareness of the risks of severe allergies. Is this something you plan to continue?
Absolutely, that's what it's all about for me: what happened to Eve didn't need to happen. So if I can help make people aware of the risks, and the need for information, that's important – that's something that really matters. Our *Give With A Kiss* campaign has been a massive success, raising over two million pounds to help create a safer environment for allergy sufferers – and now a percentage of the proceeds from 'The Coldest Day' is going to AnAlert, so that's all the more reason for people to buy it. Buy two!

What's next for you?
I'd like to carry on with the music, that's the focus for me now.

Chapter 32

The Jonahs – four kids barely old enough to shave – were here to get signed. The press were here to praise or to bury them, depending on what the mood was this week. The A&R folks were here to maybe – just maybe – be impressed, and the public was here because each of them had won an online draw for special VIP guest passes to an exclusive music industry showcase event, i.e. they'd been lured in to make up the numbers, and give the illusion of buzz.

Me? I was there so I could drink alone in company – at the kind of event I could go to every night now, if I wanted, courtesy of my label. The drink, at least, was adequate and in no short supply. The company, though, was shocking. The punters looked like they'd been bussed in from a suburban sixth form college: nest-haired girls in short-short skirts trying to look dirty; squeaky-clean boys in checked shirts and box-fresh Vans. By comparison the journos and A&R men looked creased and dusty, ravens huddled amongst the tourists. They were uniformed alike in skinny black jeans, with black pointed boots that needled something I was trying to forget.

I had plenty of time to observe all this, sat on my own at the bar: apart, and looking down at the people waiting in front of the stage. I had on my shades, despite the low lighting. The last thing I wanted tonight was to be recognised. I'd left the flat and made my way here because I was sick of myself. I was sick at the thought of my column inches in the *Daily News*. Sick of dialling Eilidh's number, hearing her phone ring out. But the sickness was contagious; it attached itself to everything and everyone. I saw the girls laughing, shouting to make themselves heard, and all the time performing, sure they were being noticed by the boys and the men; watched by each other, if no-one else. Watched by their selves. My lip curled. What did they have to feel excited about? If anything happened tonight, anything that mattered, it wouldn't be to them. They were background. Extras. Part of a mechanism that was meant to propel four young men into the public eye. They thought they were part of the show; they were rent-a-crowd, that was all.

I bought another pint: flattening lager in a glass warm from the washer. I was drinking doggedly, without any particular pleasure. It was either that or not drink, which didn't feel like an option.

Down in the pit, there was a push for the front, leaving a dark tidemark of industry folks. A few faces were familiar: I spotted Dylan, the A&R guy from my own label; Suzy, a scarlet-haired Dubliner, some kind of PR; a skinny Mancunian called Al, who wrote for a music monthly. He'd interviewed me for a feature on digital-only releases. Now when he saw me, he nodded, raised his drink, and I raised mine in return. I was pleased. He had a flat way of speaking razor-sharp words, came over as a serious muso constantly amused by the quirks of this odd business. I liked him more than most of the people whose numbers were in my phone. I had an idea he could be a friend.

A wave of claps and cheers signalled the Jonahs' arrival onstage – the extras playing their parts to perfection – and the band launched straight into a sugary piece of guitar-pop. After a minute, my teeth were aching. After five, my glass was almost empty and I was thinking of leaving. But then Al arrived at the bar in search of a refill, and I thought I might as well stay.

'Hey, I'll get that.' I waved a tenner at the barmaid, ordered the drinks for both of us.

'Very kind,' said Al. 'Enjoying the band, are you?'

'It's so fucking sunny it makes me want to open a vein. What about you? Are they indie-pop saviours or are they pissing on the grave of the Lemonheads?'

'D'you know, I can't even be bothered to form an opinion.' He surveyed the crowd, which was nodding and jigging just out of time with the beat. 'Think they've found their audience, though.'

We watched without speaking for a while. The Jonahs were competent, I had to admit. And the extras seemed to like them. When the song ended, the lead Jonah decided to introduce the band one by one, soliciting whoops and cheers for each member.

Al leaned in close, like he was about to share a confidence. 'This lot will grow up to buy your music,' he said. 'Twenty years' time. Watch 'em.'

I stared at him. He was smiling with one side of his mouth, one eyebrow raised.

'They wake up and realise they've wasted their youth – not that the realisation will stop them wasting the next twenty years as well. They're starting to count their wrinkles. They're filled with a kind of free-floating sadness, even though the saddest thing to have happened to most of them is still their dog dying while they were away at uni – or maybe Jessica or Timothy chucking them just after they graduated.' He was watching the crowd now; he'd turned away from me like I wasn't even there. 'And they'll listen to your song – feet up on the sofa – and get all teary over their third glass of wine.' He glanced at me. 'Must feel good to know you're providing a public service.'

I didn't know if I should try to laugh or offer him outside. I was still figuring it out when he added, 'Except they won't be listening to you, will they? Cos you'll be long gone by then. Take the money and run. Smart move.'

He set his pint half-drunk on the bar.

'Well, that's ten minutes I'll never get back; don't know why I even came. See you around, Campbell Johnstone.' He was checking his phone as he made for the exit, better offers beckoning from each corner of the city, leaving his words to bounce around in my head where they echoed, dueted with Eilidh's: *I don't know why you're even here.*

By the time I decided I should have hit him, he was nowhere. I drained my glass, and signalled the barman to pour me another.

'This done?' His hand closed round Al's abandoned drink.

'Aye. It's done.'

In the background, the band were still playing: underneath, a dark diminished chord thrummed inside me, a rolling, growling judder that threatened not to fade, not to die. Something about me felt explosive – not helped by the lager pressing inside me. I left my drink, set my shoulders to barge through bubblegum pop, feeling grimly satisfied when the teenybop crowd melted out of my way.

When I got back to the bar, some girl was in my seat.

'Oh, sorry,' she said, as I reached across for my drink. 'Were you sitting here?'

I shook my head, grunted.

'No, go on.' She slipped down from the stool. 'I didn't mean to nick it.'

'It's fine. Honest.'

She got the message that I didn't want to talk. Still she stayed standing, a few feet away, and the stool stood in between us.

Eventually I turned to her. 'This is stupid. Take the seat.'

'Are you sure?'

'Aye. Go on.'

'Thank you.' She hoisted herself up, fairly gracefully. Her dress came down to her knees, and I thought how the other girls here would have had their knickers on show with a similar manoeuvre. It was a summery thing she was wearing, and the green of it fluttered at the side of my vision. Also just visible: crossed bare legs, the bounce of one Converse-clad foot.

The bad chord had eased. I could hear the Jonahs clearer now, and I liked this song better. It was still ice-cream and sunshine, but more original. More heartfelt. All the time I was facing the stage, I was wanting to turn and take a proper look at the girl. I wanted to let my eyes slide up her legs. She'd had a kind of a

French style about her, long dark hair all scooped up and back, and, I thought, brown eyes.

I thought brown. But I couldn't be sure.

At the end of the song, I sneaked a glance over my shoulder – wanting just to check. But the bar-light was dim and pink-tinted, and I couldn't see for definite.

'You want your seat back?' She'd caught me staring.

'No, no, I just ..., wasn't sure what colour your eyes were.'

She opened them wide, surprised. Brown they were, chocolate brown. Warm, melting chocolate. And then they narrowed as she smiled, and then they closed as she looked down, hand lifted to shield her face from my stare and I thought, she's shy. How sweet to meet a girl who's a little shy. How unexpected.

'Sorry,' I said. 'Didn't mean to embarrass you. Look – can I get you a drink?'

I thought she'd say no; then when she nodded I thought she'd ask for something mixed and fashionable.

'Thanks,' she said. 'Just, a beer?'

My heart went soft.

Her name was Rosie. When I told her mine was Cam, there was no sign of recognition. She had no idea who I was, as far as I could tell. Tonight, I was just like everybody else.

The band was so loud we couldn't talk much, and by the time we'd finished our drinks they were still going strong.

'I don't suppose ... would you fancy going somewhere else?'

She swung herself down from the stool, bag on her shoulder: ready to come with me. 'Yeah, sure,' she said. It was as easy as that.

Outside, the night air was tepid and smelt of hot pavement. I wasn't quite sure where we were. Hackney: I didn't know these streets. 'Any ideas where we can find a pub?' I said. 'Just, like, a normal pub?'

'I know a place...' she said, and reached towards me, took hold of my hand. Small fingers, cool and dry. Girls' small hands amaze me; it felt like an awful long time since any girl had slotted hers into mine. Cody and I had not held hands, as far as I could recall.

We walked for a few minutes, Rosie and me. The air was still around us, the street deserted, or else I didn't notice any other passers-by. Our arms swung slightly. We talked about the band. Her voice bore a trace of Yorkshire that matched the pint she'd been drinking: it was black pepper on strawberries, a spice to her sweetness, unexpected and right.

'So how come you're on your own?'

'Oh, my friend had to work late, so ... I got stood up.'

'Oh. Shame he missed it.'

'She,' said Rosie, and as she spoke she smiled up at me.

The pub, when we found it, was just right. Windows too high to see in from the street: inside, worn floorboards and wooden pews, drinkers who glanced at us without interest.

'I'll get these,' she said.

Drinks poured, we slid into an empty booth. Gazed at each other.

'Still brown,' I said.

She laughed. 'And yours are–' She broke off; leaned back in her pew. 'I've just realised who you are.'

The night teetered on the brink.

'Oh yes. Who's that then?'

'Well. You're Campbell Johnstone, aren't you.'

I grimaced. 'Guilty as charged.' Her smile had vanished. 'Does it bother you?'

She looked uncertain. 'No? I'm not sure. Should it?'

I shrugged.

'Does it bother you?' she said.

'Does it bother me being me?' I phrased it like that to make fun of her question: how could it bother me to be me? I expected her to laugh at how ridiculous it sounded. But her face stayed serious.

'If you like. Being you; being ... known. The way you are.'

I opened my mouth. Closed it again. Gazed at her big brown eyes. 'I hate it.'

She nodded, eyes wide with understanding.

'I ... *despise* it.'

And somehow I was telling her all about it. There was something so sweet about her, so genuine, that she made my world seem like a tainted, shameful bazaar.

'The people who read those papers,' I was saying. 'What's wrong with them? Their lives are so empty they need to fill up their heads with ... with soap operas, with real life stories – but they're never real. They're never real.' God, I was drunk, drunker than I'd thought, and I should shut my mouth but it felt so good to tell her. It felt so good to tell the truth.

'You hate it,' she said, nodding.

'It's a game! It's all a publicity game. You don't read that crap – do you? I bet you don't, you wouldn't, I know you wouldn't. It's just morons. Idiots. They're buying my song and it's just – terrible – they don't have ears! They can't hear a good song from a bad song from a...' I was losing my thread. I couldn't speak fast enough to get it all out. 'And the next one, if there's a next one, that'll be just as bad, whatever they say ... and people will still buy it. They think – they think it's me they're buying! Like I'm for sale, like my life is for sale. And the worst thing is, the thing of it is, I need it. I need it now, don't I? They've got me.'

There was more, much more. I kept talking, and she kept listening, and we kept the drinks flowing. I was well on the way to achieving my original aim of getting steaming, while Rosie seemed able to hold her liquor. That was Yorkshire for you.

'I don't know anything about you,' I said at one point. 'Tell me about you, what do you do, where are you from, tell me everything.'

But she smiled, gave small answers – 'Honestly, there's nothing much to tell,' she said – and soon we were back to me, to my twisted world, how it fed me and drowned me.

'My friend doesn't like me any more,' I was saying, much later. 'She was my best friend. I try to phone her and she just ignores me. But now it doesn't matter because I've met you. Actually I think she hates me, now. Which is fair enough. Fair enough... It's all my fault, see.'

Rosie listened. Accepted. Understood. I could tell her anything. I suppose it was like confession because afterwards, I felt bleached. I felt like a pristine page, waiting for a new chapter.

The night fragmented. Broken and sparkling. Neon in the rain. We separated, somehow. *Come home with me*, I remember saying, more than once, and her saying, *Not tonight*, and smiling, *not the first night*. And her modesty, her reticence, made me feel I was already in love with her. And she was right: I was too drunk even to remember this, and I knew I had to hold it, to record it just as it was. I wanted this kept forever.

Chapter 33

I woke up dreaming not of Eve or of Rosie, not of Eilidh or even of Cody, but of water: deep, deep lakes of pure, sparkling water, and with a throat so dry that when I swallowed it was like knives in sand.

I should have left my aching head on the pillow, slept off my hangover, but my eyes kept popping open. I was light, and calm, and floating.

In the shower I let my mouth fall open, water streaming over and in, so clean and good. Rosie. I remembered; and through the god-awful hangover I felt something like joy.

I recalled the exact tone of her voice, the shape of her accent. My desire to hear her voice again was so fierce that I took the battery out of my phone with shaky hands, hid it from myself on the top shelf of the wardrobe. And then I covered my red eyes with my hugest shades, and left the house, locking temptation behind me because if I called now, I knew I'd fuck everything up. I had to wait.

Had she still liked me by the end of the night? I was pretty sure she had. I wondered if I'd made a fool of myself by talking so much. Complaining so much. I wondered if I'd meant all I said. But most of the time, as I followed the Thames west, I didn't think at all. The river passed through me, fat and brown; the dusty streets passed through me, and the leaves and the grass. A sliver of last night: her dress, and me thinking: green, that's what's missing in all of this. I wasn't sure now what that meant, if it meant anything. I didn't interrogate it. Didn't want to question anything about last night. I walked on, through dappled light, letting myself be empty. A good kind of empty. Pure. Waiting. Ready.

I spent all day walking, stopping in parks and cafés. Basking in the thought of her. When I got back home it was dusk, and I could have slept where I stood.

The phone was ringing. The landline. I rolled over, ignoring it: let it ring off. And then I thought, Rosie; it could be Rosie. I was out of bed and staggering down the hall when fuzzily I realised she couldn't have this number, and then the phone rang again and I still somehow thought it might be… I snatched up the receiver, coughed and growled my voice awake.

'Hello?'

'I take it you haven't seen the *Mercury*?' said Amanda. Her tone could have sliced my ear off. 'I'll summarise. The headline is: you're fucked.'

Exclusive:
CAM'S FANS ARE MORONS
Inside, we reveal how Cam:
- **SLAMS his own single**
- **Calls fans IDIOTS**
- **Admits he CRAVES publicity**

Our attractive undercover reporter posed as an audience member and got close to Campbell at a music industry showcase event in London's fashionable East End. Over a long evening of drinking, Campbell spilled his heart out to our reporter and even tried to bed her at the end of the night.

'This song they've released is a load of sh*t,' confessed Campbell as he drank pints of Hoegaarden and chatted with our reporter. 'But people are buying it because they're idiots, they're morons – they're buying it because of the whole Eve thing.'

Later, the barman-turned-singer said, 'Eve's death has given me this whole new life and in a way I am grateful for that.'

Our reporter secretly ordered soft drinks for herself while Campbell downed pint after pint of strong lager and told her, 'These stories are cr*p written by people with no morals for people with no brains.

'And the worst thing is that I need the publicity. They've got me over a barrel.'

A friend of Campbell has recently hinted that there may be more than meets the eye to Campbell's relationship with tragic star Eve Sadler. 'What the papers are saying, it wasn't like that. They are being sold a story but there's two sides to every story.'

Campbell has been involved with charity Anaphylaxis Alert since Eve suffered a fatal heart attack following a severe allergic reaction. Eve was known to have suffered extreme reactions to peanuts and shellfish in the past, and Campbell had been eating peanuts shortly before the couple shared a kiss on the night she died – the so-called 'kiss of death'.

A definite link was impossible to prove.

Campbell recently led the charity's *Give With A Kiss* campaign – working intimately with Anaphylaxis Alert employees like the attractive blonde fundraiser pictured (left).

The singer has been keen to talk about how the proceeds from his single 'The Coldest Day' will go to Anaphylaxis Alert. But we can reveal that **JUST 10%** of the cash will find its way to the charity's coffers, with the rest swelling Campbell's own bank balance.

Chapter 34

Amanda's voice was relentless, drawing blood with every line. After the first few sentences, my head shook: no, that's wrong. That has to be wrong. All the heat in my body whooshed to the surface, scalding my skin, and in seconds evaporated. My teeth began to chatter.

'Don't leave the house,' Amanda was saying. 'I'll be round as soon as I can. We need to figure out how we're going to play this. If we can play it.'

When she'd hung up, I stood in the box of my flat. An army of fear waited outside. I was back where I'd started. But this flat was no safe house. A brittle shell, an empty cell: how long was I meant to hide away in here? I clenched my jaw, trying to control my chattering teeth.

I lifted the phone again. Ordered a cab, for as soon as possible.

Planning, acting, doing, moving: anything but thinking. I couldn't think, not now, not about Rosie. The non-existence of Rosie. In the bedroom I pulled my suitcase out from the wardrobe, splayed it on the bed. Toothbrush. Razor. Underwear. T-shirts. Dressing as I packed. My laptop. Linda's photographs. My phone: I dropped it into the case, with the battery still separate, because nothing good could come from checking it now. My folder of cuttings: I threw it in, too, and hid it under a jacket, wanting it out of my sight.

I flinched when the phone rang, had to force myself to answer. Just the taxi, waiting for me out on the street. My getaway car.

I crouched, reached under the bed till my fingers touched card. Eve's memory box. I weighed its lightness in both hands. If I left it here, what would happen? Would it find its way home to Mariella? More likely it would end up out on the kerb, waiting for the rubbish truck, with everything else I was leaving behind. I tucked the box into my case, cushioned by clothes.

I was moving quickly now: guitar in one hand, case in the other, I let the front door close behind me and jogged down the stairwell. At the bottom, I paused for just a few seconds – preparing myself for what lay in wait. Then – head down, shades on – I flung the door open, and legged it towards the street.

As I hurried through the courtyard, Amanda appeared at the entrance; walking towards me, phone pressed to her ear. She saw me: her phone-hand fell to her side, and she broke into a trot.

'I said, *stay inside!*' she hissed, but it wasn't her fury that froze me. It wasn't Amanda at all.

It was the figure I saw over her shoulder, ten paces behind, smooth blonde head held high as she blocked my escape.

'*You.*'

Mariella spoke like a landowner addressing a serf. Amanda turned, and I saw her bristle. I wanted to say to her, *Help me, save me.* I wanted her to put an arm round me, steer me inside, back up to my cell. Instead, she took a step back, folded her arms. Referee position.

I put down my case, my guitar.

Mariella stalked towards me. She stopped a few feet away; close enough so I could see the sharp lines tugging down from the sides of her mouth, and how the whites of her eyes were palest pink.

'Do you have the first idea what you've done?'

She waited, actually waited for an answer. I felt myself start to shake. Wrapped my arms around my chest, trying to conceal it. Wishing now that Amanda would vanish; like this might be no more than a nightmare, if it went unwitnessed.

'I really don't think you do. So let me tell you. In your twisted brain she wasn't really *real*, was she? People who happen to be

251

famous, how can they be real? With proper feelings, and families. And then she's dead: how could it matter? Maybe that's what you thought.'

I took a breath, ready to deny it, but she swept straight on.

'But it does matter. It matters that you have clambered to notoriety on the back of her achievement. That you have been scrabbling about for cash and for consequence, and you have trampled her memory underfoot. And in telling your little lies about her, you've made sure that every day, every single day, *we* have to read more and bigger lies – her father, and me. Every time we walk past a newsagent. Every time we pick up a paper.'

I stared at a space just to the left of Mariella's head, skewered by her awful articulacy. I kept staring as my eyes began to blur. As the trees in the courtyard shivered, singed by shame.

'She's been stolen from us, from her family, do you understand that? And quite clearly you've no intention of stopping, and my patience–' Her voice broke; she took a breath. 'My patience has run out. It's never going to be enough for you, is it?'

Dry-mouthed, I managed to croak: 'It is – it's over...'

'She'd be disgusted. Disgusted with you. And the worst thing is that she did actually, once, care about you, though God knows why because you're nothing but a nasty little liar–'

A car blared its horn over her words: it was my cab, calling the end of the round, calling the end of the slaughter, but there was no way I could reach it with Mariella square in front of me. It seemed to startle Amanda into motion; for a few seconds, I thought she herself was making a run for my taxi – abandoning me, and I couldn't have blamed her – and then I saw she was marching towards a man half-hidden behind a tree. I saw his lens flash straight at me. Me and Mariella.

'You're on private property,' Amanda was yelling. 'I'll call the police if you don't leave right now.' She was trying to block his line of vision, but he danced off to one side, pointing and shooting, ignoring her threats.

'Where are you from?' called Mariella. 'Are you from the papers? I'll give you a quote. Come here and I'll give you your bloody quote.' She pointed at me. 'This man is a parasite, living off the memory of my cousin Eve, and he's a *liar*, and he meant *nothing* to her! Nothing!' Her voice cracked as she tried to make herself heard over the taxi's horn. And all the time the camera's eye was on me, its shutter-jaws working, snapping picture after picture as Mariella rounded on me once more – her face no more than a foot away so I could smell her, perfume and tobacco, so I was brushed by her breath as she said, 'I'll tell you the one thing I do believe.' Her chest rose and fell. 'Out of all those tawdry stories.' Her eyes, watered blue, were ringed with shadow. She drew a rough breath, but her voice was precise, her words a bulls-eye.

'You killed Eve. I believe it. The world believes it. And you believe it, too.'

Chapter 35

All I wanted now was to be unseen; so the nuclear-bright, soaring spaces of the airport were my version of hell. I kept my eyes hidden and showed them my money: hundreds of pounds for the next seat to Glasgow.

At the departure gate I sat, looking neither left nor right, ignoring the flap of passengers turning the pages of their tabloids. At football in second year, me and Kyle Mathieson both jumped for the ball and knocked heads instead. His skull was like concrete; he had the tiniest bump, and I was concussed. Dazed and sick, unbalanced, the world knocked out of alignment. That's how it felt now. And of all the fallout, I could only think of Rosie's hand. How it had felt in mine; the space it had left, that my fingers now curled around.

She must have felt it, the connection between us; no-one could tell me that wasn't real, and so mutual it was unbelievable. She felt it, and she disregarded it. She must have thought I deserved this.

She'd said, hadn't she – at one point she'd said, *Do you want to talk about it, what really happened the night Eve died?* What *really* happened. Even through the drink, that should have set bells ringing. And it almost had: my head and hers had been close, nearly touching, and I'd pulled away so our thoughts couldn't overlap – convinced she'd share my vision of Eve's scarlet eyes, or be frozen by my helpless terror.

What was her name, not-Rosie? Oh, not that it mattered. It didn't make a difference who she was, except that I wanted to track her down and do violence to her, to see fear in her big brown eyes, to sour her soft sweetness. She was a sharp-clawed little bitch, and – I did myself the kindness of assuming – a fucking great actor. But I must have wanted, needed to believe. How pathetic did that make me?

Bit by bit, now, through my dazed consciousness, the bigger implications were taking shape.

My musical career, such as it was, was over and out. No doubt about that. If I'd been coasting on the affection the public had for Eve, this morning I'd crashed to a halt. All that was left was a crumpled wreck, steam still rising. *Give With A Kiss* would be damaged too: the Campbell Johnstone usernames silenced, discreetly deleted; the torrents of cash drying to a trickle; Hilary cursing my disgrace.

That photographer: whatever paper he worked for, I'd be on the front page tomorrow. Mariella's accusations would be reported as fact. Which, in fact, they were: sharp-cornered truths lodged inside me, somewhere near my lungs, stabbing with every breath.

A quote floated past, in Amanda's voice. *A friend of Campbell has recently hinted that there may be more than meets the eye to Campbell's relationship with tragic star Eve Sadler. 'What the papers are saying, it wasn't like that. They are being sold a story but there's two sides to every story.'*

I knew how it worked: maybe there was no friend. But that quote: it sounded ambiguous enough to be real. Eilidh? Roddy? Even Duncs? *Memory's a funny thing*, he'd said. And Roddy, on his leaving night: *You can't believe everything you read, eh Cam...* Yes, it could have been either of them. Not Eilidh. I didn't think it was her, only because the words were too coy. Only because she wouldn't, any longer, describe herself as my friend.

That's what I was thinking when a man's voice said, 'Excuse me?' I looked up and a stranger said, 'I thought it was you.' And then the world exploded in pain as his fist crunched into my face.

My hands shot up – too late to protect myself – warding off

the next blow. But he was walking away. I saw him, through the bars of my fingers: in no hurry, shaking his hand; gone, into the crowds. Simple, swift: justice delivered. He didn't want anything more, only to give me what I deserved.

'Oh my goodness, are you okay?' A woman was pressing a wad of tissues into my hands. On the white concourse, my shades lay broken, insect-like, and blood was drip-dripping from me, from my mouth: small drops, slow, perfectly round.

'It's okay,' I told her, tried to tell her, though my mouth couldn't move enough to form the words. And it was okay. It absolutely was. If he was a fan, if he'd loved her – and he must have done; loved her from afar, so she was as real to him as anything else in his life, as real or maybe more so – then, fair enough, pal. Good on you. His pain was more than mine. His love was more than anything I'd professed.

Blood spilled through my fingers, soaking through the tissues. 'Can we get you to a First Aid point?' the woman was saying, but her voice was very far away. The blood pooled in my palms. It ran down my wrists, and painted the cuffs of my shirt: graceful and unstoppable, white becoming red.

PART FOUR

The final stretch
Is straight and long

Chapter 36

'What are you doing up here in the dark?'

Eve's head pokes up into the attic, then the rest of her too, as she scrambles through the open hatch. I knew she'd be the one to find me.

I'm about to tell her there isn't a light, but then I see she's looking at a switch on the wall. I've been up here for ages and hadn't noticed it. But at least in the dark Eve can't see my face, which is totally on fire.

'I like the dark,' I say. And where I'm standing, under the skylight, there is actually a bit of light, even though it's heavy and grey and raining outside like it has been all week. There's enough light to read, just about.

Eve is perched in front of the opening. When she stands up, the weird frilly skirt she's wearing makes a triangle against the light from the landing below. She tugs at the skirt, rearranging its frills. 'But if you've given up, it's only me that's left!' She folds her arms.

'Where's Roddy, and Jean?'

'Jean gave up ages ago, all she wants to do is sit with her Walkman on. I think Roddy's downstairs watching telly.'

'And Duncs is off being a dick somewhere, probably.'

She stares like she's a bit shocked. Good. But then she says, 'It's just because he's a teenager.' She sounds like a miniature adult, with her posh, swoopy voice.

'Aye, right,' I say, 'and aliens came and stole his brain on his fourteenth birthday and now even if he messes up the whole holiday, nothing's his fault, ever – cos he's a teenager.'

'But also, it's been raining.'

She means it's not all his fault this week's been a washout. Cabin fever, Mum calls it. And yeah, the rain is part of it – but it's basically Duncs. All that smirking every time Mum opens her mouth, and rolling his eyes, and ignoring whatever she says. Mum does say stupid things, pretty often actually – but if I acted like him I'd get killed. And plus, even though he's turned into one big sulk, he still laughs at Jasmine's jokes. Even when they're not funny or they're jokes for adults, he laughs as though he gets them, and when I ask what's funny about it – because I *know* he can't explain – he rolls his eyes at me too, like, *You wouldn't understand*. And then he gets a total beamer. It's like somehow Duncs thinks it'll wind Mum up, if he's nice to Jasmine and horrible to her, cos he kind of steals a look at Mum when he's laughing. But I've seen Mum and Dad giving each other secret looks like they're laughing too, at him, and that's even more annoying – because what's so secret? And if they are laughing at him, they could be laughing at me too.

'I don't think your mum should have let him help make up the hunt,' I say. 'The clues are rubbish this year.'

Eve's not really listening to me. She's stepped over to where the floor ends, to the place where there's only beams and dark fuzzy gaps between them. She's judging the distance, about to jump towards me, beam by beam. But if she comes over here, past the broken chair and the ancient hoover and the piled-up picture frames, she might poke her nose into the decorations box – and if she does, she'll find it. *Sexual Manners For Modern Lovers*: the book I found hidden inside a box of much more boring books; that I buried under the decorations just a minute ago, when I heard her climbing the ladder. Even Eve'll know from the title that it's a rude book, and she'll know I've been reading it, because it doesn't belong in there with the lights and the tinsel.

So before she can jump, I jump instead, take monster steps till I'm standing beside her. I look round for a way to distract her. Close by, there's a rolled-up rug that could make a good seat. I plonk myself down.

'Comfy here,' I say, and straightaway she comes to sit beside me.

Actually it's not that comfy. It's kind of hard and saggy at the same time, and it's rolled with the rough side out. I'm picking away at a scratchy knot when Eve starts to giggle.

'What are you laughing at?'

'*Twinkle, twinkle...*' she sings.

'Eh?'

'...*little star.*' She points. I look down: there's a star, a glittery star, hanging on my sleeve, hooked from the decorations box. Eve reaches out, plucks it off.

'You've been in the Christmas box,' she says, and she stares at me, eyes black in the half-dark, smiling like she knows, knows everything. It's like everyone knows everything apart from me. Duncs laughing at Jasmine's jokes. Mum and Dad swapping looks. Jean away in another world, eyes shut, ears closed by headphones. *Sexual Manners For Modern Lovers*, with its hot, secret feeling and its promise of pictures in my head, its soft furry pages and its tiny writing, its exciting words that run off into long confusing sentences so the secret feeling turns into a knot in my stomach. I'm scraping my hand across the rough backside of the rug, scraping my wrist till it hurts. It feels like there's a question inside me, pressing in my body and my head.

I don't know what Eve has done with the star; her open hand is damp and hot and sparkling when she reaches out and takes hold of mine. And the question inside stops me from yanking free, stops me from moving at all, even when she leans in and kisses me on the lips – because I want to see, I want to know, I want what's hidden. And then I do move, inside the frills of her skirt, to push them up and aside – because here, away from everyone, Eve will show me, Eve will let me–

Metal squeals. The shake of the ladder. I jerk back: Roddy or Duncs.

'Who's up there? Cam, is that you up there?'

It's Duncs, climbing fast.

Eve wide-eyed beside me, skirt at her waist. I grab it and yank it down. Glitter on my hand. I scrub on my jeans, scrub and wish that Eve would vanish too, that Eve was never here.

'We're looking for the clue,' I whisper. My voice sounds urgent, panicked.

She stares at me.

'Don't tell!' I say. And when she doesn't speak, I say it again, 'Don't tell.'

Chapter 37

To everyone who loved Eve, I owe an apology, and it was the notorious exposé in the Mercury *that made me realise it.*

The day I heard about that story, I knew I'd hit rock bottom. I'd fallen head over heels for 'Rosie'; we'd spent a special evening together, and I had opened up to her. I'd told her how hard it was for me to cope with my newfound fame. I had no idea that this apparently sweet and smiling young woman was being paid to do a hatchet job on me.

Much of what was quoted in that article was taken out of context. You can't always trust what you read. Some of it was exaggerated. Some of it was fiction. But there are two sides to every story and there was some truth in what they wrote. And I understand now that, for my fans, what I said about them was as much a betrayal of their trust as what 'Rosie' did to me. I understand too the anger that people felt, all those people who had loved Eve. I only wish I could apologise.

I only wish I could...
I only wish...

I only wish I knew how this thing is meant to end.

Outside, the constant rain is glossing the rooftops, shining the dark slate. How many days have I been here, holed up in Duncan's flat? Wait. I'll count. I'll try to count. I can tell you it's autumn now, and it was summer when I got here. I can tell you the year swivelled weeks ago, that the nights now are long, much longer than the days. I can tell you it's cold, though I haven't been out-side – not since the Tesco man was late with my order and I had to make a night-time dash for the corner shop. It's cold up here, in my hiding place. I could turn the heating on. But that would mean I'm here, really here, when I'm still pretending to be nowhere. I sleep on unchanged sheets. I keep my case packed. When dark-ness falls I draw the blinds, turn on the smallest side-lamp.

I can tell you I'm out of time; that Duncs is due back soon – perhaps as soon as tomorrow – and by the time he gets here, I need to be gone.

Forty days. That's how long it's been. Sounds like an age, but it's nothing, really. It's not long enough. As long as I'm here I'm nowhere, and as long as I'm nowhere–

I haven't been wasting this time-out-of-time. I've been busy; I've been working. Like Amanda told me, there's a deadline for my life story. Though Amanda's been hard to get hold of lately. I've stopped leaving messages, since she doesn't call back. Stopped using my voice altogether: kept in touch with just the occasional text to my mother, so she knows I'm alive. So no-one comes look-ing for me.

Sometimes the story's come easy: the pen worrying at the page, speeding along the feint-lined tracks, till my hand cramps into a claw. Other times the shadow of Eve has sat with me – aged eight, or ten, or twenty-seven – and scowled and grabbed my pen-hand in her fist till the biro scratches, buckles, tears the page, or stops dead for the rest of the day. She never leaves entirely: she's here in the DVDs Duncs has tucked away at the back of the shelf, a library complete from her first costume dramas to the latest, last films – none of which I can bear to play. She's here in Linda's photos, spread over the sofa and the floor: Eve and Jasmine smiling up at me, preserved in colour and sun; Glenelg close enough to touch, and my own face smooth and innocent of everything to come.

I've written as the days shrink and the nights stretch, inven-tion and explanation sliding one over the other. What might have happened. What could have happened. What sounds like it should have happened. Like I once said to Duncs, memory's a funny thing, and who's to say how it really was? Or like the *Write Your Life* book says, the one I got from Amazon: don't be a slave to the facts; memory's a melting pot of reconstruction and fiction.

This morning I woke from a dream so perfect it hurt to open my eyes. We were up north, with Jasmine and Eve. Everyone was together: Duncs, Roddy, Jean, even Magnus and Eilidh were there. We were young. It was summer. We were searching for treasure.

I lay for a while, staring at the ceiling. Then I got up, thought about showering, boiled the kettle, made coffee, sat on the sofa, notepad on my lap: and the fresh page in front of me was a fall off the edge of a cliff.

Nothing left to write.

I've reached the end, and it's no kind of an end.

Those other books I ordered. The bestsellers. The biographies. The comebacks. They sit stacked in the corner, half a dozen high. I pick one up, skim the closing pages. Another. Another. They don't just end. They have endings. They have – light. Redemption. The crack addict turns her life around, with the love and support of her ideal man. The (rich, celebrated) abandoned son and his father are reconciled. The widower comes to terms with his loss, achieves a new happiness with wife number two.

I've written right up to the edge. Up to the morning I walked out of the flat, suitcase in one hand, guitar in the other. Right up to: *You killed Eve.*

I shake my head, sharply. The biro gripped tight. *Mariella*, I write, *was understandably upset.*

'Because of the papers,' I say to myself. 'Because of the story.' I write, *She had read that morning's story, in the paper, and understandably–*

You killed Eve.

'I know.'

The pen falls from my hand.

You killed me.

I know. I know, I know.

On the bed, staring at the ceiling, at the top of the building across the way, and a patch of white sky. At filthy glass, city-smeared.

I know.

So. It's pretty clear that I can't go on.

What I mean is, I can't go on *knowing*. Knowing it's true in any number of ways. For instance. One: we wouldn't even have been there, in that courtyard in that hotel, if I hadn't been jealous, so consumingly, seethingly jealous, of what she was, and what I'd never be. Two: I kissed her – *I* kissed *her* – and then like a child protested that it wasn't me, that she made me, that *she started it.* Three: say it – I was embarrassed. For seconds, when every second counted, I freaked out, I froze, I was *embarrassed* by her rattling and gasping, right there in front of me, embarrassed by her dying. Is that enough? Wait: there's more. Four: I helped myself to her life, thank you very much. Just as if I deserved it. Just as if it was mine to take. Kiss and tell: whatever they wanted to hear – the press, the public – I told.

Don't tell.

It was me, of course, who said that. Not Eve. Up in the attic, in the rain. As the ladder shook, as Duncs began to climb. Me who whispered in sudden fierce terror: *Don't tell.*

And Eve, loyal Eve, never did.

I'd done my best not to know this. Not to know any of this. Had done a good job, for a while; and made sure no-one else knew, either. And if I could go back to not knowing, I think I would have a future. Something could be salvaged, from all of this. But as it is…

Oh God. Something else I wish I didn't know: what comes next.

I sit. Propel myself forward, and up onto my feet.

266

Begin to erase myself.

The notebooks slump, finished, around the living room. I gather them into a pile; search in Duncan's desk till I find just the thing: a huge padded envelope. I almost smile, at the thought of Amanda's face when she opens it up and these scrawled, soiled spiralbound pads slide out onto her desk. I shove them all into the envelope, tape it closed, ready to pack into my suitcase.

I would leave them behind, but every trace of me needs to be gone when Duncs gets back.

In the bedroom I gather a small pile of dirty clothes. My suitcase lies in the corner. With my foot, I flip it open. There – bookended by my good shoes – is Eve's memory box.

I crouch, take it in both hands and lift it onto the bed. Piece by piece, I empty it. Her diary. Her small treasures. The Christmas-tree star, still shedding its glitter. Her photographs. Jasmine's clues. I spread them across the quilt: hover my palms above them, expecting to feel a tingle or a pull. There should be an energy about these objects, a crackle of the life she'd had so much of: a sense of that tenacious, eager, lonely little girl.

Nothing.

I pick up the sheets of paper with the treasure hunt clues, read them once more. The first clue sends my song running through my head: *From a place that's the same / Forwards and back...* I wince: but still, in the dark of the room, of my mood, of my life, still the words possess a glow of sun, and the sense of somewhere magical. A crack of light.

Eve, did you ever see it? The place where the treasure would have been, if Jasmine hadn't died? Did you ever go back there? Did you trace the route, solve the clues? That night: I remember her saying she hadn't been back. I think I remember her saying that. And yet all these years she'd kept the clues: like a possibility. Kept them in a box with all her souvenirs of me. I'd thought it a mistake, but now – now I see it's a message. It's something I can do, on her behalf. Something, maybe, that she dreamed of doing *with* me. I don't expect … I mean, she's dead, she can't forgive me, and even if she could I wouldn't dare hope she might. But–

What do you say, Eve? A bargain. I'll do this for you, because it's the least, the most, the sum of all I can. I'll make the pilgrimage you never did; I'll search for your treasure. And if somewhere along the way there's a sign, not that I'm asking, but if, somehow, I feel – forgiven…

A part of me flickers: still hoping for redemption.

And if not, not: and that far north-west seems a right place for endings.

Chapter 38

I stand on the far side of the street, where Chris-from-the-*News* and all the rest of them had gathered to hunt me. My hands are shoved deep in my pockets: drizzle coats me head to foot. It took an hour to walk here, more exertion than I've had in weeks, and I feel like an invalid, my heart tripping fast under delicate skin, breath coming short and shallow. The idea of a bus or even a taxi, and the chance of recognition, too awful to contemplate.

I'll give it a couple of hours. I don't know whether Duncs has rented the place again, whether new tenants might be in residence. Don't know if my stuff will still be there – the things I left behind. But I have to chance it.

Time crawls; I count out twenty minutes, and when I check my mobile, ten have passed. After fifty minutes the windows are still dark, and I'm soaked and shivering. There's a storm on its way – a real, proper storm. Not here, and not tonight. It'll hit tomorrow: the north-west. I looked at the forecast online when I checked the bus times. *Don't travel*, it said. *Stay indoors. Red alert.* At first I thought I'd put off the hunt, just for a day or two – but then I saw how perfect it was: a sign, if anything, that I'm doing the right thing. Because if this is to matter at all, it needs to be hard, even dangerous.

Another few minutes waiting, and I'm ready to take a risk. I walk as though I belong: cross the street, and let myself in to the tenement. Up the steps, drip-dripping, the scuff of my shoes echoing in the stair. When I reach the top, I stop to catch my breath. I tense myself: reach out, and tap on my old front door.

I count sixty seconds before I knock again, louder.

Another sixty seconds.

The keys are clenched in my fist. Running excuses through my head – *I'm so sorry, I didn't realise there were new tenants; just hoping to pick up some things I left behind* – I slide the key into the lock: I'm in.

As soon as the door snags against a pile of mail, I know the flat is empty. I call out anyway. 'Hello, anyone there?'

The silence stays intact.

In the dark I fumble my way to the bathroom, the only room with no window. I grab at thin air till my fist closes around the pull-cord. Light spills, invisible from outside, just enough for me to see my way round the flat.

When I open the bathroom cabinet, I find my abandoned toiletries just where I left them. The rusting can of shaving gel, the blunted razors. Tension leaves my body. No-one is going to disturb me. The place hasn't been scoured.

I sling the backpack down from my shoulder, open it up. Everything I need is still here.

Chapter 39

Early morning: the coach pulls out from the station in last night's rain and darkness. I hide my face against the window. Let the city pass through my reflection. Early risers, walking to work; shops lighting up, raising their shutters. Normal life. I sink into my seat, into nothing, into stasis. A Citylink coach on a dual carriageway, the forgiving darkness: there's comfort in this.

I haven't felt comfort in the longest time. Even the word's been missing from my vocabulary. Now, child-like, I reach for it: the pad of my thumb rubs, rubs the rough plush seat that cradles me. Self-pity rises in my throat. I fold my arms tight. For five hours I move without effort, carried north.

When we reach Shiel Bridge, I force myself up and off the coach. Straightaway the wind catches me, shoves me off balance and muffles my ears. Nobody else gets off; I've barely touched the ground when the driver pulls away. I watch the distance stretch between me and my seat, till the coach rounds a corner, is gone.

I'm abandoned. I stand at the roadside, zip up my top, push chilled hands into pockets. Mountains rise around me. The huge sky presses down, promises nothing, threatens everything. I'm no bigger than one of these pinecones that scatter the side of the road. All I hear is wind. I wait in thin October sun, shiver and wait – till the local coach arrives, to take me the last, longest, highest ten miles.

Now I'm the only passenger. *Don't travel. Stay inside.* But the storm is holding back, so far. Again I press close to the window, but this time I'm watching glens disappear, watching trees sink into a carpet of brown-gold-green as the road climbs and turns and climbs, and the altitude pops in my ears. The engine grinds. My seat shudders. I'm trying to remember: to overlay this arrival with the half-dozen times we made the same journey, me and Duncs packed in the Volvo, Roddy and Jean in the car behind. But the palm-prickling view doesn't feel familiar. It's the nearly-there feeling that gets me, cramped and giddy. That and the twisting, tacking road, which always made me sure I was going to be sick; and Dad's completely unreasonable refusal to stop. Not so unreasonable, it turns out: the bus hauls us along the single-track road, past sheer thousand-foot drops. I swallow.

On to the summit, into the sky. Great sun-streaked valleys drop away, yellow and green, and we carve our way between shining stretches of water – sea to the left, loch to the right – and it's shocking and beautiful and gone too fast as we start our long, slow descent.

A large stone house at the side of the road snags the past. It's not Eve's house, but it's similar: tall and lonely, surrounded by a sprawl of crumbling barns. It's gone in a moment, and we're down near the edge of the village, red-brown tumbles of bracken rolling in on us, houses settling closer to each other till they line the narrow road. As we pass Glenelg's community hall I stand, move to the front of the coach, and by the village shop the driver lets me off.

It takes a few moments for me to trust the ground, after so long in motion. I stand still, breathe gusts of cold air, bright and fresh and beaded with wet from recent rain. From the sea. The air chills my nostrils, filters into the bones of my face: cheeks, jaw, eye sockets. It creeps through my layers, gathers round my ankles. From here, I can feel the sea, and smell it. For now, though, it's out of sight.

It's not a memory, exactly, but there's something familiar about the way the village nestles in the crook of the mountains we've just passed. I court it, waiting to feel more: a significant moment, back in this place. But what sweeps through me is more prosaic. Hunger: if I don't eat something right away, I'm going to keel over. My rucksack is lightly packed with what I thought I might need, scavenged from Duncan's: canteen of water; the purple waterproof I found stuffed in his wardrobe, left behind by some old girlfriend. But I didn't think of food.

The bell announces me into the shop, a *ting* that hangs in the dim, close-packed space. The woman at the counter raises her eyes. She greets me without smiling. Her eyes are searchlights, tracking me as I sidle round the shelves.

'We're just closing,' she warns.

I grab a king-size Mars and a packet containing a plastic poncho. Glance at the clock hanging behind the counter.

'Closing early, for the storm,' the woman explains. She looks at the poncho, then back at me. 'It's going to get bad out there. You'll want to be inside.'

Her stare is shameless. She recognises me: even this far from the centre, my face is known. The thought horrifies me. And then I realise: just as likely she's staring because my face isn't known. I attempt a smile, and pocket my change. Make my escape.

Outside, I eat – in full view of dozens of houses, but feeling less visible. Fuel for the hunt. They'd always been in the afternoons, our treasure hunts. We used to race our lunch, push away our plates half-full, till an adult reminded us: you're going to need that fuel, who knows how long it'll take? And then, with the hunt under-way, each new discovered clue might yield something to keep us going: Smarties, wine-gums, orange Clubs or – my favourite – Pez: columns of tiny sugar bricks. All that sweetness; I can taste it on my tongue.

Something moves at the corner of my eye. I glance round, already stepping away so as to avoid conversation. But it's just a dog, more collie than anything else, black and white and bouncy. Dancing towards me, nose held high. *Food.*

I scan the road: no sign of its owner. It trots up close, fixes me with begging eyes.

'Sorry.' I shove the last of the Mars into my mouth, and a gust catches the wrapper, hurls it away. 'Bad for you.' I hold out my empty hands to show I've nothing to offer. It gazes, unblinking.

I swallow the last melting crumbs of chocolate, tongue the caramel from my teeth. 'You going to help me?' Its ears flick at the sound of my voice, and it cocks its head like it's waiting for me to start. The hopeful, crazy thought shudders in me that the dog, with its big, dark eyes, could be a sign. A search companion, sent by Eve.

'Alright, then.' From my pocket, I retrieve a page of clues, clutching it against the wind. I've folded it so only the first clue is showing. As much as I can, I want to do this properly.

Here's where we'd have stood, or hereabouts: me and Roddy and Eve, waiting for Jasmine to start us off, to read out that first clue. Three of us where there should have been five; we'd have been feeling reduced. Always, the kids had exactly balanced the adults. That year, it would have been tilted. I could guess Eve would have been happy: she and I thrown further into each other's company – though she might have missed Jean, I suppose, having another girl around. And me... I imagine myself, thirteen years old. Kicking the ground. Angry at Duncs and Jean for growing up ahead of me. Not bothering to hide it. Catching Roddy's eye and pulling a face. Pretending not to listen. But I knew I'd have listened, really. Because I'd still have wanted to win.

Nearly twenty years late: it's time for the hunt to begin.

In the empty street, with the dog paying close attention, I read out loud:

The hunt begins
Where starts the track
From a place the same
Forwards and back

The first part, I had solved long ago, and it would have been just as easy for us kids. It was barely a riddle; it was a starting shot. But the second part:

> *A traveller's rest*
> *Where land meets shore*
> *Look for the tallest*
> *Tree of doors*

'Traveller's rest,' I repeat, for the benefit of the dog. 'Well, we know what that is. That's got to be a hotel, eh? That's got to be the inn.'

Left: I set off walking. The dog seems to hesitate, then trots after me. It's good to get going, to spark up some body-heat inside my fleece. I can feel each cold breath all the way down into my chest. Wind skelps my face, boxes my ears like the world is trying to resuscitate me, and the daylight, unmediated by window-glass, is the first that's touched my skin in weeks.

'See?' I say to imaginary Eve, and my words are gusted away. 'Here we go: we're off, at last.' I'm trying to carry a sense of her with me. Really, though, it's myself I'm talking to. Myself and the dog.

A couple of hundred yards down the road, the Glenelg Inn appears. Behind it lies a tree-lined stretch of green, and behind that, I think, is where the grass dips down to shingled beach, and sea.

Where land meets shore / Look for the tallest / Tree of doors.

But for Jean, I'd have been stumped. I'd have wasted precious daylight, pinballing from tree to swaying tree, saying, *door ... door*, with nothing opening in my imagination. Settling in the end for any tree with a hidey-hole at the root. Did Jasmine think we'd know this? Did she count on Jean, too – forgetting she wouldn't be here? I squint into the sun, knowing enough to edit out the pines, but not quite sure beyond that how an oak looks, from a distance. Spreading. Ancient. English. Of course, the right tree might not even be here any more, might have blown down years ago, like the coming storm is threatening now. But there is one that stands taller than the rest. It rises from the highest part of the slope, wind bending its branches.

I cross the car park, onto long grass that wets the hems of my jeans. The tree grows as I approach, soars between me and the sun. I step into its shadow. In the sudden dark, my outstretched hand is swallowed, and only touch tells me it still exists: tree-bark against my palm, rough and damp. A spread of leaves slips underfoot and I stoop to pick one from the ground. It tugs in my hand, bronze, brittle, with the scalloped edges of an oak-leaf.

'Looking good,' I say to the dog, before I realise I'm on my own. I turn, scan the slope for a flash of black-and-white. My companion's nowhere to be seen. 'Hey!' I call. 'Hey, dog...'

I let my leaf go. Circle the tree, running my hand right around, fingers catching on its creviced bark. Even the lowest branches are out of my reach; far too high for ten-year-old Eve. I crouch, sliding on rotting leaves: grit my teeth, and delve into the mulch.

The hollow is neat, compact, half-hidden by ridges and roots. Two inches wide, and twice as high; and empty, of course empty. Because Jasmine didn't hide these clues: or if she did, they've long since rotted away. But a hollow is enough, is the best I can hope for: a space that might once have accommodated a slip of paper, or the thought of it. I take the list from my pocket, read the third clue over and over till I'm sure I have it by heart. Then I tear it free from the sheet: I fold it and post it into the hollow. Casting around for something to hide the entrance, I spot the line of stones edging the grass. Two of them balanced against the roots make an adequate door.

I stand. Wipe my hands on my thighs.

I want to text Jean, to tell her *thank you*. But my phone shows the blank of no reception. I hold it up, walk back the way I came. Still no signal. I turn, and turn, and around me the sky turns, sunless now, and suddenly heavy. Wind rattles in exposed branches, in curled dead leaves. The cold wet rot of autumn blankets me. And I understand that the door between worlds has blown shut, and I'm on the other side.

> *A pirate sleeps*
> *Beneath the yew*
> *At his head*
> *Lies the next clue*

Yews won't grow down by the shore: Jean again, keeping me right. And a yew is a tree of death. There's one obvious place to try, if I can find my way. When I rejoin the road I hope the dog might be waiting for me – but blind houses squat to my right, to my left, and there's no sign of anything living. The shop is closed, wooden boards across its windows; the whole village hunches. Locked down.

Rain's on its way, the sky starting to spit; I pull up my hood, and the wind laughs and yanks it straight back down. But the graveyard isn't far. It's sealed behind high fences and stern gates, behind spikes and barbed wire; when I reach for the gate, it opens easily. Invites me in.

Muted space, and soft ground: thick layers of moss fed on human remains, on all that's left of us. Good for something, then, for this if nothing else: slow release fertiliser. Maybe that's why the earth feels uncertain. Impatient. Like it wants me close, wants to open wide for me.

There could be a hundred gravestones here, or twice that many. All weather-worn; some paper-thin, their inscriptions lost. I start a slow circuit round the edge of the yard, where trees droop like mourners. MacLeod. MacLeod. Grave after grave, an extended family affair. Now, if you live and die where you're born you're a hopeless failure. You're meant to strike out on your own, find success far from your beginnings. I think about where I might end up – where my parents will, and Duncs – and then

I don't. Don't think. Don't think, either, of Eve, and what they did with what was left of her – slotted into a niche next to her mother, or somewhere alone. That summer: Jasmine died and I was thirteen and incurious. Never considered where she'd be buried. When Mum and Dad went to her funeral, I must have thought they were travelling here. Not six hundred miles south. An English rose to commemorate her – commemorate them. They never belonged here, playing at being Highlanders. This graveyard wouldn't have wanted them. But the moss, and the earth: they want me. I walk and it feels like sinking: moss swallows my feet the way the lichen has shrouded the north-facing gravestones; dark ivy coils and threatens to grab at my ankles. I try to imagine Eve aged ten and Roddy aged twelve, searching for pirates on the high seas, adventuring through their summer. But why – why would a pirate be buried here? Buried at sea, surely – or outside the kirkyard wall. Buried in disgrace. Like … like a suicide.

The silence here smothers me. Not even a distant bird calling. Like nothing is alive except for me; like nothing is alive. Just the faintest rattling sound, as I make my circuit – the rattle of bones, or what's in my backpack.

With no image of a yew in my mind, I look under every tree. Bend close to the smell of decomposing leaves, into the cold and wet, to the black rot riming my nails as I shove and scrape the sludge aside, as my hands search for stone and sink instead into slime and nettles. Until, finally, something solid. A gravestone laid into the ground.

The carving is worn, the letters unreadable by sight or by touch. But the skull is clear enough: a pirate sleeps, X of the crossbones marking the spot.

I run my fingers round and under the beaded edge of the stone, searching out the crevice where Jasmine would have stuck the clue. There's nowhere to wedge a fold of paper. Behind another stone, perhaps; or held in place with tape.

I drill the next verse into my head. Then, carefully, I tear it away, fold it up. I choose a rock – and drop it, almost, as a scurry of slaters crawls from the sudden light. With a shudder I brush the stone free from insects and earth, and lean it against the pirate's bed, with the folded paper sandwiched in between.

> *Both in the sea*
> *And on the beach*
> *When the tide is out*
> *It's in your reach*

Too fast. A feeling of panic. If it's too easy, there's no point. If it's too fast – In this motionless place I feel speed-sick, like being dizzied by the turning of the earth. My foot expects the ground to shift. But I take a step, steady enough, a series of steady steps. Back through the graveyard, through the gate: smack into a wall of wind. Not laughing now – it's angry, winding itself up into a rage. I knew the storm was coming – but Glenelg was always summer; I couldn't imagine it pitting itself against me like this. I push on, under a bruised sky, towards the next clue – bending into the wind, shoving myself against it – one hard-fought step at a time. In my trainers I stumble down the stony beach, slipping on rolling pebbles, sinking into dark tidelines of weed.

High tide. The gale stirs up the sea, chops it about; it hurls itself onto the beach, hauling off shingle with every crash. It's a mob – immense, furious – it could break me in an instant, and it wouldn't be personal because I'm nothing, not even a pebble. Across the seething water, Skye is so close I could spit on it – but as I watch, the peaks of the Cuillins are swallowed by dark, low cloud, barging in from the west, taking the mountains, taking the hills, till the whole island disappears, and all that's left is the ocean.

I stumble along the beach, away from the village. As kids we would have been running, shouting; throwing flat stones into the sea to make them jump through the waves. I trudge. Wind snatches my breath, makes me gasp. I have an idea what I'm looking for: some kind of a groyne or pier – and it's not long till I see it before me. A steel jetty, jutting out, joining land and sea.

Both in the sea / And on the beach / When the tide is out / It's in your reach.

But the tide is in, and the clue is out of reach.

Where the jetty stands, the shore slopes sharply down. The legs of the structure are submerged: a depth, I'd guess, of three feet, maybe four. Around it, sea shoots into the sky – ten feet or twelve or twenty – and arcs, and falls. I stand at a distance, and the spray slaps my face, blurs my eyes.

Perhaps it's enough to have found the spot. To know where the clue would have been: somewhere on the jetty's underside. I have the next clue in my pocket, after all.

Or I could wait until the tide goes out. I raise my arms, acting King Cnut: 'Back!' And I laugh at myself, and my laughter sounds shocking and I realise the storm is all I've heard since I called after the dog: wind and ocean in my ears, and the rattle at my back.

I take a step towards the sea – ducking the spray – but it catches me, hammers me with salt-water. I gasp; splutter; spit. There's no way I can stand up to this. Another wave smashes, heaves the stones from under my feet. I stagger. Step back. Look around. Not a creature in sight, human or animal.

Before I can let myself off with excuses I set down my pack, and start to undress. Unzip my top, shove it into my bag. Unlace my shoes, bunch my socks inside; climb out of my jeans and stow them along with my fleece. I keep on my shorts and my T-shirt, though the wind fights me for them. My skin explodes into goosebumps. I wait for the next wave to pitch and crash, and when it sucks itself back I follow it into the sea.

It's instant. Agony. Sharp and aching both at once. Stones crunch and slide, and before I can retreat the first surge of tide slams me onto my knees. I scrabble for something to grab, but the next surge is a punch in the face, a mouth full of salt and a nose full of water. I battle for breath, and in the seconds before the sea comes back at me, I thrash to my feet, and – *brace*. Water crashes over me. Hauls away. One step deeper, and – brace. *Crash*. Another step: brace. *Crash*. On, till I'm in grabbing distance of the jetty, and I catch it – cling to it, battered and drenched – and in the next gap between waves, I duck underneath.

Around me sea churns, flings water and salt up into my stinging eyes. I cling to the jetty, limpet-like. Overhead, a grid of supporting beams, junctions and corners and slots into which a clue could be wedged. As I peer up, a wave explodes around me, grips and sucks and drags me, and I lose my hold on the strut, grab instead at the steel matrix above. And as the wave draws out to its farthest point, I see it. I blink and blink, because it can't be true. After so many years, it can't be here.

A cross of silver duct tape.

Jasmine at low tide, hiding her clue, well ahead of time.

I close my eyes, cling tight, wait for the next wave to flatten me – and then I work fast, tug and peel with wet fingers to reach a spider's web parcel, cocooned in cling film, which I hold in my fist while I wait again for a wave to do its worst before I can duck back out into open water. Take small careful steps – bracing against every wave – till I reach dry land.

'I found it,' I say to no-one, through chattering teeth – so cold I'm ready to cry, but fired up, too. I keep the clue loosely clasped in one hand, use the other to strip off my soaking T-shirt, fight my way back into my fleece, tug my jeans over legs frozen a matching shade of blue. Then I crouch, back to the wind, and gently, tenderly, begin to pick apart the layers of plastic that wrap the paper inside. My fingers shake from the cold that's burrowed into my bones. It takes me a long time to reach the soft white at the centre. It's almost pulp, a precious, fragile thing. It shreds itself into tissue strips as I try to unfold it, but I can see the ghostly strokes of magic marker capitals, and – though I can't read it really, though there's barely a letter that's survived – taking the page from my pocket, I imagine I can see where words overlap.

On dry land
Bound south-east
The next clue's found
At hanged man's feet

'I found it,' I say again – and for the first time, I can imagine Eve alongside me. Flickering from ten years old to twenty-seven, and back again; approving, in all her ages, of the trial I've put myself through. *Now you're starting to suffer*, she seems to be saying. And I want to argue – tell her I've been suffering now for months, but in the context... Disgrace, public humiliation, alienation, the judgement of the world upon you: yeah, yeah. Poor you. It doesn't stack up, does it? Not when you're talking to a dead woman.

But this, now, is real. I'm shaking: seriously, violently, unstoppably. I remember stories of overboard sailors who froze in minutes, whose bodies seized up and slipped from the surface of life. The brief thrill of discovery, of the real clue there from so many years ago, turns to something dark. I let it go, the sad scrap, let it float away, into the sea.

Socks, trainers back on. Wet T-shirt shoved into my pack; I pull out the woman's waterproof and stuff my arms in the sleeves. They stop inches short of my wrists. The fabric yanks my shoulders back, barely meets across my chest. As I unfold the poncho from its packet the wind catches it, ripping it, but I layer it on top anyway. If someone sees me now, recognises me now... I can only imagine how ridiculous I look – but I need this extra covering. I need the warmth.

From Jasmine's sheet I tear the latest clue, reach up and place it on the jetty, under a flat stone.

Bound south-east.

I turn my back to the sea.

Hanged man's feet: I'm thinking of swinging corpses, and shivering, and marching up the beach, moving fast to beat the cold – so when a stone rolls underfoot and my bad ankle turns, I'm flat on my back, breath knocked clean out of me, before I can even swear. My backpack – the glass inside, essential for later – expecting the worst, I feel through the fabric: somehow, it's intact. More than I am.

I haul myself upright. Stagger, as my ankle stabs. Limp to where the beach turns to grass, and on to rejoin the road. Too fast? Too easy? Maybe someone's up there listening to my worries, because this sure as hell is going to make things harder. Moisture leaks from my eyes; the wind drags it across my skin, stealing the wet and leaving a rough tidemark of salt. The road is a dark straight line, stretched to the horizon.

Hanged man; hanged man. There was a time, well into Jean's floaty-scarf years, that the Tarot was co-opted into her range of accessories. For a few months she carried her cards everywhere; the only time she was ever in trouble at school was for giving readings in the common room. I remember Eilidh angry and laughing, both believing and not, because Jean had seen four kids in her future. I'm trying to think, now, what she saw for me: I can't. I can't remember.

It's from Jean I know the cards can represent something quite different from what they seem to. The hanged man: he could be life. But everything around me shouts the opposite: the dregs of light bleeding from the sky, the world's edges disintegrating. Thunder rattling round the horizon. Leaves rotting under my feet.

South and east. I hobble on, leaning back now into the wind that's forcing me on from behind. Each step is a negotiation with my ankle, and my jeans are sanding my still-damp skin. Okay, I tell myself; this is meant to be tough – and then the clouds lower and loosen, and the real rain begins.

It's just a few fat drops at first, but inside of a minute it's hammering down. It soaks through torn plastic, through the borrowed waterproof: floods through stretched seams, finds where the zip won't meet. It drenches my jeans, underpants, skin; flows through my shoes with each frozen step. Rain blurs my eyes, and batters down till I can't see the world in front of me, and still I wade on – blind, but I have to keep looking, left and right, up and down – or the hanged man could escape me.

At a distance, Eve follows: pleased to see me drowned, frozen, limping towards the gallows. I can feel her so strongly, I actually look back over my shoulder, as if I'll catch her drifting – bodiless, impervious to the rain, but visible even so.

'I'm doing this for you,' I shout, and water runs into my mouth. I'm self-conscious enough to wince at the sound of my voice, even as reality fades with the daylight. Reality is rain shattering off a path that's become a river. Reality is one stabbing step then another. Reality is what I left behind by the tree of doors. No living thing has passed me since: not a car on this road, not a gull at the shore or a crow overhead. Is this still south-east? Have I missed the clue? Will I be walking forever? The wind cuts straight through my soaking clothes. The hedgerow looks like a welcoming nest, and for the first time I begin to think I might not make it. That I might fail – not in the face of impossible clues, but through my body saying: enough. Saying this cold and wet and wind and gathering dark is too much.

How did Jasmine expect us to solve this? Through the fear, I can still feel aggrieved on behalf of teenage-me. Too hard. Not fair. I'd have given up long ago. Didn't care enough, not unless somebody challenged me: made it a competition. What was winning to me, twenty years ago? A fat handful of jelly beans, a prize wrapped in shining paper, hauled out from its hiding place and into the sun. And today, if I get there. If I win. What will be my prize? What will be waiting for me? A missed step, a sudden fall – the thump of a trapdoor – weightless for just a second, falling or flying. Then the crack, and all you are is dead weight, and a slow, circling swing.

I make myself breathe, fighting the wind. Hitch my hands into the too-high pockets of the water-not-proof. In one pocket, something round and hard. I turn it, guessing it: conker.

A conker.

I stop, braced against the gale. Yes, a conker. And I know now whose jacket this is: I remember her picking it up, both of us searching for another – the idea that we'd soak them in vinegar, string them and have a battle like we'd done when we were little. But it was a bad year for conkers, last year, the wet summer leaving them sodden and soft so they crushed when you broke apart their green spiked shells. This was the one of the few good examples we found. She found it: Eilidh did. Walking in Queens Park.

I couldn't be more wet. I am shaking. And I think, suddenly, that she can rescue me, again. Help me, Eilidh: save me, just once more. If I speak to her, tell her what I'm doing, where I am and why. And how the path is leading just one way, and I'm closer and closer to the end and Eve is not going to help – why should she? Eve is not going to let me squirm off this hook – and I don't want, I don't want to reach this destination… Eilidh will find the error in my logic. Eilidh will show me the off-road. Eilidh will tell me how to make it okay again. In the corner of my mind's eye, a flash of colour; of hope.

My phone still shows no signal. I stare at the screen, willing the bars to appear: a single bar, please... Stretch it up to the clouds, trying to shelter it with my hand: spin it this way, that way. Nothing. If I can get to higher ground… The road is hemmed with head-high tumbles of bracken, laced with brambles and nettles. A couple of steps, and I know there's no way I'll get through unscathed. I push on. Sliding back through the mud. Thorns grabbing, catching: my jeans, Eilidh's waterproof; little ripping sounds, and a Morse Code of blood along my arm. Scrambling, step by step up the steep slope, grabbing bracken in slippery handfuls, and checking my phone as I climb. Nothing. Nothing. And then, at last, a single bar. A flicker of life.

My face is suddenly hot: relief, and apprehension as I wait for the call to connect.

An automated voice says, 'You have dialled an incorrect number.' I shake my head. Disconnect. Call again.

'You have dialled an incorrect number.'

I go back to my contacts. Choose Eilidh's London number.

It rings. It rings four times and then a real voice answers, a living human voice. The world exists, still, somewhere impossibly distant.

'Hello!' I almost shout it, over the hammering rain, and I realise the voice belongs to Eilidh's German lodger and I manage to say, nice and clear, 'Please can I speak to Eilidh?'

'I'm sorry,' says the woman, whose name I don't remember, and it's hard to hear over the gale howling round me but what she says is something like, 'Eilidh isn't living here any longer.'

I make an *oh*, but my voice fails me and it's only a shape. I cough. 'Where has she gone? I didn't know she was leaving.'

'Yes, she has left for six months, maybe, or maybe it could be a year or more. Who is calling?'

'*Left*, where? For a *year*? Where has she gone?'

'Who's calling, please?'

'It's Campbell. It's her friend, Campbell.'

'Ah, then I'm sorry, Campbell, I can't tell you where she is.'

'Can't tell – you mean – you don't know? Or you mean *me*, you can't tell me?' Her name: if only I knew her name I could use it, and she'd soften – Elke? Gisela? Heike? – she'd tell me. I know she knows.

'Okay, I think I can't help you so goodbye.'

'No, but wait, it's important, it's really important–' Before I can beg, she's gone. I can feel my face twist in disappointment. Rain ricocheting off my hood, off Eilidh's hood. The phone slipping in my hand.

I rearrange my face, make my voice ordinary. Call the last number I have for Eilidh.

'Hi! Janice! It's Campbell here.'

'Campbell!' I can hear the astonishment in Eilidh's mum's voice. 'Lovely to hear from you,' she says. I imagine her sitting down, slowly. 'How are you keeping, how have you been?'

'Oh, I'm fine, thanks.'

'We've not heard much about you lately, your mum was saying, you know ... she was saying she's not really spoken to you...' A pause. 'But you're well, are you?'

'Aye, I'm good – I'm good.' The words are torn from my mouth, and I want to cry at the thought of her warm, dry house, clean and bright and familiar to me, like a second home. I swallow, a sharp lump spiking my throat. 'I just, I was wondering – is Eilidh there?'

I count three, four, five seconds before Janice answers. 'Eilidh's gone away for a while. She didn't, obviously, say much about it – or I'm sure you would have heard – but - - know what she's like about people making a fuss.'

'But, where's she gone?' A spasm of shivering seizes me. I wrap my free arm around my chest, folding in on myself.

The line stutters and the wind shrieks, and I don't catch what she says. It sounds like Namibia.

'Sorry – where?'

'You know, in Africa. You've actually just missed her.' Like Eilidh's popped out to the shops. 'Come to think of it, you might - - at - - but - - in touch, Campbell, when she's ready.'

I can't keep the shiver out of my voice now. 'Is she okay? I mean, is she–'

'Yes, oh yes, she's fine. She was fed up, that's what she said. Had enough. Maybe you know - - what all that's about than I do.' Janice's voice comes and goes, the signal weakening, breaking up. ' - - needed a holiday if you ask me, but she's not the holiday sort, is she - - next best thing, I suppose. And - - all I can tell you.' Through the breaks and gaps she sounds genuinely sorry.

'Thanks. Thanks, Janice.'

'Listen, Campbe - - ll you?'

'What's that? The signal's not great.'

' - - said call your mother, would you? She - - from you.'

'Sure. I just – could you maybe give her a message? Eilidh, I mean.'

' - - course I will.'

But I don't know what I want to say, and the pause stretches into embarrassment, and when the signal dies I just hang up. I just ... give up.

It's a slide-scramble down to the road, skidding a diagonal through wet grass and mud and walls of bracken, splashing into a puddle a little further down the road from where I left. As I land, my phone gives a beep, and I grab for it thinking, Eilidh – a message – that was fast–

Low battery.

I turn it off. Start to trudge once more.

Blinded by the rain, I nearly walk straight past it; would have done, if it wasn't for the banging. Like something trapped and trying to break out. Close by, off the path to my left.

It's a wooden structure, only a foot or so taller than me. You could hang a child, or a dog – or a sheep. That must be what it's for: shearing, or dipping, or whatever else humans do with sheep that I don't know about. The structure itself is set back from the road, behind a wooden grid of pens, and the banging is an unbolted gate blowing on its hinges.

I catch the gate. Step inside. Enter the next pen and the next, until I'm standing right beneath this thing that, size aside, does look just like a gallows, shuddering in the gale. The scale should make it comical, but I've never felt less like laughing. Five down. Two to go.

Like everything else about me, the paper in my pocket is soaked. Shit, Eve, I'm sorry; your mother's handwriting. The ink has run. Eve kept it for all those years, and within a day I've ruined it. But the words of the next verse are still clear enough.

> *A road where one*
> *Turns into two*
> *Will signpost you*
> *Towards the clue*

At the base of the gallows, where the post is sunk into concrete, I leave the clue, weighted with a handful of pebbles. Rain pounds it within seconds. I imagine the words blurring into illegibility, and turn away.

With every step, now, water sluices through my shoes and socks, like I'm walking a river gorge. My jeans wrap me heavily, an icy embrace. I huddle into Eilidh's jacket – as though it could get any tighter round me. That brief flash of hope has left the sky even darker.

And what, anyway, was her jacket doing at my brother's flat?

In his wardrobe.

In his bedroom.

I stop dead, as I think it through. What this means.

The night in Moulin, when he chased after her to see she was okay.

The lift she gave him to London.

The caff in London Bridge. Tea and bacon rolls, and Duncs telling me, *She's no your biggest fan.* Telling me nothing.

Eilidh and Duncs. Okay, yes: that, I can just about see. But there's something else – a bigger shape behind the two of them. To do with Duncs and his hidden collection of Eve on DVD; his white knight act, when he heard about Cody and me. Supposing Duncs had wanted something I had – something he couldn't even try to take from me? How tempting would it be, how natural, to take something else instead? Something – someone – he thought *I* might want?

But Eilidh – I don't want Eilidh, do I? Not like that.

Wind urges me into a forward stagger. For a moment I want to take it off, her jacket. Leave it here in the mud. But that really would be spiting my face. No: not like that – and even if I did, well, it can't matter now. None of it can matter now.

The cold is hurting less, now. Pain becoming numb. Thoughts turning to ice.

Ahead, there's a fork in the road. A sign emerges from the dusk, fragmented by rain, swaying in the wind. In white letters it tells me, *Dun Telve*. And from here on, I know: I know where it's going to end. I almost smile; because Jasmine's finishing place is perfect.

The last clue would have been taped to the signpost – not too high – somewhere a small ten-year-old could reach. I read it several times, till I'm sure the eight lines are ingrained in my mind, and then I reach up and wedge it, soaked and folded, tight between post and sign. Sorry, Eve. Out of reach. But we know now, anyway, where we're going – don't we?

> *Here the right choice*
> *Could prove wrong*
> *The final stretch*
> *Is straight and long*
> *A ring in a ring*
> *Circle the prize*
> *The top of a compass*
> *For those who have eyes*

It's clever. *A ring in a ring / Circle the prize.* I should have guessed, of course. Really, the first time I read the clues I ought to have guessed.

Jasmine's right about straight and long; too long for Eve, too dull for Roddy and me. But then, chances are we'd have had our bikes. As we ran out of places close by Eve's house, as we all grew older, the hunts would cover more ground till eventually we'd biked from clue to clue. For me, though, it's one sodden step after another, and as I trudge, the first line drums in my head. *Here the right choice / Could prove wrong.* Was that what it went back to – one wrong choice – to press a kiss on a half-willing girl? Or was it wrong heaped on wrong, till the whole tower collapsed?

This pilgrimage – my being here – it had felt like the right choice, the only choice. Now, though, it feels like the cold is chilling my thoughts into some kind of clarity, like the rain has rinsed them clean. I'm trying to do penance for Eve – who is dead, dead, dead – while a whole long line of the living waits for me to make amends.

(The crack in Mariella's voice. Eilidh's expressionless face; her front door clicking shut.)

Why had I chosen to make my reparation to the dead and not the living? Because it was easier. Because, however I might imagine Eve travelling alongside me, the dead don't answer back. I stop in my tracks, sickened, as I realise: with me and the dead, it's still all about me.

I turn on my useless phone, start a message that can't be sent from this signal-less limbo.

Message to: All

No. Backtrack. I start again, still pacing. Discarding contacts. One by one, scores and scores. Gone. Gone. Gone. There are just these few that I keep. Duncs. Jean. Magnus. Mum and Dad. Roddy. Eilidh's number too, her *incorrect number*; I keep it, for all its redundancy.

Message to: All
Sorry.

Delete: it's not enough, it's nowhere near enough. But I can't think of anything else, and so I type it out again.

Sorry.
Save to draft

I slip the phone back into my pocket.

When I look up, a crack of lightning is splitting the sky to the east. The daylight's almost gone: fifteen minutes, no more. I pick up my pace.

I can see from here where the answer must lie.

The brochs. Iron-age roundhouses, half-ruined: drystone, hollow-walled. A ring in a ring. It could be one of two; but I guess Jasmine would have chosen the nearest, the most complete: Dun Telve. It hunches in long grass, a dark stone mound. We played round here sometimes, as kids, pretending these were our castles; that we were under attack from invading armies, running sure-footed up and down the slope. Now my approach is stumbling, the gale shoving me into a run, my feet catching dips and hillocks hidden in the half-light. Over fallen stones, come undone from the intricate jigsaw of drystone, I step into what's left of its circle. Into shelter. Above me the squalling sky is almost as dark as the shadowed walls that curve their arms around me.

The top of a compass / For those who have eyes.

North? Was that what she'd meant? I spin till the wind is in my face, then make a quarter-turn to the right. Climb over wet, mossy stones till I reach the wall. It's well intact here, with no obvious place to hide anything. I run my hand over the stones, up, left, right; I crouch and poke around in the grass at the base of the wall. Searching for nothing. How will I know when I find it?

A ring in a ring...

What made the brochs such magical places to play was their double-wall structure – forming secret passageways, with the remains of stairs as old as the Iron Age. A ring in a ring. I skirt the inner wall till I reach a place where it's disintegrated; step over the rubble and edge my way inside, in between the walls.

A moment comes to me, sharp through the darkness: me hiding, Roddy and Duncs beside me, sandwiched in here and smothering giggles as Eve runs a circle round the broch, searching for us, calling my name, searching for me. We had bolted, of course, the three of us, before she could follow our trail into this dark passageway.

I wish I'd thought to bring a torch. I reach for my phone; launch the flashlight app. A chilly glow falls on the stones. Stepping cautiously, I make my way along the passage: stop, when I think I'm as near to due north as I can get. The walls on either side are knobbled with stones jutting out at all levels. Jasmine would have chosen somewhere we could easily reach. With difficulty in the narrow passage, I lower myself to a crouch, and pan my phone across the walls. And then I see it.

The gap is perfectly sized and placed. It looks empty at first – but when I hold the light closer, something glints pale in the gloom.

So eager to reach it, somehow I drop the phone. It cracks off stone, and the light goes out. Hell. I stare into the dark, willing my eyes to adjust. Scrabble around in the wet earth, till my fingers meet plastic. I can feel the case has cracked open: I press it back together, press *on*, whispering, *Please, please...*

Hallelujah, it works.

Carefully now, I reach into the gap. My fingers meet something small and light; several objects. I clutch, bring them close to my face.

Bones. The feather-light bones of a long-dead bird. The weightless pebble of its skull. I open my hand, let them fall to the ground. But this can't be it. I reach back into the gap and run my fingers across the rough surface, collecting earth, lichen, emptiness.

All I can offer her, at the end, is bones, dirt, dust.

I let myself slump to a sitting position, knees pressed to my chest. This must have been the place – here, or hereabouts. Jasmine had written the clues, but whatever the grail she'd had in mind, she had never hidden it; or, if she had, the treasure's long since claimed by some random, lucky child. Of course: how could it be otherwise?

Pointless. All of it, all along: ridiculous. I'd managed to convince myself it mattered – solving the clues, making the pilgrimage; convinced myself it's what Eve would have wanted, that she was there alongside me, ready to forgive. But all I'd achieved was to postpone the inevitable. Well. It's done now, what I came to do.

The first part of what I came to do.

Inconceivable: a world without you in it. That's what I've always thought. But now, I can conceive of it, quite easily. A world without me: where everything carries on, the grass growing over the Iron Age stones, the sun setting and rising again; where secretly the people who know me are relieved I've gone.

I wonder whose face will be the last I see in my memory, as memory becomes a closed loop – and crackles and fades, and me with it, fades from existence. I let my eyes close. See the dark full stop of my eyelids. In the drop and lift of the wind, in the blood in my ears, I imagine I hear a melody: so stretched, so slowed, it's impossible to name.

At the edge of everything: where circle meets circle, where land meets sea, where light meets dark. At the edge of the longest, darkest night, drenched with glittering, invisible rain. In between the walls of this two-thousand-year-old safe place: and I do not want to go, I do not want to go, but there is nowhere else, nowhere safe, nowhere home – and I made a bargain, didn't I? And no sign of a sign.

Bird bones, hollow and light: I will be bird bone, I will be scoured, all that remains of me will be clean and white and true.

Lick my lip, the raised scar line, the cut from a stranger's punch, the cut that bled hot and salt into my mouth, and I spat and swallowed and saw the blood in her eyes, blood on snow, white soaked scarlet and everything at an end: for her, for me; for me because for her. And the blood in me is cold as sleet but it wants to carry on, it's racing, my whole self pulsing with being alive.

But this is only fair.

A neat place to do it. Sheltered. Hidden. Where a sick animal can crawl and hide and do its dying in private.

Phone on a stone beside me. Unzip my sodden bag, to find what I need. The whisky. The pills. How long since the doctors prescribed them? Ten years, almost. One sort after another, to help me sleep and smile and function but I could never take them, not a single one, because it was pills that had brought me to that place. I kept them – only because I didn't know what else to do.

Now: now I know. Now, they'll help me sleep. Last night I popped them free of their foils, into the vitamin tub – determined to do it right, make it easy to knock them back – and they looked like new.

The tub rattles in my hand. The cold is worse now I've stopped moving, now the sun's gone, but it won't last much longer. And the fear – but there's no fear. No fear. Just terror.

A series of simple actions. Crack the cap on the whisky. Unscrew. Swallow. Grouse blazes down my throat: wish I'd got something better, a good malt, not settled for the bottle at the back of Duncan's cupboard. Wish I'd braved an off-licence, bought their most expensive bottle. Had that much self-respect.

Wedge the whisky upright. Open the plastic tub. Tip the pills into my hand: half a dozen, a dozen. Weightless as bird bones. Flat round tablets. Plasticky ovals. The tablets stick to my palm. Catch dry in my mouth and throat. Need wave on wave of whisky to push them down. I cough and cough but keep them safe inside me. Capsules are smoother. Shiny. Easy. My heart slamming in my ears. Another handful: swallow, and swallow. My throat, my stomach, on fire.

Keep on. Keep swallowing till nothing is left. Until my hands are empty.

Inside, the mess of pills and whisky begins to disintegrate, and I start the final action.

To wait.

STORMS BRING CHAOS TO HIGHLANDS AND ISLANDS

Parts of Scotland were blasted yesterday by the worst storm to hit the North West for over a decade.

Hurricane force winds brought chaos to the Western Isles and North West Highlands, causing widespread damage to property and leaving thousands without power. Roads were blocked by fallen trees and localised flooding, while ferry services north of Oban were cancelled and the Skye road bridge was closed to all traffic.

Police advised against all travel and warned people to stay indoors, and businesses and schools were closed as the Met Office issued a red alert, its highest warning.

A woman narrowly escaped serious injury when a tree fell on her car near Gairloch. Fire station crews used cutting gear to release the driver.

Stornoway coastguard helicopter rescued a man from the Sound of Sleat, where he had been canoeing when he got into difficulty in rough seas. The man was winched to safety.

In Glenelg there were reports that former pop singer Campbell Johnstone had been walking in the area, with locals expressing concern that Johnstone was inadequately prepared for the weather.

Forecasters warned that the conditions are expected to remain unsettled for the next few days, with temperatures dropping to $-3°C$ overnight and the possibility of snow.

• • •

Hello, you've reached Margaret and Bill. We're not at home so please leave a message, and we'll get back to you.

'Hi Mum, hi Dad ... it's Duncs, you're probably both at work... Just to let you know I got back yesterday – and, I was thinking about maybe coming up at the weekend, so let me know if that's okay... Oh, also, just wondering if you've heard from Cam at all? Cos I

think he's been staying here, or – yeah, it definitely must be him...
I mean, I haven't seen him, but someone's been here anyway, using
the computer and stuff, and I'm pretty sure... So I'm just, really,
wondering what he's up to. I can't get him on his mobile. Anyway.
Speak to you later.'

•   •   •

Magnus to **Duncan**
Is Eilidh with you? Did you see story in Herald today?
Tues, 17 Oct, 09.24

Duncan to **Magnus**
Yep, about to take her to airport. What story?
Tues, 17 Oct, 09.25

Magnus to **Duncan**
Have emailed link.
Tues, 17 Oct, 09.27

•   •   •

From: Magnus MacDonald <magnus@magnus.restaurant.co.uk>
To: Duncan Johnstone <duncan_johnstone@gmail.com>;
Cc: Eilidh MacDonald <eilidhmac99@hotmail.com>; Roddy Wardlaw
<rwardlaw1999@hotmail.com>; Jean Wardlaw <jean@infocus.net>

Subject: Storm brings chaos to Highlands & Islands

2nd para from end. Should we be worried?

https://heraldscotland.com/news/storm-brings-chaos-to-highlands-
and-islands.1965270

Duncan to **Magnus**
R u at restaurant? Pick u up? Going to look for C
Tues, 17 Oct, 09.35

Chapter 40

They drove up through the tail-end of the storm, Duncs and Magnus and Eilidh: through ill-tempered bursts of rain, and left-over winds that had battered themselves down to buffeting gusts.

From Glasgow to Glencoe was one long overtake, the speed limit irrelevant. Further north and west, the road emptied, and they began to pass the wreckage of the night before. Drystane dykes half-collapsed. A roof of corrugated iron blown clean off its barn. Still they barely dropped below seventy.

Around Fort William, Eilidh thought of calling the police. It took a long time to get through. The constable at the station in Kyle promised to do his best: they were stretched, of course, but they'd alert all officers, have them on the lookout.

Duncs edged up to eighty.

Just out of Fort William, with a hundred miles to go, a lorry lay slewed across both lanes. Duncs swore, and threw the road map into Eilidh's lap: which way? They doubled back, turned onto a twisting B-road that took them past trees torn up from the roots, a power line down, and then to the edge of a newly-formed lake, where the tarmac vanished: twenty metres across, maybe, and unknowably deep. Duncs eased off the accelerator: set his jaw, and sliced slowly forward. Forward, with water halfway up the tyres; water up to the chassis. The three of them holding their breath, mentally shoring up the engine's drone. They were almost through when they heard the worst: a cough, and sudden silence.

Duncs gripped the wheel. Turned the ignition. Again. Again. Nothing.

Magnus and Duncs knee-deep in water, pressing their shoulders to the car, sliding and splashing; Eilidh in front, trying the engine – till they rose from the flood, and at last, on the twentieth try, the engine caught, and ran.

Four hours on from leaving Glasgow they reached Shiel Bridge, and the Glenelg road. Duncs gambled on it staying empty, rammed his foot down till something ahead made him hit the brakes, hurling them forward and back. A metal gate, ripped from its post. The three of them leapt out, grabbed and dragged it clear, into the undergrowth. A few miles further on, they did the same with a massive branch tangled round with great ropes of creeper.

Finally, they were grinding uphill, mist swallowing the precipice to their left – pushing on till they reached the summit and started to drop – racing towards the village, the street littered with seaweed hurled by the wind a hundred yards inland – and they sped on along the Arnisdale road, because they knew exactly where they were going, where to look.

Daluaine. Eve's old house.

Twenty years since he'd been there, but Duncs drove them straight to the gate. The three of them jumped out of the car, ran to the front door. Rang, and knocked, and rang; and after an age an elderly woman appeared. But the police had already been round, she told them – and no, she'd seen no-one the last couple of days, and yes of course they were welcome to check the grounds.

Duncs led the way. The back garden. The shed. Even the henhouse. Nothing. But next door: the farm, with its sullen barn... They took the shortcut, over the tumbledown wall. When they knocked at the farmhouse, there was no answer; only a dog that barked and barked and barked. Duncs stared at the barn, its blank walls, its roof painted dried-blood red. Stared, and hesitated: urgency turning, suddenly, to fear. In the end it was Magnus who led the way, Eilidh a few steps behind: who pushed at the barn door and found it open; stepped into the gloom and, after a long minute, came out shaking his head.

They were silent on the way back to the car. They'd been so certain. A bus schedule downloaded to Duncan's computer; a newspaper story; a phone call to Eilidh's mum, from somewhere outside. Three clues that had pointed them here – but they'd guessed them wrong. Perhaps the whole thing was a wild goose chase.

Unless…

In the passenger seat, Eilidh frowned, shook her head. It was a ridiculous idea: and yet…

She told them about it, Magnus and Duncs: about the last treasure hunt. How Eve had kept the clues for all those years. How Eve's cousin had bequeathed them. It was somewhere to look – if Eilidh could only remember. Could she? She squeezed her eyes shut. *The hunt begins / Where starts the track / From the place the same / Forwards and back.* And, *A pirate sleeps / Beneath a yew.* The first two. That was all. But it wasn't enough. It wasn't enough. The last clue was what they needed.

And then she realised: the only other person who might know.

The three of them in the car. The engine running. Eilidh on the phone to Jean, talking fast but clear. The last clue would be a place to start – and if they had no luck they could work their way back, back to the start of the track, and somewhere along the way…

The silence when Eilidh finished explaining. Five seconds. Ten. Twenty.

'Jean?'

'Yes,' she said. 'Yes: a ring in a ring.'

'A ring in a ring!' Eilidh called it out. 'A ring in a ring!'

Another few seconds – Duncs had always been quick with the clues – and they were racing back the way they'd come. Ten minutes drive to Dun Telve: they did it in five. Abandoned the car at the side of the road, splashed and slid uphill. Stumbled into the broch. Saw nothing.

In the circle, Duncs stood and turned, turned till he recognised the way in. North: he ran; they followed.

That's where they found the body.

A ring in a ring, the space between the ancient walls: curled face-down in vomit, bluish and cold, and wrapped up in plastic.

That's where the hunt ended.

That's where they found me.

PART FIVE

A ring in a ring
Circle the prize
The top of a compass
For those who have eyes

Chapter 41

I heard the story a little at a time.

How it was Magnus who turned me, touched my neck, fingers searching for a pulse that wasn't there. Magnus whose face told the others: *nothing*. Magnus who knew not to give up – who, in his army days, had survived expeditions in sub-zero temperatures and heavy snow, who knew you're not dead till you're warm and dead. And after the best part of a minute, he felt it. The faintest flicker.

How it was Duncs who climbed to the highest point, stretched and spun – *come on, come on* – till he found an emergency signal.

How it was Eilidh who wiped the vomit from my face and mouth, making the clearest path for my imperceptible breath. Eilidh who peeled off what she could of my wet layers of clothes, who covered me in their jackets and fleeces and in that narrow space laid herself alongside me, warming me gently, gently, till the air ambulance came.

It wasn't the tablets that damaged me. I'd probably thrown up half of them, and whatever was left passed through harmlessly enough. It was cold that almost killed me. Severe hypothermia – and after that, after they'd warmed me through with intravenous fluid and blood transfusions, it was pneumonia, and fluid on my lungs. For a week, every breath was a knife in my chest. Sitting up in bed was a feat. A few minutes' conversation left me exhausted, shaking and clammy. But I wanted visitors all the same, quietly sitting, or talking without expecting an answer. They'd flown me to Inverness, and for a week Mum and Dad stayed nearby, spent hours each day at my bedside, reading or chatting or even napping as I slept and half-woke and slept again. Duncs and Eilidh came often, together and separately – and a couple of times, when he could leave the restaurant, Magnus came too.

Gradually, I felt stronger. I moved from the ICU into an ordinary ward. I still couldn't take a deep breath without a fit of coughing, but before long I could walk to the bathroom and back, then to the dayroom – and after another week they wanted my bed, and I was discharged.

It was arranged that Duncs would drive me home: back to Moulin, where I could rest, keep warm, keep recovering. He arrived at my bedside just after lunch, Eilidh in tow.

'One thing I won't miss,' I said. 'Hospital food.'

Eilidh took my bag, and Duncs offered an arm.

'Thanks. I'm okay, I think.'

We shuffled down the corridors, me setting an invalid's pace.

'God,' said Eilidh, 'slow down a bit, would you? You're wearing me out.'

I would have laughed, but I didn't want to spare the breath.

Cold air hit my chest as soon as we stepped outside, and I stopped for a coughing fit. I was grateful to Duncs for parking right by the exit. He opened the rear door for me and I clambered in, heart racing from coughing, and the longest walk I'd managed in weeks.

Round the other side of the car, Eilidh opened the back door, while in front Duncs leaned over, swung open the passenger side. Eilidh glanced at me; passed me my bag, and clicked the door shut. Slid in beside Duncs.

'Okay?' he said.

I slumped, eyes closed. 'Okay.'

I dozed for an hour, maybe more, and when I woke and looked out of the window it took me a while to figure out where we were – or rather, where we weren't: the A9, our road home.

'Where are we going?'

Duncs glanced at me in the mirror. 'Just a wee detour.'

'How're you holding up back there?' Eilidh called.

'Aye, fine.' I was, actually. The sleep I'd just had. Being out of the hospital. I watched the road moving past. There were still signs of the storm: trees with the spiky stumps of ripped-off branches, or lying where they'd fallen, cavernous trenches gaping at their roots. I thought about home, and all the things I needed to do once I got there. Empty my bank account. Make an anonymous donation to AnAlert. Sell my guitar: I felt a pang at the thought, but there was no way round it; it had to go. I had to come out of this with nothing. Make a trip to Glasgow, to collect my suitcase from the coach station locker – if it hadn't been destroyed by now – and burn all those notebooks I'd scribbled with lies, with my fictional memoir. Issue a statement, a setting straight of the record: for Mariella. For Eve's father. For her lover – her real lover – the man I'd written out of his own story.

And after all that, the only thing left that I could offer: to disappear. To make sure they never heard about me again, never opened a newspaper to see my face, never skimmed a website and caught on my name.

I wasn't sure yet where I'd go, what I would do.

Outside, a sign whisked by, making me blink: we turned left, and Duncs dropped down a gear as the road lifted into a climb.

'Are we…?' But I didn't have to ask. I knew where we were. 'What are we doing here?'

'There's just something we thought you might want to see.' Eilidh had twisted round in her seat. 'It's my idea, and if it's a crap one just say and we'll turn around, go straight home.'

I didn't say anything.

'It was dark when you were here, yeah? At the broch, I mean?'

'A dark and stormy night,' I said. 'Yep. Never darker.'

She turned back round. 'Almost there,' she said.

The walk from the lay-by was maybe twenty metres, and by the time we reached the broch my lungs were going like I'd sprinted it.

'Give me a sec,' I said. It would improve, the breathlessness: that's what the consultant had told me. There was some scarring on my lungs, from the infection, but there was a chance, a good chance, the damage wouldn't be permanent. I might not want to be running marathons, he'd said, and smiled at his own joke.

'Okay: what are we looking at?' I didn't want to be here. I was bundled in two jumpers and a down jacket, hatted and scarved and gloved, I was actually hot and even so, I could feel myself shivering.

Eilidh started to walk. Heading north, for the gap in the inner wall.

The top of a compass / For those who have eyes.

Was it some kind of punishment? For putting them through this? Did they want me to relive it with them – imagine what they'd found, how they'd felt – their fear, their horror?

Duncs was beside me. 'Alright?' he said. 'Honestly: you should take a look at this.'

I followed Eilidh.

At the thought of going back there, back inside, a hot sourness rose in my throat. But she stopped just short of the opening. Crouched down, facing the wall.

I did the same.

'Here,' she said.

It was a curve, a scratch in the stone. I followed it round, down to a sharp bend, up again and round, down to a point.

A heart.

I pulled off my glove, stretched out to check with my fingers. Shallow, neat: carved with a penknife, perhaps. Definitely: a heart. Floating below and to the right was a crescent moon, more deeply etched. Up to the left, a corresponding symbol. Three horizontal lines, and an upright scratch.

E

♡

C

I ran my fingers along the lines. What I felt was her determination. Eve crouching by the wall, knowing we'd just been here, knowing I'd hidden here from her, knowing I'd dodged her again. Penknife in her hand – I even remembered it, or thought I did, a tiny red toy of a thing just a couple of inches long. Eve working the feeble blade into the stone. Digging it in, scraping away. Crumbs of stone falling. Frowning, concentrating. Her fierce little heart, her vandal heart. The knife skiting over the stone, jabbing her other hand; Eve crying out, annoyance and pain, sucking her cut finger and carrying on. Finishing the tail curve of the C. My C. Sitting back on her heels, hurt finger clutched in a fist, smile on her face. Satisfied.

Blood and grit: Eve was here, far more than she'd ever been in a plaque and a rosebush, in a garden of graves six hundred miles south.

I pressed my palm against the carving, absorbing it, trying to understand it with the whole of my self. What it meant: everything, or nothing. But they'd brought me here – Eilidh had brought me here – so it couldn't mean nothing.

I tried to speak, found myself coughing instead, and coughed and coughed and eventually managed to get the words out.

'I never saw it.' I looked up at Eilidh, who was standing now, hair lifting in the wind. I stood up too, an effort that left me dizzy: balanced myself with a hand on the stone. 'But how did you know? That I hadn't seen it?'

She was smiling, but somehow she didn't look happy. 'Because you never do,' she said. 'Because it was under your nose.'

I stared; and she turned away to see where Duncs had got to. He was waiting by the entrance, casually perched in a splash of sun, on a wedge of Iron Age wall. He waved when he saw us looking.

'You two,' I said, and hesitated. Eilidh said nothing. She wasn't going to help me. 'You and Duncs. Is it...?'

She was gazing past him now, off into the distance, at the hills and the cloud-blown sky. For a minute I thought she wasn't going to answer; and then she shrugged.

'We'll see,' she said, hands buried in her pockets. 'I'm still going away, you know.'

'To Namibia?'

She nodded. 'Still sorting it all out. In the new year, I think.'

'You'd be there already, if it wasn't for me. Really sorry I fucked up your plans.'

We hadn't talked yet, about any of it: me and her, and where I'd brought us to. And though we seemed to have scrambled free from that terrible place, I wasn't sure where we'd landed up. I couldn't expect normality – I knew that. But if I worked hard enough, for long enough, at fixing what I'd broken – between me and Eilidh; me and everyone – perhaps I could succeed.

'Oh well,' she said. 'Mice and men. And it's not all bad.' She meant Duncs, I supposed; I didn't ask. 'We'll see,' she said again – and her smile this time was smaller, and more real: like she was amused, and didn't plan on sharing the joke. 'Nobody's back-up. Remember?'

We stood for a moment longer, without speaking. Then she walked away, back towards Duncs.

I lingered by the wall. Beside *E loves C*; the stone heart that meant or didn't mean I was forgiven.

Eve had been happy here; we had all been happy. It was an unreachable happiness, locked in the past. Magical, and gone. And yet – her message to me belonged, too, in the past; but here it was, present in these walls that had existed for two thousand years and would be here as long again. The thought made me breathless, but not from fear.

I tipped my head, stared up at the clouds that streaked and stretched across a cold blue sky; at the stars invisible beyond, unimaginably far. Then, blinking, I brought my gaze back down to earth, to where Eilidh and Duncs stood close together, just inside the walls of the broch. Not touching, not talking. Just waiting for me.

As I watched, Eilidh raised her hands, made a loudhailer. 'Ready to go back yet?' she called.

I nodded: almost.

It was nearly winter: soon enough it would be Christmas. Roddy would be back for the holidays, and Jean home too, for a few precious days. We'd see another New Year in, all together for 'Auld Lang Syne' – and afterwards everyone would scatter: to Glasgow and Berlin, to Namibia, America, Kazahkstan. So the circle widened, year by year – and however far from the centre, I was part of it, still; in Moulin, or Glasgow – or even here at the far north-western edge of everything. Because I had an idea, now, that I might come back to Glenelg. Come back in the spring; ask at the inn, see about getting a job. I had plenty experience, after all. It was something I could do – in a place remote enough that I could become invisible. A place that was right for endings, and maybe for beginnings. Where treasure, of a sort, had always waited for me.

In the meantime: yes. I was ready.

I started to walk: to the slant of sun where Duncs and Eilidh waited; to the warm backseat of the car, and the start of the track back home.

Acknowledgements

Special thanks to Mum and Dad for providing a writing bolthole; to Bessie, for long hours of companionship; to Katy and Tristan for Glenelg; to Jason Donald, Ed Group, Mandy Haggith and Anya Stern for being such brilliant readers; to Ruth for fact-checking, though all errors are my own; to Juliet and all at Lutyens & Rubinstein for endless patience and enthusiasm; to Craig and Sara at Saraband for working so hard to produce the best possible book; and to Aidan, always, for everything.

About the Author

Jane Alexander was born in Aberdeen in 1974 and lives in Edinburgh. She trained as an illustrator before swapping sketchbooks for notebooks; since then her short stories have won national awards and been widely published. This is her first novel.

Join the treasure hunt online at
janealexander.net/join-the-hunt